A
Widow's
Hope

Mary Ellis

HARVEST HOUSE PUBLISHERS
EUGENE, OREGON

Cover photo © Abris / iStockphoto

Cover by Abris, Veneta, Oregon

A WIDOW'S HOPE
Copyright © 2009 by Mary Ellis
Published by Harvest House Publishers
Eugene, Oregon 97402
www.harvesthousepublishers.com

Library of Congress Cataloging-in-Publication Data
    Ellis, Mary, 1951-
    A widow's hope / Mary Ellis.
        p. cm.—(The Miller Family Series ; bk. #1)
    ISBN 978-0-7369-2732-1 (pbk.)
    1. Amish—Fiction 2. Widows—Fiction. 3. Widowers—Fiction. 4. Farm life—Fiction. 5. Holmes County (Ohio)—Fiction. I. Title.
    PS3626.E36W53 2009
    813'.6—dc22

2008047156

To the love of my life and best friend…
my husband

~

I can't imagine how dull life would
have been had I not met you.

Acknowledgments

Thanks to Mrs. Carol Lee and Mr. Owen Shevlin, who welcomed me into their homes and opened doors for me in the Amish community.

Thanks to Dr. Mike Longo, who pointed me in the right direction many times.

Thanks to my lovely proofreader, Mrs. Joycelyn Sullivan.

A special thank you to Mrs. Petersheim of the Swartzentruber Amish, and to Joanna and Kathryn, members of an Old Order Amish community.

Thanks to my wonderful agent, Mary Sue Seymour, who had faith in me from the beginning.

Finally, thanks to Kim Moore and everyone on staff at Harvest House Publishers for welcoming me into their loving family.

And thanks be to God—all things in this world are by His hand.

One

Lancaster County, Pennsylvania

Baa. Baa. Baaaaa. Hannah Brown nearly dropped the clean dress she was hanging on the line into the dewy grass. But she couldn't help herself. Every time she heard a sheep bleat, her heart jumped like a new human mom when her infant cried. Hannah pinned the garment to the clothesline and hurried to the pasture fence. Seeing nothing amiss, she breathed a sigh of relief. It was only a couple lambs energetically vying for their mother's attention. One never could completely relax with a flock of sheep. A lamb might escape the pasture and get lost, drown in the swiftly flowing creek, become entangled in the blackberry briars, or wander into the road. Then there was the possibility of a hungry predator selecting one of her beloved creatures for his evening meal.

Hannah lifted her long Plain dress and stepped up on the bottom rail so she might survey the orderly farm her late husband had so cherished. Two years had passed since his death, yet hot tears still stung the backs of her eyes when she remembered what a kind soul Adam had been. There was much to be said for a girl marrying a childhood pal and later her best friend as they grew to adulthood.

She came to love the quiet man who had loved his God, his farm, and his wife…in that order. Hannah wasn't complaining. Romantic love with heart-pounding sensations and runaway emotions was for fancy people. Practical Hannah had her house to run, a man who worked his land with deep faith, and their thriving business. Taxes must be paid on Amish farms same as on any other, and the sale of wool and spring lambs adequately supplemented the farm's income. Her nightly devotions had been filled with praise and thanksgiving for all she'd been given.

Only one prayer had gone unanswered during their six years of marriage, the prayer for a baby. No sons had come to carry on her husband's name and someday help with the plentiful chores. No baby for her to cradle in her arms and sing lullabies to in the evening. No little girl to teach to sew and knit and bake delicious cookies. No child to fill a heart that overflowed with love. Now that she was widowed, she might never know the joy of hearing a little one utter "mama." Would she spend the rest of her life alone and die a heart-broken old woman? *There were worse things in life,* she remembered as she willed herself not to cry.

She was reminded of Psalm 34:4: "I sought the Lord, and he answered me; he delivered me from all my fears." Hannah blinked several times to help her stop wallowing in self-pity and turned her attention on two rams squaring off in the far pasture. She didn't hear the footsteps until the person was right behind her.

"They are not going to do anything different than be sheep, even if you watch them all afternoon, sister." Her younger brother, Thomas, stepped onto the rail beside her and pulled a long blade of Timothy grass to chew.

"Must you sneak up on a person like that?" Hannah asked, a little peevishly. She tried to wipe away her tears discreetly before her observant brother noticed.

"I thought surely you would've heard my buggy coming up the lane. That right rear wheel must be out of round. It makes an awful lot of racket." He swatted at a pesky gnat and then peered down at his sister. "Say, why are you crying? Is it because you're selling me your farm? It doesn't have to be so. I told you that. I can move here from *mamm* and *daed*'s, and we'll manage things together. We always got along reasonably well growing up." He tugged on one of her *kapp*'s ribbons.

Hannah hopped down from the rail and slipped an arm around her brother's waist. "And when you get your courage up to ask a certain red-haired gal to ride home from a singing with you? Maybe even ask if you might court her? What then? No newlywed wife wants to share her household with a bossy sister-in-law."

Thomas jumped down too and placed a hand on Hannah's shoulder. "You're not bossy—maybe a little opinionated, that's all. And I do believe you're putting the horse way before the buggy." He gazed off across the rolling pasture and distant hayfields. The sun's rays reflected off the golden heads of winter wheat like fire. "You've got no call to move to Ohio to live with Julia unless it's what you really want. Your home will always be here on this farm, with *mamm* and *daed* down the road, and me—even if I end up a bachelor all my days."

Hannah chuckled to herself. Her handsome brother needn't worry about finding a wife. She'd seen too many female heads glance in his direction during Sunday preaching services. "*Danki*, Thomas, but I miss Julia. Her *kinner* are growing up quickly, without their loving aunt offering her two cents' worth. And Julia could use my help in the garden with canning and herb drying. Her hands are growing stiffer each year. Besides, the sale of my wool could help Simon buy land for his two sons. They'll need their own farms someday, and land isn't getting any cheaper."

Hannah started walking toward the house. "Are you hungry?" she asked over her shoulder, wishing to change the subject. "Let's have some of the stew I've been simmering all morning." She didn't want Thomas to see how uneasy she was about her relocation to Ohio. She wanted to help Julia with her four lively children—two boys and two girls. And Julia had assured her that the sheep would be welcome. But Julia's husband was a deacon in their district—a district a bit stricter than Hannah's own in Pennsylvania. He'd found her opinions too liberal during her rare visits in the past. Could she meld into the Miller household and offer assistance instead of disruption?

"And what about Simon Miller?" Thomas asked, easily catching up to her with his long strides. "He's a stern man and rules his household a bit firmer than your Adam did, I reckon."

It was as though her little brother had read her thoughts, something he'd done often while they were growing up. She stomped up the porch steps a bit noisily for a grown woman. "It's not my place to judge my brother-in-law, Thomas, nor yours. Julia writes nothing but positive things about what a good husband and father he is, and what a good deacon he is in their district." She pushed open the door and entered the kitchen, fragrant with the smell of home cooking.

Thomas washed and took his seat at the table, looking abashed. "You're right. Sorry."

She patted his arm lightly after carrying over the kettle of thick stew. "Nothing for you to worry about. Simon and I will get along just fine."

In her heart, Hannah wasn't so sure, but what choice did she have? She'd run her home efficiently during her marriage and managed to keep the farm going with her *daed*'s and Thomas' help after Adam's death. But she couldn't depend on their kindness forever. Her father was getting old, and Thomas had his own life to plan. She had to trust—and pray—for a smooth transition into Simon Miller's household. Picking up her spoon, she found her appetite had vanished.

She ate two spoonfuls before pushing the bowl aside. "I received a letter from our sister the other day. Would you like to read it?"

"Why don't you read it to me?" Thomas said as he ladled more stew into his bowl. He broke off another piece of brown bread and looked up expectantly.

Hannah drew a breath and read aloud the letter that had warmed her heart and given her courage:

My dearest Hannah,

I hope this letter finds you well, along with mom, dad, and Thomas. And I truly hope you are not working too hard between the spring planting of the fields and all the chores your critters entail in the springtime. I trust you're not starting seeds to bring with you because I have more than enough sprouted for a huge vegetable and herb garden once the soil warms up. And if there's some plant you favor that I've forgotten, you'll have plenty of time to soak seeds once you're settled in.

We are counting the days until we can welcome you to our home. All is well with us. Little Leah is busy embroidering your name on three hankies while Emma plans to bake a lemon cake with sour cream frosting on the day of your arrival. I told her it was your favorite. My boys are glad you're bringing sheep along, and not more cows to milk. Even Simon has been checking and repairing the fences so that our shepherdess can keep track of her flock. As for me? I look forward to having my loving sister near me again. Your sunny disposition has never failed to lift my spirits. And I can use your help in the kitchen as my hands are not as capable as they once were.

I know it is with great sorrow that you leave the farm you and Adam purchased as a young couple, but Thomas will care for it just as well, and you will still be able to visit. The Lord never closes a door without opening another. I am eager for you to meet Simon's brother, Seth, who also lost his spouse a couple of years ago. He is a kindhearted, hardworking man with a sweet little daughter to bring up alone. He has asked about your wool business more than once when I've mentioned you during meals. Now I must close, but soon I will have your helpful counsel whenever I need it.

Your loving sister, Julia

Hannah smiled as she refolded the letter and placed it in her apron pocket. So like Julia to try to matchmake even while hundreds of miles away. She thought back to the time Adam had come courting. Julia had had a hand in encouraging Adam to court her and see Hannah as more than a good friend. But Hannah wasn't a young woman with dreams spinning around her head, wearing her hopes on her sleeve. At twenty-eight, she would gladly spend the rest of her life as a widow if only God had blessed her with several *bopplin*. But she had no babies and probably never would.

"Your *sunny disposition*...who is Julia talking about, sister?" Thomas asked, breaking her reverie with his teasing.

Hannah swatted his arm lightly but couldn't help but smile. "Julia's been gone for some time. She must have forgotten my true nature."

"It is that true nature I will sorely miss." Thomas brushed a kiss on her forehead before heading outdoors to his chores.

Lately Hannah had felt neither helpful nor sunny, knowing Simon had originally insisted that she sell her sheep or give them to Thomas before making the move.

Hannah's place was with her sister. So like Ruth, that is where she would go. But she would not move without her sheep. Caring for those animals, the gentlest of God's creatures, allowed her days to be productive and meaningful. But they might be more than the Miller clan ever bargained for.

Holmes County, Ohio

Simon Miller swept his hat from his head as he entered the livestock barn and wiped his brow with his handkerchief. When his eyes adjusted to the dim light, he spotted his two sons sitting side by side, milking cows. The heifers chomped noisily on hay from their trough, not paying much attention to the boys' small hands. "Awfully warm for March, no?" Simon asked.

"*Jah*, sure," his elder son agreed, glancing up briefly. Matthew at twelve years old was growing so fast Julia was always lengthening his trousers. Wiry and fleet as a fox, the boy hurried wherever he went. He wasn't much of a student, but his love of the farm equaled Simon's own, and he seldom had to be told what chores needed to be done.

"Put some elbow to it, Henry, or you'll still be sitting there come dark." Simon chuckled at his younger son, who usually worried about angering the heifer by pulling too hard or not warming his hands enough. He was as different from his brother as the hawk to a dove. Although not lazy, Henry meandered through his chores, easily distracted by an ant colony or a cloud formation or a newborn calf. Although he was usually quiet, when the child did start talking, he poured out a bucketful of questions.

"Finish up, sons, and get that milk into the cooler. Your *mamm* will have dinner on the table soon. And I for one am hungry."

"Me too," they answered in unison, and even Henry worked the udders faster.

Simon walked slowly to enjoy the sun slanting over his white frame house. Sunset was his favorite time of day. With the chores behind him and night coming on, he looked forward to a good meal with his family. Julia was an excellent cook. Her pies and cakes were the best in the district. His mouth watered at the thought of her fresh peach cobbler.

They didn't need Hannah Brown coming to live with them. They would be able to manage fine until his daughters were old enough to take on more of the household chores. But the Bible was clear on the topic of widows and orphaned children. It was his responsibility to take in Julia's sister and provide a home for her. He was a deacon in the district. What kind of example would he be setting if he allowed her to struggle on her farm alone? With only one brother back home and an aged father, Hannah should not remain her parents' burden.

But did she have to bring sixty smelly animals that produced no milk, no cheese, and no butter with her? And wool was scratchy, no less. *Ach,* he mumbled, trying to put the move from his mind for the tenth time that day. He'd crossed paths with Julia's sister during some of her previous visits. The woman appeared to have an opinion about everything. It wasn't an Amish woman's place to be so forthright. And he'd seen books on her mantel that had no place there—books of higher learning and agricultural references. Everything he needed to know about farming he'd learned from his *daed* and would pass down to his sons. He didn't need any textbooks to teach him about crop rotation or natural pesticides. Adam should have put a stop to all that book learning after their marriage, but Adam had been too lenient with Hannah. Even Julia admitted it. Julia had said Hannah would lose interest in studying once children came. But poor Hannah and Adam hadn't been blessed with God's greatest miracle of all.

Simon walked up his back steps where a welcoming lamp glowed in the window. He whispered a silent prayer of thanks for his four healthy children. It wasn't easy to be widowed at such a young age with an active farm to manage. He pledged to be patient with his sister-in-law when she arrived, remembering Romans 12:12: "Rejoice in hope, be patient in tribulation, be constant in prayer."

He would let Julia deal with her sister because the house was a woman's domain. He had a problem to solve with his own sibling. His younger brother, Seth, had been widowed for more than a year and a half. Time to at least start thinking about marrying again. Seth's little girl needed a mother, and what's more, Seth needed sons. One skinny little daughter wouldn't help in the fields during the years to come. Seth had a hay crop and a corn crop, and he needed *kinner.* Simon yearned for the day his brother remarried and once again had a loving wife to set his table with a meal, mend his shirts, and keep the house clean. Seth usually ate cold sandwiches with pickled beets or chow chow twice a day. Only his fried eggs or oatmeal in the morning broke the routine. That wasn't right. Never a baked chicken, slice of smoked ham, or piece of spiced apple pie with ice cream dripping down the sides.

With a glance over his shoulder, Simon spotted his boys closing the barn door behind them, and he entered the kitchen feeling
immensely blessed. He would make it his business, no, his duty, to
see his younger brother remarried and settled into a happy home.

~

Seth straightened his spine at the sound of horse hooves. He was
refitting a mule harness with new buckles at the anvil so it would be
ready for spring planting. A buggy was coming up his lane, and Seth
recognized the horse as his brother's. But it wasn't Simon who stepped
down and tied the horse to the hitching post but his sister-in-law,
Julia. And she was carrying a large wicker hamper. Seth wiped his
hands quickly against his leather apron and hurried to meet her.

"*Guder mariye*," she called as he approached. Her cheeks were
flushed from the cold, but as always there was a smile on her pleasant face.

"Good morning to you, Julia. What have you in the basket?" He
couldn't help but grin in anticipation. "Something good to eat, I
hope?"

He reached to take the hamper, but she sidestepped him and
headed for the house. "No, just a basketful of baby kittens. Simon
was concerned you might have too many mice this spring after the
mild winter."

"*What?*" Seth followed Julia up the steps, across the porch, and
into the house.

She managed to stay beyond his reach until she set the basket
on the table with a mischievous grin. "I hope you like calico with
white paws."

Seth lifted the lid cautiously, not wishing for a dozen little kittens
to scamper in all directions. He needn't have worried. Inside was a
pie tin of biscuits, a stuffed chicken smelling of sage and chestnuts,
and an entire custard pie. "You tease me, Julia. This is much better

than a litter of mouse catchers." He leaned close and inhaled deeply. "What kind of pie? Banana cream?"

Julia walked to the sink to wash her hands. "I tease you because you should laugh more. And the pie is lemon cream," Julia replied, laying her wool sweater on a chair back.

"Oh, mercy. My favorite," Seth uttered before heading for plates and forks. "Phoebe," he called in the direction of the stairs. "Come down. Your Aunt Julia is here, and she's brought lunch for us." Seth set three plates on the table with a clatter, but Julia picked up one to return to the cupboard. "I've already eaten. But I'll have a cup of coffee with you and Phoebe." She tucked a lock of her dark hair back under her *kapp*.

"Coffee it is," Seth said as he reached for the pot on the stove, shoving aside the frying pan. His attempt at making pancakes yesterday had been a disaster, and he hadn't had a chance to scrub off the burned results. He noticed Julia eyeing his kitchen while she thought him distracted—the wilted geranium on the windowsill, the stack of unsorted mail on the counter, the laundry Julia had washed on Monday that he still hadn't put back in Phoebe's bureau. It was a far cry from the tidy kitchen his late wife had kept.

He moved the laundry basket closer to the steps. "Don't think I don't appreciate your washing our clothes, Julia. I've just been busy getting ready for the spring planting." He poured coffee into a chipped cup while Julia went for the pitcher of milk.

"I know that, Seth. Your outdoor chores take all your energy this time of year. I'll take the clothes up before I leave, and Phoebe and I can put them away together."

"That child," Seth said, his impatience growing.

"Wait, Seth. Let's talk a moment before she comes down." Julia smiled in her bashful fashion as she often did when about to venture into touchy matters. "Has she said anything this week? Has she raised her voice in song or praise? Has she talked *at all*?" Distress knit her brows and creased her forehead.

"She prays silently before meals and before bed, as do I. God doesn't require that we shout loudly to the heavens." Seth knew Julia meant well, but he wished she'd stop worrying about his daughter. Phoebe had simply chosen to be quiet for a time. "When she's ready to start talking again, she will, and making a big fuss won't hurry things along."

Julia set the chicken on a carving platter, along with a sharp knife and large fork, and then pulled back the foil covering the biscuits. "I agree, but it's been almost two years since Constance's passing. And I'm worried that if Phoebe doesn't resume talking soon, she might never."

Seth exhaled a weary sigh. "It's not been two years; it's barely one and a half. Don't worry so about Phoebe. There's not a thing wrong with that child."

At that moment, the subject of their discussion leaped from the bottom step and hurtled herself across the kitchen, her face aglow with pleasure on seeing her aunt. Julia swept the five-year-old up into her arms, still easy to do as Phoebe remained small for her age. "Hello, dear Phoebe," Julia said, bouncing her on her hip. There was certainly nothing wrong with the hug she delivered to Julia's neck or the huge grin on her sweet face.

"Let's all sit and bow our heads," Seth said when Julia set the child down. After prayers, Seth sliced off a chicken leg for Phoebe and a breast and wing for himself. He then spooned stuffing for them both.

When the child began to eat with gusto, Julia settled back in her chair. "Come back to our house on Sunday afternoon after the preaching service and noon meal. Phoebe can play with her cousins, and your *bruder* will breathe easy that you are not starving to death here by yourselves."

"*Danki,* Julia. I'll come if it's just going to be family." He leveled his sister-in-law a knowing look, one he didn't need to explain. Julia and Simon were determined to see him remarried to somebody—anybody—in the district. He often felt like an animal on the auction block in Kidron during one of their fix-up evening meals.

Seth was happy with how things were. His marriage to Constance had been good, but he wasn't ready to remarry. With God's grace, he and Phoebe would continue to manage on their own. He had more pressing matters on his mind than matrimony. He needed a cash crop, another business to augment his meager farm income. Land taxes kept going up while the price of grain fluctuated too wildly to be counted on.

Another source of farm income, that's what he needed.

Certainly not a new wife.

Two

Lancaster County, Pennsylvania

The first rays of dawn were filtering through the muslin curtains when Hannah awoke on Sunday. She heard her mother below, already bustling around the kitchen. She, her father, and Thomas had come early to help get ready because services were to be on her farm that day. The sounds of her mother fixing breakfast reminded her of growing up and made her homesick before she had even left!

Hannah parted the curtains to gaze out on the dark, rich earth of newly turned fields. A red-tailed hawk soared on the wind currents, seeking out a tasty breakfast. A mist hung over the stand of pines on the ridge and spoke to her heart of peace and tranquillity. *Never grow too fond of things of this world. God's greatest creation is the hereafter.* One of her grandmother's favorite expressions drifted back, but Hannah didn't know how not to grow fond when surrounded by such beauty. Would Ohio have hills as lush and green? Would the fields offer as bounteous a harvest in the fall? Would the meadows bloom with violets, wild hyacinths, and trillium to sweeten the air as she counted her flock? She knew she was being silly. She'd visited Ohio several times, and the landscape wasn't much different than the one beyond her window. But still her heart hung heavy as she washed her face and hands and rolled her hair into a tight bun.

Her *mamm* turned from stirring the oatmeal when Hannah entered the kitchen. A plate of sausages waited on the table, along with a stack of toast. Butter pooled in the center of the top slice. "Are you hungry, my daughter?"

Hannah's eyes filled with tears while a lump the size of a goose egg blocked her throat. *When did my mother grow so old? When did her dark hair become streaked with silver and her back so stooped?*

Hannah couldn't answer the question; speech was impossible. Luckily her father and brother marched into the kitchen with news of another newborn lamb and plans of where to park the carriages that would soon fill their driveway. Much of their yard still remained soggy from the spring rains. After sitting, they bowed their heads and offered thanks for the meal, perhaps their last together for some time. Thomas and her father were soon eating quickly. Much remained to be done before friends and neighbors arrived for the preaching service, including removing or rearranging the furniture so that long benches could be set up.

Hannah glanced at her father, who was scraping the last of his oatmeal with a crust of bread. Deep lines and creases made his face resemble a county roadmap, one that showed every lane, farm trace, and cattle crossing. The backs of his hands were splotched with sunspots and calloused from years of hard work, while his nails were jagged and torn. The thought that she might not be here when her parents reached the end of their days gripped her heart like an iron vise.

"What's troubling you, daughter?" her mother asked as the menfolk hurried back to their preparations.

Hannah carried their plates to the sink. "I'm fine, *mamm,* just a little nervous about moving my sheep." There was much more on Hannah's mind than her flock, but she had no desire to add to her mother's worries.

"*Ach,* your animals will be fine. The livestock hauler that your *bruder* hired has plenty of experience and assured Thomas they will arrive safe and sound. It is you I'm concerned about. Thomas says you might be having second thoughts. Is that so? It's not too late to change your mind."

Hannah looked into her mother's face. This woman had taught her to sew, and bake, and cook, and quilt, and dry herbs and flowers, and whiten sheets, and remove berry stains from tablecloths. How could she get along without her? And how could she admit she was frightened by the prospect of a lonely future? She reached out her hand and forced a smile. "I'm looking forward to living with Julia and Simon on their farm. I can't wait to spend time with my nieces and nephews before they're all grown up." At least all that was true.

Her mother opened her mouth to speak and then cocked her head at the sound of the first buggy. Whatever comment she had remained unspoken as the kitchen filled with women and children. They brought side dishes and freshly baked bread for the lunch, which would be served after the three-hour service. Jugs of lemonade and tea were carried to the cold storage while extra paper products and plates were stacked on the counter. Young people sought out others of their own age to chat before the deacon called everyone to their seats. Then came hymns to recite, several sermons to ponder, and silent prayers to offer up.

Hannah immersed herself in the service and the meal afterward surrounded by the people she'd known her whole life. While toddlers napped and children played, everyone shared fond memories with her. Hannah soon grew weary of all the attention. But no sooner had she longed for solitude than people began to drift off to their buggies, waving goodbye and wishing her a safe trip. Soon even her parents retired upstairs after the long day. They and Thomas would accompany her to Lancaster to catch her bus. Hannah took the few minutes she had to herself to walk around her farm—the place Adam had brought her as a young bride. She said goodbye to her barns and sheds and the rushing creek with an oak plank bridge built by her husband's hands.

"Guide me, Lord. Show me Your will. Give me courage and

strength." Hannah sent up her prayer and then slept soundly that night, her last in Pennsylvania for a long time. The next day she packed a trunk of clothes and things from her hope chest, leaving behind most of the household items for Thomas. She took the quilt made by her mother and the trivets forged by her dad. She packed the books Thomas would have no use for, hugged her family good-bye, and tried not to dwell on when she would next see them. After boarding a bus westward bound, she vowed not to shed one more silly, self-pitying tear.

The bus ride to Ohio took most of the next day. Hannah arrived at the Canton station hungry, tired, and cramped from sitting too long in one position. She was more than a little cranky. Fellow passengers had insisted on talking loudly, making a nap impossible. Looking around the station, her heart lifted on spotting Simon's familiar face and fell when she noticed he was alone. Her sister hadn't come from Winesburg to meet her. She would have to ride back without Julia's tales of the children's antics for company.

"Hello, Simon." Hannah greeted him with a smile.

"Welcome, Hannah." Simon Miller reached for her satchel and then headed for the door.

"Wait, I must retrieve my trunk," Hannah called, just as a porter wheeled over a cart holding her large, battered trunk.

"*All that?*" Simon asked in disbelief. "What have you there? There's little you needed to bring, Hannah. Our home is as fully stocked as those of Pennsylvania." He dug into his pocket for change for the porter and began dragging the trunk toward the door.

"Let me help you, Simon." But each time Hannah bent down for the other handle, he dragged the trunk beyond her reach. What a sight they must have made in the bus station as they made their way outside.

"Where's your buggy?" she asked, giving up on the handle.

"Too far for the horse to go. I hired a neighbor to drive." With that a van pulled to the curb, and the driver helped Simon load the trunk inside with more grunts and groans than Thomas and her father had uttered. There was nothing for Hannah to do but climb into the backseat while Simon sat next to the driver.

"How is my sister?" Hannah asked, once the van was underway.

"She is well, *danki*," Simon replied shortly.

"I had hoped she would meet my bus," Hannah said, leaning forward in the seat.

"It's her arthritis—a flare-up." Simon neither turned in his seat nor elaborated more on Julia. His full attention was focused on the road ahead.

Further attempts on Hannah's part for polite conversation resulted in equally brief responses. She soon tired of hearing "*jahs*" and "noes" and settled back against the seat cushion. It was then she noticed why Simon's attention was riveted to the windshield. The light snowfall that had greeted her in Canton had turned into a true snowstorm. March always seemed to deliver a final winter wallop before the arrival of spring. The drive, which should have taken fifty minutes, took more than two hours as traffic snarled into great backups, and at times the van seemed to float across the pavement. The Amish have no great confidence in vehicles, especially on slick pavements in near whiteout conditions. How could the driver tell where the road was in the slanting blizzard at such high speed? Hannah spent most of the trip praying with her eyes closed.

By the time the van finally arrived at the Miller farm Hannah had an upset stomach and white knuckles from gripping the door handle. "We'll just leave this here on the side of the driveway," Simon said to the neighbor as they struggled to get the trunk out of the van. Hannah's heart sank with the thought of it becoming covered with snow overnight. She bit down on her tongue and walked toward the house. At long last she would be greeted by her loving sister and see her nieces and nephews.

But the house was dark and silent when she followed Simon inside. A sole kerosene lamp burned low on the kitchen table when they entered.

"Your room is at the top of the stairs, the second door on the left. We'll get that trunk to the porch and deal with it in the morning."

"*Danki*, Simon," Hannah murmured.

"*Gute nacht*, Hannah." Simon finally met her eye, looking tired and worn. The trip from Canton had frayed his nerves as well, and his forty years were well apparent on his thin face.

A pang of regret at causing additional work for her sister's husband added to Hannah's already queasy stomach. As she climbed the steps to the small room she would call her home, an odd sense of foreboding gripped her. Had she made a serious mistake? Had she been too hasty to sell her farm to her brother without even attempting to manage it as partners?

She had no business here. She would be an intrusion into her sister's life and a thorn in the sole of her brother-in-law's boot.

Tears ran down her face in earnest as she closed the bedroom door and set her satchel in the corner. Hannah knelt beside the neatly made bed and bowed her head in prayer. At times she cried more than prayed, but finally she was able to crawl under the covers and sleep. When she awoke the next morning, she greeted the beautiful, white-blanketed world of her new Ohio home.

～

"Surprise!" They all shouted in unison as Hannah entered the kitchen. Hannah looked around at the assemblage and smiled. Her sister, Julia, looked as pretty as ever with her brown eyes sparkling with animation. Simon nodded, looking more rested than he had the previous evening. The deep purple shadows under his eyes had faded. And the shining faces of her nieces and nephews warmed Hannah's heart. She glanced around the room, fragrant with the smell of bacon frying and biscuits baking, and felt her eyes fill with tears. Here they all were—the reason she'd come to Ohio—her beloved family.

"Why are you crying, Aunt Hannah?" asked Emma, the eldest of Julia's *kinner*. "Do you miss Pennsylvania already?"

"Oh, no." Hannah hurried to the girl's side and squeezed her shoulder. "My tears are joyous because I'm so happy to see you." She reached to pat Leah's forearm and offered the two boys her best smile. They both blushed and squirmed on their wooden kitchen chairs.

"Sit, sit, sister Hannah. We need to get our meal underway. The chores won't get done by themselves," Simon said.

Hannah slipped into the chair on his left, and all heads bowed in silent prayer. After bowls and platters were passed and everyone had filled their plates, Hannah was asked to describe in great detail what she'd seen along the way. Four pairs of eyes watched her curiously as she described the farm fields, forested mountains, and small towns she'd observed from the bus window.

But no one was more riveted than Emma. The young girl watched Hannah as though she were a beetle under a magnifying glass. Impressionable—that's what girls were at her age. Hannah vowed to show her most congenial side whenever the youngster was nearby.

"Eat, sons," Simon ordered. "Aunt Hannah will still be here after the cows are milked and the horses fed and watered. I don't want you late for school." Both boys ate their breakfasts with zeal and were soon pulling on wool caps and heavy jackets.

"How much snow fell overnight?" Hannah asked, remembering the blizzard. She was grateful it hadn't hit while the bus had been twisting through the Alleghenies.

"Almost eight inches," Julia said, refilling Hannah's coffee cup. "I hope that's the last of it for a while. I'm eager to get my seeds into the ground. It might be another four weeks until the soil is warm enough even if the snow melts quickly." Julia pulled back the kitchen curtain to reveal long icicles hanging from the porch gutter. "And it's not above freezing yet."

"I am ready for spring to come," Hannah said, sipping the strong coffee.

"It will arrive when God deems it's time, not because we are ready."

Simon spoke sternly as though addressing *kinner*. Then he tugged his black hat down over his ears and headed out the door.

Hannah glanced at Julia, who smiled lovingly as he shut the door behind him.

"Do not be alarmed. That is his deacon's tone of voice, and we've gotten used to it."

Hannah nodded, studying her sister, who looked the picture of contentment. And why shouldn't she? Her farm was tidy and productive, her children healthy, and her husband a good provider and loving father. For the briefest moment, Hannah envied her sister and immediately felt ashamed.

"Tell me about your wool business, Aunt Hannah. Mother says you card, spin, dye, and knit—all with wool from your own sheep." Emma's eyes glowed with excitement. "And that you have a loom for weaving your own cloths."

"I do." Hannah said. "My *bruder* is packing it up today. I hope it won't become damaged in shipment. It's coming on the same truck as my flock."

Julia's face brightened. "When it warms up in the spring, we'll find space to set it up in the barn."

"Oh, no, mother." Emma looked aghast. "Not in a barn with the cows and horses tromping in with muddy feet. Maybe father can turn part of a loft into a workshop where we can keep the floors properly swept."

"Maybe so, daughter. Or we can just hang a sign to remind the livestock to wipe their feet," Julia said with a grin. "Now hurry and get ready for school. Don't be late." Julia reached for the bottle of aspirin on the windowsill and shook two into her palm.

"Can't I stay home with you and Aunt Hannah? I can tell your hands are troubling you, and it's baking day. I can peel and core apples for pie faster than anybody."

"*Jah*, that's true, but I'll have Hannah's help. You're excused from the breakfast dishes. Now hurry along."

Emma's face clouded with disappointment.

"We'll have need of a pie taster when you get home," Hannah said, offering Emma a wink.

"Tasting is more fun that peeling and coring!" Emma said. "I'll see you after school, Aunt Hannah…and welcome." Her cheeks flushed bright pink before she sprinted to the stairs.

"I'll start on those dishes," Hannah said, rising from the table.

Julia studied her younger sister as she cleared the table. Hannah had grown so thin since their last visit. Her dress hung on her frame as though made for a much larger woman. When she filled a pot with water and carried it to the stove to heat, she at least didn't wince or struggle with the weight. *Ah, good.* No sign yet of the arthritis that robbed Julia's hands of movement and flexibility and caused her daily pain. Hannah's back was still straight as an arrow as she washed the plates and cups and set them in the strainer to dry.

As though she felt the perusal, Hannah glanced back over her shoulder. "What are you thinking, sister? If I do a chore not to your liking, don't be shy about instructing me in the Miller ways."

Julia laughed. "The Miller ways must be the same as yours because we had the same good teacher, our *mamm.*"

While Hannah wiped down the countertops, Julia set out the baking supplies, Julia's mind drifting back to their girlhood. Hannah, at seven years younger, had loved to follow her around while she ran errands to nearby farms. But she hadn't minded because her sister had the gentlest heart of anyone she knew. Hannah had been the one to return baby birds to their nests and rescue baby skunks that had fallen into a dry well. She would beg their *daed* to stop the buggy for every stray pup or kitten she would see and cry and fuss when he didn't oblige.

Hannah, the *eegesinnisch* one, her father had called her. But her willfulness was seldom to benefit herself. She didn't understand yet that Amish rules didn't allow livestock to be treated as pets, nor a farm barn to become an animal shelter. "Her heart is too big," *mamm* had said after *daed* had disciplined Hannah. She had crawled onto a frozen pond to rescue a cat that had fallen through the ice.

But Julia doubted that a heart could ever be too big.

Now as a grown woman Hannah tended her lambs as though they were her *kinner*. Children—that's what Hannah needed—children to love and nurture and watch grow into adulthood.

Hannah would be a good influence on the girls—Julia knew her kind and gentle ways would teach Emma and Leah the fortitude that arthritis robbed her of. And Hannah's unflagging energy would make up for her own diminishing strength in the years to come.

Julia rubbed the backs of her hands before picking up an apple to peel and core, shaking away her selfishness. She'd been thinking how wonderful it was to have Hannah as part of her family and not what Hannah might want.

Whether Hannah admitted it or not, she should remarry. Twenty-eight was too young to reconcile herself to remaining alone and childless. Julia watched as Hannah dried her hands on a towel and carried over two bowls of apples. She was still so pretty with her clear green eyes and hair the color of ripe wheat. Her skin glowed with health and vitality. Their district still had several unmarried men of Hannah's age if Hannah didn't care for the match that Julia had in mind.

"What are you thinking, sister?" Hannah asked, lining up apples to be peeled. "You look like your mind is working harder than necessary for pie making."

"I was just thinking it might be time to invite Simon's brother and his daughter for dinner. It's our duty to make sure those two are getting enough to eat."

～

Seth pulled up on the reins as the buggy neared his brother's house. The warm sun had melted the snow from the roadways, but the fields and meadow still lay under a blanket of white. He'd considered taking the sleigh for the four-mile ride but feared getting bogged down in a low, soggy area. Phoebe loved sleigh rides, but he'd been asked to come help, not create another problem should he get mired in mud. He lifted his daughter from the buggy and set her on the higher ground. "Go run to the house to see what your Aunt Julia is doing." The child scampered off, her braids bouncing on her shoulders. Soon he would speak to Julia about sewing some head coverings for Phoebe. She was no *boppli* anymore.

Simon came from the barn, wearing boots well above his knees. "It's my gutters," he called. "They're blocked, and my cistern's not filling up. We'll need plenty of water come summer. Can you help me clean them out and the downspouts too?"

"That's why I'm here," Seth said, pulling on his beard. "Your boy said you had problems with the well, not the cistern. I'm in luck. It's a better day for scraping gutters than digging down into a water well."

"*Ach,* that son of mine don't know the difference between a well and cistern. All he knows is he turns the spigot and out comes water," Simon said, slapping Seth on the back. "Let's go for the ladder."

They walked to the storage area on the lowest level of the barn and spotted the ladder leaning against the wall. "Julia tells me her sister is coming from Lancaster," Seth said, picking up one end. They carried the forty-footer around to the far side.

"*Ach, jah.*" Simon's reply was more of a grunt as he stumbled over a hidden tree root along the path.

"Julia will be glad for the extra help." Seth tried to take most of the ladder's weight as his brother started to slip on an icy patch.

"We've got two daughters. Emma will be home for good come May. She'll be done with school."

"For the company then. Women never seem to run out of things to talk about."

"We spend all Sunday afternoon visiting after preaching services. That should be plenty of gabbing time."

Seth smiled. It was more than enough for his quiet brother, who found most conversation a waste of perfectly good air. "No need to beat around the bush when the rules are clear" was Simon's favorite explanation as to why his sermons were so short. Seth didn't continue along that line. Instead he said, "Let me go up. My arms are longer. You hold the ladder."

Simon didn't argue, as he wasn't fond of heights. Seth slipped on gloves and climbed. Once at gutter level, he began to scrape out the debris that had accumulated.

"Matthew, come help us," Simon called. "You follow behind and pick up the mess that your uncle drops down."

Matthew dutifully ran for a bucket and started gathering up the dead leaves and twigs.

"Aunt Hannah has a big flock of sheep," Matthew said when he'd caught up to them. "And soon they'll be arriving. At least they're not more cows for me to milk."

"You've not seen them, boy. You don't know if the flock is large or small since we have no sheep at all," Simon said. "Mind where you're stepping. Your *mamm*'s rosebushes are beneath that layer of snow."

"When is your aunt due to arrive?" Seth asked from the top of the ladder.

Matthew looked up, confused. "She's here already, uncle. She came two nights ago and brought this great big trunk, and pap said that nobody needs to drag around that much stuff. And pap put the trunk under the porch under a tarp and told Aunt Hannah she could take things out a little bit at a time." The boy's face revealed nothing out of the ordinary with his tale.

Seth stopped scraping out the gutter and looked down at his brother, trying not to smile. Simon's cheeks had reddened from the cold.

Simon adjusted his grip on the ladder rails before replying. "We have a houseful of useful things. Hannah needn't have brought so much."

"Maybe she wanted something to remember her home in Pennsylvania," Seth said casually.

"Pap said women shouldn't try to run a farm by themselves. It makes them too independent. She should've sold long ago and moved back in with grandpa and grandma."

Simon tugged on the sleeve of his son's wool coat. "Were you listening in bed when you should've been sleeping? *That's* what makes people too independent." He gave Matthew's arm a shake.

Seth came down the ladder to move it further along the roofline. "Run a farm by herself? I thought Julia had mentioned her sister got married awhile back."

"*Jah*, but her husband died two years ago." Simon tried to lift the bottom of the ladder from its position, but it started to totter precariously along the gutter board. Seth hefted the weight easily and moved it over eight feet.

"So she sold her farm then?" Seth stretched the kink out of his neck and noticed two turkey vultures soaring high in the clouds. The birds were returning—a sure sign of spring.

"Sold it to Julia's younger *bruder*." Simon eyed his son close by, his bucket already brimming with debris. "Go dump that on the compost pile and tell your *mamm* we'll be ready for lunch in thirty minutes. You can collect the rest and burn the branches later."

Simon waited until the boy had run off before speaking. "That woman tests my patience."

"Who, Julia?" Seth asked, starting back up the ladder. He was eager to put the gutter-cleaning chore behind them. The wind could cut right through a man's flesh despite the bright sunshine.

"No, not my wife. Her sister." Simon's voice was low and pained. "But I'm glad to take her in. It's my duty and Julia loves her so."

"What seems to be the problem?" Seth glanced down, surprised that his brother would mention the matter. He vaguely remembered Julia's sister from their wedding in Pennsylvania—a skinny scrap of a gal with big green eyes like a cat and plenty of freckles. Didn't have an ounce of meat on her bones, but she'd seemed tame enough. Seth couldn't fathom how that little filly could so rile Simon but wasn't eager to participate in a conversation that wasn't any of his business, especially when he had little experience with such matters.

"I nearly threw my back out hefting that trunk from the bus terminal. Do you know what that trunk was filled with?" Simon braced his body weight against the ladder to keep it steady.

"Rocks from her favorite creek bed?" Seth reached to scrape out a sodden clump, surprised at Simon showing his impatience like this.

"Might as well have been! Books and more books! Books on farming and crop rotation and herb varieties and birds and bugs and, of course, sheep. Just about everything that lives or grows on the earth. Why would any woman need so many books?"

"Sounds like a way to pass time during a long winter."

"*Jah*, sure, but spring is almost here. Those books could have stayed behind in Pennsylvania." Simon glanced back at the house.

Seth got the distinct feeling it was more than books that had stirred vinegar into his brother's tea on this fine afternoon.

Just then the subject of their conversation stepped out onto the porch. At least that's who Seth assumed the woman to be. Half a foot taller than Julia and still willowy, she walked to the rail and dumped coffee grounds into the flowerbeds. Seth stared, trying to get a better look, and almost lost his balance on the ladder.

"Mind your footing," his brother called. "We've only got another dozen feet before we'll go round to the other side."

The two men finished the dreary chore, amazed at how many leaves managed to blow in when no tree overhung any part of the barn. After washing up, they headed for the house, their faces and hands stinging from the cold.

Seth followed Simon into the warm kitchen and hung his hat on a peg. The savory smell of onions and celery filled the air and made his mouth water. Phoebe was already at the table with her cousins. She grinned when she spotted him.

"Chicken soup," Julia announced, setting a basket of biscuits on the table. "Good and hearty for my hard workers." She patted Matthew's head lovingly.

The woman at the oven turned and met his gaze. Those green cat eyes had turned the color of pine boughs after a rain since he'd last seen her. Seth had planned to say something welcoming and friendly. He'd planned to reintroduce himself, as it had been many years since Simon and Julia's wedding day. But all he could do was stare into the woman's sweet, gentle face...and wonder how this small creature could possibly have upset his brother so.

Silence spun out as the woman waited for him to speak first. When he didn't, she took her seat and looked at Julia.

"Seth, do you remember my sister from Lancaster? Hannah Brown." Julia's voice revealed her fondness. "Hannah's come to live with us. Let's be thankful for that along with our food."

Perhaps a buzzard had plucked his tongue while he'd been busy on the gutters, as speech still wouldn't come. Seth could do no more than nod before bowing his head in silent prayer. Luckily for him, with five *kinner* at the table there was enough conversation that he didn't feel uncomfortable. As Matthew and Henry described the antics of their least favorite milk cow, Seth was able to steal glances at Julia's sister. She looked barely old enough to be courting, let alone widowed already. Her skin resembled the color of that first perfect peach, picked from the highest branch early in August. He forced himself to study his soup and not stare like some young whelp about to ask a girl to take a ride in his courting buggy.

"Phoebe? Do you and your *daed* have cows?" Hannah asked his daughter.

The child stared at the new face with utter terror.

"*Jah,* they have cows," Emma answered. "Not as many as us, though. Uncle keeps a few beef steers too."

"Has your *daed* allowed you to try your hand at milking yet?" Hannah asked, softening her tone to put the child at ease.

"A girl's got no need to learn barn chores. I'd say there's enough to do inside the house," Simon stated emphatically.

"That there is, husband," Julia agreed, passing around the plate of biscuits. Seth helped himself to his third.

"Any new calves born at your farm, Phoebe?" Hannah attempted conversation with the youngster for the third time.

Phoebe's big brown eyes filled with tears, and she looked as though she'd met a bear on the path to the milk house.

"She doesn't talk much, Aunt Hannah," Emma said.

"But she's a real good listener," Leah added as two big tears ran down Phoebe's cheeks.

Hannah looked stricken as she briefly made eye contact with Seth.

"It's all right," Seth said to Phoebe, stroking her back gently. When she crawled into his lap, he wrapped his arms around the trembling child. Any time his daughter was upset or afraid, it tore the hole in his heart wide open again.

After Phoebe settled down, Seth turned to Hannah, who was studying the contents of her soup bowl. "Phoebe will get to know you soon enough. She's shy with strangers," he said, feeling his communication skills weren't much better than his daughter's.

Phoebe was naturally quiet, more so since Constance's passing. But Seth had never seen her so completely terrified of a person before. Of course, Phoebe only saw the same people in the district over and over, whether at Sunday services or at the neighbor's where Phoebe stayed while he worked his fields. In the fall, she would start school. When she was around other children more, his little robin would break from her shell.

What he couldn't figure as he sopped the last of the soup with a bread crust was why he too had suddenly lost the ability to speak in the company of the widow Brown.

THREE

Hannah awoke to a beautiful Sabbath morning feeling grateful for a day of worship and rest. The last few days had flown by quickly, getting the sewing and darning caught up and the spring cleaning started. The women had scrubbed floors and washed walls and windows and made the whole house sparkle. But she wasn't complaining about the hard work. Not since childhood had she known the joy of family living. She hadn't realized how lonely she'd grown. Despite the fact her parents and Thomas had lived nearby, many days would pass without her speaking to anyone other than the fat yellow barn cat.

At the Miller farm, there seldom was a quiet moment. There always were meals to fix or dishes to do besides the daily dusting and sweeping. With spring plowing underway, a cloud of dust blew in every time the door opened or someone threw up a window for some fresh air.

Hannah enjoyed the afterschool time most of all. The *kinner* would rush into the kitchen with shining faces and playground tales while they ate their snack of chocolate cookies and cold milk. Then the boys would hurry to their chores to allow for some playtime before supper. The girls talked of what they'd learned that day, especially Leah, who loved school, and reading most of all.

Each of the children was a unique child of God: Emma—modest and reserved, always the peacemaker between her two brothers; Matthew—hearty and energetic, eager to show his dad how capable a man he was becoming; Henry—shy and quiet, yet never sullen, eager to help his mom with opening jars or carrying kindling; and Leah—dreamy and playful, with a big heart for such a tiny girl, curious about even the lowly spider spinning its web. Hannah had grown to treasure them all in the short time since her arrival. How silly she'd been to question whether she'd made the right decision to move.

Now as she washed her face and hands and tidied her hair, the night of the blizzard seemed a long time ago. Only one thing troubled her as she put on her best Sunday dress...little Phoebe Miller. Was no one else concerned that the child never spoke a word? There wasn't a thing wrong with her hearing. Hannah had noticed her nodding answers and laughing enthusiastically at her cousins' stories. Seth doted on his daughter—spreading her bread with jam, cutting her meat into smaller pieces—yet seemed unconcerned by her extreme shyness. Hannah had thought the child would bolt like a startled deer if she had asked one more question.

But what business did she have questioning how a child was reared? She had no *kinner* of her own to provide practical experience. Her prayers for a baby had gone unanswered during her six years of marriage to Adam. *God had His reasons,* she reminded herself, shaking away her sadness and worry over Phoebe.

Seth Miller seemed like a kind, thoughtful man. If something were amiss with his daughter, he surely would have taken notice.

Hannah joined the Miller family in the kitchen for a pancake breakfast before they walked out to the carriage. Simon, who'd been out readying the horses, sat waiting for them, looking thunderous. "Hurry along," he called. "A deacon should never be late, and it's more than ten miles to the Crumleys'."

Hannah stepped up onto the second bench behind Julia and

Simon, seating herself between the two girls. Matthew and Henry sat in the very back, preferring to view where they had been instead of where they were going. It was indeed a long drive to the farm holding the preaching service, and Hannah was grateful Simon had brought heavy lap robes he'd warmed atop the woodstove.

Simon hunched down in his heavy coat from the strong wind that managed to blow inside the enclosed carriage. He didn't look much larger than his wife, who leaned into his side for added warmth. Hannah had noticed Seth Miller was very tall with big hands and long fingers. He had to weigh at least fifty pounds more than his older brother. *Funny how siblings often turn out completely different.* She was much taller and thinner than Julia, who'd always been sturdy and well rounded. Both Miller men possessed thick heads of hair, Simon's lightly streaked with gray, and both were soft-spoken. However, Seth often boomed out a hearty laugh when something tickled his funny bone.

It was Julia who loved making them all laugh. But Simon seldom chanced much more than a halfhearted grin. Perhaps he feared his face wouldn't return to its natural position.

Hannah bit down on the inside of her mouth as penance for such unkind thoughts. Simon had opened his already full house to take in one person more, so perhaps she could show a little more gratitude. Soon the carriage turned down a rutted lane leading to a large, rambling house. Many carriages were parked neatly side by side, promising a full house for the Crumley family. She clasped her nieces' hands tightly as Simon maneuvered around the driveway puddles.

"*Guder mariye,* Mrs. Brown. I'm glad the snow you brought from Pennsylvania decided not to stick around," a voice spoke over her shoulder.

Startled, Hannah turned quickly and stepped down into five inches of icy water. It immediately seeped through her worn boot soles and chilled her foot to the bone. "Goodness, Seth Miller," she exclaimed, stamping her foot to keep it from freezing into a solid block. Her surprise stemmed more from seeing the subject of her musings for the last half hour than the shock of a wet foot.

"Beggin' your pardon. I didn't mean to startle you," Seth said, tipping up the rim of his hat. His face had turned the color of pickled beets, but his eyes twinkled with merriment. "I'll send over Mrs. Crumley to help. Maybe she can supply you with some dry socks before the preaching starts."

Before Hannah could stop him, he picked up his daughter and strolled off, disappearing into the crowd milling about before services began.

She stamped her foot again—this time from her embarrassment rather than as an attempt to keep the blood flowing—as Emma and Leah giggled. This was her first day in her new district, and the first impression she would make on Mrs. Crumley and the other women was that she couldn't watch where she walked and that she expected a busy wife to drop what she was doing to find a stranger some dry socks.

Hannah followed Julia and the children into the Crumley parlor where long rows of benches had been set up, knowing very well that some things were much more uncomfortable than a wet foot. At least when she glanced in Seth Miller's direction on the men's side of the room, he offered her the smallest of grins.

Simon and the other deacons passed out hymnals, and soon all gathered were reciting traditional German hymns familiar to Hannah from back home. Another deacon read Scripture; Simon delivered a short sermon; and then they bowed their heads in silent prayer. After the bishop delivered the main message, Hannah chanced a peek at Seth. She hoped he hadn't been offended by her sharp words. He'd been looking in her direction too and flushed deeply when he met her eye. They both looked down at their hymnals so quickly, it could have been mistaken for some sort of race.

A lengthy list of announcements of new births and people who were ill followed the benediction. Hannah wondered if she would ever come to know and love the people of this community as she had those of Lancaster County. A widow had few opportunities to social-ize and make new friends even if she had a mind to. Right now all she wanted was her flock to arrive. The busier she stayed, the easier it would be to forget her old home. With her heart in Pennsylvania, she had a hard time concentrating on the words of the closing hymn.

Soon Hannah was caught up in the flurry of moving benches and setting up tables for the noon meal. The women served the men their sandwiches first. Then it was their turn and the children's. Hannah refilled coffee cups and fetched lemonade for those who preferred something cold to drink. Julia introduced her to so many welcoming faces that her fears of just a short while ago seemed foolish. It was some time before she could stop meeting new people and rest her back against Mrs. Crumley's comfortable sofa.

"Aunt Hannah," Leah said, peering outside from the parlor window, "would you push me on the swing? The boys are gone from it."

When Hannah nodded in agreement, the child ran to get their capes. Hannah looked out to the side yard, where, sure enough, the swing hanging from a sturdy branch sat empty.

"I'll come too," Emma said, shrugging into her long cape. "I'd love to get some air." As the three stepped onto the front porch, Hannah spotted Simon walking from a knot of men. It was the first time she'd seen him alone since the noon meal, and she wanted to mention how his sermon had touched her heart and maybe take the opportunity to thank him privately for opening his home to her.

"Emma, please push your sister for a while. There's your *daed,* and I'd like to speak with him for a moment."

The two girls ran toward the tree before other *kinner* got the same idea, while Hannah headed in the deacon's direction. As she crossed the lawn, a young man of about sixteen with the clean-shaven face of the unmarried approached Simon from the row of carriages. A deacon had many responsibilities in his district, and Hannah would simply have to wait her turn.

"Wait up, Deacon Miller," the youth called.

Simon turned, shielding his eyes from the sun's glare. "Amos, how's your grandmother? I heard today that she's ailing." He had to crane his neck to look into the lanky young man's face.

"She's in bed with a bad cold, but she's starting to feel a little better. Pap sent me home after service to check on her—see if she needed anything."

"That was good of you. Go into the kitchen if you missed the noon meal. I'm sure Mrs. Crumley has something left over to feed you." Simon nodded then turned to walk off.

"No, deacon," the boy called. "It's you I mean to speak to. I passed by your farm on the way home, both comin' and goin'. On the way back, I saw an eighteen-wheeler sitting in your driveway. I feared it be might be lost...looking for some English farm...so I stopped to ask the driver his business." The boy drew a deep breath and tipped his hat back on his head.

Simon's forehead furrowed into deep creases. "A truck, you say?"

"He wasn't lost," the boy continued. "He said he was lookin' for the Simon Miller farm. Said he had sixty head of sheep to deliver. I told him he'd found the right place." The youth paused for a moment for Deacon Miller to collect his thoughts.

It took little time for Simon to exclaim, "On the Sabbath?"

"That's what I thought too. I told him to sit tight and I'd fetch you."

It was then that Amos noticed Hannah hovering behind the deacon, probably because of the expression of complete joy on her face. Her sheep had arrived! Not just her business, which generated cash for the always-increasing land costs, but her warm, cuddly, gentle, lovable sheep. She certainly had her favorites and had named almost half the flock. A few even seemed to prick up their ears when she called their names.

"My sheep!" she exclaimed with great pleasure as she stepped up to the two men.

∼

"*On the Sabbath?*" Simon repeated at exactly the same time Hannah spoke. The deacon stared at Amos as though he must have heard wrong. "That English driver can't unload those sheep on the Sabbath." Simon could feel the sandwich he'd eaten earlier take a nasty churn in his stomach. "How would it look to the young people whom I instruct in the *Ordnung* if I go accepting delivery of livestock on the Sabbath?"

"Don't know about that," Amos replied, looking uncomfortable.

The sheep I don't even want in the first place, Simon thought.

"You say my sheep have arrived?" Hannah asked.

"What do you know about this, Hannah?" Simon asked, turning to face her. "Why did your *bruder* set up delivery for today? He should've known we couldn't unload a truck on the Sabbath." Amos saw this as his opportunity to get away from a personal family matter, and he started walking toward the Crumley kitchen.

Hannah looked bewildered. "There must have been a mistake by the English trucking company—some confusion. Thomas never would have scheduled delivery for today."

"Well, they're parked in my driveway right now, according to Amos. And that truck's wheels are probably sinking into the soft gravel with all the melt-off we've had this week. We'll be lucky if it doesn't get stuck and have to stay with us all week." Simon heard his voice rising in pitch and volume, and quickly tamped down his temper.

"*Jah*, right. We mustn't let that truck get bogged down. We'll just release the sheep into the fenced pasture you said I could use and get that driver on his way. I'll tend to them tomorrow. We sure don't want to be charged for any extra days." Hannah dug her fingers down into her apron pockets, looking cold and nervous. Her nose had turned the color of ripe cherries.

"No, Hannah, I'm sorry. He'll have to drive off and come back tomorrow. I'm a deacon in this district. How would it look if I started breaking the rules just to suit our own convenience and pocketbook?" He hoped that would settle the matter, not having any desire to argue with his sister-in-law on the day she'd been welcomed into their community.

"But Simon, I have many spring lambs that I haven't sold off yet. They're not weaned. I need to get them off that crowded truck before they get trampled. They'll need to find their mothers and nurse. The longer they stay in tight confinement, the greater the chances of losing them. They're still babies." Hannah had stepped forward and seemed to be looming over him.

"No, Hannah. I'm not rushing home to deal with your sheep. I'll send Seth back to the farm to talk to the truck driver. I can't leave the Crumleys' yet. He'll arrange for him to come back. That's all I'll say on the subject."

Simon turned his back on her unhappy face before he changed his mind. He didn't need to start giving in to the whims of women. What had Julia's little brother been thinking? Simon wasn't so sure it had been a misunderstanding on the part of the English trucking company. Thomas probably didn't count ahead his days when he'd arranged delivery. That young man usually had his mind on sneaking off to the pond for a swim in warm weather or grabbing up his fishing pole, according to what Julia had told him.

The more Simon thought on the matter, the more it irked him. Hannah should have stayed home with Thomas to help him manage things, at least until he married. Without a wife, Thomas probably needed her help with household chores. Now she'd moved to Ohio with her pack of smelly beasts that served little purpose other than eat all day long. At least cows produced food a person could eat. And a cow could always be sold for meat once it stopped producing milk. But nobody he knew ate mutton in America. And from what he'd learned from Julia, Hannah was reluctant to sell off her spring lambs to the packinghouse. That's why her flock kept growing larger and larger.

Simon glanced skyward to the heavens, hoping an easy answer would be forthcoming. But he saw only a flock of mallards flying in V-formation on their path north. "Sheep," he muttered, and went in search of his brother.

∼

Julia glanced out the Crumleys' kitchen window as Hannah came up the porch steps. Her nose was running, and her eyes were filled with tears. At first Julia thought it merely the effects of the cold wind until her sister drew closer and she saw sorrow on Hannah's usually cheerful face.

Julia threw a shawl around her shoulders and stepped outside so they might speak in private. "What happened, little sister? Won't my two selfish daughters give you a turn on the swing?"

Hannah looked up, her face awash with misery. "Oh, Julia. There's been some kind of mix-up. My sheep have come. The truck sits in your yard right now. But it's the Sabbath, and we can't unload them. Simon is sending Seth back to the farm to tell the truck to return tomorrow." Two big tears slipped from her eyes, but she hastily wiped them away. "I'm worried about my newborns. I don't want to break Sabbath, but I don't want them to suffer either."

Julia watched Hannah bite down on her lip, her usual behavior when she thought she might have said too much. "*Ach*, always something to worry about. Why don't you ride back with Seth to the farm? Then you can see for yourself that your sheep are fine. It's not against the *Ordnung* to feed and water animals; we did so before we left for services. Seth can straighten out the mix-up while you fetch some food and water. I don't think that will require much labor." Julia pulled Hannah into her arms briefly, feeling her shiver from the cold and her anxiety.

"*Danki*, Julia. *Danki* so much," Hannah whispered and strode in the direction of the Crumley barn.

～

Simon had no sooner marched off toward the house than Seth spotted Hannah Brown coming in his direction. At least she looked happier than his brother had been. Seth led his horse from the corral and began walking toward his buggy. He'd been itching to leave anyway when his brother had approached with his request. He wanted to put Phoebe to bed and get to his evening chores. He hoped he wouldn't lose his ability to talk as he had the other night at dinner.

"Afternoon, Mrs. Brown," he said, grasping the horse's bridle to bring him to a stop when she drew nearer. "I hope your foot has warmed up by now."

· "Good afternoon. My foot is fine. And please call me Hannah. After all, we are family by marriage."

"All right, Hannah. Simon tells me your sheep have come. That must set your mind at ease."

"Not at ease yet. Has Simon asked you to go to his place?" She looked up at him, her lashes long and darker than her hair.

"*Jah,* I'm heading there now. Soon as I hitch up the horse and collect Phoebe." He tried to focus on the budding trees overhead or the horses prancing in the distance. It seemed that every time he looked into her face, he became nervous.

"May I ride home with you then? I'm ready to leave now. I'll just tell Julia if you agree." Hannah's smile set two dimples deep into her cheeks, adding to her still youthful prettiness. She tucked in a stray lock of hair that had escaped her *kapp* in the breeze.

"*Jah,* sure." Seth might have said more on the way to the house but his tongue had stuck to the roof of his mouth. He considered asking Hannah to fetch Phoebe to save time but remembered how scared the child had been of a new face. No sense causing a ruckus if Phoebe decided to fuss. When he found his daughter with the children in the parlor, he couldn't find Hannah. But by the time he hitched the horse into the traces, he spotted her sitting on the second bench of his carriage. "What are you doing back there, Hannah? Come sit up front with Phoebe and me. There's enough room, and she'll stay warmer wedged between us."

Hannah obliged by climbing into the front. Phoebe looked upset, but she didn't start crying. Once on the road, Seth questioned his decision to suggest she sit up front. The seat wasn't all that wide for three of them, and he hardly knew the woman. She belonged in the backseat where she'd originally put herself. Now he'd have to sit with this stranger only inches away, and he couldn't think of a single intelligent thing to say.

Hannah broke the uncomfortable silence by speaking first. "I'm grateful for the ride, Seth. I can't wait to check on my sheep. They've suffered enough on the trip. You know how livestock can get banged around in those trucks, especially on twisty mountain roads."

"*Jah*, that's true," he agreed, clucking at the horse to pick up the pace.

"I'm anxious about them and eager to get them off that truck and into their new pasture." Her voice was filled with emotion.

"Hold on a minute. My *bruder* wants me to tell the driver to come back tomorrow. He refuses to take delivery on the Sabbath."

"Hmmm," she agreed, nodding enthusiastically. "And that's what we'll do too, unless the driver can get them off and maneuvered into the pasture without our help. Maybe I can ask one of Simon's English neighbors to help." Hannah glanced at Seth with a hopeful smile.

"I don't know about that. Simon doesn't like asking for help unless it's some kind of emergency. I don't rightly think this qualifies." Seth looked away, not liking to disappoint a woman.

"Oh, but it does." Hannah smoothed the folds from the lap blanket and tucked it around Phoebe's legs. "I've got baby lambs in that truck. I fear they'll get trampled if not released. They've probably been separated from their mothers during the whole trip. You know how loading animals can turn into a melee. Some might die if they can't nurse." Her voice had dropped to barely above a whisper. "And then there's the matter of the truck wheels sinking into the soft ground."

Seth gave his beard a pull, trying to sort all this out. The matter had been crystal clear when his brother had explained the situation. But Hannah had made some excellent points. Nobody wanted to see any lambs die if they could be unloaded without much help on their part. Simon didn't need a tractor-trailer mired in his driveway. And he sure wanted to help the widow if there was any way he could.

In the end, Hannah Brown got her beloved flock off the truck and properly fed and watered. Seth joined her at the fence rail once he'd thanked the English driver for his extra work. She was watching her brood wander over the low hills toward the riverbank. Phoebe squealed with delight upon spotting twin lambs nursing from their mother. Hannah thanked him profusely for asking the driver to unload the flock.

He had a feeling, however, that Simon wouldn't be quite so pleased even with the truck safely on its way back to Lancaster.

As Seth counted the large number of new lambs, it occurred to him how a sheep operation might be exactly what he needed to increase his farm revenue. They would be far less labor-intensive than expanding into a full dairy operation. This could be the idea he'd been asking for in his nightly prayers.

He watched as Hannah retrieved her crook from under the porch and then marched off through the meadow looking like Bo Peep from the picture books. His heart tightened uncomfortably against his chest wall. He probably shouldn't breathe so deeply in the cold air. Hannah Brown seemed to be a kind, gentle soul—one he could learn from if he wanted to start his own sheep operation.

Simon had forgotten how it felt to be lonely. He enjoyed the loving companionship of a good wife and four healthy *kinner*. But Seth remembered the days after Simon first met Julia while they had been visiting an aunt and uncle in Pennsylvania. After their return home, his shy, backward brother had stumbled through his chores like a lovesick duck after its mate had been killed. He wrote her a letter every night, although most he burned in the woodstove instead of mailing. He invented excuse after excuse why he needed to travel back to Pennsylvania until finally their mom and dad made him admit the truth—he was in love.

His private, circumspect brother was head-over-heels in love with Julia. Their father had taken pity on him and sent him to live with their uncle for a year so that he and Julia might court properly, even though it left their farm shorthanded.

Simon may have forgotten what loneliness felt like, but Seth hadn't. Usually his chores kept him too busy to dwell on it, but every now and then it would creep up on him like a snake in the woodpile.

For some reason, Hannah had become a burr in the sock of his older brother. And until that matter straightened itself out, he could at least be her friend. Everyone needed a friend, especially a widow who had moved to a new land.

Especially a widow with sparkling green eyes and skin the creamy color of that first perfect peach of summer.

FOUR

"Oh, good grief," Hannah muttered with both hands planted firmly on her hips. "With an entire pasture around you, must you all crowd into one small spot?" The question had been directed at brown speckled animals without enough manners to glance up from their munching. Most were muddy up to their bellies, their wool not looking like anything *Englischers* would want to knit into sweaters or hats.

She tightened the shawl around her shoulders and scanned the nearby fields. The sun felt warm on her cheeks and soon would melt the last lingering snow along the fence line. A few of the animals had wandered away from the gate to graze. But most, true to their reputation, preferred to remain close to where Seth had placed two water troughs. Since their arrival, they had already eaten the new spring grass down to roots and churned the area in which they had congregated into a sea of mud.

She stepped up onto the lowest fence rail. "You are not pigs," she called. "Do not turn this into a pigpen."

Again her beloved flock refused to dignify the chastisement with a response. At this rate, the entire pasture would be reduced to swampland. And Simon wouldn't be happy about that. She knew she'd annoyed him yesterday when she had asked Seth to ask the driver to unload. But what other choice did she have? This morning she had prayed for a smooth transition of her wool business with a minimum of disruption to the Miller household. One glance at her mud-caked flock told her that was not to be.

Hannah didn't wish to appear ungrateful, but the field Simon had given her was too small. Her sheep were used to grazing over a much larger area—and on higher ground. A pang of longing filled her heart for her beloved Lancaster County. Spring had already arrived back home, bringing snowdrops, windflowers, and the first purple crocus. Her neighbors had finished plowing and tilling their fields, and some had even begun to plant hay and wheat. The farms of Holmes County seemed weeks behind those of Pennsylvania. But something else was curdling her morning glass of buttermilk. Hannah knew she should have waited to move the flock from Lancaster County until the sun had a chance to dry things up. With snow still melting in the hills, the pasture was far too wet. This was the first sunny day since her arrival. She'd just introduced sixty animals onto land where the grass hadn't had a chance to come in. Her hungry mob could quickly overgraze even a lush pasture. "Humble yourselves, therefore, under God's mighty hand, that he may lift you up in due time. Cast all your anxiety on him because he cares for you." The Scripture she'd read last night in First Peter reminded her to be patient—not the easiest assignment.

At least she hadn't lost any of her new lambs enroute. As she watched a playful pair trying to nurse, Hannah felt something tickling her left temple. A crawly sensation coupled with a muffled buzzing sent a shiver up her spine. A bee or hornet had crawled under her *kapp!* Though she possessed no fear of any of God's creatures, she preferred stinging insects keep to themselves. With a shriek, she jumped down from the rail and yanked off her *kapp*. Even after shaking her head side to side furiously, she still heard the insistent buzzing as the insect crawled closer to her scalp. In sheer panic Hannah pulled the pins from her bun and shook out her hair. Her thick hair fell across her shoulders and down her back in a tangle, but the bug finally flew off. With her heart pounding in her chest and her breath coming in great gulps, Hannah laughed at her overreaction. The bee was probably just as glad to be rid of her. Bowing her head, she closed her eyes and whispered a silent prayer as her heart rate returned to normal. It hadn't stung her! The early hatchling would live to taste summer nectar, and she wouldn't have a painful goose egg on her forehead.

Hannah repinned her hair and replaced her *kapp* before walking into the boggy pasture to count the sheep and check for any injuries she might have overlooked during unloading. Hurt or sick animals often hid in the middle of the flock, so as not to be singled out by coyotes or other predators. As she wandered further from the gate, nothing appeared out of the ordinary among the tired, cranky beasts. She prodded animals lying down to their feet with her crook. Their bleating and complaining sounded particularly unhappy, as though they were displeased with their new Ohio home. She knew most of them were probably hungry and would need supplemental feed.

Just as her thoughts turned to Julia's strong coffee or a soothing cup of chamomile tea, Hannah stepped into an old gopher hole. Icy cold water immediately filled her boot. "*Ach,*" she muttered as she tried to pull out her foot, which had become wedged in the narrow hole. When she finally got her foot loose, the boot remained behind in the smelly muck. Reluctantly she reached into the hole to get her boot back.

Hannah Brown, twenty-eight years old and an experienced farm wife, stood balanced on one foot, with a muddy boot in one hand and a muddier foot held aloft, and no dry place to sit down and sort things out. The bottom ten inches of her dress were wet and encrusted with mud. Her stockings had turned the color of a sheep's underbelly, and even her white apron was speckled like a robin's egg.

Back home, she would have been wearing Adam's old muck boots, which reached her knees. She used to tuck her long skirt inside the boots, allowing only enough leeway for easy movement, and then stomp through the fields without soiling her clothes. Nobody had lived close enough to witness her unladylike appearance. Now she lived in a houseful of onlookers, including four impressionable *kinner*, a deacon in the district, and a sister who desperately wanted her to adjust to the community. Still, she might have to pull them out of the trunk.

Hannah considered her limited options: She could tromp into Julia's spotless kitchen and leave a messy trail in her wake. Or she could go to the pump house to clean up—but then she chanced running into Simon. She probably looked as silly as she felt and preferred keeping a low profile. Her third option involved washing her feet in the stream with temperatures barely above freezing. But the icy water that flowed down from melting snow asked no questions and offered no suggestions.

She decided to chance on freezing to death and headed toward the creek.

After washing out her sock and shoe, Hannah leaned back on her elbows and laughed at her predicament with her feet knee-deep in cold water. This wasn't the first time she'd made a mess of things. And it certainly wasn't her first foolish decision. But it was the first time she didn't have the sympathetic eyes of Adam as her only witness.

Hannah Brown, surrounded by six people, including four children, felt very much alone.

But alone or not, her sheep weren't getting enough to eat, and that problem wouldn't go away on its own. Replacing her sock and boot, she shivered all the way back to the house. With some of the money Thomas paid her for the farm, she would buy feed to last several months. By then the grass should have thickened up in the pasture. She had relied on Adam in such matters but no longer had that luxury.

She dug through her trunk under the porch and found her books on the care and feeding of sheep. Without Adam or Thomas or her *daed*, Hannah had only books to tell her what to feed, how much, and how often. But somehow the cracked leather bindings and creased pages of her texts reassured her. Even the smell of mildew didn't offend her senses as she scanned the index. Books had become her only friends in her new land, so until she made others of the human variety, she would take comfort here.

~

Simon Miller wasn't a happy man. Although the unloading of the sheep on the Sabbath had been accomplished without breaking the *Ordnung,* he still felt his authority had been challenged. He didn't like how Hannah had questioned him in front of teenaged Amos. Young people needed to see good examples of respect and deference, not someone debating a deacon. And how did Hannah talk Seth into her idea? Seth must have persuaded the driver to unload the livestock by himself. Yet Seth was as levelheaded and practical as they came, not a man who'd humor female whims. How lucky, Simon thought, that Julia was nothing like her willful sister. Julia never questioned his decisions. Her infrequent advice was well intentioned and well timed. She was a helpmate and a loving support, not a woman caught up with her own ideas. Adam Brown surely must have had the patience of Job to deal with his wife.

Simon turned his attention from the gelding he was grooming to the darkening sky. He gave his beard a thoughtful pull and prayed it wouldn't snow. He needed to plow and disk his fields. He wanted to sow his wheat seeds before the heavy rains came. Yet the high ground was still frozen while the low remained too wet to cultivate. He had finished straightening all the bent implements, sharpened all the cutting blades, thoroughly sanitized the milking parlor, whitewashed the sheds, and cleaned the barn from top to bottom. Now he was itching to get his fingers back into the dirt. Nothing smelled as sweet as newly turned earth to a farmer. Even the cackle from crows would be music to his ears if only he could start plowing. Soon the age old cycle of rebirth would begin as winter released its grip on the land. This year Matthew would be old enough to drive a team of horses by himself, while Henry could ride along with him. Emma would finish school in a couple months, so she would be home to help Julia whenever the arthritis flared up. Julia wouldn't need Henry as much in the garden or with kitchen chores.

It was Emma who had him worried. Her fascination with Aunt Hannah seemed boundless. And Hannah Brown wasn't the kind of example he wanted for his daughter. That very morning Simon had seen Hannah pull off her *kapp* and take all the pins from her bun. She had shaken out her long hair as though it were a source of great pride. Vanity—pure and simple! What kind of behavior was that for an Amish woman?

A short while ago he had seen her on the riverbank with her feet dangling in the water when she was supposed to be counting her flock. He couldn't imagine the cold water had felt good. Some people would use any excuse to shirk their duties for a few minutes of playtime. How tired could tending sheep possibly make a person? He planned to speak to the widow about her vanity and laziness before Emma started to emulate her. Hannah was no longer living on her own—under his roof she must follow his rules.

He unhitched the horse from the crossties before he brushed the coat down to bare skin. After returning the gelding to his stall, he spotted the subject of his irritation duck beneath the porch. What could she possibly be looking for among the old implements stored there? Then Simon remembered her battered trunk and felt a little guilty. He should have dragged it inside the barn or into the cellar, out of the dampness, but the two of them could do that later.

"Good afternoon, Hannah," Simon greeted. "What are you looking for?"

Hannah glanced up. Two heavy books were balanced on her knees, while several others had been stacked on a straw bale near her feet.

"Good afternoon, Simon. I've found what I sought—a description of the proper mixture for sheep feed, especially good nourishment for nursing mothers." Her face radiated with joy.

Simon swallowed his irritation at finding her nose buried in a book. At least her *kapp* was back in place. "The grass in my pasture isn't to your liking?" he asked.

She shook her head. "Oh, it'll be just fine come summer. But for now, I'd better buy feed, or they'll eat the grass so low it might kill the roots." Her attention returned to the page where various grains with percentages of additives were listed. "I've brought some of the down payment Thomas paid before I left Pennsylvania, so it'll be no problem to purchase feed—just to tide us over until the grass comes in." Her finger trailed down one column and up the other making comparisons.

No problem? Where exactly was she planning to buy this feed, and who would take time away from chores to help her? Simon was about to voice his concerns when a booming voice over his shoulder startled him out of his boots. He turned so quickly he bumped his head on the overhang while his hat fell into a puddle. He found himself face-to-face with his younger brother. Speaking to Hannah about keeping a proper appearance around the farm would have to wait.

～

"The first sunny day and you two decide to move the parlor out of doors?" asked Seth, surveying the curious scene before him. His *bruder* was stooped under the porch while the widow Brown sat on an upended milk crate. Books and papers were spread around her feet as though she were sitting before a cozy living room fire. She glanced up and met his eye. Unless he was mistaken, Hannah looked pleased to see him.

He swept his hat from his head and bowed, feeling a little silly with the gesture. "Good afternoon, Mrs. Brown. I would have thought Julia could find indoor accommodations for you. It's a big house." He was grinning like a schoolboy.

"Hello, Seth. It's good to see you." She bobbed her head politely. "I wanted to thank you again for helping me yesterday, and I wondered if you were going to a grain elevator anytime soon. I need livestock feed." Her cheeks had flushed to bright pink, which on her looked very pretty. "I need sheep feed, and I looked up the perfect blend in one of Adam's old reference books." She tapped a forefinger on the worn leather binding.

"Now, Hannah, we shouldn't impose on Seth for errands we could do ourselves," Simon said, ducking out from under the porch. He rubbed the bruised spot on his forehead. "I'm sure he's busy getting ready for spring planting. I'll take you later in the week when I call on shut-ins as deacon."

Impulsively, Seth spoke up. "I had planned to ride into Mount Eaton today for extra seed corn. It has the largest feed supply in the three-county area. Have you been to Mount Eaton? You're welcome to ride with me and Phoebe if you like." He hadn't planned to make the trip today. He wanted to burn the brush pile of tree branches that had accumulated over winter and clear the fields for plowing. He'd stopped only to drop off the cutting blades Simon had promised to sharpen.

"May I?" she asked. "*Danki,* Seth. My hungry sheep won't like waiting until later in the week for something to eat." Hannah began loading her books back into the trunk.

Seth caught his brother's expression when Hannah quoted his exact words, yet she seemed oblivious to her effect on the man. He bit down on the inside of his cheek to keep from grinning.

Simon slapped his damp hat back on his head. "Matthew and I will move your trunk to the barn while you're at the grain elevator," Simon said, "to get it out of the damp air."

"Oh, would you?" she asked, finishing her repacking. "That would be better, *danki,* Simon." Hannah rose from the milk crate and ducked her head beneath the overhang.

It was then that Seth got a good look at her appearance. Her cape hung askew, and the hem of her dress was caked with dried mud. Mud had also spattered across her white apron. One leather boot was dusty while the other looked soaking wet. Grime streaked across one cheek, and there was a dot of something suspicious on the tip of her nose. Several tendrils of wheat-colored hair escaped her *kapp* and framed her face.

Simon blanched at her unkempt appearance, and a muscle began to twitch in his right cheek.

But Seth's opinion of Hannah went up a notch or two. He liked a woman not afraid to work hard, and working on a farm meant getting dirty. Judging by her appearance, the widow must have worked very hard that morning. "Looks like you've already been busy today, Mrs. Brown."

Hannah glanced down at her skirt then rubbed the palms of her hands on her apron. "Oh, my, I look a sight. I forgot how muddy fields get this time of year. I'll change into something clean and meet you at your wagon in ten minutes."

Simon shuffled his feet in the gravel and kicked at a rock. "Seth just arrived, Hannah," he said, sounding peevish. "Maybe he's not ready to leave right this minute."

Seth stepped between the two and said to Simon. "Let's unload the tools I brought for you to sharpen, *bruder*. It'll give Mrs. Brown time to change and Phoebe a chance to visit with her cousins. Then we can be off."

Shaking his head, Simon stalked away, allowing Seth a moment to speak to Hannah. She stood only inches away in a state of disarray he'd never seen his wife or *mamm* in before. Yet she met his gaze with cool assurance.

"*Danki*, Seth. You've come to my rescue twice in two days." She smiled sweetly before stepping past him and heading toward the house.

Once again, Seth found himself speechless. Hannah possessed a confidence not commonplace among Amish women—at least his

Constance hadn't had it. Constance had asked his opinion and advice even with matters in which she was experienced. And work directly with livestock? Not his late wife. She didn't enjoy the few times she'd helped him milk cows. Constance had been afraid of grown animals. Only the newborns had interested her, and only when he'd carried them out of the pasture. The house had been Constance's domain. But even on the hottest days of summer, after an afternoon of canning fruits and vegetables, she'd always greeted him in a freshly pressed dress.

The widow Brown hadn't appeared the least bit embarrassed that she was muddy from head to toe. She might never have noticed if he and Simon hadn't stared. Yet even in disarray, Seth had to admit she was a fine-looking woman.

And that one errant thought made Seth feel ashamed...as though he'd been disloyal.

Inviting Hannah to go to Mount Eaton had been a mistake— one that became more apparent when he told Phoebe that Hannah would accompany them. The child ran upstairs into Leah's bedroom and refused to come out. Forcing her to do so would only cause a scene. And he didn't want Julia to fret over his daughter more than she already did. So after they unloaded the tools and finished the shopping lists, he found himself riding ninety minutes to town with a woman who robbed him of his ability to speak.

But he needn't have worried. Mrs. Brown seemed to have words for them both.

"Where is Phoebe?" Hannah asked, once settled on the seat beside him. "I thought you said you brought her today."

"*Jah*, she came with me but decided to stay with her aunt instead," Seth said, not meeting her eye. It was true; Phoebe clung to Julia like pollen dust. But Seth didn't mention that his daughter didn't like strangers and usually bolted like a rabbit if one came around. Now that Hannah lived at Simon's, Phoebe would get used to her in time.

"She's a lovely child, well behaved. You must be very proud."

He looked at the woman sitting so near it made him nervous. He smelled the scent of raspberries but dared not ask why. "*Jah,* she made her *mamm* and me proud. She was the apple of Constance's eye. Gentle like her too, and smart."

Hannah smiled, leaning back against the bench. "I wish I could have met Constance, and you could have met Adam. How he loved springtime. Of course, spring comes earlier in Lancaster County than here in Holmes and puts on a better show. I'm sure the meadows back home are already covered with wildflowers and the skies filled with songbirds. I haven't seen any birds here other than crows and hawks."

Seth slapped the reins against the horses' backs to pick up the pace "If you ask me, birds do nothing but peck away the new seeds if they're not planted deep enough and wake a man up with all their squawking. I've got no use for birds until late summer when they can't do too much damage."

Hannah pondered this for a moment. "What about spring flowers—white trillium, wild violets, and grape hyacinths? Are they also nothing but a thorn in your side?" Her voice sounded teasing and playful.

Seth slanted her a glance. "*Jah,* if they shoot up in my hay or cornfields. They will sap all the minerals and nutrients from the soil. Now if they have the sense to grow in my backwoods, I can appreciate them." He felt a lonesome ache, remembering the bouquet of violets he once picked for Constance and left in the center of her kitchen table. She'd acted as though he'd given her the sun, the moon, and all the stars.

Hannah tilted her head to the side. "Ah, that means the flowers back home are more sensible than Ohio's because the ones I mentioned grow only deep in the forest." She appeared to be biting the inside of her cheek.

"Is that right? What do you call all those pink flowers that spring up everywhere in my pasture? They cover just about everything over until I get the field plowed under."

She turned to face him. "Does it grow so thick it trips you when you try to walk through it?"

He nodded but kept his focus on the road.

"It's probably crown vetch, but I would need my plant book to make positive identification. That ground cover works great to control erosion if you seed it along a riverbank."

He shook his head. "Don't know why anybody would plant the stuff. It moves in uninvited and then takes over if given half a chance. Like that kudzu vine I read about down south."

"Oh, you enjoy studying books, do you?" she asked. "I have several you might want to look at." Hannah relaxed against the seat back and straightened her skirt. At least this one wasn't spattered with muck.

Seth moved away from the subject of her library of reference books, knowing his brother's opinion. "What do you have in mind to buy at the feed store? Today they'll be busy as hens at a corn spill with everybody eager to plant their first crop."

"I need a grain mixture to feed my sheep. You know, back home most of the corn, wheat, and rye would be in by now. They would wait to sow only soybeans and, of course, vegetables." She gazed at the fallow fields they passed on the right.

Seth pitied her homesickness yet felt obliged to defend himself and his fellow neighbors. "Look there, Hannah—plowing and seeding on our left." He pointed at an Amish man driving a team with his son following behind with the seed bag. "Looks like the Holmes County farmers aren't quite as lazy as you thought."

She turned toward him on the seat. "Oh, *es tut mir leid,* Seth, if I sounded like that. I only meant that the Lancaster Valley must get more sunny March days." Her face looked truly apologetic.

"You probably do get more sunshine. We get lots of clouds that blow down from Lake Erie in early spring, but they'll be gone soon.

Constance loved April. She used to say the month was God's blessing for remaining faithful all winter."

"What a beautiful sentiment. I will try to remember it. Those clouds blowing down from up north probably bring quite a bit of rain. I hope not too much—my pasture is already wet enough to grow rice." She shivered and clutched her cape more tightly around her shoulders.

Seth felt oddly guilty, as though personally responsible for cloudy days, too much rain, and the chilly breeze buffeting the wagon. "I've been to Lancaster County enough times to know they get their share of bad weather, Hannah."

She laughed, not the reaction he expected. "*Jah,* that's true enough, but the air back home definitely smells sweeter. Do you have a paper mill nearby? Or maybe a meat-packing house?" She asked with such sincerity he tamped down the anger inching up his spine.

He shook his head. "No, nothing like that, Mrs. Brown. What you smell is good, old-fashioned farming—manure being tilled into the soil for fertilizer. Several farms on this road are certified organic. Their produce will fetch a good price in the fall. Some of the farmers have contracts with whole-foods markets. Everything they grow is bought up at a negotiated price even before the seeds are sown. Something to think about for the future."

"*Jah,* organic produce is becoming more popular all the time. I've been reading a lot about it."

Just then the wheel hit a pothole in the road, and the wagon lurched to the side. Seth instinctively reached for Hannah's arm to steady her. The feel of her skin was soft and warm. The brief touch caused a heady sensation followed by a pang of guilt.

"Better hang on," he instructed. "I put that handle there for my Constance to hold. No sense landing in a heap on the floorboards."

Hannah grasped the handle with both hands. "*Danki,*" she said quietly.

He hadn't meant to sound so gruff. But he didn't like the way one touch of a woman's hand had affected him. He was eager to get to town and get their errands finished. This skinny whelp of a woman was having an odd effect on him—one he didn't like.

~

Hannah discussed the feed mixture with the clerk at the grain elevator, who agreed with the book's advice. She purchased the sheep feed and watched the men load it into the wagon. Seth said he had his own errands to run and insisted she wait for him in a small café. As she sipped a cup of strong coffee, it occurred to her that she unwittingly made Seth nervous. But he had an unsettling effect on her too.

He had such affection for his wife, Constance. How tender were his memories of their life together. Just for a moment, she envied his devotion. She doubted Adam would have spoken that way about her. He had been a man of few words, especially when it came to expressing his feelings. And did she deserve such devotion? The way she spoke of Lancaster County with such enthusiasm made her seem unappreciative of the home Julia and Simon had made for her.

During the drive back to Winesburg, she kept quiet and bowed her head. Last night before bed she had read Galatians 5:26: "We must not be proud, or irritate one another, or be jealous of one another."

Seth might have thought her napping, but she was praying instead. She prayed to be delivered from her own pettiness and jealousy. God had shone His grace and mercy on her many times, and she should be grateful for all her blessings.

But she couldn't help but wonder...would a man ever love her again? Would she know the affection she'd shared with Adam, born of deep respect and common goals? Dare she hope to find the kind of love Seth had felt for Constance?

The unpleasant cackle of a mockingbird offered her little assurance as Seth's wagon turned into the Miller drive. "Wake up, Hannah. You're home."

Home, indeed. If only she could feel that way.

FIVE

Three of the four Miller *kinner* ran toward them with bright, shining smiles as the wagon rumbled up the driveway. The boys aimed their enthusiasm at Seth, while Emma reserved hers for Hannah.

"Good afternoon, Aunt Hannah. How did you like Mount Eaton?" Emma asked, her dark lashes framing her blue eyes. The young woman grew prettier with each passing day.

"Very nice, *danki*. I found everything I needed." Hannah stepped down and gave the girl a hug.

Seth set the brake and jumped from the wagon, pulling several little bags from his coat pocket as he approached the group. "Fire-hot cinnamon," he announced as he handed one bag to the boys. Henry grabbed the sack, and he and Matthew sprinted toward the barn. "Sweet lemon drops," he said with a grin in Emma's direction.

She stepped forward and took the gift shyly. "*Danki*, uncle."

Hannah watched with amazement. He must have bought the treats while she was having coffee, and apparently selected their favorites. She'd better try harder if she wished to become anybody's *favorite* aunt, she thought, reaching for her purchases from the pharmacy.

"Let me help you with those," Emma said, popping a lemon drop into her mouth. She grabbed two plastic bags from behind the bench and headed for the house.

If Emma had been pleased to see her aunt, it couldn't compare with the unbridled joy on Phoebe's face when she walked out the back door and saw her *daed*. The child jumped down the steps, flew across the yard with her pigtails flying, and hurtled herself into Seth's arms.

Seth responded with a hug usually bestowed on someone who's been gone a very long time. "My Phoebe, my Phoebe. How goes your day with Aunt Julia? Have you helped her or merely tormented your cousins?" He swung the child in a wide arc before settling her on his hip.

Hannah watched them as her eyes filled with tears and a lump the size of a duck egg rose in her throat. Phoebe's little arms clung to her father's neck as though her life depended on it, while Seth brushed a string of kisses across her head.

Will I ever know the unconditional love of a child? Will I ever feel a small heart beating against my breast and know that, at least for a while, that child's devotion belongs to me?

She didn't think so. If God hadn't seen fit to make her a mother during her years with Adam, she must serve Him in a way that didn't include motherhood. As many times as she had faced the harsh truth, it didn't get any easier to swallow.

"Hello, Phoebe," Hannah croaked, once her voice returned. She stepped closer as Seth set the child down. "If you check your *daed*'s pockets, I think you might find a surprise."

Seth grinned over Phoebe's head. "I was holding off until I got a full report from Julia."

Phoebe, however, wasn't waiting. Her tiny fingers found the bag of gummy worms in Seth's coat. She tore it open in no time at all.

"They're her favorite," Seth explained, reaching for the other shopping bags.

"Should I help you unload the feed?" she asked.

Seth looked startled by the question as he handed her the bags.

She had often helped Adam because there were only two pairs of hands of their farm.

"No, I'll drive around the barn and get Matthew and Henry to unload. You go up to the house and take Phoebe with you. Julia can use you two more than I can." He ruffled his daughter's hair as she tried to hide behind his leg. Part of a candy worm hung from the side of her mouth.

"Come, Phoebe. Let's see if Leah knows the proper way to eat a blue worm." Hannah held out her hand and held her breath.

The child didn't take her hand, but she did break into a fast dash for the back door. Hannah started to follow her and then turned back. Seth was still watching her.

"*Danki*, Seth, for taking me to buy the sheep feed."

He tipped up his hat to meet her gaze. "*Gern gschehne*, you're welcome. I was glad for the company."

Hannah felt a flush of warmth up her neck and face and didn't like it one bit. She didn't need to react like a silly schoolgirl after a simple shopping trip. She hurried after Phoebe with an almost identical pace.

Inside Julia's tidy kitchen, Hannah launched into her share of the tasks with zeal. Scrubbing, peeling, and cubing potatoes allowed her to focus energy on something less confusing than Seth Miller. Once she set the pot of potatoes to boil, she sat at the scarred oak table and found her sister watching her. "What can I help you with next?" she asked.

Julia's dimples deepened in her cheeks. "If that had been a race, you surely would have won, sister." Julia was basting two chickens with pan drippings while Emma tore lettuce and sliced vegetables for a salad, humming softly as she worked. "You may set the table if you like," Julia said. "How did you like the ride to Mount Eaton? What did you and my brother-in-law find to talk about along the way?"

Luckily Julia hadn't noticed Hannah's flushed face or trembling fingers until the strange attack of nerves had passed.

"We mainly discussed the difference between Lancaster farms and those here in Ohio," Hannah said, setting the stack of plates and silverware on the table. "And Seth talked a lot about Constance. She must have been a wonderful wife and mother."

"*Ach,* no one could bake like Constance. Her cinnamon-raisin cakes and lemon bars were the best in the district." Julia licked her lips as though she could still taste them.

"Yours are just as good, *mamm,*" Emma insisted. "At least they were till your fingers got so stiff. And with my help, yours will be just as good again."

Emma's loyalty to her *mamm* warmed Hannah's heart. "I can't wait until the next baking day," she said. She glanced around to make sure no other *kinner* were close by and then whispered, "Does Phoebe ever speak? I mean when she's with people she knows well?"

Emma looked up from the cucumber she was peeling. Julia cocked her head as they heard giggling from the girls on the steps. She waited until Leah and Phoebe ran outdoors, letting the screen door slam behind them. "*Jah,* she speaks," Julia said. "At least she used to when Constance was alive. She learned to talk early and hardly ever stopped to take a breath. But when she lost her *mamm,* she stopped." Julia slipped the roasting pan back into the oven for a final browning.

Hannah checked that the girls were still headed toward the swing as she took glasses from the cupboard above the sink. Then she couldn't stop herself from asking, "Isn't Seth worried? Hasn't he taken the child to see a doctor about this?"

Julia slanted a look at her daughter. "Emma, why don't you get a quart of green beans from the cellar?"

"*Mutter,* I'm fourteen years old—not a baby anymore."

Julia didn't say a word. The arch of her eyebrow proved sufficient.

Emma set down the paring knife and headed for the basement steps. "Okay, I'm going."

Julia waited a minute before continuing. "The doctor in Walnut Creek said there's nothing to worry about—that she'll start talking again when she's ready." Her tone indicted she didn't agree with his assessment.

Hannah swept potato peels into the bucket headed for the compost pile. "And what do you think?"

Julia didn't ponder her answer. "I think he should take her to a specialist in children's grief before her condition becomes permanent." Then she added in a softer voice, "But I am alone in that opinion." Julia took up Emma's peeling but soon stopped as her face blanched with pain.

Hannah pulled the peeler and cucumber from Julia. "For what it's worth, you're not alone anymore." She clasped her sister's hand for several moments. The simple touch of a sister soothed and lifted her spirits.

"Why don't you find the girls and the menfolk and tell them we're ready to eat?" Julia said.

Hannah quickly slipped on her cape and headed outdoors. The spring evening air felt refreshing after the overheated kitchen. She spotted Simon and Seth near the barn and gave them a beckoning wave. "Supper," she called. When they waved back, she headed toward the sheep pasture where all five *kinner* stood huddled in a tight circle. As Hannah crossed the yard, she saw Emma bend low to speak to Phoebe, who appeared to be rubbing her eyes. The grim expressions on Matthew's and Henry's faces caused Hannah to pick up her skirt and run.

"What's wrong?" she hollered. "What has happened?"

The question needed no answer as Hannah joined the group. A large ewe stood guard over her unmoving offspring just inside the fence. Hannah knew without getting any closer that the creature was dead.

"It's dead, Aunt Hannah," wailed Leah. "Why did the baby lamb die?"

Emma looked into her eyes with sympathy while Phoebe kept her head buried in Emma's skirt. Even the boys looked sad, though they had undoubtedly seen death before. It was part of the farming life.

Hannah inhaled deeply, feeling miserable herself. "Probably pneumonia," she said. "It happens sometimes, Leah, and there's not much we can do to prevent it. The baby's lungs weren't strong like the other lambs, and so it got sick."

That much was true, but it wasn't the whole story. The flock had probably become overheated on the truck and then subjected to the colder weather and perhaps a draftier barn than the one they were used to. She opted not to fill in the details, but she'd be surprised if she didn't lose several more over the next week or two.

Leah nodded her head, accepting the explanation with resignation.

Phoebe, however, burst into wracking sobs. Despite everything the other *kinner* said, the child continued to cry.

Hannah stepped forward, crouched down to Phoebe's level, and gently pulled her from the folds of Emma's skirt. "Phoebe, we don't have to be sad for the little lamb. He or she is already in heaven, playing with the other lambs that died before it. It will see its mama and its brothers and sisters someday when they get to heaven too. God cares for even the birds of the air; it says so in the Bible in the book of Matthew."

For a moment, Phoebe turned her streaming face up to Hannah and appeared temporarily mollified.

Then the voice of Simon Miller boomed from behind them. "You *kinner*, get on up to the house! Your mamm has dinner already on the table." They didn't have to be told twice but started sprinting toward the house.

He waited until the children were beyond earshot and then raised his hand and shook his finger at Hannah. "Our Lord didn't hang on the cross for sheep. I'll not have you making up stories just to placate a child. Animals die. That's part of life on a farm. And I won't let you misinterpret or change His Word. Not in my house!" His voice shook with anger.

The blood drained from Hannah's face, while the bottom seemed to fall from her stomach. "Simon, I'm sorry. I didn't mean to—" she stammered, but he had already turned and stalked away from her. She felt ashamed and frightened, yet she couldn't understand the error in her deed. Didn't the Savior bid the children to come to Him, and didn't He tell His disciples to be more like them? Hot tears streamed down her face. Soon she was awash in misery, no different than little Phoebe a few minutes ago.

"Aunt Hannah?" A voice called out, and Emma emerged from behind a tree. She ran to her aunt, holding wide her arms. "Are you still crying for the lamb?"

Hannah quickly wiped her face with her apron and accepted Emma's hug. "No child. Not anymore. I've said a prayer, and now I'm at peace with the matter." She forced her lips into a smile. At least the girl hadn't overheard her *daed*'s admonition. Hannah couldn't have handled that.

Emma's young face brightened. "Oh, good. Let's go in to dinner. I'm pretty hungry, aren't you? We're having fried chicken."

Hannah thought her heart would break with her niece's tender concern. "You go inside and tell your *mamm* I'll eat something later. I want to look for signs of sickness among my other animals." When Emma didn't move, Hannah added more firmly, "Go on, Emma. I'm fine, but I want to check my flock."

Reluctantly, Emma walked to the house, leaving Hannah alone with a very heavy heart.

～

"Tell me, dear *ehemann*, why don't you like my sister?" Julia asked. With the unusually quiet dinner over, the boys gone to evening chores, Emma and Leah upstairs, and Seth off with Phoebe, she had a few moments to talk with Simon. Much food remained for leftovers as no one's appetite had been up to par.

"I like your sister well enough, *fraa*. That is not the point," Simon said, after taking a sip of coffee. "But I won't have her changing the Word of God for her own purposes." He pulled what remained of the cherry pie closer for inspection.

Julia finished wiping down the counters and settled into the chair opposite his. "She was only trying to comfort a child."

"I understand, but that is no excuse." Simon pushed away the pie tin, apparently changing his mind. "It is dangerous to make up stories of false gospel. I read from the chapters of Scripture sanctioned by the bishop every night in this house. I won't have her implying that sheep have souls and are worthy of a place in the hereafter."

"I doubt that was her intention." Julia reached out to place her hand on Simon's. "I think there's something else bothering you. I've never seen you get so riled up when explaining the *Ordnung* or correcting others in our district for errors in judgment." She tightened her grip on her husband's hand.

Simon looked up, his face redder than the rooster's after discovering the hens ate all the feed. Then his pinched and sour expression softened. "*Ach,* there is more nettling me than her story to Phoebe. I fear my *bruder* may be growing fond of the widow Brown." The words hung ominously in the kitchen like the announcement of the seventeen-year locusts.

Julia counted to five before responding. "And that would be so terrible? You fell in love with one Kline sister, and I don't think our marriage turned out disastrous."

Simon rolled his eyes but also suppressed a smile. "Hannah is nothing like you, wife. There is no similarity whatsoever." He talked softly, glancing back at the door.

"I'm not sure that's a compliment. She has many good qualities that I would love to share."

Simon appeared to be growing weary of his wife's prodding.

"Whatever favorable attributes the widow has or doesn't have should be another man's concern, not my brother's," he announced, as though settling the matter.

"You are probably worried about nothing. I've seen Hannah show no special interest in Seth. And if she should develop an interest at some point, and if Seth was of like mind, I see the match as a good one."

Simon looked as though Julia had just declared corn should be planted in January and all Amish homes should forever more be painted purple. "No, Julia. I'll not have it. And I'll ask you not to encourage such a thing." He struggled to his feet, throwing down his napkin. "I'm sure there's a perfectly good Amish man looking for a wife like Hannah Brown. And with any luck, he lives on the other side of Tuscarawas County." A mottled red hue crept up his neck as Simon grabbed his coat from the peg and headed outdoors.

Julia could only shake her head and then bow it in prayer. If the plans of her heart were ever to come true, she was going to need divine help.

~

Seth had thought dinner would never be over. Although his sister-in-law's cooking had been delicious, no one seemed to have enjoyed the roast chicken and parsley potatoes. The girls only pushed the food around their plates; the boys' appetites were far smaller than normal; and even Simon had eaten little of his wife's handiwork. Julia had kept glancing toward the back door during the entire meal.

He had heard about the dead lamb and comforted his daughter as best he could. And he understood Hannah's concern and desire to check the rest of the flock. But something was wrong. There was more to it than a lost animal, but he knew better than to broach the subject at the dinner table.

After pushing Phoebe on the swing until the child grew bored, he fixed a plate of food from the leftovers in the refrigerator. Hannah still wasn't back from her chores. The woman must be getting hungry.

They'd eaten little on their trip to town—only half a sandwich on the way there and an apple on the way back. Judging by her appearance when she returned from the pasture this morning, she must have walked long and hard. Seth placed the tin of chicken and vegetables in the bottom of a basket and poured milk into a Thermos. He wouldn't be much of a friend if he didn't see what was taking her so long.

After thirty minutes of hiking up and down the small hills and valleys, Seth finally spotted Hannah leaning against a swamp willow by the creek. Her shoulders were slumped, her head bowed. Surprisingly, her dress appeared to still be fairly clean.

"Good evening, Mrs. Brown," he called. "You're a hard woman to find despite your opinion this pasture is too small."

Hannah's head snapped up and her shoulders straightened. She had dozed off against the tree trunk. "Seth Miller, you have a talent for sneaking up on people." A smile turned up the corners of her mouth. "But I am rather glad to see you." One lock of sandy hair had escaped the pins and hung beneath her *kapp*.

Seth settled himself on a log near the bank, setting the basket next to him in the tall grass.

"Why didn't you come in to supper? You almost missed Julia's roast chicken. That would've been a cryin' shame."

Hannah tucked the lock of hair behind her ear and dug her hands deep into the pockets of her cape. "I...I couldn't come in until I checked my flock to see if I had any more lambs down. I made sure no toxic weeds that could be nibbled by hungry critters had sprouted. Lupine, milkweed, larkspur, chokeberry—all can be poisonous, especially in the spring. Rhododendron, laurel, and azalea are toxic and need to be pruned so they don't overhang the fences. Even acorns left behind from last fall can cause kidney damage to sheep."

"I remember hearing about that once," Seth said, impressed with the widow's knowledge.

The corners of her mouth drooped. "And then there's the matter that…I angered your *bruder*…again." With the second admission, she turned her focus to the ground.

"So you had a run-in with Simon. Were you planning on staying out here all night? Come sit, Hannah, and have some supper. I brought it to you because you hadn't come in." He pulled out a checkered dishtowel and handed it to her.

"*Danki*, Seth, but I couldn't eat out here. It's too cold and wet for a picnic."

"Either you eat some of this dinner, or I'm taking you back to the house right now, without the opportunity to tell me what my *bruder* said that got you so riled."

Hannah gave him a steady glare, one that made him remember the times he couldn't string two words together in her presence. Then she gingerly stepped down to the stones of the riverbed and began washing her hands in the icy creek water. "Very well, Seth. I'll eat your dinner. You drive a hard bargain."

She sounded amused, but Seth saw lines of worry crease her forehead. Once she finished washing, he reached down and pulled her up the bank.

Hannah dried her hands on the checkered towel and settled herself on the log. "I do think I might be able to eat a bite or two."

He handed her the container with a chicken leg, breast, and wing, along with a scoop of potatoes and buttered green beans. Hannah spread the towel across her skirt, bowed her head to pray, and began to eat. And eat. And when she was done, she had eaten most of the picnic dinner.

"Milk, Hannah?" Seth asked, suppressing a grin. He knew better than to comment on a woman's hearty appetite.

"*Jah, danki.*" Hannah took the cup of milk and drank two long swallows before dabbing her mouth with the towel. She leaned back against the tree with a satisfied sigh. "I was hungrier than I thought," she said, a dimple forming in her left cheek.

He had never noticed that dimple before. "You walked quite a distance trying to find all your lambs. And it's chilly today—much easier to work up an appetite."

"That must be it. I don't usually eat that much." Her smile triggered a dimple in her right cheek as well.

Seth had to look away and concentrate on the water rushing over the jagged rocks to gather his composure. He didn't like the effect Hannah had on his emotions. "Tell me what happened between you and Simon," he said in a quiet voice.

The smile and dimples faded away. Hannah screwed the top back on the Thermos and appeared to consider her words carefully. "After I saw you menfolk, I spotted the *kinner* by the pasture gate, so I went to get them for dinner. They had found a dead lamb, and Phoebe... was all upset. She was crying up a storm." She glanced up from beneath her lashes, but Seth kept silent.

"Emma tried to console her but had no luck. So I tried to calm her down by...by telling her about lambs in heaven and how she would see all the animals that died someday." Two big tears slipped from her eyes and ran down her face. She swiped at them with the dishtowel.

"Go on," Seth prodded, sorry he had brought up the topic. He didn't want the widow to become distressed all over again.

"Your *bruder* overheard my story and became angry. He accused me of trying to change the Word of God to suit my purposes. I surely wasn't trying to change the Good Book." She turned to face him with watery eyes the color of dark moss.

At that moment Seth yearned to wrap his arms around her and calm her as he'd done with Constance many times in the past. He could cradle her head against his chest and stroke the tension from her shoulder blades. Then he could dry her tears with his bandana and promise her problems wouldn't look so grim tomorrow. But he didn't dare; this woman wasn't Constance.

Seth took off his hat and ran a hand through his hair, growing more confused by the minute. He shouldn't interfere with his brother's business. Simon was a deacon in the district and had every right to correct a church member breaking a rule or straying from their way of living. But if he knew his brother, Simon hadn't used the kindest voice to straighten out the matter.

So instead Seth tried to think of something helpful to say. "Once Simon cools down, he'll realize that wasn't your intention. You were only comforting my Phoebe, and I thank you for trying."

Hannah looked up with red-rimmed eyes. "Do you really think that?"

"I do," he said, setting his hat back on his head. "But I'd better get you back to the house before Simon starts looking for you. Then you'll hop right from the frying pan into the fire."

Hannah rose from the log and picked up the basket. "You're right about that. *Danki* for supper and for hearing me out." She brushed the leaves from her skirt and tightened the ribbons of her *kapp*. "Besides my sister, you're my only friend in the district," she said as she started walking toward the house.

Seth stood rooted to the spot for several moments, mulling over her words. That he was her only friend both pleased and frightened him. He did enjoy her company and even found her somewhat attractive. She wasn't afraid to work hard, even if it meant getting dirty. Her gentle heart loved all God's creatures—but that's what had landed her in this stew. He didn't want her to get the wrong impression. He certainly wasn't in the market to start courting again.

His interest lay in her flock. He wanted to learn the ins and outs of sheep farming to see if he should expand in that direction. Now that she might have sick animals on her hands, he could help her treat them and learn the business at the same time.

It just would be a whole lot easier if his new friend didn't have the sweetest smile in the entire county.

Six

Hannah loved this time of day, the time before the sun burned the dew from the grass. The pine trees along the fence and up in the hills glistened like gemstones as she counted her lambs in the early morning light. All appeared healthy as they nursed from their mothers. She was right in thinking it must have been pneumonia that killed the lamb. The runny eyes and crusted nose had told her as much. Just the same, she continued to search for invasive plants that she might have overlooked during her inspection of the pasture yesterday. Sheep were not the smartest of God's creatures and snacked on just about anything in their path.

After filling the trough with the grain mixture, she forked hay into the large round bin. Soon the animals came running to eat, one following another in long rows. Simon had left the hay wagon near the gate to make her morning routine easier. His sons had offered to help with feeding, but she preferred doing her own chores. Time outdoors with her sheep was time well spent, even though few Amish women shared this opinion. It gave her time to think, to sort things out—something not always possible living with noisy *kinner*.

Seth Miller was the subject of her musings. It had touched her deeply when he had brought dinner to her and demanded that she eat. How did he know her stomach was growling loud enough to scare off crows? Few men would worry about a woman who wasn't their wife. Was Seth simply showing kindness to a newcomer, or could he possibly have thoughts of a different nature? She had to admit he was good-looking with his broad shoulders; thick, dark hair; and large, gentle hands. Yet it wasn't his handsomeness that appealed to her. His affection for Phoebe warmed Hannah down to her high-topped shoes. All Amish fathers loved their children, but not all men showed their love so plainly. Phoebe was a lucky little girl, as Constance had been a fortunate woman to have Seth for a husband. As Hannah watched the ewes contentedly chewing their hay, she wondered what she would say if Seth asked to court her. She hadn't thought about courting back in Pennsylvania, but since coming to Ohio the possibility of remarriage had crossed her mind more than once.

It would be nice to have someone care for her again.

It would be wonderful to become Phoebe's new mother.

And the possibility of *kinner* of her own someday? Hannah nearly dropped the water bucket on her foot. A baby of her own to hold and love and fuss over...the idea made her breath come in quick gulps. Turning her face skyward, she uttered a silent prayer that if this was God's will, let it be done. And quickly, before she grew too old.

After finishing her chores, Hannah hurried to Julia's warm kitchen. If there was a person who might know where she stood with Seth Miller, it was Julia. Nothing scuttled beyond the scope of her hawk eye. And she might have some insight on how to win his heart. Every woman alive, both Amish and English, knew that the pathway to a man's heart was through his stomach.

Hannah fervently hoped that wasn't the case. Seth had reminisced fondly about his late wife's cooking and baking. Hannah's own domestic skills, though adequate to keep meat on Adam's bones, would never win any ribbons at an English fair.

"Julia?" she called in the empty kitchen. "Where are you?"

The countertops shone, and the room smelled especially fragrant.

Julia usually set a pan of water atop the woodstove into which she dropped herbs, apple bark, or flower petals. Their scent wafted through the house whenever a fire burned. A vase of daffodils, probably picked by Leah, adorned the center of the table. *Little girls are a special gift from heaven.* The thought she might have one of her own someday made her want to sing.

"In here," Julia called from the front room.

Hannah found her sister seated at the worktable under the window. Patterns, fabric, and sewing notions were spread across the entire surface. "With the bright sunlight, it's a good day to start new dresses for Leah and Emma," Julia explained. "And Phoebe also needs some white prayer *kapps.* She's getting too old to run around without a head covering."

"I'd love to help you, sister," Hannah said. "How are your hands today?" At least Hannah's sewing skills were better than her culinary ones. She especially loved to weave at her loom. Remembering that her loom still sat unassembled in bundles and boxes gave her a pang of homesickness.

Julia rubbed the back of her hands one at a time. "Not so bad today. Another reason to get some sewing done. Let's pin the pattern to the cloth I bought last week."

Hannah held up the material. Although plain, it was a lovely shade of a robin egg blue. Emma would not be able to wear such light colors much longer—soon she would become baptized and join the church. "Tell me, sister, how much longer till your brother-in-law starts looking for a wife?" Hannah asked, not one to beat around the bush.

Julia's eyes grew round as saucers. "Who do you mean?"

"Why, Seth, of course. Most Amish men look for another wife after a couple years of mourning, especially if they've got children needing a mother."

The look of shock on Julia's face faded, replaced by a sly smile. "I wouldn't know his personal plans. Why do you ask?" She spread the cloth across the table and smoothed out the pattern on top.

"I was just curious. It was sweet of him," Hannah said quietly, "to bring me dinner and fetch me home when I was afraid to face Simon." Hannah concentrated on securing the pattern to the fabric. "He seems a nice man. I'm surprised other women in the community haven't set their sights on him."

Julia laughed. "I believe he receives pans of baked goods and jars of preserves on a regular basis. And more than one woman, single or widowed, waits to ask his advice after Sunday services about one thing or another."

"Do you think he has his eye on someone special?" Hannah didn't look up from pinning the pattern.

"Hannah Brown, have you set *your* sights on Seth?" Julia asked, dropping the pins she'd been holding.

"No, absolutely not. I only wished to inquire on the situation *if* I were to have an inkling in his direction." Hannah's fingers flew around the edge of the pattern, pinning it down as though short on time.

"*If* you developed an inkling, I believe you would find the field wide open." Julia's smile spread from one side of her face to the other.

"Hmmm," Hannah mused, "I doubt your husband would approve of the match."

Julia's silence spoke volumes as she ran the sharpening block against the edge of her shears.

"He might try to dissuade Seth or say things that wouldn't put me in a favorable light."

Julia laid her hand on Hannah's forearm. "Simon would never bear false witness against you or any other person. And he's not a man to prattle on with gossip or opinions."

Hannah felt her cheeks grow hot. "I'm sorry, Julia. You're right. I'm being foolish and wasting time on matters of no importance. I have plenty of things to concern myself with other than who Seth Miller decides to court, when he gets around to courting at all." She stuck a pin through the fabric and straight into her thumb. "Ouch," she said, and quickly pulled back her hand before any blood could stain the dress.

Julia was studying her closely. "Shall I get you a bandage?"

"No, I'll go," said Hannah, sucking on her thumb. "I want to make us some tea to clear my head before you think I've taken leave of my senses."

Setting the kettle on the stove, she contemplated Julia's words. *I believe if you were of such a mind, you'd find the field wide open.* Why did that information send her spirits soaring? Just last week she'd thought she would be content to live the rest of her life alone. Now her thoughts kept drifting to a man whose eyes sparkled like crystal prisms when he laughed.

She shook away the notion as the taste of blood soured her stomach. *What in the world would Seth see in me after having a wife like Constance?* But if there were any chance he might be interested, she'd like to give it a try. And she hoped the pathway to that man's heart had nothing to do with recipes or cooking ability.

～

The afternoon of sewing and sharing stories from their childhood passed pleasantly. There was no more talk of Seth Miller or any other man, except for tales of the antics of Julia's sons. Before they knew it, they'd finished two pots of tea and had cut out and basted together both girls' dresses. Tomorrow they would sew them on the treadle sewing machine, but now they needed to fix dinner. Julia's beef roast had been in the oven for two hours. "This cow is cooked," she said, drawing out the words like her Missouri kin. She set the roaster on the stovetop to cool.

"I like beef so tender you can cut it up with your fork," Hannah said as she mashed up the boiled potatoes. "You can't do that with rare meat." When she went to the fridge for milk and butter, she spotted Seth's carriage as it pulled into the yard. "Seth's here," she announced, feeling uneasy. She regretted revealing her feelings about Seth to Julia.

"*Jah*," Julia said, "he helps Simon with the spring planting after he finishes his own chores. He has the energy of two men." Julia leaned over the sink to look out the window. "*Ach*, good. He brought his sweet Phoebe along. We can give her the new *kapps* we made after supper."

"If I had known they were coming, I would have boiled more potatoes." Hannah wished she had kept quiet this afternoon. Now she would be nervous whenever Seth's name was mentioned.

Julia peered into the mixing bowl. "That looks like plenty of mashed potatoes to me. Why don't you check your critters while I finish up dinner? I'll call Emma to help make a salad." Julia smiled and motioned with her head toward the door.

"All right, I did want to make sure no other sheep have taken sick." Hannah washed and dried her hands, and then caught her reflection in the small hallway mirror. Her skin looked as pale as biscuit flour, the center part of her hair was crooked, and her dress hung from her shoulders like a feed sack. Had she lost more weight? There had been nothing wrong with her appetite last night down by the creek. She'd noticed Seth watching her and felt a little embarrassed. Now even a simple thing like eating had become complicated!

Hannah noticed Phoebe alone by the pasture gate as she carried over the water buckets. The child stood on the bottom rail, her gaze fastened on a lively lamb frolicking among the tall buttercups. Luckily, the animal's eyes looked clear and its nose dry.

"That baby is having fun on this nice spring day, no?" Hannah asked, setting down the buckets.

Phoebe eyed her cautiously and then shook her head up and down. Her attention returned to the lamb chasing a bumblebee from flower to flower.

"Is that lamb your favorite, Phoebe? Would you like to pet him?" Hannah held her breath waiting for the reply.

Phoebe nodded enthusiastically for her answer. Luckily the lamb's mother was a pleasant enough ewe, accustomed to Hannah and not overly protective of her young. When Hannah entered the paddock and lifted the animal, mama offered a complaining *baaa* but didn't become agitated. Hannah carried the baby to the fence and held it in between the rails. Phoebe stroked the soft head and velvety ears. The lamb began to lick Phoebe's fingers, much to the child's delight. She giggled and grinned at Hannah, showing a space where she'd lost her two front teeth.

"Would you like to have this lamb, Phoebe?" Hannah asked on sudden impulse. "You could give him a name, and he would be yours."

The child's face glowed with joy.

"We must check with your *daed* to be sure it's all right with him. And the lamb needs to stay here with his mother so he can nurse, but I know how you can find him and tell which one is yours." Hannah pulled some long white ribbons from her apron pocket and began braiding them together. She and Julia had used the ribbons to make new *kapps* for Leah, Emma, and Phoebe. When she finished, she tied the ribbon collar around the lamb's neck just as the animal was growing restless.

Phoebe buried her face in the snowy wool and whispered in a barely audible voice, "Joe."

"What?" Hannah asked. "What did you say, Phoebe?" Her heart thumped against her chest wall as Hannah realized the child had spoken.

"I believe she has named him Joe," Seth said from over her shoulder. He'd come up without their notice. Hannah looked up to meet his gaze, and their eyes lingered longer than necessary. "A right suitable name for a sheep, I'd say. Unless, of course, Joe is actually Jolene."

Seth laughed before bending low to examine the critter. "Nope, Joe will do nicely. And *danki* for the gift, Mrs. Brown." He patted the lamb's head and then his daughter's while Hannah stood mutely.

Apparently when Phoebe regained her ability to talk, Hannah misplaced hers.

Finally she managed a sentence. "You're welcome. I hope you're not mad. I know I should have checked with you first, but the lamb could stay here with us indefinitely." Hannah smoothed out the wrinkles in her skirt. She had to do something, look *anywhere* other than into his handsome face.

Phoebe giggled and ran along the fence as Joe rejoined the other sheep. Her head poked in and out between the rails as she kept track of her new pet.

"Not to worry," Seth said. "But it does bring up a matter I wish to discuss with you." He swept off his hat and ran a hand through his hair. For the first time Hannah noticed a few strands of silver near his temples. "I want to start my own sheep business, Hannah, and I'd appreciate any suggestions you can give me. The price of wool is shooting up in these parts, as well as the price of lamb meat, especially if I were to get organic certification for my operation. Even without it, I'm thinking this might be the cash crop I need at my place." He rested his boot on the bottom rail and pulled up a long weed to chew.

Hannah's mouth dropped wide open. Seth Miller was seeking her advice? Unlike flaky piecrust or uniform quilt stitches, this was the one area she excelled at. "I'd be happy to offer advice, Seth. I'd even be willing to part with some of my spring lambs to start your flock, once they're weaned of course." She hoped she didn't show on her face the excitement she felt in her heart.

"I won't take charity from a widow, except for the gift of Joe to Phoebe. I'll pay you a fair price for any livestock you decide to sell." He watched two ewes rubbing their heads together. "What breed of sheep are these? Might as well start my education tonight."

Hannah swallowed, feeling a strange dryness in her throat. "These are a Cheviot and Merino mixture. Most sheep are crossbreeds these days, but you can still find pure if you look hard. I'm thinking of adding some Lincoln to my flock. I'm sure you've seen them—they're heavy wool producers."

Seth scratched his jaw as though deep in thought. "Say, there's a livestock auction in Kidron every Thursday. How 'bout you ride over with me and make sure I pay a fair price for any I decide to buy. You could point out what I need to watch for." His skin was already tanned from a few sunny days in the fields.

Hannah suddenly felt like running for the wooded hills. During their outing to Mount Eaton, she'd felt comfortable and composed. Now that she'd voiced the idea flying around in her head, she suddenly felt like a girl at her first Sunday night singing. "I'll check with Julia to make sure I'm not needed here, but if she can spare me, I'd love to ride to Kidron." She tied her ribbons in a bow before her *kapp* blew off in the stiff breeze.

Seth plopped his hat back on his head as Julia stepped onto the porch and began waving. "It's settled then. If your sister can spare you for an afternoon, you can begin your sheep lessons on the ride to Kidron." He nodded and then strode toward his daughter, who had crawled halfway through the fence rails. "Come, Phoebe, let's get washed up for dinner. You can see that Joe is already eating his supper." He swung the child up to his shoulder as they walked to the house.

Hannah stood watching Phoebe's lamb for several minutes as it hungrily nursed from the ewe. Maybe her move to Ohio wasn't such a mistake after all. Tonight after supper she would write to her parents and brother. Lately she'd been reluctant to write for fear her unhappiness would spill onto the page and cause them worry. But with Seth's announcement and Phoebe speaking in her presence, Hannah's spirits lifted.

If only she could smooth things out with Simon and not ruffle any more of his feathers, she just might have reason to celebrate. Hope welled in her chest as she remembered Psalms 34:4 "I sought the Lord, and he answered me; he delivered me from all my fears."

With that she picked up her skirts and began to run toward the house and her supper.

~

Seth carried Phoebe all the way inside and straight to the sink, where they washed their hands as he held her aloft.

"Something wrong with that child's legs, Seth Miller?" Julia asked, carrying a platter of sliced meat from the stove. The rest of the family was already seated at the table.

"Her legs are so short they barely reach the ground," he said, swinging her into the chair. Everyone laughed. Everyone except Simon, that is. Seth's *bruder* drummed his fingers on the tabletop until Hannah hurried into the room. She breathed heavily, as though she'd been running.

"Sorry if I kept you all waiting," she said over her shoulder at the sink.

"Let's bow our heads," Simon said tersely, barely allowing Hannah time to sit down.

Seth folded his hands and gave thanks not only for the meal but also for God's guidance in a difficult decision. Taking on another type of livestock was no small undertaking. An investment must be made not only in animals, but in food, medication, dietary supplements, lumber to build lambing pens, and new fencing to divide his pasture. He would also need a dog trained for herding and guarding against predators. And that was only the beginning. If he were to do his own shearing, more equipment would be needed down the road. But he felt he'd made the right choice. Sheep had always appealed to him as he drove the county backroads. And his opinion hadn't changed since Hannah moved her flock here. The gift of the lamb to his daughter had been a nice gesture, considering how Phoebe had carried on the other night. And he uttered thanks for Phoebe's one spoken word. "Joe" might not be much, but it was a start. He couldn't wait to tell Julia that maybe his daughter's long period of silence was over.

"There's gonna be a gathering, Seth," Simon said, accepting a glass of iced tea from his wife. "This Saturday at Robert Yoder's place—about the price of corn going through the roof. It's the only thing some men want to plant this year. Both grain elevators are plumb out of seed corn and have to truck bags in from another state."

Seth stopped his woolgathering and turned his attention to Simon. "With so much corn going to make ethanol, I see why many farmers don't want to put in wheat or soybeans," Seth said, surprised that Simon would discuss the topic at the dinner table. He seldom talked of business matters in front of women and children.

"Farm families still need to eat. I'm sticking to my wheat and rye crop, planting only enough corn for livestock feed," Simon said, sliding several pieces of beef onto his plate.

"And for sweet corn on the cob, *daed*," Emma said, reaching for the bowl of mashed potatoes.

"What about popcorn with lots of melted butter poured on top?" Hannah asked as she passed the bowl of pickled beets to Leah.

"My corn is sweet enough without drowning it with butter, Hannah. That's just an excess I won't have in my house." Simon's brows beetled together over the bridge of his nose.

"*Jah*, of course," Hannah agreed, "but we must not forget about corn relish, corn muffins, and, of course, corn bread stuffing in our Thanksgiving turkey."

Seth saw the light from the kerosene lamp dance in her green eyes as she spoke.

Henry rubbed his stomach in a circular motion, but Simon's expression turned thunderous. "Why don't we just concentrate on the bountiful food set before us and not worry so much about meals yet to come?"

With that, the family finished dinner in silence. Even Julia's cheery demeanor faded. Hannah didn't take her eyes off her plate and seemed to be clenching down on her back molars. *What is wrong with Simon?* Seth wondered. Why was he acting like a burr had gotten in between his shin and sock? Most of his wrath seemed directed at the widow, yet Seth couldn't imagine Simon would still be angry over her mistake yesterday. Correcting someone who misinterprets the Bible or questions Amish ways was everyday business for a deacon. Seth ate his plate of beef, beets, and potatoes but found he had lost his appetite for second helpings.

"If you're finished, *bruder,* I'd like your help in the pump house. That well of mine is acting up again."

"But you haven't had your coffee," Julia protested. "And we've got apple pie for dessert, made by Emma all by herself."

"We'll have coffee and dessert later, *fraa.* I want to see why we're not getting enough water before it gets too dark." Simon rose from the table with a weary sigh. The last few months seemed to have aged him by years.

"Emma, save a piece of pie for me—a big piece," Seth said. "I can't wait to try your creation." His niece blushed prettily. He glanced at Hannah as he left the table. She resembled a hapless moth caught in a spider web. He would try to talk to her before heading home and thank her again for Phoebe's gift.

Matthew followed them to the shed that housed the pumping apparatus. Their windmill used an intricate system of valves and pulleys to provide water to the kitchen sink and bathroom. Simon had added onto the house many times since accepting it from his parents and had changed how the water lines ran. Nothing worked right forever, so Seth was glad he'd learned about mechanical things at an early age. Matthew appeared to share those interests. He hovered nearby with a can of lubricating oil.

"What do you say about planting every tillable acre in corn this year?" Simon asked while Seth took apart the pump housing. "That's what many men in the district are planning to do." Simon stood with his hands clasped behind his back, peering curiously over Seth's shoulder.

"If *all* of us double our production, what'll happen to the price of corn when we flood the local market?"

"David Brower at the Farmer's Exchange says he'll buy every bushel brought in this year at a fair price. They'll load it into boxcars and ship it out of state."

"*Jah,* that so?" Seth tightened each bolt he could get his wrench around, hoping that would increase the amount of water pressure. He was eager to finish the task and see if Hannah might want to join him for a cup of coffee and piece of pie.

"He'll sign a contract committing to a certain price if a farmer meets a minimum," Simon persisted. Matthew leaned his head in so far Seth couldn't see what he was doing. He gently backed the boy up with his elbow.

"How can you promise a set number of bushels with seeds barely in the ground? What if there's another drought? I've seen corn come up fine in the spring only to wither right down to the roots. And do you remember that year we got so much rain we could have raised rice or cranberries?" Seth found a particularly loose bolt and gave it a few twists with the wrench. "There, I think I fixed the problem."

"Maybe you have another idea for a cash crop this year? I thought you said you wanted to save money to buy the land adjoining your English neighbor?"

"Well, because you asked, I do have something under my hat brim." Seth straightened his back and clamped a hand on Matthew's shoulder. "*Danki* for your help, Matty. That grease went a long way in tightening everything up."

His nephew beamed while Simon clucked his tongue. He didn't approve of nicknames, especially not ones shortening the name of a Bible book.

"Go on up to the house, son, and tell your *mamm* we'll have that coffee and pie now," Simon said.

Seth tried to hide his disappointment. If Simon were present, the widow would probably hide in her room if not run all the way to Wooster. "I'm thinking of adding a flock of sheep. I like what I see of Mrs. Brown's operation. I can sell off the lambs and sell the wool sheared from their backs. There's always a market for wool." He replaced the protective housing around the pump carefully.

Simon looked as though he'd eaten a wormy apple. "You're pulling my leg! Trying to get my goat." Great blotches of crimson flushed his cheeks.

Seth laughed. "No one tries to kid you, *bruder*. You should know that," he said, wiping his hands on a rag.

Whatever additional comments Simon had on the matter were drowned out by the uproar outside. "Dad! Dad! Uncle Seth!" yelled the boys.

Both Henry and Matthew burst through the door looking as though they'd spotted an approaching tornado. "Come quick!" demanded Matthew.

Simon reached for his son's shoulder, alarm replacing his annoyance. "What it is, son? What's happened?"

"It's Aunt Hannah's sheep! Two of the rams got into a tussle, and the whole flock started stampeding. They broke down the fence on the far end of the pasture and then kept running. There's not one critter left in the paddock you put them in."

Matthew and Henry stared at their father, waiting for the significance of this to sink in. It took only a few moments. "The north end? They broke through the fence on the *north* end? That's where I got my crop of wheat coming up!" Simon shouted at no one in particular as they hurried into the yard.

Despite his shorter legs, heavier frame, and elder years, Simon ran pell-mell for his newly planted field with Seth close on his heels. Matthew and Henry wisely hung back a few paces. Seldom did their *daed* yell without restraint.

Seth uttered a quick prayer that the damage wouldn't be severe.

This was one prayer not to be answered.

Simon and Seth stared where just that morning acres of waving green shoots had broken the soil and stood at least six inches tall. One could hardly imagine a flock of animals, fewer than a hundred, could possibly wreak such havoc.

But if there was a plant still standing upright in the field before them, the two brothers did not see it.

SEVEN

With the dishes done and the kitchen floor mopped, Hannah thought she and Julia might be able to enjoy a cup of sassafras tea while Hannah read aloud Thomas' letter. Leah had given it to her after bringing up the afternoon newspaper and mail. As Hannah slipped into a chair, sudden commotion in the backyard postponed catching up on news from home.

"What on earth?" Julia asked, hurrying to the window.

"What's happened?" Hannah felt a shiver of dread snake up her spine.

"Oh, my goodness. It's your sheep. They must've broken through the fence and escaped."

Hannah jumped to her feet, shrugged into her cape, and fled out the door in a flash. Knowing her animals, a rambunctious ram had probably spotted better grass on the other side and led his friends to tastier eats. She ran as hard as she could toward the pasture where Simon, Seth, and the boys were shouting and waving their hats furiously.

By the time Hannah arrived, her heart was pounding like a locomotive, blood throbbed in her ears, and her chest felt gripped by a tight fist. Speech was impossible.

Not that she would have had much to say after surveying the

damage from the high knoll. Much of the pasture that only yesterday had sported new growth had been churned into muck. The remaining wheat sprouts were so widely spaced apart that the entire crop would have to be replanted. And many of the animals were still moving in the direction of the neighbor's farm. Willing herself not to cry, she joined the men in trying to stop the stampede and turn back the flock. It was no easy task. Sheep had the habit of following other sheep rather than the commands of mere humans.

While Seth worked on repairing the busted fence rails, Simon, Henry, Matthew, and Hannah rounded up the confused and agitated animals. By full dark, almost two hours later, they had returned about two-thirds of the flock to their paddock. The rest would have to wait until daylight. The family could only hope no predators would take advantage of the situation tonight and cull the herd.

Hannah approached her muddy and exhausted brother-in-law as he closed the gate behind him. "Simon, I'm so sorry about your crop. I shall pay for your seeds from the proceeds from my farm, and I'll help you replant. Please forgive me…and my sheep." She hung her head and focused on one healthy wheat shoot apparently missed by the melee. When she finally glanced into his face, she saw more sorrow and fatigue than anger.

"Go to the house, Hannah," said Simon. "Have Julia draw you a tub. We'll not speak about this when we're both tired." He walked past her with the faltering step of a much older man.

Hannah turned her shoulder to the stiff wind and crossed her arms over her chest, hugging herself. It was too dark to see if the boys were still in the pasture. Goosebumps had risen on the back of her neck as she picked her way over the rutted earth. For the second time in a week the idea of sleeping on pine needles under a tree as opposed to inside the house crossed her mind. Shaking off the cowardly notion, she approached the welcoming light of the kitchen.

"What you need is a dog—a sheepdog—Mrs. Brown." A disembodied voice drifted toward her from the darkness.

If the tone hadn't been so warmly familiar, she would have jumped out of her laced-up boots. "I had a dog, Mr. Miller, back in Pennsylvania. My brother Thomas had grown so fond of old Jack I didn't have the heart to take him when I moved." She stepped up onto the porch. The creaking chains of the porch swing gave away Seth's location in the complete darkness. "I'd planned to check the classified ads for a new dog once I'd settled in and had a chance."

Seth stood and walked into the glow from the window. Despite having to be equally tired, he managed to look remarkably handsome. "I'll find you a proper dog, Hannah, if not before then during our trip to Kidron next week. They've got a bulletin board hanging in the auction barn with just about everything under the sun for sale. A shepherdess shouldn't be without a good herding dog." His gaze held hers for a long moment, and then he touched the brim of his hat to her. "Good night, Hannah."

His voice sounded so soothing she was tempted to run after him. "Wait, Seth!" she called. "What about Phoebe?"

The skin around his eyes crinkled into a web of tiny lines. "I haven't forgotten about my daughter. She's long asleep, and I only hope the odd way I smell doesn't wake her." He laughed as he headed into the house and up the stairs.

Hannah felt a pang of longing as he disappeared. True to Simon's suggestion, a tub of water was waiting in the bathroom. Dropping her soiled clothes into a heap, she slipped into the bath. The warm water soothed her aching muscles and tired feet, but little would salve her troubled soul. A dozen questions danced through her head: Would Simon demand that she sell her sheep? What if he replanted his crop and the sheep broke out again? She couldn't bear another night like this one. Simon and Seth had enough chores without having to do some of them twice. No easy solution came to mind as Hannah washed her long hair and then rinsed it with the pitcher of fresh water next to the tub. Julia had left her nightgown and a thick terry cloth robe on the chair. Hannah dressed and crept quietly into the kitchen.

Wrapped in a shawl over her dressing gown, Julia waited at the table with a teapot and two mugs. "Feeling a little better?" she asked when Hannah emerged from her safe haven.

"Much, *danki* for the bath," Hannah said, blotting her hair with the thick towel.

"Come, have a cup of tea with me before bed," Julia said. "And read our brother's letter to me."

"Tomorrow I will, sister. Right now I just want to go to bed and put this day behind me."

Julia patted the chair next to hers. "No, read it to me tonight. You will sleep better with your mind on something other than your own woes."

Too tired to argue, Hannah unfolded the letter as Julia poured tea into the mugs.

My dear sister,

Have you settled so easily into your new life at Julia's that you can't spare a single thought for those left behind? Mamm and daed send their love to you and to Julia's brood. I send a plea for help. I might be in lieb or was bit by some nasty spring bug. Do you remember Catherine Hostetler? She is the fourth daughter of Isaac and Sarah over on Route 33. I saw her at a Sunday night singing and can't get her out of my head. I asked to drive her home two weeks in a row, and she turned me down, preferring to go home with her brother instead. I asked her to take a ride in my buggy, and she said she needed to can the rest of the apples in cold storage before they turned brown. How can I talk to her? She seems so shy, and I am not a very forward man myself.

> *Your bashful brother,*
> *Thomas*

P.S. Give my nephews and nieces a big hug from me and tell them I'll see them this summer.

"My word. The solution is easy," Hannah said, after taking a swallow of tea. "I'll write him tomorrow and tell him to haul the last of our apples in the cellar over to the Hostetler farm. He can explain that I moved away without using them up, which certainly is the truth. He'll get a chance to talk to Catherine when he asks her to can them for him and when he picks up the finished jars. With any luck, the Hostetlers won't have enough canning jars, and Thomas can take Catherine to town to buy more." Despite her tiredness, Hannah straightened up in the chair.

Julia grinned over her mug while Hannah furrowed her eyebrows.

Hannah needed only another minute to ponder. "Then he can ride over to the next singing with someone who lives close to him. When it's time to go home, he can ask the Hostetler *bruder* for a ride. He'll have a chance to talk to Catherine all the way home." She finished off her tea and poured a second cup to carry upstairs.

Julia rose unsteadily to her feet, gripping the arms of her chair tightly. "Sounds like you've come up with a good plan."

"I've only just begun." Hannah set the teapot on the stove and Julia's mug in the sink. "Thank you. You were right. I do feel better after thinking about someone other than myself." She kissed her sister's forehead and climbed the stairs to her room.

She said her silent prayers, the ones she'd prayed since childhood, but added some special pleas for mercy toward her wayward sheep and a few words of thanksgiving for the special man who'd showed her more than simple kindness. Seth gave her hope for a new and meaningful life, one in which she wouldn't be alone anymore.

~

Seth Miller slept soundly that night and woke up refreshed. Answers to his prayers had come to him long before the morning sun. Washing and dressing quickly, he carried a still-sleeping Phoebe to the buggy. She would stay with his neighbor who often watched her while he worked his fields. He took the bag of leftover seed from the barn and a change of clothes for both of them. With eight children of her own, Mrs. Lehman didn't mind one more under foot, especially not one as quiet as Phoebe.

Jacob Lehman was only too happy to help once Seth explained his plan. His three sons loaded their extra wheat seed into the wagon while Jacob hitched up his two Belgian draft horses. Seth moved his bag of seed to Jacob's wagon, and with Phoebe asleep on the Lehman sofa, returned home for his plowing team. His buggy would remain in the Lehman yard for the day, his driving horse in an empty barn stall.

By the time the sun cleared the horizon, shining light on the ruined hayfield, Seth and Jacob were almost to Simon's farm by the back lanes. Both were eager to help.

Simon stood on his porch enjoying his second cup of coffee. He, Hannah, and the boys had finished the sheep roundup and returned all of them to the hastily repaired pasture. Hannah was off counting and recounting like a dutiful mother hen. The smell of sizzling bacon and frying eggs whet his hearty appetite, but the sound of wagon wheels rumbling up the drive kept him from heading to breakfast. He stared at three young faces bobbing into view and recognized the sons of his closest Amish neighbor.

"*Guder mariye,* boys," Simon said. "Why are you out so early?"

"We're here to help you replant your hay, deacon," the older one called. He was a tall, gangly youth, who could use a larger portion of his *mamm*'s cooking. His strawberry-colored hair hung down in his eyes, in need of a trim. The boy didn't stop to offer further explanation but clucked to the horse to keep moving toward the back fields. Simon stood on his stoop, speechless for the first time in a while.

He didn't have long to wait.

"*Guder mariye, bruder,*" Seth called, coming around the house.

"What are you up to, Seth? I didn't expect you here today after our late night yesterday. Have you no chores to do?" Simon appeared to be stifling a grin.

"They're done. It's a work frolic, even if a small one at short notice. Jacob Lehman and I had nothing better to do on this bright, sunny day, and we both had extra seed taking up valuable barn space, so I said why not help my brother replant? With three teams plowing and all the *kinner* following behind and dropping in seed, we'll be done by lunch and looking for something else to do." Seth swept off his hat and then repositioned it playfully on the back of his head.

Simon's joy couldn't be contained as he spotted Jacob in the distance, bringing his plow and team. "I'll have Julia make another pot of coffee and start fixing sandwiches," he said. "Come in for a bite of bacon and eggs before we go to the fields. I know you haven't had any breakfast and must be hungry." He rubbed his hands together while organizing details in his mind. "I'll check with Jacob and his boys to make sure they've eaten. Then I'll pull my sons from their chores and look for my girls. I need to find Hannah too. I know she'll want to be part of this." He started down the steps and then paused to meet his brother's eye. "*Danki,* Seth."

Seth touched his hat brim in response and headed toward the wagon for the seed. The mention of Hannah's name caused an odd jolt of anticipation. His brother was right. He must be hungry for his gut to be all aflutter. He would unload the sacks, grab something quick to eat, and hope he wasn't coming down with something.

Hannah still seemed to be sticking in Simon's craw. Yesterday's sheep stampede through his crop hadn't helped matters. Instead of growing accustomed to an extra female in the household, his pique had increased with the passing of time. But once Seth presented Simon with his second God-given intuition of the early morning, her sheep would no longer be a thorn in his side.

Once the work frolic began, no one had time for thinking. Henry and Hannah followed his plow, dropping in evenly spaced seeds as the blade cut furrows into the earth. Emma and Leah walked behind

their *daed,* while Jacob had two of his boys for helpers. His eldest son
and Matthew tamped and raked long rows, making sure the seeds
were adequately covered with soil. Jacob whistled while Leah and
Emma sung gospel tunes they had learned from Julia. With the sun
warming the back of his neck, Seth felt the first sweat on his brow
as he rolled back his cuffs and shed his coat. It felt good to be back
in the fields after a long winter.

When they stopped to rest the horses, Seth watched white, lacy
clouds scurry across the bluest of May skies. The world looked a far
different place than it had yesterday when dozens of critters eluded
every attempt to corral them. With a solution to their dilemma
almost in his back pocket, Seth felt like humming himself.

By two o'clock, they had reseeded the entire field. The boys would
finish covering the seeds during the afternoon. Mrs. Lehman came
by with Phoebe and her girls to help Julia prepare lunch for the
hungry workers. They set up a table outdoors where they spread out
an array of sandwiches, cold pickled vegetables, and fresh-baked pies.
The meal looked like an oasis under the maples when they returned
from the fields.

Seth ate his fill of ham and Swiss cheese sandwiches with more
than his share of pickled beets. He drank two tall glasses of lemonade to wash the dust down his throat and stole glances at Hannah
across the table during the entire meal. She looked surprisingly fresh
for someone who'd just spent almost as much time in the sun as he
had. Her heavy black sunbonnet had been replaced with a white *kapp,*
revealing newly sun-burnished cheeks and a shiny-penny smile. He
thought only Constance ever looked prettier sipping iced tea and
laughing with the girls. She sat with the women, chatting amiably
with Emma. He couldn't wait to tell her his idea and see the look
on her face. Someone as kind and thoughtful as the widow wouldn't
want to cause turmoil in her sister's house indefinitely. But Hannah
didn't meet his eye once during the meal—furtively glancing only
at her brother-in-law. Simon, on the other hand, looked like a father

who'd been given his first newborn son. And the satisfaction on his face was all the thanks Seth needed.

Only one thing still remained to straighten out—the problem of Hannah's sheep. Simon hadn't responded to his plan to expand with sheep with the anticipated slap on the back and "good luck to you." But surely he would see the wisdom behind this idea.

Seth waited until the Lehman family packed up and left by buggy, wagon, and draft team, and then he followed Simon to the barn. The afternoon milking still needed to be done. The cows couldn't milk themselves.

Simon nodded when Seth entered the barn. "*Danki* again for arranging the work bee," he said. "Extra hands make light work of any task." Simon forked hay into the cattle troughs.

"Happy to help." Seth picked up the other pitchfork. "I've got another idea brewing that I wanted to run by you." He tried to control his growing excitement. "I told you I wanted to add sheep to my livestock. The way I see it, Mrs. Brown's sheep have just about overstayed their welcome at your place. And they don't seem to like the particular cuisine of your pasture." Seth glanced up at his brother, expecting at least a small laugh, but Simon looked bewildered.

Seth squashed any further attempts at humor. "Well, I've got a pasture already thick and green on good high ground. I say we move Hannah's sheep to my place." He jabbed the pitchfork into a full bale and leaned his weight on it, waiting for Simon's hearty approval.

Simon stood with his jowls slack and his mouth in fly-catching mode.

Seth realized he hadn't approached the subject tactfully. "I'm not saying there's anything wrong with your pasture. It's fine, to be sure. I'm only suggesting a temporary move to my farm until your grass has a chance to come in. We also need to replace those rotted fence rails. The repairs I made last night will only tide you over. Plus, I'll be able to learn the business from the widow while the sheep are with me to prepare me for my own flock. Hannah and I are going to the auction in Kidron on Thursday to see if any decent animals are up for sale." Seth pulled the fork from the bale and finished filling the trough. When he glanced back, Simon was staring at him.

It probably was the heat of the unseasonably warm day coupled with the exhaustion of replanting the entire field the day after staying up so late. Added to that, there was the pleasant surprise of the neighbors coming to his aid so quickly. But Simon looked ready to faint. He lowered himself to the milking stool nearby. "I don't know if that's such a good idea," he said, slowly pulling on his long beard. "I promised Julia that Hannah…and her animals…could move in with us. Julia won't like the idea of my sending half the bargain away."

This wasn't what Seth had expected. "I'm sure Julia will see the common sense behind the suggestion."

"Unless this is the widow's desire—and I can't imagine her wanting to be separated from her sheep—I can't go along with your notion. We can talk more about this later, but right now I need to feed and water my horses and help the boys with milking." He struggled to his feet using the stall wall for support, his short break over.

Seth once again felt he was making trouble rather than offering a practical solution. He told Simon good day and scratched his head all the way back to his team of Percherons.

Why did he feel like any involvement on his part with Julia's sister wasn't welcome? Had Hannah complained that he was acting too forward? That wasn't the feeling he had when they were together. But Seth didn't want to cause problems for Hannah—she managed to create enough on her own. He would let her behavior on their trip to Kidron settle the matter. If she was relaxed and comfortable with him, he would offer his pasture for better grazing. And if not, he wouldn't pester her for any more advice. He could just as well do what she did—open a book and read.

～

Simon dragged his milking stool into the open doorway and sat down heavily. He didn't permit smoking in any of his buildings, not even by himself. But tonight he would enjoy half a pipeful of Ohio-grown tobacco as he collected his thoughts and said his prayers. With the chores finally done and the rest of his family asleep, he allowed himself this one rare vice before going to bed.

The day had pleased him beyond measure. Everyone—young, old, male, female—had worked together in Christian service. He had participated in work frolics more times than he could count but seldom had been on the receiving end. It felt mighty good. He said a special prayer of thanks for Seth, who'd worked longer and harder than anyone.

Simon arched his neck to study a sky studded with twinkling stars. The moon was just breaking the horizon in the east, promising to shed cool light on his satisfactory Plain world.

"*Daed?*" A female voice called from the darkness.

Simon nearly tipped over on the stool. "Emma! What are you doing still about? I thought you'd gone to bed more than an hour ago."

The eldest of his *kinner* stepped into the pool of kerosene light. "I was waiting in the kitchen to talk to you, but you didn't come in." She was wrapped in her mother's handmade shawl over her heavy robe.

"What is it, child? What's so urgent it couldn't wait till morning?" Simon labored to his feet once again.

"I was wondering if you could clear out the loft area in the main barn. It's not being used for anything right now—just for storing a bunch of old junk."

"That's not junk. Those are tools left by your grandfather that still might be useful one day. What do you want the loft for, girl?"

"I thought we could clean it up and set up Aunt Hannah's loom. It could be our workshop. Aunt Hannah said she would teach me how to spin and weave and knit."

"Did your aunt ask you to speak to me about this?"

Emma looked surprised by the question. "No, *daed*, I love the new sheep and want to start spinning and carding wool. Aunt Hannah said they would soon need their spring shearing. I can't wait to see that. She showed me a beautiful throw for the back of the couch that she wove on her loom." Even in the thin glow of his lantern, there was no mistaking excitement in her eyes.

"Since when do we want fancy decorations for our front room, Emma?"

"It wasn't fancy—just a plain navy blue—but it would be good and warm for cold winter nights." She smiled pleasantly, reminding him so much of Julia.

Simon studied his daughter in the wavering light. *When did she start using logic and reason when she wanted something? When did she start sounding like an adult?* Before he knew it, boys would be comin' round to court Emma, and he sure wasn't ready for that!

Then Simon remembered he had promised to give Hannah space for her weaving. With the spring planting—and replanting—he'd forgotten all about it. "*Jah*, Emma, when Matthew and Henry get home from school tomorrow, they can help me clear it out. But you and your aunt will be responsible for sweeping it and whitewashing the walls. Can't rightly see how you'll keep the mice out of there. They'll be nesting in her wool if you're not careful."

Emma threw her arms around his neck and hugged tightly. "*Danki*, papa. I will appoint one barn cat to stand watch so no mice come into our new workshop." She kissed his cheek and then turned and ran for the house. All her former grownup behavior vanished when she sprinted like the leader in a footrace.

Simon shook his head and moved his stool out of the doorway. He suddenly felt every one of his forty-one years. The next time he saw Seth, he would tell him he'd given his idea some thought. It might not be a bad idea to move the flock to his farm, at least temporarily. And setting up the loom and making the loft into a workshop might be good ideas too. The weaving would get Hannah busy with normal female activities instead of stomping around wet fields in her late husband's boots. He didn't want either of his daughters developing overly independent tendencies or too much interest in manly pursuits.

This might just be the best thing for all concerned.

EIGHT

Julia winced in pain as she washed and dressed the next morning. The chilliness of the bedroom stiffened her already painful joints. Luckily no one was around to hear her moans as she fastened the hooks and eyes of her garment. As usual, Simon had risen before dawn to begin his chores before his first cup of coffee. The boys would milk and feed the cows, water the horses, and load Aunt Hannah's hay wagon before getting ready for school. Emma was probably also up, baking bread or buttermilk biscuits for breakfast. But no doubt little Leah would still be fast asleep.

As Julia pinned her hair into a tight bun, she noticed the dark circles beneath her eyes and deep-set lines around her mouth. Yesterday's work frolic had taken its toll and put her behind with her everyday tasks. She felt tired and haggard after preparing meals for so many hungry workers. She hadn't minded the extra work, especially after seeing how happy Simon was with the entire crop replanted. But her arthritis was getting worse by the day. Soon she wouldn't be able to hide the truth from anyone.

Today her knuckles refused to bend, she couldn't lift her arms waist high, and her knees ached almost beyond bearing. How would she finish the new dresses for the girls in addition to her ironing? With Emma almost done with school, Julia would soon have full-time help with the housework. If she could only hold out until then, maybe Hannah wouldn't realize how bad off she was. If her sister knew the truth, she would neglect her wool business to do more around the house. Julia wouldn't allow that. Hannah needed to make a life for herself instead of doting on her. Then maybe her little sister would smile again.

From her window, Julia watched Hannah walk to the barn with a definite spring in her step. She would begin sweeping and cleaning the loft even before Simon moved out the heavy equipment. That kind of energy was the only thing Julia ever coveted. She smiled as she imagined Hannah with her broom flying over the wide planks, stirring up a cloud of dust with cobwebs hanging from her *kapp*.

Simon had told her when he'd come to bed that they would set up the loom today. Then he'd turned his head on the pillow and fallen deeply asleep, exhausted from the replanting. Julia had lain awake for a long while before sleep came. And it hadn't been her aches and pains that kept her tossing and turning until the wee hours.

Struggling down the stairs, Julia saw that Emma had already built up the fire in the woodstove and prepared a pan of biscuits to bake. Swallowing three aspirin with a glass of water, she let out an exasperated sigh. What had made her sleepless the night before continued to trouble her this morning: Hannah had made no progress in capturing Seth's attention, even though Julia knew she liked him.

How could Hannah so easily concoct solutions for Thomas' courtship problems yet be unable to help herself? What a clever idea to take the cold-storage apples over to Catherine. And showing up at a singing without a ride home would work too. Thomas was shy, so talking to Catherine while in her brother's company might smooth things out. But Hannah hadn't a clue what might win Seth. Her brother-in-law might be interested in sheep farming, but seeing a woman stomping through a swampy meadow with mud up to her knees was never going to win a man's heart.

Seth needed to see Hannah for the kind, sweet-tempered woman she was—a woman who would make any man a fine wife, especially Seth, who had a motherless child to raise. Time was running out. What if Simon found out that Hannah's forthrightness had landed her in trouble with the ministerial brethren back home? Plain people loved taking trips to visit family or interesting places, same as fancy folk. Many of their neighbors traveled back and forth to Pennsylvania whenever time, chores, and their pocketbooks allowed. What if someone in the district got wind of Hannah's admonishment back in Lancaster? Simon would be furious—angry with Hannah, and with her, for not telling him sooner.

Reputation meant everything to Simon. If it became known around their community that Hannah had been called before the elders and threatened with shunning, Simon wouldn't be able to hold his head as high. Hannah was a Kline and she was a Kline. One hint of disgrace reflected on the entire family.

Julia loved her husband only second to the Lord, but Simon wasn't known for his patience or understanding. "Bad company corrupts good morals," according to Simon. Hannah would be labeled as a troublemaker and a bad influence. Seth, who understood the price of living in a close Amish community, might squash his growing interest in Hannah. Any fondness he possessed would wither on the vine, and they'd both be denied the chance of finding happiness again.

～

A haze of dust hung in the air from Hannah's sweeping as Simon surveyed the almost empty loft. He felt another twinge in his lower back as he hefted the last large piece to move—an old-fashioned walk-behind plow. Henry and Matthew tried their best, but they were too small to take much of the weight. It might be time for another visit to the chiropractor once he finished cleaning out the loft.

"Please, Simon, let Emma and me help," Hannah begged for the third time in half an hour. "Five sets of hands can lift better than three."

"No," he said. "You'll have plenty to do once we move the rest of the tools and implements out." Simon walked backward carrying the plow and hoped he didn't tumble over the edge before reaching the steps.

"Careful there," Hannah cautioned. "Six inches to the edge. Don't get any closer."

Like a mother hen, she repositioned herself every few feet or so to supervise the movement of the plow. "You're getting close to the steps. Almost there."

Why anyone had decided upstairs was a good place to store a heavy piece of equipment, Simon didn't know. "Hold up, Matthew. Let me start my end down first," he instructed. Glancing over his shoulder, he moved one foot down and shifted his weight. His back began to spasm in protest. He could sense Hannah bobbing her head left and right behind him, and it made him nervous.

"Henry, watch that your fingers don't get pinched along that wall," Hannah called over his shoulder.

"Please, Hannah, move out of the way." Speech proved very difficult with the weight of the plow. Simon could barely draw a breath.

With great effort the three slowly lowered the plow several steps. Simon glanced back and spotted Hannah standing at the bottom. "Move away from the landing. If I drop my end, I don't want it crashing down on you." Simon gritted out the warning through his clenched teeth. With Henry and Matthew at the top end, all the weight rested on him. He felt the color rise up his neck into his face from the strain as the plow began twisting to the side.

"Stay back, Emma!" Hannah ordered before hurrying up the steps to grab the plow. Her hands gripped the bottom edge just as the plow began shifting downward.

"Come down the steps, boys," Simon ordered. "Now!"

Although Hannah was neither large nor strong, her help made all the difference. After three quick backward steps, the four of them set the unwieldy plow down on the barn floor with a loud clatter.

"*Danki,* Hannah," Simon said, straightening his spine very slowly. "That piece was heavier than I thought."

"You're welcome," she said, also out of breath. "If not for me and my loom, this plow could've stayed where it was forever." She wiped her grimy palms on her apron.

"I'll get us some lemonade and oatmeal cookies," Emma said merrily, as though this were a cider-making frolic—more fun than hard work.

"You will do no such thing," Simon ordered. "You will wash your hands and head to school. Why didn't you leave with Leah?" It occurred to him only at that moment that today was a school day.

"Ah, *daed,* I'm almost done with school anyhow. I thought I'd stay to help Aunt Hannah clean out and whitewash the workroom. The boys are home today." She smiled with her pretty, toothy grin.

With his breathing back to normal, Simon rested his hands on his hips and angled a glare at his eldest child.

"Oh, is *that* what you thought, Emma? The boys have been excused for planting season." He didn't need to raise his voice or say anything more. The tone did the trick. *When did my daughter start deciding if and when she would go to school?*

"Sorry, *daed,*" Emma said, much deflated. "I'll hurry and try to catch up with Leah. See you after school, Aunt Hannah." The girl disappeared through the doorway without a backward glance.

Hannah nodded her head and then headed up the steps, carrying her broom, bucket, and mop. "Study hard," she called.

"Matthew, Henry, help me move this out of the way until I decide where to store it," Simon said. "Then carry the remaining small tools down and store them under the stairs. Work with your aunt as long as she needs you and then see if your *mamm* needs anything done."

Simon was eager to get to his fields, but he'd noticed Julia's fingers were worse than ever.

He would help Hannah set up the loom after lunch, but he wouldn't disrupt his entire schedule for any more foolishness. The loom would keep Hannah busy in women's work, which would be good. But Emma seemed far more interested in what her Aunt Hannah was doing than in learning from Julia. Again he thought moving the flock to Seth's might be a good idea—Hannah would have time for her weaving, and Emma could help in the kitchen where she belonged.

"Pa? What are we waitin' for?" Matthew asked. He and Henry stood at their end of the plow, watching him curiously.

"Doin' some thinking, sons. Just figuring a few things out."

With Julia's sister living with them, he found himself doing that on a regular basis.

~

Hannah awoke Thursday morning to a hot, stuffy bedroom. She threw the two small windows wide and savored the cool breeze on her face.

Sunrise. A pinkish sun was just breaking the eastern hills, indicating rain later in the day. Hannah didn't care. That's why God had made umbrellas. Nothing could dampen her high spirits that morning. She was about to spend most of the day with Seth Miller.

His invitation had sounded like a pleasant diversion from daily chores, besides a chance to compare her new Plain community to the one back home. But during the past few days, she'd grown giddy with excitement over the prospect of seeing him again. She hoped her exuberance wasn't written across her forehead. She didn't want to behave foolishly with two young girls in the household. Amish ways didn't permit a woman to act interested in a man. She needed to keep her feelings hidden until his were fully known. But telling herself not to feel excited would be like telling a hen not to scratch in the dirt.

Hannah filled her lungs with the clean air, lightly scented from the magnolia blossoms near her window. Magnolia trees weren't commonplace in northern Ohio, and often a late frost ruined their early pink flowers. But not this year. Pink petals covered the ground after a full week of glorious blooms.

She hurried through her sponge bath and slipped into her favorite dress, one made by her mother as a parting gift before she moved. The deep shade of green would complement her eyes and tone down her sunburned nose and a new crop of freckles across her cheeks. "Why worry about your clothing? Look at the lilies of the field and how they grow. They don't work or make their clothing, yet Solomon in all his glory was not dressed as beautifully as they are." Her grandmother's favorite Scripture came to mind, which the old woman had recited whenever a girl exhibited a bit of vanity. Hannah smiled at the sweet memory of her grandmother, wishing she could still sit at her feet, smell her lilac fragrance, and receive the wisdom and serenity that comes only with age.

When they had heard of her trip to Kidron, Matthew and Henry volunteered to do her morning chores so she and Seth could get an early start. As she wound her hair into a bun, she spotted them driving the hay wagon into the pasture. Buckets of water to fill the tubs sloshed in the back. Emma had offered to count lambs before school while Leah volunteered to help her *mamm* with breakfast. *What good kinner they are.* Hannah whispered a prayer of gratitude for her nieces and nephews, and a second thanks that none of them asked to go to town. But it was a school day, and yesterday she'd seen firsthand what Simon thought about children skipping their lessons.

Julia was busy stirring a pot of oatmeal when Hannah reached the kitchen. The snaps on her sleeves were still undone. "Let me help you with your cuffs," Hannah said. "Are your hands very stiff today?"

"No more than usual," Julia replied, but deep shadows under her eyes told a different story. "Just roll back my sleeves to keep them out of my way."

Hannah did as she was told and then went to the cupboard for plates and cups. "What can I help you with on this lovely morning?"

"Oh, my, take the biscuits from the oven before they burn! I almost forgot them. Then just set out the jam and preserves. I won't have you soiling your best dress before your trip to Kidron."

The comment on the dress made Hannah feel a little silly. She felt her cheeks flush as she pulled the pan from the oven. "Just in time. They're perfect, and this isn't my Sunday best. I'm only going to a livestock auction to help buy some sheep."

"With Seth Miller," Julia added, pushing the oatmeal off the burner with her mitt.

"With Seth and Phoebe Miller," Hannah said, carrying three jars of preserves to the table. She hoped the butterflies in her stomach would settle down.

"With Seth alone," Julia corrected. "Phoebe is upstairs in Leah's bed. She came down with a cold after spending the day with the Lehman brood. She'll stay here with me so I can keep an eye on her."

"Seth's here already?" Hannah's voice sounded like a tree frog's.

"*Jah,* sleeping till noon never was a Miller trait." Julia's brown eyes twinkled with mischief. "He's helping Simon with chores since Simon's back is acting up. Then they'll come in for breakfast. Afterward, you two can be off to Kidron. Be sure to try some of Jasper's homemade ice cream while you're there. And bring me home some licorice hard candy."

Hannah stood motionless by the table, her fist of silverware held aloft like a bouquet. *Simon's back is acting up?* Seth must do his brother's chores because Simon strained his back clearing out a workshop for her. Maybe instead of fretting over the color of her dress, she should concentrate more on not being so bothersome.

Julia plucked the knives and forks from her hand. "Whatever's got you stymied—don't worry. You must know your way around a livestock auction. Kidron's will be no different than those back home." She gave the pot a final stir. "Please call the girls, Hannah. The oatmeal is ready."

Hannah hollered up the stairs and finished setting the table. She really didn't know everything about livestock. Adam had always been with her during purchases. Now Seth would be looking to her for sound advice. What if she couldn't remember a single thing she had learned about traits and characteristics?

At that moment the kitchen door swung open, and Matthew and Henry stomped in, followed by an energetic-looking Seth and a slightly stooped Simon.

"Cinnamon oatmeal with buttermilk biscuits?" Seth asked, sniffing the air like a bloodhound. "My goodness, Julia, you read my mind. That's what I was hoping for." Seth squeezed his sister-in-law's shoulder affectionately.

"You say that no matter what I make. One day I'll fix you creek mud pies with pond water to drink and see if you gush then." Julia lowered herself slowly into the chair, but only Hannah noticed her wince with pain.

"Good morning to you, Mrs. Brown," Seth said in her direction. He touched the brim of his hat before setting it on a peg. His manner was reserved and formal. "I hope you're ready for a long day."

"*Guder mariye. Jah,* I slept soundly last night," Hannah replied.

The girls flew into the kitchen and took their seats. After prayers, everyone passed jars of jam and ate their fill of the meal. No one dawdled on the sunny day. Simon kept watching his wife; Seth kept glancing at Hannah; and Hannah didn't know where to look. When she noticed the inviting twinkle in Seth's eye, she was too afraid to look anywhere but at her oatmeal for fear her feelings would be revealed.

As soon as breakfast was over, everyone hurried in different directions—everyone but Hannah and Seth. Even Julia excused herself and abandoned the kitchen. Hannah cleared the table and filled a sink with water. She wanted to start on the dishes but wasn't sure how early the auction started. Farmers were an early lot.

"Shall we get going, Hannah?" he asked.

The question ended her dilemma. Putting the dishes into the sink to soak, she decided she would have to make it up to Julia tonight. "All right, but let me get my shawl in case the evening turns cool."

Seth downed the last of his coffee. "Have you packed something for our lunch?"

Hannah felt her stomach twist into a knot. Any other Amish woman would have risen early enough to pack a proper hamper. *I am no good at this courting business,* she thought, but she answered with a weak smile, "No chance this morning. Can we buy something there?"

"Sure. I'm itchin' to try one of those sausage sandwiches with all the grilled peppers and onions." Seth rubbed the palms of his hands together as though in anticipation. "Why don't you fill a jug with water while I hitch up the horse? I'll meet you outside." He set his cup in the sink, grabbed his hat, and was gone before she could ask any more questions.

She filled the jug, packed some small carrots and apples into a totebag, and ran for her purse and shawl. *When did I become so addlebrained?* By the time she reached the hitching post, Seth had brought the buggy around the corner of the house.

"You look rather nice today, Hannah," he said, reaching for her hand as she stepped into the open carriage.

She nodded politely but didn't reply. *What is proper behavior between us?* The *Ordnung* didn't have such clear rules for widows and widowers as for young people courting in the blush of youth. She didn't want to appear bold or pushy. It would be more prudent to appear unfriendly than reckless.

Seth gave her little opportunity to appear one way or the other. He filled their drive from Winesburg to Kidron with interesting tales of Phoebe's antics with her new lamb, Joe. Hannah had insisted they take home both the lamb and ewe once she saw how attached Phoebe had become. Joe was growing quickly and was now nibbling grass, as well as nursing from his mother. Hannah enjoyed hearing Seth talk about his daughter while they passed the tidy farms along the way. She yearned to ask if the child had said anything else besides "Joe" but didn't dare.

"What news do you hear from home? Are the Lancaster County farmers ready to cut their first crop of hay? Is their corn already up to their knees?"

Hannah turned on the seat to catch the playful gleam in his eye. "What do you mean, Seth Miller?" Then she remembered their discussion during the last outing.

"Seeing how Pennsylvanians are so ahead of us Ohio boys." He shook the reins over the mare's back to pick up the pace.

"I got a letter from my brother the other day, but he didn't mention any *June* harvest this year," she said wryly. "Instead he was interested in how to properly court Miss Catherine Hostetler and was seeking my advice."

Seth appeared to be biting the inside of his cheek. "You are an expert on animal husbandry *and* rules of courtship, Mrs. Brown? I knew you'd studied many a textbook on sheep, but how did you gain knowledge on matters of the heart?"

"I never claimed to be an expert on either, Mr. Miller, but a woman does hear things at quilting or after church about how young men find opportunities to speak to young women." She fixed her focus on the green pasturelands and woodlots that looked much improved from the landscape on the way to Mount Eaton.

"How should a young man place himself in good standing with a gal?"

"It's simple. I told Thomas to find common ground between them, something that would give him a chance to see her again in the future."

Seth guided the horse onto the shoulder to give a car trying to pass a wider lane. "Sounds like logical advice, but did you come up with anything specific?"

"Since Miss Hostetler was canning apples, I told him to clean out his cellar of leftover apples and ask her to make something out of them. He is being both generous and seeking help at the same time. Plus he'll get to see her when he picks up the finished jars." Hannah crossed her arms over her cape, hoping she didn't sound too smug.

Seth lifted a brow. "You know, that just might work for Thomas. It's not too different from us today on our way to Kidron."

Hannah felt her heart rate quicken. "What do you mean by that?" she asked, not sure if she wanted to hear his answer.

"We've got plenty of common ground, considering my interest in ornery critters with heavy wool coats. And if nobody's selling sheep today in Kidron, I'll have to ask you to ride to Mount Hope with me. They've got an even bigger auction on Wednesdays for horses, chickens—just about everything under the sun. They're bound to have sheep." He swept his hat off to run a hand through his hair. The sun reflecting in his eyes made them sparkle.

Hannah exhaled her breath in a rush. "I sure hope you don't think I planned this as some...some..." The right words wouldn't come.

"As what, Mrs. Brown? As some courting move on your part?" He settled his hat so low on his forehead she couldn't read his eyes.

"Exactly! I did no such thing! You're the one who wanted to buy sheep, not me! This whole trip to Kidron was your idea!" She wished she'd eaten more oatmeal. Her stomach felt queasy from all the bumps in the road.

"Well, a man can hope, can't he?" He spoke softly, barely above a whisper. Then unexpectedly, he leaned over and brushed her cheek with his lips.

The action astounded and pleased her at the same time. She wasn't sure which emotion outweighed the other. "Settle down, Mr. Miller.

There'll be no more of that along the way." She hoped she wouldn't fall out of the buggy from shock.

"In that case, I'm glad we're here. Welcome to Kidron, Hannah."

As they crested a hill, the bustling town opened before her like a greeting card. Cars, buses, and buggies were everywhere. Amish and English milled about on sidewalks and congregated in parking lots. Seth tugged on the reins to slow the horse as he gently applied the brake. Ahead, a line of vehicles waited at the red light at the bottom of the hill. The pavement widened as the road approached the center of town, allowing buggy lanes on both sides.

"My word," she breathed. "I hadn't expected anything like this. What is that building?" She pointed at a rambling structure that had obviously been added to many times. Rooflines went off in many directions to accommodate the steeply sloping lot.

"That's the hardware store," he answered.

"*Hardware?*" she asked. Buses were queued in back as though at an amusement park. Cars filled most of the spaces in the parking lot, while Amish buggies were tied at a long row of hitching posts.

"Oh, there's plenty of hardware inside, for Plain and *Englischers,* besides a restaurant, bookstore, and bakery. Tourists love the place, but nevertheless, it has the best selection of cook stoves, woodstoves, propane refrigerators, and nonelectric appliances in the state. Most of it is way too fancy for Old Order, but the owners keep a good variety of oil lamps on hand—something for everyone."

"You don't say." Hannah craned her neck to watch an Amish woman cross the street carrying one baby while three other youngsters clung to her skirt. "Can we go inside later and look around?"

"Sure, if there's time." Seth clucked to the horse as the traffic light turned green. Once through the intersection, they joined two long lines of traffic funneling into a parking lot—one for cars and trucks and the other for buggies and wagons. Both types of conveyances were pulling animal trailers. Two separate worlds melded harmoniously in the charming little town while a cloud of dust hung in the air from the commotion.

"Welcome to auction day, Hannah," Seth said, as a young boy waved them into the area for buggies.

"My word," she repeated, astounded by the hubbub behind the auction barns. "Look, there's a flea market too."

Makeshift booths had been set up and an area of pavement chalked off to display all sorts of merchandise. Several Amish women were selling quilts from the backs of their buggies.

"Later in the summer, this is a good place to bring produce, cheese, wool, or anything else you want to sell," Seth explained. "Most of the English you see aren't locals, not on auction day. People come from Cleveland and Akron and all over to shop."

"*Jah*, like Lancaster, I suppose, but on a smaller scale." Hannah couldn't help but smile and shake her head. She saw an English farm wife in overalls and work boots, a Plain young woman in a heavy black bonnet, and an overdressed young girl in high heels and a short skirt standing in line at a booth that sold cold drinks. *What a collision of cultures,* she thought.

Seth jumped out and offered his hand. "I need to go to the sheep barn and register so I can get a number."

She liked the touch of his fingers despite his rough calluses.

He pulled out his pocket watch. "It's a good thing I aim to buy sheep and not cows, or we'd be too late for good selection. They sell sheep after they're done with cattle."

"No one told me what time to be ready," she said a little stiffly. "We could have skipped breakfast if you wanted to come early."

"And miss Julia's cooking? No chance. Anyway, like I said, they sell sheep and goats last. They're not that popular in these parts, seeing how ornery they can get." He winked at her from beneath his hat brim.

Hannah opened her mouth to defend her favorite species but changed her mind. Amish women had congregated in groups outside the main barn, and several pairs of eyes were keenly studying Seth. Hannah had forgotten that although she knew no one, Seth Miller was no stranger in the community. One or two Amish women looked in her direction and then spoke quietly behind their upraised hands. Hannah chose to pay them no mind as she followed Seth to the sheep and goat building, far less grand than the one for cattle.

Nothing could sour her mood. She'd come to town on a beautiful day in May to buy the world's sweetest, gentlest creature with a man who'd just kissed her. What could be finer? The possibility she might have a beau raced through her blood like wildfire.

"While I register," he said, "why don't you check out the sheep in the holding area? See if there're any you would buy, and any you would avoid. By the time the auction starts, it'll be too late to tell if they're worth the bid or not. I'll meet you outside that door in fifteen minutes." He pointed toward a white clapboard building fifty yards away.

"All right. I'll meet you there," Hannah said, watching him climb the steps to the registration counter. She noticed his broad shoulders and how his muscles flexed beneath his shirt.

Shaking away her thoughts of him, she headed to the pens and began working her way down the rows. She found a perfect group of Cheviot ewes with healthy looking coats and good conformation, sound teeth, and alert eyes. One docile creature let her pull back its gums to inspect its teeth. The other groups of animals wouldn't suffice no matter how low the bid. She jotted down the lot number of the Cheviots and walked to where Seth had indicated. Just when she thought the day couldn't get any better, she spotted a sign across the street: Jasper's Ice Cream. She hadn't felt this happy since coming to Ohio and had to force herself not to whistle a tune.

"You might be in luck," she said when Seth joined her.

"I already came to that conclusion myself," he said, wiggling his eyebrows. "Let's go inside." With auction card in hand, he took her elbow, and they entered the clapboard building together. "Perfect timing—they're getting ready to start." Seth looked as excited as a child on Christmas morning.

Hannah couldn't stop grinning as he guided her toward two empty seats in the small arena. People were filing in, taking their seats, and talking with great animation. She settled herself primly on the bench but clapped her hands when they brought in the first group of animals to be sold. *Who knew an auction could be so much fun?*

Hannah was so busy having fun, she failed to realize she was the only Plain woman inside the building. But that fact didn't escape notice of several Amish men in the bleachers.

And they didn't look pleased.

NINE

"Before the bidding starts, tell me about this breed you checked out," Seth whispered.

Hannah cocked her head to one side and considered carefully. "They're Cheviots—a robust breed that won't mind your cold winters. They graze well on hilly pastures like the ones in Holmes County. They tend to be a little excitable, but the ewes make good mothers. They produce lots of twins too. Very hardy lambs, not genetically predisposed to illness as in some breeds. Their wool is easy to hand spin." Hannah was surprised by how much she remembered.

"Good breed for meat lambs?" Seth asked, pulling on his beard.

She frowned unwittingly. "*Jah,* I've heard some say as much." *Not that I know from personal experience. I haven't sold a single lamb to a packinghouse.*

"Sounds like a good breed. What about this particular lot?" He was looking at the paper she had jotted the number on.

"You're taking a chance when you buy at auction. Some dishonest shepherds try to sell off sick animals to the unsuspecting, but those six look fairly healthy—no discharge from the eyes, not much squinting, coats look decent. I could only check the teeth of one ewe, but they weren't bad. Didn't see any manure to check for good, firm pellets."

Seth laughed, drawing attention from people seated nearby. "I won't even ask how you evaluate a critter's manure."

"Shush," Hannah murmured. "They're starting."

An Amish teenager prodded the first group of Suffolks into the auction pen.

Hannah tried to study the animals huddled together while Seth craned his neck for a better look. The half-dozen Suffolks, with their black faces and bare legs, were young and skittish. They were sold after a few bids to an elderly buyer, and an odd pair of beasts was brought in next.

"What are those?" Seth whispered, not wanting anyone to hear his question.

"Angora goats," she whispered back. "I might add some of those one day. You shear them just as you would a sheep, but you get a better price for their wool. Always a decent market for angora, unless keeping warm in winter goes out of style with the English. Plus, you never have to worry about a goat eating the wrong plant in your pasture and poisoning itself." She wished she'd taken her own auction number. "I hate to say it, but they are smarter than sheep."

Seth scrunched up his features with contempt. "Goats—no thanks. A goat chased me up a tree once when I was a boy. That varmint wouldn't let me down for two hours. I got a whippin' on top of that for being late for supper! I suppose my pap wanted me to risk getting butted all the way home by those horns. Didn't seem fair to me."

Hannah held her fist to her mouth to hold back laughter. "What did you say to the billy goat? I'm sure you said *something* that started the disagreement."

Seth watched the proceedings in the ring with a grin that stretched from one side of his face to the other. He leaned over to whisper in her ear, "I said his mother and sister were a pair of worthless grass-eaters, same as him."

"I knew it! You provoked him. I happen to love goat's milk and goat's milk cheese and goat's milk fudge." Hannah folded her hands in her lap.

Seth tore his attention from the ring just for a moment. "None of which can you get from a billy."

Hannah opened her mouth to argue, but right then the group of Cheviots darted into the arena. "That's the lot I examined. Don't look too excited, or the price will bid up quickly," she instructed, trying to look as nonchalant as possible.

Soon an Amish farmer established an opening bid, and two other farmers, both *Englischers,* joined in. Others had recognized the quality of the stock not usually found at auction barns. The bidding hopped back and forth around the room in lively fashion.

Hannah nudged Seth. "Now might be a good time to jump in with your number card," she whispered. "Hold it high to get the man's attention when you call out your bid."

Seth sat motionless, content to watch the action as an interested observer.

"Seth," she said, "those Cheviots are worth the price." She poked him in the ribs with her index finger.

But by the time the words left her mouth, the bidding was over. An English farmer and his son marched down to sign a paper at the desk. That lot of sheep was ushered through the door on the right while the next lot was paraded in on the left. Hannah chewed the inside of her lip. *Am I being too pushy?* She looked around at the human occupants in the arena and noticed for the first time several pairs of eyes on her instead of on the livestock down front. Three elderly Amish men were frowning in her direction.

Hannah folded her hands in her lap and offered no further bidding advice.

Seth seemed content to merely watch the goings-on anyway. Within ten minutes the whole business was over, and people began to file out. It was then that she noticed all the other participants were male. The air seemed to go out of her lungs.

Hannah could say nothing, but she felt the stares of several Plain people on her.

"Are you hungry, Hannah?" Seth asked, once outdoors. "Let's go find the booth that sells sausage sandwiches. I'm starved and have been thinking about them all morning."

"All right," she answered. "That sounds good." The buyers leaving the barn scattered in all directions, going about their business. *I probably imagined those men staring at me,* she thought.

Seth took her arm as they crossed the street to a vendor selling lunch and cold drinks. Hannah waited at the picnic table while Seth bought them sausage sandwiches with baked beans and cold iced tea.

"*Danki,*" she said, unwrapping her sandwich. "Next time, I'll provide the lunch."

"So there will be a next time? I'm glad to hear it." He took a bite of his sandwich with gusto.

Hannah felt a blush rise up her neck but knew anything she might say would only heighten her embarrassment. She began eating instead. "I'm curious. Why didn't you bid on the Cheviots?" she asked after dabbing her mouth with a napkin. The onions and grilled peppers were greasy but delicious.

Seth took a long swallow of tea. "I had no intention of buying today, Hannah. I only wanted to see what was available and gauge the going price. Never buy the first time you see something. You'll usually regret it." He looked toward the street where several teams of draft horses were leaving the parking lot. They pulled trailers loaded with new livestock.

She nodded in agreement. "That's true. You might find a private owner willing to sell part or all his flock, and you'd be taking less risk."

When Seth finished his sandwich, he took a small white card from his pocket. "Remember the bulletin board I told you about—the one that hangs in the auction barn?"

Hannah wrapped up the rest of her sandwich to take home. "*Jah*, you said someone might have herding dogs for sale."

"You are in luck." He set the card on the table.

Hannah read aloud. "For sale: Border collie pups, twelve weeks old, weaned. No AKC papers but trained to gather and work hard. Nonaggressive. Gentle with animals and people." She grinned with joy. "I love border collies. They're usually good-natured dogs."

Seth rose from the bench and gathered their wrappers. "You wait for me here. There's a pay phone on the street. I'll see where these dogs live and how much the owner wants for them."

By the time Hannah finished her tea, Seth was back. "Let's go into Kidron Hardware; then we'll need to be off," he said. "It's a long way home."

He was no longer smiling, so she assumed the price was too high. No matter. She'd gotten along fine without a dog thus far.

Inside the expansive store, she soon forgot all about dogs. The place had room after room of things to see, do, eat, or read. "Oh, Seth, look!" Hannah pointed at the most ornate cooking stove she'd ever seen in her life. It had a deep oven and six large burners that would accommodate the biggest pots. "You could get a lot more canning done with that."

"Mighty fancy, wouldn't you say?" He crossed his arms over his chest, staring at the appliance as though it were an alien beast.

She laughed and shook her head. "Fancy" wasn't the word. Besides the bright enamel paint, it had shiny brass knobs and curlicue filigree trim everywhere. Only the most progressive Amish district would allow such a thing.

"People would come from far and near just to see it," she said. "Not that I would like that." She ran her finger lightly down the oven handle. "What does it use?"

"Propane," Seth answered, moving to the next monstrosity. "Look at this bottled gas refrigerator."

Hannah walked over but was losing enthusiasm. The appliances were garish and showy. "Do Amish people ever buy these things?" she whispered.

"Not many. Mostly it's tourists who are worried about power failures who buy them. Take a look at the price tag."

Hannah did so and almost fainted. It would take a lifetime of shearing wool to afford one. "It's a good thing I don't care for it." Although the stove wasn't to her taste, she found herself almost skipping into the next building.

Here they found more practical things to consider—beautiful crockery, oil lamps in every color, hand-tooled weather vanes for the house or barn. Hannah didn't know what to look at first but ended up with two handblown hummingbird feeders for her nieces. Seth bought simple woodworking planes for the boys. Both nephews were interested in making birdhouses.

"Look at this," Hannah exclaimed. "Do you think Julia would like it?"

Seth peered over her shoulder. She caught his clean scent of piney soap and just for a moment contemplated what it might be like to be married. Would he enjoy shopping trips to town with her? Would he keep her company and help make difficult decisions? She'd loved how her *daed* always went inside stores with *mamm* instead waiting out in the buggy or talking to other fellows.

Seth took the baking pan to examine. It was similar to an iron skillet but had dividers to separate the batter. Small reverse indentations on the bottom would leave impressions of ears of corn on each muffin as they baked. "For corn bread?" he asked. "I think she would love it."

"Good." Hannah pulled it back before he tried to pay for it. "Now you go find something for your *bruder*. We mustn't come home empty-handed for him."

Home. She'd said the word as though they shared the same. She'd better be careful—one kiss on the cheek did not make for serious courtship. Seth often kissed Julia on the cheek with brotherly affection, so Hannah shouldn't jump to conclusions.

"I know just the thing for Simon," he said, striding off into the next room of tools. Apparently he hadn't noticed her poor choice of words.

Hannah waited several minutes for him to return, and when he didn't, she decided to see what was keeping him. She spotted Seth talking to a young woman in a navy dress with a stiff black apron. Not a smidgen of dust, or wrinkle, or hair out of place could be seen anywhere. And when the girl tilted back her head to laugh at something funny, Hannah saw she was quite pretty. An older woman, all in black, stood nearby, presumably the girl's *mamm*.

Hannah pressed down the folds of her skirt and tucked some stray locks under her *kapp*. She felt as though she'd just come in from slopping the hogs and feeding the chickens. Just as she was thinking of joining the group, Seth tipped his hat to the two women and walked back to where she stood rooted to the floor.

"That was Leah's and Emma's teacher, and soon to be Phoebe's. We must pay for our gifts and get going, Hannah, or we'll be out way past dark."

"Can I treat us to ice cream cones for the ride back?" Hannah asked. Suddenly her confidence had evaporated after seeing the pretty woman talk to Seth. Everything had been easy when she held Seth's attention like a captive bird. Here in Kidron, many women noticed the handsome widower with a fine farm and sweet daughter to bring up.

"Sure, but we had better hurry."

They headed for the cash register without a backward glance at the teacher. "What do you think?" he asked, setting down a rooster weathervane. "It's for Simon."

"Perfect," she answered, remembering licorice hard candy for Julia in the nick of time.

Soon they were enjoying ice cream cones and headed south out of town. Hannah didn't want the day to end. She loved Julia and her family, but living in someone else's home wasn't the same as having your own. Perhaps one day she would again have her own home... and maybe...

"A penny for your thoughts," Seth said. "And since I didn't buy any sheep, I've got money to spend."

Hannah's woolgathering stopped on a dime. No way could she admit thoughts of courtship and marriage after one peck on the cheek. So instead she chose her words carefully.

"I was just thinking that double chocolate swirl ice cream with chunks of dark chocolate is probably the best-tasting thing ever invented."

She leaned back on her seat to enjoy the ride home, hoping the horse walked very, very slowly.

∼

Seth knew the way home from Kidron like the back of his hand. And if he fell asleep at the reins, he was certain his horse would bring them safely home. But for some reason everything on the way back looked different. Maybe it was due to the sweet woman sitting beside him, trying not to let her ice cream drip. Unfortunately he'd made a mess on the floor of his courting buggy with his cone, but he didn't mind a bit.

Courting buggy? He hadn't thought about anything like that in too long a time to remember. But that's what the trip had felt like—going on an outing away from the inquisitive eyes of Hannah's *mamm* and *daed*. But instead of parents, they'd left behind her sister and his brother. Odd how things sometimes turned out. *Am I courting Hannah Brown?* He'd certainly kissed her on the way into town. He'd chosen that precise moment in case she became angry—they could go their separate ways until she cooled off.

But she hadn't become angry. She might have said, "No more of that," but her beautiful green eyes said something different.

He was glad he'd spent the day with Hannah instead of going to a meeting at one of the brethren's farms. According to the grapevine, some men in the district wanted to form an alliance to lease available land and plant corn. They sought to make a good profit if the price kept skyrocketing as it had been. And nothing in the *Daily Journal* indicated corn prices would be going down anytime soon.

Seth favored the old ways—plant only what you need to feed your family and pay your bills. He didn't need to get rich. He remembered hearing a passage of Scripture once about a rich man and the eye of a needle. That's one reason why shepherding appealed to him—it was a good, simple life. Or maybe it was the pretty shepherdess by his side that had him thinking so.

As they rolled toward the next town, turkey vultures soared on high wind currents while the setting sun warmed their backs. Mount Eaton was the only town between Kidron and Winesburg. There they would rest the horse before turning south and heading for home. "Are you warm enough, Hannah?" Seth asked. "That breeze will get chilly once the sun drops behind the hills."

"I was plenty warm until I finished eating my ice cream," she said, and scooted closer on the bench.

He decided not to reach for the lap robe yet for fear she'd move away. He would be happy to ride all the way to Columbus if Hannah kept smiling like that. The possibility of his getting remarried someday didn't sound half as impossible as during those dark days after Constance's death. He'd been so consumed with grief he had made a silent promise never to remarry.

That might be one promise the Good Lord might forgive if he broke.

He remembered Proverbs 31:10-11 about how wonderful a wife could be in a man's life. "Who can find a virtuous and capable wife? She is more precious than rubies. Her husband can trust her, and she will greatly enrich his life."

Hannah plucked at Seth's coat sleeve to get his attention. "What's got you preoccupied, Seth Miller?" she asked. "Your brow's so furrowed you could put in a short row of beans."

Seth laughed deeply from his belly. That's one of the things he liked best about Hannah—her sense of humor and the wonderful sound of her laughter. But he was in no position to quote Scripture on remarriage until he was sure of his feelings—and could figure out hers.

"I was thinking about something I'd read in Corinthians," he answered truthfully.

"*Jah?*" she asked. "That's not one of the books of the Bible the bishop approves of."

"I know, but someone recommended the book after Constance died, so I read it several times. It gave me a sense of peace."

Hannah stared at the row of white houses with their lights coming on as the buggy rolled into town. "*Jah,* me too. I've read my share of the Good Book when sleep doesn't come during difficult times." Her words were barely audible over the clopping of the horse's hooves.

Seth didn't question her about this but took her hand and held it until they reached the traffic light. Just past the center of town, they found the watering troughs and a place to rest the horse.

"Do you think I'm a rebellious woman?" she asked. "For reading Scripture on my own?" She turned her moist, shiny eyes toward him.

He had to look away as he brought the horse to a halt at the trough. "No, nothing in Scripture could do you harm, but I wouldn't mention it to Simon. A deacon would look differently on the matter."

"*Jah,* that's true." She squeezed his hand and then hopped down from the buggy. "I'm going inside that café. Be back in a jiffy."

The touch of her hand soothed him like a cool drink on a September afternoon. How he'd missed a woman's gentle touch. Yet he'd had no desire to court before this, preferring to wrap himself in a heavy coat of grief. He hoped to muster the courage to kiss her again before the night was over. Then he'd know for sure where he stood. Although conversation came easily between them, she often kept a cool distance, especially in front of her family.

God had a plan for him, and Seth hoped the plan included Hannah Brown.

Once the horse had rested and they were headed south again, he broached the subject he'd been chewing on all day. "There's something I've been meaning to talk to you about, Hannah. And it's part of the reason why I was lookin' today instead of buyin'." He tipped up his hat brim so as not to miss her reaction. "I think I might have the perfect solution for your problem."

"What problem are you referring to?" she asked, turning to face him on the bench.

"The problem with Simon's pasture, of course. You said it was too small and the grass too sparse for proper grazing. Plus there's the possibility the sheep might break down that fence again."

The look flashing in her green eyes wasn't the reaction he had expected. He watched her suck in a lungful of air. "Did Simon come to you about my sheep?" she asked, lifting her chin.

"No, this was my idea." He slapped the reins on the horse's rump. "I think we should move your flock to my place. I've got a good pasture that's come in thick and green. It's on higher ground than where your sheep are now, with sturdy fences in case they get another notion to stampede like wild horses." He chuckled until he caught the annoyed expression on her face.

She wasn't laughing at his joke.

"So you and your *bruder* just sat down after dinner and decided what was best for *my* sheep?" She crossed her arms, hugged herself tightly, and appeared to be clenching down on her back teeth.

"Are you getting cold, Hannah?" He reached behind the seat for the lap robe and spread it across both their knees. "No, I came up with this solution. I thought I could take your sheep temporarily until Simon's pasture comes in. You could teach me the business at my farm before I buy my own flock of sheep. I would have to quarantine any new animals I bought today away from yours, and I didn't like that idea."

Hannah pulled the lap robe up to her chin. For a moment, Seth thought she would pull it over her head. She sat like that for a full minute before she replied, "If Simon wants to move my flock temporarily until his grass comes in, then I have no choice but to go along with his decision."

Her voice sounded as though it hurt to talk, like the time he had his tonsils out.

"But in the future, Seth Miller, I'd oblige you to speak to me first before coming up with any more *perfect* solutions."

Her words hung in the air like mist on a cloudy day.

No more was spoken on that particular subject. In fact, no more was said on any topic at all during the rest of the long ride home. And Seth began to feel a little guilty about the kiss and wanting to move on with his life. His thoughts of courting again seemed premature.

~

The tree frogs were beginning their nightly chorus when Julia heard the buggy rumble up the driveway. She could tell something was wrong the moment Hannah jumped down from the carriage and stomped across the yard. She was carrying several bags that Seth didn't help her with. Nor did he walk her to the door, which wasn't like Seth at all. Something went wrong during their outing. They must have had a spat.

Julia put the teakettle on the stove and added kindling to the smoldering embers. When Hannah entered the kitchen and removed her heavy black bonnet, her expression confirmed Julia's suspicions. Hannah pulled on her white *kapp* and slumped into a chair.

"What's wrong, Hannah? What went on in Kidron?" For a fleeting moment, Julia feared Hannah had done something to draw attention from the district elders and was scolded in front of Seth. But she quickly dismissed the notion—the ministerial brethren would never embarrass someone in public.

"Oh, sister," Hannah moaned. "I thought Seth Miller was different from the other men I've met since Adam's passing." She kept her voice low and her head down.

Julia slipped into the opposite chair. "What happened? Do you want to tell me?"

Hannah released such a weary sigh one would have thought the weight of the world rested on her shoulders. "On the way to Kidron, we got along so well. We talked; he asked my opinion on matters; and he actually *listened* to my answers."

Julia suppressed her impulse to smile at this.

"We got along so well," continued Hannah, "I thought...I was starting to think we might make a life together...that I might find the contentment I'd known with Adam. He even kissed me on the cheek right before we arrived in town." Her fingers reached up to touch the spot where he'd kissed her. "We spent a wonderful day— eating greasy sausage sandwiches with grilled onions and chocolate chunk ice cream and looking at the livestock for sale and all the fancy stuff in the giant hardware store."

Julia shuddered at the bizarre combination of food choices but remained silent.

Hannah's face glowed with the reminiscence as though she plucked it from the past, rather than from a few hours ago. "He said he wanted to talk to me on the way back." The corners of her mouth turned down.

Julia clenched her back teeth with anxiety. *Did Hannah take an auction number and start bidding herself on livestock?* Plain women didn't venture into traditional male roles in their conservative community, not without stirring up a cloud of gossip. *Did Seth take offense at her sitting in the auction?* Julia struggled to her feet and took the kettle off the burner before the whistle woke every one up.

"What did Seth say? What did he want to talk about?" she asked, unable to contain her curiosity.

"He said he had a perfect solution to my problem—a problem I didn't know I had! He would take my sheep away from me because the grazing here is thin and move them to his place. That way Simon's pasture would have a chance to grow, and my flock wouldn't trample any more crops or bust down the fences again."

A single tear slipped from Hannah's eye. She wiped it away quickly.

Inwardly Julia breathed a sigh of relief. Hannah hadn't drawn undue attention to herself after all. "I thought Seth went to Kidron to buy his own sheep," Julia said. Relief was soon replaced by growing irritation with her brother-in-law.

"That's what I thought. But why spend good money when he can just take over my flock?" Hannah's lower lip trembled as she met Julia's gaze.

Julia wanted to wrap her arms around her sister and comfort her, but she first had to get to the bottom of this. "Surely Seth would never just take your sheep. He would at least offer to buy them."

"They're not for sale!" Hannah sobbed. "I love them." Tears started to stream down her face.

Julia went to her and wrapped an arm around her shoulders. An unsettling notion crept into her head. "Did Seth say Simon had suggested this?"

Hannah pulled the hanky she kept tucked in her sleeve and blew her nose as she shook her head. "He said it was his idea, but it's for everyone's good. Everyone but me."

Julia released the breath she'd been holding.

The rest of Hannah's story gushed forth. "I didn't talk to him all the way home from Mount Eaton. I know I should have discussed this like an adult, but all my emotions rushed to the surface. I was afraid if I said anything at all, it would be mean and spiteful." Hannah buried her face in her hands. "I pouted instead of expressing myself calmly."

"This is a simple misunderstanding," Julia soothed. "Everything will look differently in the morning, and you and Seth will put this behind you."

Hannah looked up, her reddened eyes brightening slightly. "Do you really think so?"

"I do. You must be exhausted. Go get some rest."

"*Danki*, Julia. Good night."

Julia had voiced the words, but in her heart she wasn't so sure. She and Hannah were sisters—Julia had been on the receiving end of Hannah's silent treatments after an argument.

At the time, she would have greatly preferred an unladylike hair-pulling instead.

Julia released a sigh as Hannah climbed the stairs to her room. How she wished Hannah and Seth would stop putting up barriers and just get to know one another. She wanted Hannah married again and settled, not attending auctions as an independent woman. Until then people would watch her every move. And Julia hoped she married soon before the ministerial brethren observed something they didn't like.

The trouble she had in Pennsylvania could start all over again.

TEN

Julia had been right about one thing—the world did look better in the morning. Hannah rose earlier than usual to arrive first in the kitchen. She started a pot of coffee, mixed up pancake batter, and lined up sausage links in the frying pan before heading to her chores. Emma or Julia would have an easy time of breakfast now.

Outdoors, May had exploded into flowers everywhere. Dogwood, redbud, azalea, rhododendron, and apple, pear, cherry, and crabapple trees competed for the showiest display with their fragrant blossoms. Hannah loved spring with its longer, sunnier days. Soon the pasture grass would grow thick and lush, providing plenty of food.

In the meantime, she corralled her nephews to help move the grain troughs and water stanchions to higher ground, away from the gate. She would gladly walk farther and work harder to keep her sheep where they were. The decision about their move, however, rested with Simon. If he wanted them moved, Hannah must go along. This was his household, and she had no say in the matter.

But neither did Seth.

She tried to muster the anger she'd felt yesterday toward him, but all she felt was profound sadness. How gentle his touch had been. How tender his lips had felt on her cheek. And how she had wanted him to end her loneliness. He'd given her hope—hope that she would once again know love, hope to have a home again, and hope she might one day have a child. But thanks to her quick temper and sullenness, that hope was lost. No man wanted a woman who pouts. Her *mamm*'s warning had come back to haunt her: She was *eegesinnisch*—willful, but she didn't know how else to be. Her sheep were all she had left from her old life.

"Be still and know that I am God!" How much easier said than done.

At least her frisky lambs gave her reason to smile. They frolicked and played like human children on the warm spring day. Her stomach growled to remind her she'd eaten nothing since Kidron, so she headed inside to wash up.

"There you are," Julia said as Hannah entered the kitchen. "*Danki* for starting breakfast."

"You're welcome." The smell of fried sausages and maple syrup whetted Hannah's appetite as she poured coffee. Hannah noticed that the plates on the table were dirty other than two. "Am I late?" she asked. "Has everyone else already eaten?"

"*Jah,* Simon was going to Winesburg and wanted an early start. I hurried the children along because I wanted Matthew to take a note to Seth on his way to school." Julia was rubbing the backs of her fingers and wrist.

Hannah tamped down her anxiety at the mention of the sheep-napper's name, handsome and tenderhearted though he was. "I'm sure the *kinner* are glad school is almost out for the year." Hannah bowed her head for prayer and then loaded her plate with food.

Julia took a more modest portion on her plate. "I've asked Seth to come this afternoon to help Simon move the furniture in the living room. I want to wash the floors and walls to get ready for the preaching service at our house. Simon's back is still acting up, although he won't admit it. Besides, I bought a turkey breast on sale at the store that I want to use up while it's fresh." As Julia reached for the cream, Hannah noticed her fingers were bent over, clawlike.

Hannah grabbed the pitcher first and poured cream into Julia's cup while she took several deep breaths. "I could've helped move furniture just as well," she said, not ready to face Seth Miller yet. More water needed to run under that particular bridge!

"Can I ask you to fix dinner tonight, Hannah? Our neighbor came down with the flu, so Emma is going to her house after school. My fingers are awfully bad today, and I'd like to look in on Mrs. Lehman myself. I've got a great recipe for turkey casserole you can make that I'm sure everyone will enjoy. Phoebe especially loves noodle casserole with peas and mushrooms."

Hannah set down the pitcher before it slipped from her fingers. "Of course. I'd be happy to help," she replied quickly. *But I don't know if anybody else will be too happy once they taste it,* she thought. Then an idea occurred as she recalled how shrewd her sister could be. "Is there another reason you asked me to cook? One that might involve the fact you invited Seth to dinner?" Hannah perched her hands on her hips.

Julia feigned a look of innocence that fooled no one. "Me? Trying to mend something that ought not to have been broken in the first place?" Julia leaned over to whisper even though the women were alone in the room. "Time is a'wastin', sister. Many women in the district have their eyes on Seth, but he is fond of you. I'm sure of it. But if you wait too long to patch this little misunderstanding, he might think you're...ah..." Julia's cheeks flushed a bright pink when the right word didn't come to mind.

Hannah laughed at Julia's stymie. "Let's see...disagreeable? Stubborn? Pushy? I *am* all those things, and Seth's bound to find out sometime. I am doomed." Hannah helped herself to another pancake. After all, she was about to spend her remaining life unwed, so she might as well get as fat as Henry's prize sow.

Julia wouldn't be sidetracked. "You're also kind, generous, hardworking, and forgiving. You have many wonderful qualities that Seth will see tonight when you fix a delicious dinner. And he's bound to notice how children adore you. Even his little Phoebe is coming around since you gave her that lamb. After praying on this matter for many nights, I'm sure you and Seth are destined to be man and wife."

"Do you really think so?" Hannah asked, not liking how needy she sounded.

"*Jah,* I do, and we won't let the sun go down with you two still on the outs."

"All right," Hannah agreed. "I'll make dinner because I want to help, not because I'm promising anything else. And you'd better give me a written copy of the new recipe before you leave for Mrs. Lehman's."

Although Hannah could cook well enough, this was an untested recipe. No one had ever accused her of trying to poison people at potlucks or family get-togethers, but she was no Julia. Julia didn't need recipes, merely drawing on an innate ability passed down through generations. Hannah must have been out counting sheep when that particular gift had been passed out. She usually ventured off the tried-and-true with disastrous results. But tonight Seth and Phoebe were coming. This was her chance to turn over a new leaf—in the kitchen and with the man she hoped would ask to court her.

Hannah smiled and turned toward her optimistic sister. "You go get ready, and let me clean up this kitchen." She stacked dirty plates until the kitchen door swung closed and then turned her face up and murmured a heartfelt, "Thank You."

～

Seth stood in the middle of his kitchen not knowing where to start. How in the world had things gotten so messy? Dishes were piled high in the sink, a film of dust covered the countertops, Phoebe's sticky jam-prints decorated the refrigerator door, and the floor needed sweeping and washing. He filled the sink with water, put the kettle on to boil, and then hunted for the broom and mop. Between the spring planting, Simon's replanting, and routine chores, the house had gotten out of control. He still needed to get his vegetable seeds into the ground or the summer garden would be late. But he would straighten out his house before tackling anything else. No way would he let Julia see this kitchen when she stopped by to get their laundry.

Julia. He slicked a hand through his hair, remembering her note that morning. She'd asked him to move furniture today even though the preaching service was more than a week away. She was up to something, and he had a feeling it dealt with the widow. His sister-in-law couldn't stand to see two people alone, whether they were happy with life or not.

While Seth washed dishes, he tried to remember the conversation with Hannah. He should have approached her differently, but she had no reason to arch her back like a cornered tomcat. He should have made it clear he planned to buy his own flock, but she should have been willing to discuss the matter. Instead she'd given him the cold shoulder the whole way home. Women!

This wasn't how people acted when they cared about each other. Seth could only draw one conclusion—Hannah was content with things as they were. Any friendliness toward him was because of their family connection. He had made a fool of himself, especially when he'd kissed her yesterday.

As he wiped down counters and appliances, the memory of that one kiss crept back. And while he swept and mopped the floor, each detail of their day together returned to taunt him. She was a fine-looking woman, with eyes he could gaze into for the rest of his life. Her honesty and forthrightness drew him like a moth to a candle. But Hannah had made it clear she didn't like him making decisions or telling her what to do.

Seth threw the bucket of dirty wash water off the porch, hung the rags up to dry, and went back inside to appreciate his hard work.

Passable, livable, but by no means the standard he'd enjoyed with Constance. He exhaled a whistle between his teeth in frustration. He might need a wife, but it never would be Hannah, despite Julia's good intentions.

Seth took Phoebe down to the pond for a quick swim before getting ready to go to Simon's. He would help Simon move whatever he wanted and then stay for one of Julia's delicious dinners. But he planned to cut a wide path around Mrs. Brown. Hannah had made her feelings clear. And he certainly didn't need a wife every bit as ornery as her sheep.

Maybe his *bruder* had been right all along.

~

For an hour Julia was able to rest easy. Seth was coming to a dinner prepared by Hannah. Once he saw her and realized how silly their quarrel had been, the whole matter would be forgotten. And the new recipe for turkey casserole with plenty of pickled beets on the side wouldn't hurt either.

Her serenity lasted for only the time it took to dress and walk the length of the driveway. There she met Simon returning from his errands in town. His face in repose looked tired and worried, but it immediately brightened when he saw her.

"Where are you off to, *fraa?* I hurried back from town early so we could eat lunch together."

Julia rested her basket on the wheel. "I'm walking next door to Mrs. Lehman's. She's down with a bug. Emma is already there doing her cleaning and ironing. I left a plate of sandwiches for your lunch." Julia watched his expression fall. It did her heart good to know that after all these years her husband still enjoyed her company.

"Where's Hannah?" he asked.

"Inside, dusting and sweeping. She'll be busy fixing the evening meal tonight. I invited Seth and Phoebe to stay for dinner."

Simon's forehead furrowed into deep creases. "Hannah's doing the cooking? Is that a good idea?"

Julia leaned toward her husband. "Simon Miller, my sister kept a fine house for six years before moving in with us. I think she can manage one supper."

"*Jah,* sure, but I invited a guest while I was in Winesburg today."

"A guest?" Julia asked. Simon never used such terms for neighbors he would run into and then invite to share a meal. "Who is this *guest?* Did you run into the bishop? Or maybe the U.S. secretary of agriculture in the English world?" Julia laughed merrily as she leaned her hip on the wagon.

Simon shook his head, oblivious to her humor as usual. "No bishop, no secretary. I invited Miss Laura Stoddard—Emma's and Leah's teacher."

"You did?" Julia was downright flummoxed. "Why would you do such a thing—invite her out of the blue on an ordinary weeknight?"

Simon met her eye and then looked off toward the road. "I heard from my son as I was leaving for town that you told Seth to come. I thought it a good time for Seth to meet the schoolteacher properly. She's a bit past prime marrying age—maybe twenty-three—but still a handsome woman. Wouldn't you agree? She will be Phoebe's teacher in the fall."

Julia was past flummoxed now. Simon had never commented favorably or not on any woman's appearance since their marriage. "Miss Laura Stoddard?" she asked ridiculously.

He nodded. "All things considered, couldn't you postpone your visit next door and fix the meal yourself?"

Smug—that was the only word that would describe his expression.

"Miss Stoddard is a pretty woman, to be sure," Julia said. "But Hannah wishes to cook because my hands hurt terribly today."

Simon's demeanor changed immediately. "I didn't know that, wife. Did you take some of the pills the doctor prescribed?"

"*Jah,* soon they should bring relief." Julia straightened her spine. "What are you up to, Simon? Matchmaking?"

"It's time Seth meets eligible women in the district. Everywhere he goes the only company he keeps is men, except for your sister. And I don't think Hannah and he are suited in the least." He leaned close for confidentiality, but someone would have to have been hiding in the maple tree to overhear.

"I think they're perfect for each other." Julia crossed her arms.

"I think you're either joking or blind." Simon's fingers tightened on the reins until they had clenched into a fist. "Your sister is not resigned to the will of God nor respectful of the *Ordnung.* She tends to do whatever suits her best. A man is the head of every household."

Julia lifted one eyebrow. "Let's just allow Seth to decide and let God's will be done."

The arched brow, so effective on *kinner,* had no effect on Simon whatsoever. "God's will doesn't need your help either, wife, yet you seem bound and determined," he said, sweeping his straw hat from his head. His cowlick stood straight on end while the rest of his gray hair lay plastered to his skull. "Enjoy your visit with Mrs. Lehman, Julia." He met her gaze with a look of challenge. "We shall both sit down at the dinner table tonight, all..." He quickly counted up to the appropriate number, "ten of us, to enjoy Hannah Brown's cooking and the interesting company of Phoebe's new teacher. Everything else that happens will be up to them."

"All right, but please tell my sister there will be one more place to set for dinner. She doesn't need any surprises," Julia said.

Simon nodded politely, as though he'd just passed an acquaintance on the road, and then clucked to his gelding. The buggy rolled toward the barn while Julia walked to the next farm without an ounce of the assurance she had felt after breakfast. *Why was Simon interfering in matters of courtship?*

One meddlesome relative per household was more than enough.

~

Hannah hummed a tune as she cleaned the kitchen from top to bottom. She washed the windows with vinegar water, swept out the woodstove of ashes, and scrubbed the floor on her hands and knees. Tucking a stray lock of hair back under her *kapp*, she jumped when Simon spoke to her from the doorway.

"Hannah, there will be an extra person for dinner tonight," he said.

"I know. Julia told me Phoebe and Seth are coming." Hannah continued to rub at a black heel mark.

"*Jah*, Phoebe and Seth and one more. Ten in all." He went to the refrigerator for the plate of sandwiches that Julia had made and carried it to the porch without crossing her wet floor.

Hannah watched him leave without another word of explanation and returned to her scrubbing. Nine or ten hardly makes a difference when cooking a casserole. When she finished the floor, she rose stiffly to her feet and noticed the curtains looked dingy against the sparkling clean windows. She took them down to soak in soapy water. Later she would rinse them, hang them to dry, and iron them before putting them back up. They would look much fresher, and Julia would appreciate one less task before Sunday's preaching service.

While the curtains soaked, she kneaded and rolled out dough to make noodles. She chopped carrots and onions and brought up jars of peas, beans, and beets from the cellar. She started the bottled gas stove to roast the turkey breast and set out her baking supplies. Why have a loaf of yesterday's bread when she could bake buttermilk biscuits? She remembered Seth's fondness for them. Hadn't he eaten four or five? She glanced at the wall clock with a frown. She still had to boil the noodles, fix a salad, and set the table. A long, warm bath before changing clothes would help relieve her sore back muscles. And at some point during the afternoon, she needed to feed and water her animals.

But Hannah had always worked well under pressure.

The anticipation of seeing Seth tonight would help her sail through her chores. She ate the last sandwich from the plate Simon left behind and took a few moments to plan what she would say to smooth over their disagreement.

I'm sorry I implied you were a sheep rustler. It's just that I've grown attached to this particular group of woolbags.

No, maybe while she cut the noodles something clever would occur to her. But nothing clever came to mind then or while she rinsed the curtains and hung them to dry.

While the turkey breast roasted, she continued to draw a blank, and rolling out biscuit dough did nothing to stimulate her imagination.

Hannah decided to leave the overheated kitchen and head to her pasture. Among her sheep under the open sky, she would find the tranquillity necessary to clear her head. Unfortunately her nephews had forgotten to bring over the hay wagon in their haste to leave early. Neither had they filled the water buckets. Once she'd done both tasks and loaded the troughs with grain, she spotted a ewe stuck in the fence. "Oh, mercy," she moaned.

Getting an animal to go back the way it came wasn't easy alone. But with patience and determination, she eventually freed the obstinate creature. Rising to her feet, Hannah wiped a hand across her perspiring forehead. If she hurried she should have time to take a scented bubble bath and change before finishing dinner. But as she reached the house, she spotted Seth's buggy parked alongside the barn. *What time is it?* Was he there already to help move furniture? She couldn't run into him yet!

In the pump house she washed her hands and face and pulled off the soiled apron. If she could sneak in the back door, she would grab clean clothes and take a quick sponge bath.

"Hannah?"

Simon's voice stopped her in her tracks just as she reached the steps to her room. *"Jah?"* she answered, not turning around.

"Should I send Henry to fetch Julia and Emma home? It doesn't look like you've made much progress on dinner."

The hairs on her neck rose like quills on a porcupine. "Absolutely no need. I've got everything under control." She turned to face him and watched his gaze scan the room—the table covered in flour and dough scraps, counters arrayed with cut vegetables and their trimmings, two trays of biscuits expanding in the humid air.

Simon noticed the cooked turkey breast sitting in congealed grease and made a face. "Julia said we were having a casserole." Disappointment shaded his words.

"We are, but I've got plenty of time before dinner. Everything will be ready when we sit down." She forced her lips to smile. "Don't worry about anything," she added, and tried to shoo him back to the front room.

Simon moved as though walking through waist-deep water. At the doorway, Hannah spotted Seth taking down the calendar and a framed sampler from the wall. Luckily he didn't see her as she started a pot of water to boil and threw the noodles in before heading upstairs for her clothes. The clean dress she put on could have used a pressing, but she soon forgot about it once back in the kitchen.

Looking into the pot, she gasped and dumped the noodles into the colander. When the steam cleared, she saw with horror a blob of sticky starch. The heat from the bottled gas stove cooked things much faster than the woodstove. With a sigh she told herself that once mixed in with mushrooms, seasonings, meat, vegetables, and cream soup, no one would even notice.

Hannah cleared the table and counters, sliced the turkey, and put together the casserole. Sprinkling the top with breadcrumbs, she stepped back and uttered a satisfied "Done" as the baking dish went into the oven.

When she turned around, someone was standing at the back screen door. The jar of pickled beets she was holding almost slipped from her grasp. Hannah recognized the young schoolteacher from the Kidron hardware store.

"Good afternoon," the woman called. "Am I too early? I'm Laura Stoddard. The deacon invited me to dinner tonight." She smiled prettily.

The tenth for dinner...couldn't it have been another farmer from the district?

Hannah dried her hands on a towel before greeting the woman. "Welcome, Miss Stoddard. I am Mrs. Hannah Brown, Julia's sister. You're not too early—just in time. Please come in and enjoy a glass of tea while I set the table."

If not for the fact Hannah still had plenty to do, she might have enjoyed the schoolteacher's company. Laura seemed bright and friendly and made easy conversation. *But does she have to have such a softly rounded figure and creamy soft skin?* Hannah smoothed her skirt down over her bony hips. By comparison she could have replaced the broomstick strawman that scared crows away in the cornfield.

But it soon didn't matter how pretty the new teacher was. Within ten minutes, Julia and the girls arrived home, full of funny stories from the Lehman brood. The boys came in with fists full of dandelions, and Simon and Seth returned from the pump house.

Neither man was smiling.

Hannah had managed to get the table set, her salad tossed, and the wildflowers arrayed in jelly jars. Her silent prayer included a plea for patience and diminished jealousy.

"Hannah, the windows are sparkling. *Danki*," Julia said.

"Where are the curtains?" Simon demanded.

"Still on the clothesline," Hannah said awkwardly.

"Aunt Hannah, the casserole smells wonderful." Emma was leaning over the dish and inhaling deeply.

"What's burning?" asked Henry.

"The biscuits!" Hannah exclaimed and raced to the stove. The bottom shelf of the oven proved to be too close to the heat. When Hannah rescued them, the bottoms were burned to a crisp.

If not for two things, Hannah might have endured the shame of burned biscuits, bare windows, and overcooked noodles in the casserole. One, Simon took every opportunity to draw Miss Stoddard into a conversation with Seth. And two, Seth Miller paid Hannah not one dab of attention during the entire meal. Although he didn't entertain Laura with much more than polite *jah*s and noes, he looked everywhere in that overheated, crowded kitchen than at her.

When the disastrous supper finally ended and the kitchen had been cleaned, Hannah took two aspirin and climbed the steps to her room. She would take the Good Book from her dresser and read the Gospel of John. Only then would her feelings of hopelessness and loneliness fade away like dew with the morning sun.

ELEVEN

Julia rubbed the palms of her hands and insides of her fingers, wincing from the pain but also feeling a small measure of relief from the manipulation. She doubted three aspirin would be sufficient for what she had in mind. Instead she'd take a dose of the prescription sample the doctor had given her and pray it worked quickly.

Today a quilting bee was being held at the home of Mrs. Stauffer, who lived close to town. Julia planned to go and take Hannah with her. Arthritis had forced Julia to give up quilting, so she seldom attended bees anymore. Her fingers just wouldn't bend sufficiently to grip the fabric and make the necessarily tiny stitches. But she would make herself useful by sorting squares, ironing, and helping with the refreshments.

It had been several weeks since Hannah's less-than-sucessful dinner, and it was time Hannah got away from her four-legged friends to become better acquainted with her new neighbors. Julia knew Hannah sewed and quilted beautifully, despite her preference for outdoor activities. Her neat, small stitches would be much appreciated by the accomplished quilters. Even more important, it was time the women of their community got to know Hannah better. Human nature unfortunately casts doubts or misgivings on one who keeps herself apart from others for too long. Hannah needed to expand her circle beyond family, flock, and occasional outings with Seth.

Besides, Julia had heard rumblings through the grapevine about Hannah. An afternoon with the camaraderie of other women would do them both much good.

Gazing out the kitchen window, Julia smiled as she watched her sister return from the pasture. She looked like a nursery rhyme character, with her Amish head covering and her crook in hand. "There you are," Julia said brightly as Hannah came inside. "I'm glad your chores didn't take too long. Why don't you hurry and change into a clean dress, and we'll be off. I've already asked Simon to hitch up the buggy."

Hannah looked quizzical as she washed her hands and arms at the sink. "Off where?"

"To the quilting bee at Suzanne Stauffer's house. I mentioned it the other day. Suzanne's eldest daughter is to be married after the harvest, and we'll be putting together a wedding ring quilt for her."

Hannah frowned and shook her head with exasperation. "I plum forgot about it. Sorry," she said, sitting down at the table.

"There's still time. It's not far away." Julia pushed the plate of toast within reach and then went for the coffeepot.

"I can't, Julia. I sent word to the vet to stop by today on his rounds. I have no idea when he'll get here. Some of my ewes have developed eye infections. I need to treat them with antibiotics before they get worse, or the problem will spread through the flock." She spread the last slice of bread with jam and took a bite.

Julia drew a deep breath. "Couldn't you ask Simon to watch for the vet? I'd like the women of Winesburg to get to know you better. Besides, it'll be fun—you'll see."

Hannah looked horrified as she set down her toast. "Absolutely not. Simon has plenty of his own work this time of year, and the flock is my responsibility. I won't be a bigger burden to him than I already am, especially not for a social outing. I know there will be enough capable hands there without my calloused pair. I'll go next time, but right now I need to consult my herbal book for a salve remedy. Why buy something if we can make it better right here?"

Before Julia could think of a rebuttal, Hannah grabbed her toast, kissed her on the cheek, and hurried back out the door. Julia exhaled with exasperation. Just once she would like to pave an easier road for her sister. Without an alternative, she collected her sewing basket and headed for the buggy. The horse snorted with impatience until the two of them were trotting down the road toward town.

Much goodwill could be garnered from a social outing, Julia mused on the way to the quilting bee. And much harm from wagging tongues could be avoided.

Julia had been right to be worried.

All eyes turned in her direction when she walked into the front room. The other women were just sitting down at the large quilting frame. "Julia," called Mrs. Stauffer, "I've saved you a place by me." A folding table had been placed next to the frame with stacks and stacks of colorful fabric squares. "Come do your sorting here where there's more room. We will work inside instead of under the trees. My knees say it's going to rain later."

"That could be why my hands are so bad today," Julia said, shoving her basket of notions under the table. She pulled the piles of fabric toward her.

"I thought your sister would be joining us today," a young woman called from down the frame.

Julia glanced up from her cloth squares, startled to see eight pairs of eyes fastened on her. "She was disappointed that she couldn't. The vet is stopping by later today to treat some of her sick animals."

"*Jah,* her sheep business. I heard about that," the woman added. She glanced at Sarah Miller and nodded solemnly.

"It's not really much of a business. I keep her too busy helping me in the house most days," Julia said. She rubbed the backs of her aching hands.

"You're lucky to have your sister close by," Suzanne Stauffer said. "Mine moved to Ontario last year where she and her husband could get land cheaper. Letters are nice, but I still miss her terribly." She arranged the swatches Julia handed her onto the marked cloth and began to pin them securely.

"She is a blessing to me," Julia said, handing around small piles matched for color to the rest of the women.

"That I know," Suzanne nodded, but the others remained oddly silent.

Julia thought maybe they were intent on their quilting until a couple of hours later when she went to the kitchen to start making sandwiches. She'd finished sorting and matching, and had even cut more squares until her hands seemed to lock in one position. The hostess joined her in the kitchen after a few minutes.

"There is talk in the district about the widow Brown," Mrs. Stauffer said softly without preamble.

"Whatever about?" Julia stopped spreading butter on the thick slices of bread.

"The elders didn't like her bidding in the auction barn in Kidron. They said she should've waited outside and let Seth do the buying. It's not proper womenfolk behavior."

Julia set her knife down abruptly. "Hannah didn't buy or bid on anything as I understand. Seth wanted to see what was available and gauge the going price."

"This isn't my opinion, Julia. I'm only telling you what's being said. It might have been all right if they were married, but they're not." Suzanne began to slice and arrange tomatoes, cucumbers, pickles, and peppers on a blue platter.

"They never will be wed if gossip gets back to Seth...or Simon," Julia whispered to Suzanne. She trusted the woman despite not knowing her all that well.

This is just like the time before in Lancaster, she thought, but said it to no one.

As Suzanne finished fixing the tray, she glanced toward the door before continuing. "I'm afraid there's more talk too. Even worse." She lowered her voice to a whisper. "Word has gotten back to the ministerial brethren that Hannah has been quoting Scripture."

Julia cut the last two sandwiches in half before replying, and for a brief moment breathed easier. "She knows and loves the Good Book."

"She's been quoting passages from books not approved by the bishop. Word has gotten back to him, and he's unhappy about it. They will be calling on your sister to issue a warning. If she doesn't take the situation seriously, they will threaten her with shunning." Mrs. Stauffer cast her eyes downward.

That would be the ultimate humiliation for a grown woman. Hannah was no girl during her *Rumschpringe* but a widow once firmly established in her community. Julia's eyes filled with tears, but she batted them back.

Suzanne placed her hand over Julia's. "I've spread no gossip about Hannah, nor will I. Please bring her by for an afternoon visit once her critters are better. And I will pray that this blows over quickly."

"*Danki,*" Julia murmured, gathering her resolve. "Let's serve lunch on the porch. The rain has held off, and I'm sure everyone's getting hungry after all the hard work. The wedding quilt is turning out lovely."

It was all she could do to force down half a ham sandwich and an apple. Julia concentrated on cutting her apple into the thinnest slices possible to avoid talking much. No one seemed to notice her unusual silence. Conversation was lively among the group—from the anticipation of vegetable gardens and the price of corn in the fall harvest to who might be courting whom among the youth. Two circle letters were read aloud from Lodi and Lancaster as many of the women had friends who had contributed to the letters.

Julia listened patiently and nodded appropriately, but she couldn't wait to return home. There was little she could do to shelter Hannah from the coming storm except be close by when it hit. She didn't like feeling so helpless. For the remainder of the afternoon, she stayed as far away from the frame as possible and busied herself cleaning up the kitchen, ironing, and sweeping the floor of scraps and loose threads. She was the first guest to hitch up the horse and start for home, giving Suzanne a heartfelt hug on the way out.

Questions peppered her mind during the drive home: Why was it so terrible for Hannah to sit in the auction barn, especially since she didn't actually buy? To whom did Hannah quote Scripture who knew it wasn't from approved chapters? And who went to the bishop about the matter?

Remembering Hannah's dinner last night added another dose of vinegar to her already sour stomach. Of all nights for things to go wrong! Her plan to patch things up between Seth and Hannah couldn't have gone worse. And having Simon invite Miss Stoddard hadn't helped matters. Seth resembled an angry ram with his horns caught in the fence. After the meal he hurried after the boys to help with chores as though he couldn't get away fast enough. Simon had looked disappointed, Miss Stoddard confused, and her sister embarrassed.

"Oh, Hannah," she murmured as the buggy turned into her driveway, "may God's mercy and grace be upon you."

~

With her attention riveted to a book of herbal remedies and natural cures, Hannah didn't hear the car drive up and park near the pasture. Her cherished trunk, brought from Pennsylvania, still hadn't been moved to the loft, but at least her loom and weaving supplies had been. The freshly whitewashed room had become her favorite retreat to work, pray, and study Scripture. It was easy to appreciate God's creation from the large window overlooking the pasture and fields. She would sneak up here whenever time permitted for solitude and contemplation.

The English veterinarian nearly startled her out of her shoes when he entered the barn and hollered, "Hello?"

"I'm up here, Dr. Longo," she called. "I'll be right down." It was very unladylike to yell, but she didn't want him to go searching for her in the other outbuildings. Vets were in short supply in rural communities and busy as ants under a picnic table. He had no time to waste.

"Mrs. Brown?" he asked once Hannah reached ground level. "I've received word that some of your sheep have eye infections. Let me take a look at them." He discreetly glanced at his wristwatch.

"Thank you for stopping by on short notice," Hannah said, remembering to use all English. "I'll lead the way to my flock." She strode from the barn as fast as she could without breaking into a run. "I've found recipes for both a poultice and a salve that I can make if you think it'll help. I've got petroleum jelly to use as the base if that's all right. I already have or can easily find all the necessary herbs in the woods." Hannah marched toward the pasture with her herb book tucked under her arm like a scholar.

Dr. Longo trailed close on her heels, lugging his large black satchel. "I'll take a look at your salve compound before I leave. I've brought syringes of antibiotics in case it's the same malady I saw in Wilmot last week."

The vet wasn't a bit surprised by her herbal knowledge. Most Plain folk relied heavily on natural remedies, turning to modern pharmaceuticals only when necessary.

Hannah felt the noonday sun hot on her back as they walked toward the flock. She pulled the brim of her black bonnet forward to prevent her usual summertime sunburned nose. The sheep pranced nervously with the approach of a stranger.

"Just as I expected," the vet announced after inspecting several ewes. "Pinkeye, same as in Wilmot. Luckily it hasn't spread much yet. You were wise to call me right away." He straightened his spine and scanned the rolling pasture.

Hannah noticed deep lines around his eyes from squinting. "What should we do?" she asked.

"With your permission I'll administer strong antibiotic shots to the infected animals. One shot should do the trick as long as you follow up with your salve. A poultice might be needed for that one." He pointed to one sad-looking, older sheep with especially runny eyes. "I trust you have no plans to take any to slaughter in the next several months. All meds should be fully out of their fatty tissue by then."

"No, none will be…harvested," she said, not able to repeat his word. Hannah felt a measure of relief as they walked back to the house.

He reviewed her salve recipe, decided it was fine, and gave her a jar of plain cream to use for the base. Hannah paid him in cash and because his bill was so reasonable, packed up a box of preserves and canned fruit.

"Send word to me through an English neighbor if my shots and your treatments don't do the trick," he instructed.

She followed him to his pickup truck. "Thank you, Doctor Longo. I will be diligent with the salve."

"You're welcome. Thanks for the preserves." With a wave of his hand, the vet headed down the drive.

Just as he pulled onto the road, an unfamiliar Amish buggy turned in. "It's getting to be a traffic jam on Miller Lane," Hannah said, shielding her eyes as she tried to identify the occupants. She recognized none of the elderly, somber-looking men who got out of the carriage and tied the horse to the post.

"You can turn your horse out in the paddock while you visit with the deacon," Hannah said politely as they approached, happy there was nothing unseemly about her appearance that afternoon—no muddy skirt hem or knee-high rubber boots.

The three black-clad men approached in their Sunday best. Hannah feared they might have come directly from a funeral, although she hadn't heard about any deaths in the district.

"We won't be staying that long, Mrs. Brown," a white-haired gentleman said. "And we've come to speak to you, not Deacon Miller."

A chill swept over her, despite temperatures well into the eighties. Her palms began to sweat, and the soup she'd eaten for lunch churned in her belly.

"You've come to speak to me?" her voice croaked in a tone no one would recognize as hers. "Would you like to come into the kitchen for a glass of cool lemonade?"

Nothing in their deportment indicated this visit was social, but Hannah tried to hope for the best.

"*Danki,* no." The eldest swept his hat from his head and looked down his thin nose with a stern but compassionate gaze. "As elders in your new district, Mrs. Brown, we were displeased to learn of some of your recent...activities. We're unsure how liberal the previous community where you were a member was, but here we expect our female members to behave with restraint. And more seriously, word has gotten back to the bishop that you've been quoting passages of Scripture."

Hannah felt heat rise up her neck into her face, but she also felt a measure of reprieve. Certainly if she'd been misquoting passages or applying them in an incorrect context, it couldn't be as serious an offense as dancing in the milk house while listening to a battery radio as a former schoolmate had done. She wiped her damp palms on her apron and glanced up. "*Jah,* I often find myself reciting verses that might help me or another person during a difficult situation."

Two of the men seemed to relax with her admission, but the white-haired elder's expression didn't change. "You are knowledgeable in Bible passages, Mrs. Brown?"

"Somewhat," she said. "I've memorized many of my favorites."

He nodded and gave his beard a pull. "The passage you quoted to Mrs. Lehman was from the book of Romans: 'Pay your taxes, too, for these same reasons. For government workers need to be paid too. They are serving God in what they do. Give to everyone what you own them.' And the passage you shared with your niece Emma was First Timothy 6:6-7: 'True godliness with contentment is itself great wealth. After all, we brought nothing with us when we came into the world, and we can't take anything with us when we leave it.' Do you remember them?"

"I do, indeed." Her uneasiness grew as she contemplated how her remarks to Emma and Mrs. Lehman had reached the ears of the bishop.

"In the hardware store last week you were overheard saying: 'Serving God does make us very rich, if we are satisfied with what we have.' That passage is also from the book of First Timothy. And those aren't chapters approved by our bishop. Nor, I'm sure, are they ones Deacon Miller reads to his family. Do you study the Bible on your own?" he asked.

The other two ministerial brethren leaned forward, waiting for her answer.

"*Jah,* almost every night I read several chapters before bed and after my prayers." Hannah knew what was coming but saw no alternative but to tell the truth.

"This is a conservative district. We have no assurance of salvation. We must endeavor to lead humble, productive lives until the moment of our death, never certain if we shall be deemed fit to enter heaven." He shook his head slowly, as though disappointed in a rambunctious child. "Please confine your readings to the approved chapters. Deacon Miller will assist you if you're uncertain which they are."

His features hardened slightly. "We take no joy in threatening a widow with shunning. We welcome you to our community, but we want you to conform to the *Ordnung* of your congregation. Look to your sister-in-law or any of the other women for examples for your behavior—in Kidron and elsewhere. We don't want our matrons setting a poor example for young girls approaching *Rumschpringe.*"

Hannah thought she would crumple into a pile of dust on the driveway, so great was her mortification. Threatened with shunning for the second time in her life? She felt her eyes fill with tears, but she kept them in check until the three men bid her good afternoon and returned hurriedly to their buggy.

All thoughts of a cool glass of lemonade were forgotten.

Where was Simon during this ministerial visit? She hadn't seen him all morning and had assumed he'd taken his lunch with him into the fields. Had he simply missed crossing paths with her, or had he known in advance of this warning? He must have known; he was a deacon!

Hannah stood rooted, watching the carriage roll away until it disappeared around the corner. A heavy weight of despondence and fatigue burdened her heart. She loved her family with her whole heart, but moving here had only added another burden to their lives. Now the deacon's own sister-in-law had brought shame to his household.

With legs feeling like lead, she walked slowly back to the house to change her dress for afternoon chores. She wondered if she could avoid telling Julia about the visit, not wishing to add to her worries. If only she hadn't lost her temper with Seth about moving the sheep, she'd have someone to talk to. That disagreement seemed silly now. He would never take them away from her. She had been prideful and stingy and ungrateful for his practical suggestion. The brethren were probably correct about her not setting a good example for her two nieces.

Seth. Thinking about the man with gentle hands and soft, wavy hair made her heart ache all the more. She'd had such high hopes of a new life with him, but her sharp tongue had ruined everything.

Burning dinner hadn't helped much either.

Hannah smiled, then giggled, and then laughed aloud at the disaster she'd made of things yesterday. She'd cooked a thousand meals, yet when it had counted the most, she behaved like a novice. She couldn't remember ever trying so hard to impress someone and having it turn out so badly.

Laughing felt good—if just for a few moments. But her giggles stopped when she thought about Seth in light of the new circumstance. He was bound to find out about the chastisement and would never wish to be seen with her again.

∼

Some things just weren't meant to be.

The early summer shower stopped as abruptly as it had begun. With his chores finally behind him, Seth headed to the river to wash up instead of to the tub indoors. The cool water refreshed him after nine hours of sun beating on his back. He had one more thing to do before his rest tonight, and that was to pay a visit to his brother's house. The gift he picked up that morning should be delivered before it settled into the wrong routine.

He grinned remembering last night's supper: Julia had looked nervous, Simon peeved, Miss Stoddard sympathetic...and Hannah? Hannah had looked delightful with her green eyes shining and her flaxen hair peeking beneath her *kapp*. She surely had tried her best. And that's all anyone should expect. Her dinner might have been awful, but that didn't bother him at all.

After the ride home from town, he'd pretty much figured Hannah wouldn't become his wife anyway. Some widowers were destined to remain alone. He never did have much luck saying or doing the right thing when it came to women. Constance had overlooked his rough edges, or he would never have married the first time around.

He shouldn't have told Hannah what to do with her sheep. It wasn't his place to interfere in Simon's household. But there was no reason they couldn't be friends. Not talking to one another was just plain silly. Maybe after his apology and the gift, she would consider watching Phoebe for a few days until Mrs. Lehman was back on her feet. It wouldn't hurt to ask, especially since Phoebe needed to lose some of her shyness around Hannah.

As it turned out, his gift ended up doing all the talking.

Seth had barely brought the buggy to a stop in Simon's yard when the dog he had bought leaped down and started barking. It ran straight to its new mistress.

Hannah was bent low, weeding the garden, and she was nearly knocked off her feet. "A border collie!" she exclaimed, trying to pet the prancing dog. "Seth Miller, is this dog for me?" When the dog jumped up to lick her face, she lost her balance and landed between the bean rows.

"*Jah,* it's for you," Nothing could stop the dog's exuberance until Seth took hold of the collar with one hand and pulled Hannah to her feet with the other.

"What's her name?" she asked, patting the dog's head.

"*His* name is Turnip." Seth said, holding up his palms. "Don't blame me for the sorry name. He came with it. Supposedly, that's what he likes to eat from the garden when no one's looking."

"No kidding?" Hannah asked. She put both arms around the collie's neck. The affection appeared to be mutual. "I thought the price was too high or the pups were all gone," she said as the dog struggled to lick her face.

"They were all gone. The ad hanging in the auction barn was pretty old. But the man needed to find a home for the pups' father. He has sold his farm and is moving to Akron to live with his daughter."

"Oh, good," she said, rising to her feet. "I mean, good for me. How much do I owe you, Seth?" For the first time, she looked at him and not at the new herding dog.

"Nothing. He's a gift since…I got all carried away telling you what to do. I've got no right to do that. I'm sorry." He shoved his hands into the back waistband of his pants.

"Are you sure? I mean you shouldn't be buying any expensive gifts."

"Shucks, the guy almost gave me the dog when he heard Turnip would be going to another sheep farm. There aren't that many of them around here."

"That's true," she said. She took the leash from his fingers and clipped it to the dog's collar.

Seth had forgotten he was still holding it.

"I love Turnip, *danki*. I have a feeling he'll work out just fine. Should we see how he does with the flock?"

Turnip lunged to the left and right, not accustomed to being hooked on a leash.

Seth found himself suddenly uncomfortable. Being in the widow's company still did that to him. "Nah, I need to get going. It's been a long day. Phoebe's already asleep in the back of the buggy, but that reminds me of something else, Hannah."

Speaking her name aloud had an unnerving effect on him. He feared he might start stuttering. "Could you keep an eye on Phoebe for a couple days? I've got to plow my fields and start planting another hay crop, and Mrs. Lehman is sick. I don't want to ask Julia again. She does too much for me the way it is."

Hannah looked surprised. "Watch Phoebe?"

Then it occurred to him that Turnip could be viewed as a way to get back on her good side only because he had a favor to ask. Nothing was further from the truth. "I hope you don't th…think that I only brought the dog because…"

He began to stammer after all.

"I don't think anything of the sort. Bring Phoebe over tomorrow. But I do wish you would come up to the porch and talk for a minute."

Seth started backing away from her. "No, but I'll bring Phoebe by and check how the dog is getting along. I'll take him back and find another home if he doesn't work out. Good night, Hannah. Good luck with Turnip."

Seth felt so manipulative. He nearly ran back to his buggy without even a glance over his shoulder.

TWELVE

Phoebe slept for three hours on the blanket under the black walnut tree, her faceless doll clutched in her fist. Neither the traffic noise from the county road nor the buzzing insects nor the occasional yap from Turnip broke her perfect, deep sleep. Only in childhood could one slumber so peacefully. Just for a moment, Hannah envied the ability to sleep like that as she spun her raw wool into yarn on her hand wheel. The yarn would later be dyed or left natural and then preshrunk before it was knit into sweaters or woven into cloth on her large loom in the loft.

Hannah had tossed and turned for the past two nights since the brethren's visit—fretful and worried she would make another misstep. The shame she'd experienced from the warning haunted her daytime hours as well. Hannah loved being Amish—loved the Plain world she'd been born into, married in, and hoped to remain part of for the rest of her days. The thought of being shunned—cut off from others in the district—broke her heart. Her own sister and nieces and nephews wouldn't be allowed to share a meal with her. Although Simon would be permitted to provide food and a roof over her head, he would not be able to benefit from her sheep or take anything made from her hands. She shuddered again at the thought of becoming a pariah in her new community.

But at the same time, Hannah loved reading and studying the

Bible. She hadn't promised the elders she would stop learning the Word of God and didn't think she could. But she wouldn't quote her favorite passages to others any more. She had no desire to challenge the ministerial brethren or the bishop's authority, but she didn't want to ever lose the great joy and peace she found each time she opened the Good Book.

Stretching out the cramped muscles in her shoulders, Hannah saw she'd spun two full skeins during Phoebe's nap. Nothing like the pleasure of accomplishing two jobs at the same time. "Dear, sweet Phoebe, how I long to hear your voice," she murmured in a barely audible tone.

At the sound of her name, the child stirred and rubbed her face sleepily. She sat up and stared at Hannah with huge, round eyes.

Hannah changed her dialect to *Deutsch* because Phoebe was more familiar with it. Children seldom learned English until right before they started school. Hannah had overheard Seth address his daughter in both languages. Yet no matter what question she asked Phoebe in whichever language, Hannah only received nods and gestures in reply.

"Did you have a nice nap?" Hannah asked.

Phoebe shook her head up and down.

"Are you getting hungry?" she asked.

The girl rubbed her tummy with a circular motion.

Hannah stopped trying to get a verbal response, took the child by the hand, and headed toward the house. It was time for lunch in any language.

"You go on in, Phoebe," Hannah said, pointing at the screen door. "Your cousins are already at the table. Emma will fix you a sandwich." The child ran inside, but the sound of an approaching buggy took Hannah's attention off food. Her heart lifted when she saw the sole occupant in the open carriage was young and female.

"Miss Stoddard," Hannah called, stepping off the porch and into the yard.

Laura Stoddard was smiling brightly as her horse brought her up to the side door. "Good afternoon, Mrs. Brown. Are you very busy? I'm on my way home and thought I'd visit a spell. Today is the last day of classes, and I sent the children home early."

"I was wondering why the Miller *kinner* are in the kitchen and not eating lunch in the schoolyard. Let's have a sandwich outdoors. Just give me just a minute to fix them. And please call me Hannah."

"Thank you, Hannah. I'll wait for you there." Laura tied the horse to a low-hanging branch in the shade but didn't release him from the traces.

When Hannah carried out the plate of sandwiches and pitcher of lemonade, she found Laura seated on a patchwork lap robe under the tree. Hannah noticed again how young, fresh, and energetic the teacher appeared. By comparison Hannah felt older than her twenty-eight years. Sleepless nights of tossing and turning hadn't helped matters. "I hope you like smoked turkey and cheese," Hannah said, pulling a jar of bread-and-butter pickles from her pinned-up apron. She poured pickles into the upturned lid.

"I do, indeed," Laura said as she took a sandwich from the plate. She began eating zealously, popping in a pickle slice after each bite. Halfway through the sandwich, she put it down on the napkin and stretched out her legs in the grass. "My, I worked up an appetite with all those farewells and hugs goodbye." Her smile was genuine, free of artfulness.

Hannah started to eat her own lunch but with far less enthusiasm. "I'm pleased you're willing to chance a second meal of my making. Dinner the other night wasn't exactly the best I can do."

Laura grinned and poured lemonade into the two paper cups. "I've burned my share of dinners. Breakfasts too. I have my most success with lunch because it's usually served cold. I once overcooked pot roast when the bishop and his wife were our guests for dinner. All the gravy evaporated, and the meat could have reshod my *daed*'s work boots. No one said a word about the beef. I suppose they couldn't— chewing a forkful took a full minute or more."

Both women laughed, and Hannah felt some of her nervousness drain away. "I suppose no one will be offering either of us jobs as cooks in a restaurant."

"Only if they're mighty desperate for help." Laura took a bite of the other half of her sandwich and then locked gazes with Hannah. "I hope you know I had nothing to do with the deacon's...plan." She spoke in a discreet whisper.

Hannah arched an eyebrow. "His plan?"

"Well, I don't know what you would call it, but it sure felt like some kind of a fix-up between me and Seth Miller. I must admit, I didn't see that one coming."

"That notion did cross my mind, " Hannah admitted.

"Usually I'm much better at sniffing out a setup. At my age, I've had more than my share of well-intended matches. Here I am, twenty-two years old and still unmarried."

Hannah took a few more bites. The sandwich was starting to taste a little better. "Frankly, I'm surprised you haven't been snapped up by some young man yet."

"I've had plenty of dates and a couple of serious beaus. My *mamm* says I'm being too picky, but I couldn't imagine spending the rest of my life with any of them. Until now, that is." She smiled with a twinkle of mischief in her sky blue eyes.

Hannah nearly choked on the turkey and Swiss. "You've found the right one? You've fallen in love?" she asked.

"I have, except we haven't announced anything yet. Not even to our folks. I wanted to be sure, you understand. He's from another district. My parents might get a little worried, since his district is more liberal. But I know I won't be shunned or anything like that."

Hannah stopped holding her breath. "Who is he? Where does your young man live?"

"His name is Joshua, and he lives on a farm outside of Baltic with his family. But he doesn't farm. He has worked in a sawmill for more

than ten years. They've just promoted him to night shift foreman."
Joy and maybe a touch of pride shone in her pretty face.

"God's blessings on you both," Hannah said, finishing the rest of
her lemonade. The odd tension in her shoulders eased.

"*Danki*. That's why I stopped today to talk to you. I figured out
what Deacon Miller was up to, and I want you to know…I have no
interest in Seth." Her cheeks blushed to the shade of ripe raspberries.
"I could tell you favored him, and I had no desire to trouble you."

Hannah's head snapped up. "Is it that obvious? Can even a
stranger spot it?"

Laura patted her arm. "Only a stranger who happens to be in love.
Don't worry. I'm a very observant woman—a teacher has to be so."

Hannah didn't find herself much consoled. "I appreciate your
telling me this, but it won't change anything. Seth Miller barely said
a dozen words to me that night. We've had differences of opinion
previously, and we don't seem to be well suited at all."

Laura popped another pickle in her mouth. "I disagree. Every
time you were watching the clock on the wall, or listening to *kinner*
tell a story, or cutting your food into particles, Seth was watching
you. Like I said, I'm a very observant woman."

"People watch animals in the zoo all day long, but they don't ask
to court them."

The teacher's laughter startled the sparrows from the bird feeder.
"I like your sense of humor, Hannah. I hope we can become good
friends, but I will speak frankly here. Seth will continue to watch you
forever like a kangaroo at the zoo until *someone* gives him a nudge.
He's lost his first wife, as you have suffered your own terrible loss. But
men are much more afraid to take a chance on dating again." Laura
folded her hands on her skirt, looking a little nervous as to how her
advice would be received.

Hannah brushed crumbs into the grass and pondered for a
moment before looking the younger woman in the eye and asking,
"What exactly do you suggest?"

Miss Stoddard looked ready to take on the world, or at least the entire Plain world of Holmes County. "I suggest, Hannah, that you need a break from farm chores and your flock of sheep. This Friday evening, my *bruder* and I will pick you up around five o'clock. Don't eat dinner beforehand. You're going to Berlin." She rose to her feet and shook out her skirt.

"What's in Berlin?" Hannah asked, trying unsuccessfully to keep the excitement from her voice.

"It's a fundraiser with an auction and a haystack dinner in Joshua's district. A young man working with a chainsaw fell out of a tree and was badly injured. He will recover, but it'll be some time before he can work again. He has a wife and two small sons besides a pile of medical bills." Laura looked skyward to gauge the sun's position. "My, it's getting late. I wanted to work in the garden yet today. *Danki* for lunch; see you Friday." She started walking toward her buggy at a brisk pace.

Hannah ran to keep up. "Wait one more minute. Did you also say an auction? What shall I bring?"

"Bring whatever cash you can spare because the plate dinner is by donation. Anything you can contribute to the auction would also be appreciated. I believe you spin your own wool? Have you made anything lately you might be able to part with for a good cause?"

"Of course," Hannah said. "Do you think any women might bid on one of my wool shawls? I've made a couple lap robes too."

Laura tugged the reins from the tree branch and climbed into her buggy. "I know I would certainly bid on one of your shawls." She reached down and clasped Hannah's shoulder. "No more thoughts about the burned supper. Now you have a haystack dinner to look forward to." Laura clucked to the horse, and it started to clop down the drive.

Hannah walked alongside for as long as she could, not wanting the impromptu lunch to end. "Goodbye, Laura. See you Friday," she called.

The schoolteacher leaned out and asked, "Oh, did I happen to mention Seth Miller would be at the fundraiser too? I have it on good authority." She grinned and winked before her head disappeared back inside the buggy.

Hannah Brown found herself smiling uncontrollably for the rest of the day and counting the hours until Friday, five o'clock.

～

"Seth Miller! Over here!" A voice wafted on the evening breeze.

Seth scanned the people milling outside the auction barn for the source of his name. At first he couldn't discern any familiar faces in the throng of people—some English but mostly Amish.

"Seth," the voice repeated. Then Seth spotted his friend Joshua Hershberger. It was Josh who'd told him about the benefit auction for the injured farmer. But Seth hadn't expected this kind of turnout. He'd had to park his wagon nearly a mile away as every parking spot closer for buggies or cars had been taken. Luckily he'd been able to drop off the furniture he'd made last winter and the tools he was donating at the loading dock before tying up his mare. With so many horses in town, Seth was glad he'd brought his own water bucket and feedbag.

"Joshua," Seth called. He snaked his way through the people trying to squeeze inside the barn that had been set up for quilts and handmade items.

The two women standing with Josh turned when Seth reached the group. He gasped from sheer shock as he recognized both. The taller was Miss Laura Stoddard, the teacher in Winesburg. The smaller of the two was Mrs. Hannah Brown, who was blushing like a schoolgirl. He couldn't decide if he was more stunned or delighted.

"You look like you've seen a flying goat," Joshua said.

Seth swept his hat from his head and patted down his cowlick. "Good evening, Miss Stoddard, Mrs. Brown."

"Hello," they both chimed in unison.

Joshua looked ready to burst at the seams. "Seth, I want you to be the first to know. Laura and I have been courting, and our engagement will soon be announced in both our districts."

Shock won out as his primary emotion. Seth slapped his friend on the back. "Congratulations," he said to Josh and to Laura. "Best wishes." He stole a glance at Hannah, who had crept out from behind the post. "Did you know about this on Tuesday?" he asked.

She shook her head. "No, not until Wednesday when Laura came by." She clasped her hands tightly together in front of her, apparently almost as nervous as he was.

"Sit with us during dinner, Seth. You shouldn't eat alone after coming all the way down here," Josh said.

"Is that all right with you, Hannah?" Seth asked, not taking anything for granted with his luck lately.

"*Jah*, sure," she squeaked. "It's fine." She glanced from Laura to Joshua without her usual composure.

"Let's go into the auction barn," Laura said. "I want to see if they've sold my quilt or Hannah's wool shawls yet. She donated two, both dyed black, made of the softest wool I've ever felt."

"They're not as nice as the quilt you made," Hannah said.

"Twice as nice. You're too modest." Laura linked arms with Joshua, leaving Seth next to Hannah. He hoped he wasn't overstepping his bounds when he took her by the elbow. But with so many people congregating in the doorway, they would become separated for sure if he didn't.

"Should I cut a path for us up to the tables?" he asked as the other two disappeared into the crowd.

"No," she said. "I'm not planning to bid on anything so I'm happier back here."

She wedged into a spot by the back wall that was large enough for two. "Me too," he agreed, slipping in behind her to watch the commotion over her head. "Josh and Laura have a home to furnish, whereas you and I have pretty much everything we need."

"Pretty much," she said, looking everywhere but at him.

"Look, Hannah. I'm sorry 'bout the way I acted coming back from Kidron," he blurted. "I wanted to tell you that on Tuesday night, but there were always so many people around."

"I know. I'm sorry too. I acted grumpy instead of discussing it with you like an adult."

"I didn't give you much chance."

"I didn't try very hard."

"Maybe we're both a little stubborn."

"Maybe more than just a little," she said. A smile was starting in her pretty green eyes that soon filled her entire face. "Sounds like we're two peas in a pod," she added.

"Two bulls in a china shop." He pulled on his beard.

"Two black snakes in a woodpile."

He thought for a moment but came up short. "I'm fresh out... you win," he said, and they both laughed.

"What do I win?" she asked, rocking back on her heels.

"I'm buying your haystack dinner tonight."

She shook her head and sent the ties on her *kapp* swinging. "No, Seth. I brought money, and I want to help the Schlabach family with it."

"Good. You can put it in the donation jar, but I'm paying for your haystack."

"What exactly is this dinner before you shell out hard-earned cash?"

"You've never had one? You're in for a treat, but I can't really describe it. You might get scared off."

"Fair enough. By the way, Turnip is working out fine. He's taken to my flock as though I've had him all my life."

"How does he treat the lambs?"

"Gentle as can be. No nipping—he just nudges them in the right direction."

Suddenly Laura and Josh appeared before them. "Hannah, you are not going to believe this! Your shawls fetched three hundred dollars!"

"You're right. I don't believe it," Hannah teased.

"I saw the sold tag with the price written right on it."

"Three hundred for the two shawls? I'm quite happy about that," Hannah said.

"Nope," Laura said, crossing her arms. "Three hundred *each*. And if you had brought more, I'd bet you could have sold a dozen."

"My goodness," Hannah replied. "Folks sure are generous with their money when it's for a good cause."

"That's true enough," Laura agreed, "but I heard a couple of ladies ask who made the beautiful pieces. They said they had never seen finer wool."

Hannah's face glowed with pleasure.

"I think you might have found a use for those woolbags, after all," Seth said, "since you're not fond of selling off spring lambs."

Hannah nodded. "Do you really think there's much demand for my homemade woolens beyond what Julia and the rest of the family can use?" She looked from Seth to Laura.

"Absolutely," they answered together.

Josh leaned in between the two women. "I'm getting hungry," he said, patting his ample belly. "Let's talk in the chow line about Hannah's new enterprise."

Seth nodded, and they moved to the line in the dining hall.

Inside, long tables had been set up and covered with white paper. Jelly jars held bouquets of wildflowers, and strings of tiny white lights hung from the rafters. At least five hundred people could sit down at one time while the others patiently waited their turn. It felt good to have Hannah by his side, as it had in Kidron. He hoped today would have a much sweeter end result.

Hannah craned her neck from side to side, trying to get a look as they inched closer to their supper. "Is it a big salad bar?" she asked, standing on tiptoes.

"Sort of," he said. "Soon all questions will be answered."

When they reached the front, he handed her a dinner plate and began his instructions. "First, start with crushed Ritz crackers on the bottom. Then add a layer of crumbled beef. Next build your haystack as you see fit with shredded cheese, chopped onions, tomatoes, and peppers. Then add shredded lettuce for the hay and sprinkle with peas. At the end of the line, you'll top it with either melted cheese or with sweet-and-sour dressing." He grinned in anticipation as his stomach rumbled.

"All that on one plate?" Hannah looked a little frightened.

"They don't call it a haystack for nothing. Oh, and save room for a bowl of ice cream with warm chocolate syrup."

"My goodness, Seth. Had I known about this, I wouldn't have eaten for two days."

He handed her a plate, and they both began their creations. "What are you supposed to donate for all this?" she whispered.

"Whatever you can afford to give. No one pays much attention to what people put into the donation jar at the end of the line."

Hannah's eyes grew as round as saucers watching people build stacks with near artistic creativity. "I never knew a meal could be so much fun," she said, arranging tomatoes around the edge of her plate.

"Me neither," Seth agreed, but he was referring to his dinner companion, not the food. As Hannah carefully carried her haystack to the table where Laura had found spaces, Seth dropped two twenties into the donation jar.

God had been generous in bringing the widow here to Berlin tonight. He wanted to return a small measure of gratitude.

They ate their meal with gusto. At least Seth and Josh ate their entire haystacks. Laura and Hannah tried nobly but scraped at least a third into the compost buckets.

"Any room for ice cream?" Seth asked close to Hannah's ear.

A painful-sounding groan answered his question. "I never turn down ice cream, but I can't eat another bite until Sunday. Thank you, Seth, for dinner. And thank you, Laura, for inviting me."

Laura grinned happily. "You boys, go get your ice cream. We'll wait here."

Seth and Josh did as ordered, but Seth would have rather stayed with Hannah than eat anything else. He fixed a small bowl and carried it back to the table. "Just a taste," he said to Hannah, holding out the spoon.

Instead of taking the spoon from his hand, she closed her eyes and opened her mouth, just like Phoebe did when taking cough medicine.

"Where's a bottle of cod liver oil when you need it?" he asked.

Hannah's mouth snapped shut. "You wouldn't dare."

"You're right; I wouldn't. Open wide," he said.

Hannah took the first taste, but he had to eat the rest.

"Let's get some air," Josh said after they had finished and cleaned up their table. They walked out into the warm night as the first stars appeared in the clear sky.

Since Laura and Josh seemed lost to the world, Seth cleared his throat and asked, "May I take you home, Hannah?" Before she could answer, he remembered what he'd used to deliver the furniture. "I mean…I just have my wagon tonight, but it doesn't look much like it's going to rain. And I've got a tarp for our legs and an umbrella in case my weather report is wrong." Seth hoped he didn't sound as ridiculous as he felt.

"Yes, Seth. I'd like it very much if you took me home, rain or not." Hannah was smiling as she answered.

Maybe it was the close proximity of a newly engaged couple. Maybe it was Venus, clear and bright in the southern sky. For whatever reason, he and Hannah got along fine the whole drive home. Not one argument—not even a difference of opinion. And when he pulled into Simon's yard and walked Hannah to the door, he did what he'd been thinking about doing the whole evening.

He bent down and kissed her.

～

Heavy clouds had rolled in to obscure the moon and stars, leaving nothing to light his path. Simon wished he'd remembered his flashlight, even though he'd walked this way too many times to count. Tomorrow would be a long, arduous day, and he was anxious to get to bed. He wanted to take care of his beloved Julia. She'd always taken such good care of her family; now it was their turn to worry about her.

As Simon concentrated on not tripping over a root or walking into a tree, a buggy pulled into his lane. *Hannah returning from her outing*, he thought. She might as well get a job giving buggy rides to English tourists, she gallivanted so much. Odd that Laura the schoolteacher took to Hannah in such a big way. She wasn't the one Simon hoped Miss Stoddard would have been intrigued with. But the two women had acted like longtime friends when Laura picked Hannah up to go to some auction in another district. And Seth had acted like both women had some kind of catchy rash.

Simon paused under the maple tree to get his bearings. He was surprised that Miss Stoddard's parents hadn't insisted she come home before dark. The Stoddard farm was several miles away. As he contemplated speaking to the woman about the late hour and perhaps seeing her home himself, the buggy pulled up to the porch steps.

It was no female schoolteacher who walked around to help Hannah down. It was his *bruder*.

Rooted to the trunk of the tree, Simon peered through the inky night, hoping his eyes were playing tricks on him. But the man was tall like Seth, had the same wide shoulders, and had the same bent brim where Phoebe had sat on his hat.

It was Seth who walked the widow to the kitchen door. Simon's worry over tomorrow's events just got a dose of kerosene thrown on the fire. Seth had brought Hannah home from the fundraiser in the other district. She had gone out with Miss Stoddard and then, behind her family's back, had arranged a meeting with Seth. And his *bruder* was falling into her web like a hapless spider.

Simon didn't like watching them, but he could hardly explain his presence in the pitch dark at this point. He took no pleasure in spying on two adults capable of making responsible decisions. And he certainly didn't enjoy seeing Seth lean over, tip up her chin, and kiss Hannah good night. That made his blood boil like soup left too long on a hot stove.

Thirteen

Hannah awoke before dawn and couldn't fall back asleep. Counting sheep never seemed to work for her because they all had familiar faces. She would only start worrying about runny noses, infected eyes, or ewes not producing enough milk. But it wasn't four-legged creatures that had her tossing and turning. It was a quiet five-year-old girl with silky hair and big brown eyes.

Phoebe Miller would start school this fall. The child should be learning some English words and phrases. English is what Miss Stoddard would speak in her classroom. Phoebe should be able to repeat words back to learn proper pronunciation so she wouldn't fall behind her classmates.

Phoebe needed to talk again—whether in English or the *Deutsch* she'd heard at home since she was born. Starting school was hard enough for Amish children, never having been separated from their mothers for any length of time. Their siblings comprised their daily social interactions, and Phoebe Miller had none.

Hannah punched the pillow in frustration and tried to clear her head of worries. Last night Seth had been so sweet and so attentive that she couldn't help but grow hopeful about their future. Didn't the Bible teach in Matthew 21:22 that if you believe, you will receive whatever you ask for in prayer. She had prayed last night for a future that included Seth Miller and his daughter.

What kind of person would she be if she didn't take it upon herself to draw Phoebe from her silent world? The face of Laura Stoddard drifted across her mind as Hannah tried in vain to fall back to sleep. Bolting upright in bed, an idea came to her, making any further rest impossible. She hurried to her desk for notepaper and pen. She would send Matthew on an errand as soon as his milking chores were done. With any luck she'd have the practical solution in her hands by noontime.

With a plan of action, Hannah washed, dressed, and hurried to the kitchen. Why not surprise Julia and have breakfast underway when she came downstairs? But Julia and Simon were already sitting at the table when Hannah entered the room. They were talking in soft tones and sipping mugs of coffee. An aromatic kettle of cinnamon oatmeal simmered on the stove.

"Julia, Simon, isn't my windup clock working right? What time is it?" she asked.

"Very early, sister, but I'm glad you're up." Julia looked pale and appeared to be struggling to draw breath. "We need to go into Canton today," Julia said, not one to beat around the bush. "Our English neighbors have volunteered to drive us. They have some errands to occupy their time." She paused as a spasm of pain contorted her features.

"It's time she sees a specialist and stops trying to treat this herself with herbs and salves," Simon barked. "She's in terrible pain. This bout of arthritis keeps getting worse by the day. And now she's running a fever. Her feet are so swollen she can't wear any of her own shoes."

Hannah looked from Simon to Julia, who nodded slowly. "The doc in Winesburg thinks my arthritis is rheumatoid. He wants a specialist to run tests. I didn't tell you sooner because I didn't want you to worry."

Simon scowled. Hannah sank into a kitchen chair. "Rheumatism?" she asked weakly. "I'm afraid I don't know much about that."

Julia rubbed the backs of her fingers, which were fixed in an odd position. "Me neither, but I'll ask plenty of questions while I'm there. I do know you'll have your hands full today, with Phoebe here besides my young ones."

"Don't be silly. Emma is a big help to me, and the boys will be too. I wish you would have told me about this sooner." Guilt washed over Hannah like a sudden downpour. *Why haven't I noticed Julia's increasing pain?*

The sound of car wheels on gravel drew their attention. "Oh, my, the Lees are here already," Julia said. She looked almost frightened.

Simon struggled to his feet. "Let's not keep them waiting." He picked up a hamper Hannah hadn't notice on the floor and then helped Julia get up. "Don't know when we'll be back. I want them to run all the tests they can while we're at the hospital."

Hospital. Hannah's guilt increased tenfold. She hurried to hug her sister as she walked toward the door. Her gait resembled that of a very old woman. "Don't worry about anything here. We'll be fine." Hannah didn't know what else to say. *Get well? Feel better soon?* Everything she thought of sounded wholly inadequate. "Here, take this coffee for your drive," she called, quickly pouring it into a Thermos. At least it was something productive she could do.

"*Danki,* Hannah," Simon said, accepting the Thermos but not meeting her eye. Then they clambered into the backseat of the neighbor's van and drove into the foggy dawn.

Hannah watched the red taillights vanish around the corner with a weight resting on the center of her chest. *Why haven't I noticed how bad things have become?*

She stirred the oatmeal until it nearly liquefied before the sound of a buggy drew her back to the porch. Now the constriction around her heart had a different origin. Seth Miller was dropping off his daughter.

He lifted the child down and greeted Hannah with a wide smile. "Good morning. Are you ready to face my barrel of trouble?" Eyes flashing with humor, he looked strong, fit, and well rested, quite unlike how she felt.

His daughter, however, had been weeping—her eyes were red and puffy. Phoebe clung fiercely to Seth's pant leg with both fists.

Hannah stooped to be at her eye level. "Hullo, Phoebe. I'm so happy you've come by. Can you help me make thumbprint cookies? Do you think you can unwrap the Hershey's Kisses?"

Phoebe's face brightened a bit. After Seth nudged her with his hip, she nodded yes.

"Oh, good," Hannah said. "I thought I'd be stuck with that job all by myself." She stretched out a hand to the child. "Let's have some milk and cinnamon oatmeal before we start baking."

After a second prodding from Seth, Phoebe accepted the hand, but tears looked ready to fall. "Breakfast, Seth? It's ready and not burned." She wiggled her eyebrows.

"Nah, I've gotta get going. I'm helping Noah set the block foundation for a new *dawdi haus*. Thanks just the same." Then to Phoebe he said, "You be a good girl for Aunt Hannah. No more crying. I'll be back 'bout supper time, and you'd better save some of those thumbprint cookies for me."

Seth might not have stayed for breakfast, but the look he gave Hannah before climbing into his buggy made her legs tingle down to her toes. And her stomach did a somersault for good measure.

Hannah glanced back at the man who had captured her heart and then down at his daughter. *I can do this. I can reach inside her silence and have her talking again by the time school starts—and in English. She will not fall behind her classmates or anyone else in the Plain world.*

Holding onto Phoebe's hand, she marveled at how wonderfully soft the skin felt next to hers. Knowing the love of a child was what she'd prayed for until Adam's death took that possibility away. Now hope sprung anew in her breast, even though she dared not voice that hope except in her nightly prayers.

But maybe, just maybe, Phoebe would grow as fond of her as of her Aunt Julia. And for now, that would be enough.

In the kitchen Emma, newly graduated from the eighth grade, had the boys and her sister seated at the table, patiently waiting for their breakfast. When Phoebe spotted Leah, she ran and climbed into the chair beside her.

"Oh, good, you're here, Aunt Hannah. Emma's not in charge after all," said Matthew.

Not paying him any mind, Emma said, "Good morning. Shall I serve the oatmeal?"

"*Jah*, go ahead. We've all got a busy day ahead of us. We'll be baking this morning and weeding the garden, besides our regular chores. Your *mamm* and *daed* have gone to see a doctor in Canton. You boys have your pap's morning and afternoon chores besides your own. They might not get back till late."

No arguments ensued—not even any grumbling. Only four expressions of concern gazed up at Hannah. "What's wrong with our ma?" asked Henry.

"You know how her hands and knees have been troubling her, don't you?"

Their heads nodded yes.

"Well, they've gone to see a specialist. Maybe he'll give her stronger medicine than the aspirin she's been taking so she'll feel better."

Any further details would be up to Julia, but her children seemed to accept the explanation without further questions. "And before your chores, Matthew, I need you to go to Miss Stoddard's with a note." Hannah pulled an envelope from her waistband and set it on the table.

The boy looked as though he'd been asked to dive headfirst into a snake pit. "Why? School just let out yesterday. I shouldn't have to see her till September."

Hannah bit back a smile and said sternly, "I hope Miss Stoddard never finds out about your unkind opinion of her, young man."

Matthew's cheeks colored to match the jam on his toast. "Ah, she's okay, I s'pose, but this is my first day off from lessons."

"It's just a note. And you may ride the bicycle in the barn as long as you go there and straight back."

His face brightened somewhat. "Do I have to wait around for an answer?"

Now Hannah did laugh. "Yes, and she might give you something to bring back too."

Matthew finished his oatmeal, grabbed another slice of toast, picked up the envelope, and ran for the door. Apparently he was eager for his summer break to begin in earnest.

Emma finished her breakfast almost as quickly. "Will we be able to work at your loom today, Aunt Hannah?"

"No, not today. After baking we're going to sweep the floors and dust and then we'll head to the garden to weed. Later we're going to start teaching Phoebe some English words." An idea popped into Hannah's head as she finished her oatmeal. "You can start now while I tend to my sheep. As you clear the table and wash dishes, pick up something and say the word first in *Deutsch* and then in English, like this." Hannah reached for the milk and said "*milch*" and then "milk." She did the same for the plate and cup while Phoebe watched her curiously.

Emma looked confused. "But Phoebe doesn't talk. How will she learn English words if she doesn't repeat them?"

Hannah wasn't daunted. "She hears fine, doesn't she? And just because she doesn't talk today doesn't mean she won't start tomorrow."

Emma shrugged her shoulders but glanced around the room for her first idea.

As Hannah headed outdoors into the bright sunshine, she overheard Emma pronouncing "butter" in both languages. Then Leah enunciated the word "water" slowly and carefully and splashed dish-water on Emma to underscore her lesson. All three girls broke into a fit of giggles.

Easy as pie, Hannah thought. *If I work hard and the girls help, we'll have Phoebe talking in no time—in two languages, no less!*

~

Julia never felt happier to see the kerosene lamp burning in the front window of home. The day had been long, painful, and dis-couraging. Simon had tried making polite conversation with Mr. and Mrs. Lee during the drive back, but finally he too lapsed into silence.

Their kind English neighbors, who'd waited for them long after finishing their own errands, understood. The diagnosis wasn't good. The tests confirmed what Julia's local doctor suspected—rheumatoid arthritis, a far more serious situation than painful, inflamed joints. Her immune system was attacking healthy tissue and causing per-manent damage. If left unchecked, it would wreak havoc on her kidneys, lungs, and other internal organs.

The specialist couldn't believe she had waited so long before seek-ing further medical tests. Only Julia understood why. Until today, prayers and a few aspirin a day had gotten her through. Now she faced the truth. If the medications and treatments weren't successful, she would become a complete invalid—a load on her family.

After thanking the neighbors and bidding them good night, Julia leaned heavily on Simon as she entered her home. Her heart ached worse than her feet.

Hannah sat at the table, spinning her wool into yarn. "Finally home," she said. "I was beginning to worry. Are you hungry? I've kept stew warm, and there's fresh bread, baked by—"

"We've already eaten, in Canton," Simon interrupted. "Just put it away."

Julia felt her sister's eyes studying her as she lowered herself into a chair. "*Danki,* we'll eat it tomorrow for lunch." She tried to smile.

"What did the doctor say?" Hannah asked softy. She sounded frightened and meek, like she had when they were children.

Julia waited until Simon went out to check his animals. He didn't need to hear the story a second time. "Not good news," Julia said plainly. "There's permanent damage to my fingers, knees, and feet. I'll need to have physical therapy and take strong anti-inflammatory drugs and low-dose cancer drugs to stop the joint destruction."

Hannah's eyes grew round as saucers. "Then will your pain lessen?"

"It might. If not, I'll have to start injecting medicine right into the joints. And I'll probably need surgery to remove damaged tissue from my knees and toes."

"Oh, Julia. Why didn't I see things were so bad for you?"

"Because it just got worse lately...and I didn't want you to spend all your time caring for me. You have your own life to live. I don't want to be a burden on my family."

"Your family loves you. I love you. You can never be a burden." Two large tears rolled down Hannah's sun-burnished cheeks as she hurried over to embrace.

The hug from a sister offered more relief than the shots in her knees at the hospital. "And I love you," Julia whispered into Hannah's sweet-smelling hair. Hannah's *kapp* slipped off during the hug, but Julia pulled it back in place with an extra tug on the strings. "Now tell me, how were the boys? Did they mind you without putting up a fuss?"

"Of course," Hannah said. "You've got good *kinner.* Emma was a big help to me. Even Leah pitched in with Phoebe. We're trying to start her talking again by teaching her English words for the common things she already knows. She paid very good attention to us. One of these days, she will forget her sorrow and let something slip out." Hannah's eyes sparkled with conviction.

Julia so hoped she was right. Having Phoebe whole again would be the answer to her *other* prayer concerning her brother-in-law.

~

It was dark when Seth turned into his brother's drive. At least he'd put new batteries in his lanterns so cars could see him on the drive home. He was tired and dirty. The project at his friend's house had taken longer than he'd figured because only Noah's sons were available to help. But the foundation of the new *dawdi haus* was finished. Once the mortar had set, the little home would be ready for floor joists and walls. It hadn't helped that he'd gone to bed so late the night before, but spending an enjoyable evening with Hannah had been worth the fatigue he felt now.

Hannah. He wondered if he was falling in love with the woman. And he wondered too if that was such a smart thing to do. But tonight he was too tired to consider the wisdom of kissing her good night. He knew only that the kiss had been the best thing he'd tasted in a very long time. He would leave contemplation of the rest of his life for another time. Right now he wanted to pick up his daughter, see Hannah, if only for a few minutes, take a bath, and hit the hay.

The Millers' lamp still burned in the window when he walked onto the porch. Someone was still awake. Hannah opened the door and greeted him with a smile that could have knocked him from his boots.

"Hi, Seth," she said. "Come in. You must be hungry."

Her skin looked fresh as buttercups, and he caught the scent of peaches from her shampoo. Suddenly he felt like an oaf. What woman wanted to be courted by a man who'd been sweating in the hot sun all day? His hair was plastered to his head, his trousers were dirty, and his shirt was ripped from catching it on a ladder hook. He should have at least jumped into Noah's pond.

"Hullo, Hannah," he said, hoping he was standing downwind. "I'll just get Phoebe and go on home. I'm not fit to come inside. Besides, it's late. Thanks just the same."

Hannah reached for a hamper on the counter. "That's what I thought you would say when it started to get dark. I packed up your dinner to go home. *Unburned* fried chicken and parsley potatoes. There's a jar of pickled green beans inside too. We're out of beets."

Her grin made the breath catch in his chest. "That sounds real nice. *Danki.*" He took the hamper from her grasp, brushing her fingertips lightly.

"Phoebe has already eaten and is asleep upstairs. Why not let her stay over? That way you won't have to bring her by in the morning."

Hannah looked so earnest Seth decided not to mention he'd been gone all day without seeing his little girl. Now must he go all tomorrow too? He nodded in agreement because Phoebe would only break into tears if he took her home and then left again in a few hours. "All right, but I'll come by in the afternoon for her. She can work with me in the garden cutting lettuce and pulling up radishes."

Hannah stepped onto the porch, letting the screen door close behind her. "Oh, Seth. I'm making real progress with Phoebe. With Emma's and Leah's help, I've been teaching her English words. Sort of making a game of it with these language flash cards that Laura Stoddard sent over. We hold up a picture and pronounce a word she knows slowly and carefully in both languages. She shapes her lips as though trying to say the word. I think it's only a matter of time before she starts talking again." Hannah rested one hand on her hip, looking quite pleased.

Seth feared she'd taken leave of her senses. "Were you out in the garden all day without your *kapp?* Why would Phoebe need to learn a bunch of English words when she doesn't even speak our own language?" Because he was trying to keep his voice low so as not to wake the others, his words came out in a hiss. "I know you mean well, Hannah, but I'm sure you've got better things to do with your time."

Hannah didn't seem discouraged in the least. "Have you forgotten? Phoebe starts school in the fall. She'll be with other children who'll already know some English. We don't want her to fall behind. And she needs to start talking again."

"She will when she's ready. Then Miss Stoddard can worry 'bout English and all the rest."

"Are you saying you don't want me to work with Phoebe?" Hannah looked bewildered.

"No...yes...I don't know. Fall is a long time off. What's the big hurry? Phoebe's still a *boppli!*"

The last thing in the world he wanted to do was hurt Hannah's feelings when they'd just gotten things back on track. And he wanted Phoebe to relax around her. But the *second* to the last thing he wanted to do was think about Phoebe going off to school.

Hannah mulled this over with a furrowed forehead and patted his arm. "I know what you mean. At least, I think I know. Let's give this a few days. She seems to enjoy all the fuss from her cousins and me." Hannah propped her other hand on her hip too.

"Okay, we'll give your idea a try. I don't see where it can hurt anything. *Gute nacht,* Hannah. I'll see you tomorrow afternoon."

Seth didn't kiss her or attempt an embrace—not in his current physical state. And not in his emotional state either. Phoebe wasn't ready to start school. And he wasn't either.

She was all he had left of Constance and their old life. He might be ready to allow someone else into his heart, but he wasn't about to let his little girl grow up and leave. Staying all day in a schoolroom could wait. Maybe he would hold her back a year. Learning English words could certainly wait. And Phoebe would talk again when she was good and ready.

That Hannah Brown—she certainly didn't let the dust settle before stirring up the next tornado.

FOURTEEN

A rainy day on a farm can either be a blessing or a discouragement, depending on what needs to be done. Simon needed to harvest his first crop of hay. If he could get it cut and bailed soon and the fields replanted, he might get three crops in before the first frost. But not if it didn't stop raining—no sense cutting if it would only lie wet in soggy rows.

And the stiffness in his back indicated the rain wouldn't stop soon. Julia was in so much pain, she was staying in bed for another day. According to the doctor, it could be weeks before the new pills had any pronounced effect. The inflammation might actually get worse before it improved because the physician had told Julia to stop the pain relievers that had brought some relief.

Julia had kissed him so tenderly that morning, despite her discomfort, and whispered such sweet endearments that he wanted to stay by her side the entire day. But that wouldn't get his chores done, and his children needed at least one parent active in the household.

Simon swallowed a pair of aspirin and felt ready to face the day. What he wasn't prepared for was the odd goings-on in his kitchen. Cardboard squares hung all over the downstairs rooms, each with a picture of the object it was attached to. Stove, sink, potato bin, rug, and lamp all had colorful pictures and words stating the obvious in English and what looked like a strange approximation of their spoken German dialect.

Emma sat at the table showing Phoebe the silly cards and repeating names of items in both languages. The child appeared to be forming the words with her lips, but no sounds came from her mouth. Simon glanced around the room. The table and kitchen floor were covered with crumbs, dishes were piled high in the sink, and muddy paw prints ran from one end of the floor to the other.

Simon bit the inside of his cheek and walked to the stove. *Oatmeal again—for the third morning in a row?* Only today's breakfast was dried to the side of the kettle. Someone had forgotten to remove the pot from the burner after everyone else had eaten. Looking out the window, he spotted his youngest daughter—barefoot and missing her *kapp*—returning from the henhouse. She stomped through every puddle of standing water along the path. Her dress was soaked to the knees while her hair hung wet and stringy down her back.

"Leah, come inside this instant," he hollered through the window screen.

Emma and Phoebe both looked up at his outburst. "Where is your aunt, Emma?" He poured a cup of coffee and concentrated on not losing his temper.

His eldest child smiled sweetly. "She's in her workroom in the loft, *daed*. She's making woolen shawls to sell at the next auction. Did you know that women pay three hundred dollars for one handmade shawl? I'll bet some of the English ladies will pay even more."

"That's ridiculous," he said. "No one in their right mind would pay that much!"

"Do you think something's wrong with Mrs. Stauffer's mind? Because she paid that much for one at the benefit auction." Emma gazed up with her luminous blue eyes and only a hint of a grin.

"Don't try to put words in my mouth, young lady. You know Mrs. Stauffer paid that much only because of the fundraiser. And what is going on with all these cards?"

Emma looked proud as she patted her cousin's back. "Aunt Hannah and I are teaching Phoebe English words so she'll be ready for school." She held up a card picturing a horse and repeated the name twice.

"She can't read yet, Emma. What good are those cards?" He drank down his coffee and scowled. *Ice cold. Why hadn't anyone kept the coffee warm?*

"Aunt Hannah says she'll get used to hearing the words associated with the picture, and it will help her match sounds with words."

"She doesn't talk," he argued, trying to scrape some of the oatmeal from the side of the pot.

"Yes, *daed,* but this might encourage her to try talking again." His daughter was staring as though he were slow to catch on. She turned back to her cousin and enunciated "*kuh*" and then "cow" and held up a picture of a Holstein.

Simon gave up on the dried oatmeal and took the last two pieces of cold toast. "Work with Phoebe only after your chores are done, Emma. Right now, see to this sink of dishes and the dirty floor. I'm going out to speak with your Aunt Hannah."

His eldest scrambled to her feet immediately and began to fill the kettle with water. "Sure, Pa," she said.

He slapped his straw hat on his head. In the hallway he spotted Leah, trying to blend in with the cloaks and jackets. "You get upstairs and put on dry clothes. And where are the eggs? Your basket is completely empty." The child scampered up the steps faster than a coyote after a rabbit.

His wife lay flat on her back; his house was a pigsty; his youngest looked like a drowned mouse; and his sister-in-law was busy trying to make things to sell. Earning more than one required was a tool of the devil. And what did Hannah need to buy? He provided her food and the roof over her head. Apparently the elders' warning to behave in keeping with the ways of their district had gone in one ear and out the other.

"Hannah, where are you?" he called on entering the barn.

Her head appeared in the doorway at the top of the loft. "Oh, I wasn't sure when you would be down this morning. I thought of sending breakfast up to you and Julia."

"From the barn?" he asked, scratching his nose.

She smiled patiently. "Of course not. I was just coming in to cook something fresh. The boys ate most of the oatmeal. I wanted to wait till you and Julia were ready." She brushed wool lint from her palms as she walked down the steps.

"Forget about breakfast for me. I had toast, but you can take a tray up to Julia when she wakes up." Something was making his nasal passages close and his breathing difficult. He sniffed and sneezed several times.

"Come outside," she said. "I've been spinning wool, and that puts a lot of dust and fibers into the air." Simon sneezed twice more as they stepped out into the drizzle. "Unwashed wool can be quite an irritant," she said, not paying the rain any attention.

He chose not to comment regarding irritations. "Hannah, with Julia laid up, I need you to mind my house." He kept his voice perfectly nonconfrontational.

She looked surprised and then bewildered. "Of course. I fixed breakfast for the *kinner*, asked Emma to tidy the kitchen, sent the boys off to chores, and told Leah to fetch eggs. I plan to hard-boil a dozen for egg salad for lunch." Drops of water ran off her nose, but she didn't seem to notice.

Simon stepped back into the barn and motioned for Hannah to follow. "Leah is soaking wet, even her hair. She's been playing in the rain without her *kapp*, not gathering eggs. We'll be lucky if she doesn't end up in bed with pneumonia."

Hannah lifted her chin and pursed her lips. "Simon, it's already *eighty* degrees outside, but I'll see that she changes into dry clothes immediately. And I've already spoken to her about keeping her *kapp* on. She doesn't want to comply until Seth makes Phoebe wear hers.

I've sewn Phoebe several head coverings but haven't seen any on her head yet."

"Julia never had this problem with Leah," Simon said.

"True; this has just begun." Hannah appeared to be inhaling and exhaling deeply.

"And I saw dog prints across the kitchen floor." This time his tone rose to match his mood. "You know I don't permit pets of any kind inside the house, and that includes your new collie."

Hannah sighed. "I'm sorry about that. Turnip followed Henry into the house for breakfast. Henry was testing the dog to see if he would listen to him when he called. I've already spoken to Henry and shooed the dog out with a rolled newspaper. Neither will do it again. And I plan to wash the floor as soon as I'm finished in here."

At least she looked contrite. Simon shook his head. "All right, Hannah. Please see if Julia is ready to eat something now." He stepped past her into the rain, which had increased significantly. All of his chores today involved being outdoors. He tugged his hat brim lower and hunched his shoulders against the downpour.

He would look like Leah in no time at all.

~

Hannah returned to the loft to clean up and calm her nerves. Why was Simon suddenly so critical? Who had any idea Leah would start acting like a duck? And Turnip, despite his misstep this morning, had turned out to be an excellent sheepdog. He kept the flock together and had actually herded them to the high ground where the grass had come in thick and green.

Everyone was entitled to one or two slipups.

Unfortunately, she'd gone over her quota by quite a few as far as Simon was concerned. But she must be patient. His concern for Julia overshadowed everything else. She was still learning to be Julia's stand-in. A mother had to have eyes in the back of her head and anticipate what *kinner* might do, and then head them off.

Hannah might never be as efficient as her sister—juggling tasks and responsibilities with smooth, easy grace—but she was making progress with Phoebe. The child had begun to relax around her as they worked with the language cards. It was only a matter of time. Hannah wouldn't give up until she heard the child's voice with her own ears.

Glancing back at the plastic bags filled with woolen yarn, she exhaled a sigh of satisfaction. She'd risen before dawn to work up here before anyone else was up. One of the women who had purchased a shawl in Berlin had been so impressed with it she had tracked Hannah down from the homemade label. Turned out that the *Englischer* ran a gift shop in Sugar Creek that did brisk business selling Amish-made goods to tourists. The proprietor, Mrs. Dunn, wanted everything Hannah had to sell and would pay a very good price. She was also interested in selling raw wool. There was quite a market for organic yarn among women who knitted or crocheted. Mrs. Dunn said she could sell every skein of wool Hannah supplied. And the price she promised per pound had made Hannah's jaw drop.

Never before had her sheep been so profitable.

Never before had the need to raise cash been so great. Julia's anticancer drugs and steroid injections were staggeringly expensive. Simon didn't know the true cost of her treatments because Hannah had gone with the neighbor to fill the prescriptions.

He didn't need anything else to fret over. Hannah would pay for the medications from the sale of her farm to Thomas. Between those proceeds and the sale of her wool, Hannah could take care of her beloved sister for a long time to come. She would even sell her lambs next spring if it came to that. Julia's health was worth everything to her.

Hannah moved the heavy bags close to the steps before hurrying to the house. She would tend to Leah, fix more breakfast, carry a tray to Julia, and then wash the kitchen floor. After picking vegetables for tonight's dinner, she would take the buggy to Sugar Creek. Mrs.

Dunn was attending a craft fair this weekend and needed all the wool she could supply. Phoebe would have to ride along with her, but she was certain Seth wouldn't mind. She'd be extra careful with *kinner* in the buggy.

One thought troubled her while she washed the kitchen floor. She still hadn't told Seth about the visit from the ministerial brethren. At the fundraiser, in front of Joshua and Laura, the topic hardly seemed suitable. During the ride home with his talk about the rain's effect on crops and her tales of Turnip with the sheep, it had simply slipped her mind.

She had decided to tell him last night when he picked up his daughter, and also report Julia's worsening medical condition, but he'd refused to cross the threshold. Seth had grabbed the hamper and hightailed it home as though fire ants were crawling up his pant leg.

You are a hard man to pin down, Seth Miller, she thought. But the sooner she told him about the warning—and how she planned to avoid ever being shunned—the better. It was not a good idea to keep secrets.

Hannah fried some eggs and sausage and sliced a fresh peach for Julia. With the kitchen clean, Hannah carried the tray upstairs. "Stay dry," she said to Leah and Phoebe, who were playing quietly with their dolls.

Julia was awake and sitting up. A smile stretched across her weary face when Hannah entered the room. "Oh, you spoil me," she said. "I was just about to come down. I've stared at these four walls till I've memorized every crack in the plaster and even named the spider that lives between the window and the screen."

Hannah raised the shades, revealing a watery world. "You might wish to stay abed another day. We've got more rain today—too many days in a row to count." Drops beat against the glass hard enough to rattle the frame.

"*Ach,* poor Simon. He'll never get his hay cut if this keeps up. He wanted to plant a second crop by the first of July." Julia struggled to sit up straighter in bed while Hannah plumped pillows behind her back. When Hannah set the tray before her, Julia looked pleased. "Fried eggs, my favorite, with bologna. I am hungry at long last." She sipped the coffee after inhaling the aroma deeply. "What would the world be like without coffee?"

"Much groggier." Hannah sat on the edge of the bed. "Tomorrow you'll start physical therapy. Will the neighbor drive you?"

"*Jah,* Simon found a therapist in Berlin. Mrs. Lee has a daughter there to visit during my appointment. But I can take the buggy myself once the pills start to work. It's not that far." Julia took a small forkful of eggs.

Hannah thought about the pills and the future steroid injections too. "After I fix sandwiches for Simon's lunch, I'm going to Sugar Creek if you'll be okay for a couple hours. I want to deliver my wool to the English shopkeeper. I'll take Phoebe and Leah along to keep them out of the soggy yard. Emma will be home if you need anything. She plans to cut fabric for a new dress."

Julia smiled, the lines around her mouth deeply set. "She's quite a good seamstress—much better than I was at her age. Why don't you take her with you and leave the other two with me? They can work the flash cards or play with their dolls here and keep me company." Julia pointed at the built-in window seat with a cushion big enough for two little girls. "I'd love to spend the afternoon with them, and Emma needs things from the bargain store and the fabric shop. It would be good for her to get out—she's been hovering over me worse than a mother hen. Make a couple extra sandwiches, and we'll be fine. Okay, Hannah?"

"Of course," Hannah agreed.

Emma would be great company if Julia didn't need her this afternoon. Her niece asked countless questions about the sheep, the loom, and the wool business that Hannah seldom had time to properly answer. Emma seemed genuinely interested, and Hannah wanted to encourage her whenever she could.

Julia ate every bite of the breakfast and finished a second cup of coffee. The color in her cheeks began to return with the hot food. With a plan in place to provide Julia with everything she needed to feel better, Hannah finished the morning chores humming a tune. While fixing a tray of tuna sandwiches, she thought of Ephesians 4:2: "Always be humble and gentle. Be patient with each other, making allowances for each other's faults because of your love." Helping her family filled her heart with joy.

"Aunt Hannah," Emma called from the back door. Her basket brimmed with fresh eggs—what had been Leah's task until she got distracted with deep puddles. "*Mamm* said I can go with you to Sugar Creek. I love Little Switzerland; the town is so sweet. Can we stop at the chocolate shop and maybe have supper at Sweet Thyme?" Her skin glowed with the vitality only the young possessed.

"The chocolate shop, maybe, but we'll be cooking supper at home for the rest of the family," Hannah said patiently.

"Of course, but do I have time to change my dress and *kapp?* This one's so wrinkled."

Hannah nodded, even though she thought Emma looked fine. Her niece was rapidly reaching the age where looking her best started to matter, unlike her duckling little sister.

The ride to Sugar Creek took longer than anticipated because Hannah stayed on back lanes and kept off the state routes. June meant plenty of tourists in the four-county area that was home to most of Ohio's Amish. Many of the English who came to shop and sightsee for the day weren't accustomed to winding roads and slow-moving buggies. Wherever possible, Hannah used the township roads frequented by the locals. Once in Sugar Creek, she had no trouble locating Stitch-in-Time Shoppe on the main thoroughfare. She tied her horse behind the store and found Mrs. Dunn on the loading dock.

Audrey Dunn apparently wasn't depending solely on Hannah's flock to supply her customers. A young *Englischer* of about seventeen was carrying in bag after bag of wool from the back of his pickup truck.

"Good afternoon, Hannah," called Mrs. Dunn. "What perfect timing. This is James Davis. He and his parents raise organic sheep near Charm. Between the two of you, I might be able to start supplying the customers I already have. And my assistant tells me new orders keep coming in from our website."

Hannah had heard of websites but didn't exactly know what they were.

"James, this is Mrs. Brown from Winesburg," said Mrs. Dunn.

"Good afternoon, ma'am," the young man said, sweeping an Indians ball cap from his head and extending his hand.

"Nice to meet you," Hannah said, shaking his hand.

"Afternoon, miss," James Davis said, smiling at Emma.

Emma stood as motionless as a statue in the park. Crows would come to rest on her shoulders if she remained like that any longer. Not a word came from the girl who had chattered all morning.

The young man nodded politely at Emma and then turned back to the shop owner. "I have one more bag to unload, ma'am, and then I'd be happy to bring in Mrs. Brown's wool too."

"Good idea, James," Mrs. Dunn said. "Thank you." To Hannah she said, "Come have coffee with me. I'd like your opinion on natural dye sources and colors."

"Emma, please help James with the bags," Hannah said softly. "Then you can fetch water for the horse." Hannah started to follow Audrey Dunn inside but turned back to Emma. Her niece was staring at the boy as though she'd never seen a handsome, polite young sheep farmer before.

But then again...she probably never had.

With a face quite flushed, Emma followed James onto the loading dock and toward the buggy...after a gentle push from Hannah.

Too bad, Hannah thought. Young Mr. Davis was just so...English!

～

"We were worried sick about you two," Simon said the moment Hannah stepped down from the buggy. "Here it is, almost dark, and you two women are still out on unfamiliar roads alone. And there's no dinner for the family." Simon stamped his foot, raising a cloud of dust in the driveway.

Hannah was tired from the long drive back from Sugar Creek. Mrs. Dunn had kept her longer than planned to discuss the items she wanted Hannah to make on her loom and agree on a quota of wool. Then she had to wait in a long line at the pharmacy for Julia's medicine. Emma had gone to the dollar store and the chocolate shop with James Davis after Audrey Dunn assured Hannah he was a trustworthy young man. She didn't like letting her niece out of sight, but Emma had nearly begged. And Hannah feared she would offend her new business colleagues if she didn't allow Emma half an hour in two crowded stores.

By the time they set off for home with their coffee in to-go cups, Hannah could have drunk a quart by herself. Emma prattled about "James this" and "James that" all the way back to Winesburg. But it wasn't dark. Plenty of daylight remained even with the sun below the treetops.

"We had a good map, Simon. No chance of getting lost," Hannah said, releasing the horses from the traces. "And dinner will be ready in thirty minutes. I've already washed the vegetables for our salad, and ham steaks and cauliflower won't take long to heat up."

Simon took the reins of the horse. "You shouldn't have taken Emma with you today on your little excursion. I want her home helping Julia while I'm out in the barn or fields, or visiting shut-ins in the district. Julia shouldn't be left in the hands of a six-year-old and an eight-year-old." Simon had never demonstrated such an outburst of temper before. He must be very worried about this wife.

But Hannah was also concerned about her sister—the very reason for her trip to Sugar Creek. "Taking Emma and not Leah and Phoebe was Julia's idea," Hannah said. "Emma had some shopping to do."

"Shopping?" Simon repeated the word as though it were akin to skydiving or deep-sea fishing.

"Yes, shopping," she answered, her own temper flaring like a candle in the breeze. "A young woman occasionally has to go shopping for personal needs." Hannah pulled the reins back, deciding to put the horse away herself.

"I'll take care of my gelding, Hannah. If you and my daughter are done with your *personal needs*,' I would greatly appreciate having someone fix dinner. And the next time Emma wishes to gallivant off, she needs to check with me first. I am still her father." Simon stalked off, dragging the horse behind him.

Hannah stood in the barnyard with her hands balled into fists, counting to ten...then to twenty. She had to count all the way to one hundred in *Deutsch* and English before she could enter her sister's house to prepare the evening meal.

~

The all-day rain caused a change of plans for Seth too. Because it was impossible to plant the back acreage with more field corn, he decided to head back to his friend's house. Noah would be receiving a delivery of wood today, both floor joists and framing timbers for the house for his parents. No matter what the weather, the lumber could be unloaded and stacked near where it would be used. And an extra pair of hands would be useful.

Now Seth felt glad to have left Phoebe with Hannah and Julia. Despite how much he missed his daughter, a construction site with a big, gaping hole in the ground was no place for a child—especially as Phoebe loved to race at full speed whenever she had a notion to change her location.

Noah stood on the back of a flatbed truck, directing his sons.

They were stacking the lumber close to the new house's foundation. "You're just in time," Noah called as Seth pulled into the yard. "We're almost down to the joists on the bottom of the pile. They'll be too heavy for the boys, but two big, strong men should be able to handle them."

Seth turned around to see if someone else had walked up behind him. "Oh, you mean you and me?" he said with a laugh. "Let me put my mare in a dry stall out of this rain, and I'll give you a hand."

"I hope you're still in good humor after we get the truck unloaded. I think they added roof rafters to the order too." Noah jumped down and walked over to shake Seth's hand. "You are a sight for sore eyes. I didn't expect you to stop by today."

"Unless I switch crops to either rice or cranberries, I gotta hold off till we get a few sunny days. My fields are too wet to set another crop." Seth went to put his horse in the barn and then returned and rolled up his sleeves. "Just tell me where you want to stack 'em. I'm ready."

A few hours later, they had not only unloaded and stacked the delivery but started building several walls. The men built the walls lying down on the gravel with kiln-dried two-by-fours to be stood in place later. Both setting floor joists and lifting walls could be done on Saturday when more men could come to help.

Noah offered a cold drink to Seth once their work for the day was finished. The two stood under the barn eave, looking at what they'd accomplished. "I heard the elders paid a call out to your brother's house the other night," Noah said. He pressed the cold bottle to the side of his face. The rain might have stopped, but the humidity had risen to oppressive levels.

"*Jah,* I'm sure the ministers have plenty to talk about with the preaching service at Simon's this Sunday." Seth gazed out over Noah's soybean fields. Luckily water wasn't standing in between the rows.

"They came to talk to his sister-in-law, Mrs. Brown, not to the deacon," Noah said with his customary directness. "Hearing that you two were friends, I thought I'd mention it because they were talking about shunning."

Seth's attention snapped back from the bean field. "What in the world did they go to see Hannah about?"

"She has been quoting Scripture. That is all I know. Seems they want to be the ones picking out the verses to remember." Noah pulled the bottle away from his neck and took a swallow.

"*Jah*, she mentioned she loved reading the Good Book on her own. I guess she should've kept what she read to herself. But I hardly think that should warrant a shunning." Seth set the bottle down on a rain barrel.

"They just warned her—she being new to the district and not familiar with our *Ordnung*." Noah took another sip and set his drink down too. "The elders' job is to keep younger people to our ways. They don't like it when people move from elsewhere and bring their own set of rules." Noah rocked back on his heels and pulled on his suspenders. "Boy, I hope that's the last of the rain for a while. I'm itching to cut my hayfield and plant a crop of spelt. I've got seed in my barn in open bags that I need to use before it molds. Is your hay ready to cut as soon as the fields dry up?"

"*Jah*, ready to cut," said Seth, but his mind wasn't on hay or spelt or field corn. He was worried about Hannah and wondering why she hadn't told him about the brethren's visit. If they were friends as he had supposed, she should have come to him about this instead of hiding it under a rock.

"Come inside, Seth, and stop worrying yourself. I'll bet my Elizabeth's got supper ready to eat. You haven't had good cookin' till you've tried her chicken and biscuits."

Seth slapped his friend on the back. "I look forward to that some other time, Noah. Right now, I'm eager to pick up Phoebe. She spent last night at Julia's so I didn't see her this morning. She's not all that fond of staying anywhere overnight. But thanks just the same."

Seth hurried to the stall holding his horse before Noah tried to talk him into supper. He led the animal back to his buggy and hitched her faster than usual.

"*Danki* for the help, Seth," Noah called. "And during your ride back home tonight, you can think about the chicken and biscuits you passed up." Noah waved and walked off toward his house with more spring in his step than he'd had while they were working.

Seth drove down the driveway, tired and hungry for the second night in a row. And with a bad feeling growing in the pit of his stomach.

FIFTEEN

Counting to one hundred lost its calming effect when Hannah opened the kitchen door to find the floor dirty again and the sink full of dishes. Couldn't the boys reuse the same drinking glass instead of taking another each time? But she wouldn't say anything because she and Emma had been gone, and Julia's hands were causing so much pain. Tomorrow, however, she would teach Leah to wash dishes instead of only drying. And she would explain to the boys that a glass could be refilled several times within the same day without dire consequences.

"Emma, fetch two jars of cauliflower for supper and then set the table," Hannah said as she began washing the garden vegetables she'd picked that morning for a tossed salad. Green peppers, radishes, onions, and carrots added color as well as yummy nutrition to the large colander of Bibb lettuce.

"Aunt Hannah, do you think we could visit the Davis sheep farm in Charm sometime? James invited us to stop by and see their flock. They have more than a hundred and fifty head of Dorsets, Cheviots, and Suffolks, besides crossbreeds. We might learn how to do the shearing ourselves and spare the expense." Her face was still flushed from their outing.

Hannah thought Emma would have tired of the James-the-sheep-farmer topic by now. "Mind what you're doing, Emma. Drain off most of the liquid into the sink and then pour the jars into a sauce-pot." Hannah arranged the ham slices on a cookie sheet, which she set in the oven. The ham would warm through in a hurry, and then they could eat.

Emma did as she was told but kept glancing back at her aunt. "The Davis family uses Dr. Longo for their vet too. And James said he'd like to see your recipe for an infection poultice. With a natural poultice, antibiotics wouldn't build up in the sheep's bloodstream and fat tissue." The girl placed the pot of cauliflower on the stove, turned on the burner, and sat down at the table. Setting the table had apparently slipped her mind.

"Emma, the dishes and silverware, please. Your *daed* and the rest of the *kinner* are hungry, and I'm sure your *mamm* is ready to eat." Hannah looked in the front room but found it empty. "Julia? Phoebe, Leah—dinner will be ready in ten minutes," she called up the stairs before filling seven glasses with cold milk from the jug.

Emma wasn't finished with her topic. "James, his brothers, and his dad do their shearing themselves. It saves a lot of money if you don't have to bring someone to the farm. He could give us pointers while we're there," Emma said, placing a napkin atop each plate.

The cuff of Hannah's dress stuck to something red and sticky on the countertop. Someone had neglected to clean up a spill this afternoon. "I'm not promising a visit to the Davis farm. We've got so much work to do here. Besides, I doubt we would benefit much from their advice. They use electricity in their farming operation."

"Who uses electricity on their farm?" asked Simon. He stood in the doorway to the root cellar. His hair was stuck to his forehead and a piece of cobweb hung from his white beard.

"*Daed,* what were you hunting for in the cellar?" Emma asked, springing to her feet. She brushed the web away with one quick stroke. "I would've fetched it. You don't know how things are arranged down there."

"*Danki*, daughter. I didn't realize there *was* organization on those shelves," joked Simon. "Who uses electricity, Hannah?" Simon repeated.

"The Davis family that lives in Charm," Hannah replied as she added oil and cider vinegar to the salad and put it on the table.

"We met the nicest boy today at Mrs. Dunn's shop in Sugar Creek," Emma added, all but clapping her hands and skipping around the room. "He was delivering a load of organic wool to A Stitch-in-Time Shoppe at the same time we were. He carried in our bags of wool and helped me fetch water for our horse. He knew right where the town's nearest pump was." Emma's enjoyment of the afternoon was as obvious as an advertisement on the side of a barn.

Simon stared at his daughter and then turned to Hannah. "This Davis family that uses electricity—do they attend a New Order church in Tuscarawas County?" he asked, setting his hat on a peg.

"No, *daed*," Emma giggled. "James' family isn't Amish. I believe he told me they go to the Methodist church while we were in the chocolate shop." Emma carried the pot of cauliflower to the trivet and wiped her hands on her apron. "What else can I do, Aunt Hannah?"

"Go up and help your *mamm* down the stairs. And tell Phoebe and Leah to come now," Simon said, his words like a rumble of thunder.

"Hannah, will you step onto the porch with me?"

Hannah turned off all burners so as not to repeat her burned-dinner performance and followed him out.

Simon rang the farm bell twice to call his sons to supper and then looked her in the eye. "You let my daughter go off to some chocolate shop with a stranger—an English stranger? Some *sheep farmer* that we know nothing about—him or his people?" Simon managed to imbue sheep farmer with a more ominous inflection than "English" or even "stranger."

"Mrs. Dunn, the store owner I'm doing business with, vouched for him and his family," Hannah said, crossing her arms.

"This Mrs. Dunn...you know her well?" he asked, to which Hannah remained silent. "You permitted Emma to go off alone with a boy vouched for by another stranger?"

"I let her go inside a crowded store across the street from the pharmacy I was in. She was never alone with him at any time."

"He's not Amish, woman. Not a good idea with Emma almost fifteen." Simon's face turned florid.

"They drank cups of cocoa; they didn't walk in the moonlight!" Tiredness was draining the last of her patience.

"Do you ever think? Do you ever use good judgment? I don't want Emma running around with English boys this close to *Rumschpringe.*"

"Did we not raise our daughter right? Do you think we can keep her from associating with English friends and neighbors, Simon?"

Simon and Hannah both jumped an inch from the porch floor. Julia had come to stand in the doorway unseen. Her spine was stooped and bent, but some of the pain had ebbed from her face.

"Julia," Simon said. "It's good to see you downstairs."

"It's good I've come down to intervene between you two. You might be making a mountain out of Emma drinking a cup of cocoa, husband." She leaned into Simon's side while he steadied her with a supportive arm. "If Hannah says there was no danger in the situation, I believe we can trust that. She would never place Emma in harm's way."

Hannah released her pent-up breath. Julia would shine logic and reason into the conversation.

"It's not a question of danger, Julia. I don't want my daughter to get into the habit of going off with English fellows. How does that look? I'm a deacon. My family is held to a higher standard of behavior, and that includes Hannah because she's part of my household."

Hannah thought it time to share her two cents. "I did nothing unseemly in Sugar Creek, and neither did Emma. I was delivering my load of wool to a buyer, and we met another of her regular wool suppliers."

"Your idea of unseemly doesn't always match mine," Simon said, "or the ministerial brethren wouldn't have singled you out for a warning. It's improper for you to quote Scripture to Emma from books not approved by the bishop—yet that didn't stop you. I overheard you with my own ears."

"You went to the elders instead of speaking to me privately about the matter?" Hannah asked.

Julia stepped out from his protective arm. "Why would you do that, Simon?" she asked. "Why would you go to them about my sister?"

"I knew it wasn't an isolated incident because Mrs. Lehman had mentioned it to her husband, and others had overheard her in Kidron. I thought she might listen better if it came from someone else in the district. She seems to let everything I say roll off her back without paying a bit of attention." A vein in his neck had begun to throb.

Hannah didn't like how she was being discussed as though she were in town having an ice cream cone. She stepped forward until she was almost nose to nose with her brother-in-law. "That's not true. I have heard everything you've told me and taken your advice to heart. I would have listened to this had you come to me first. I've quoted no more Scripture since then and will confine the joy and comfort I find in the Good Book to myself. I will try harder to bring no further shame to your household. But I ask you not to jump to a negative conclusion every time you hear of a situation that even remotely involves me."

Hannah felt her eyes fill with tears and didn't want to cry with five *kinner* in the kitchen wondering where their dinner was. "Please go in to supper. Everything is ready. Emma will help serve. I would like to walk for a while and clear my head. I'll try not to do anything unseemly in the pasture."

Simon reached down into the tall basket next to the door. "Here, take the umbrella." He thrust it into her hand and went back into the kitchen to his dinner, his wife leaning heavily on his arm.

Hannah walked into the mist regretting her final words. She felt petty and unkind and not filled with Christian love at the moment. The walk would do her good—maybe she would walk across the county and back. Then maybe she could be still and allow God's will to be done.

The rain would do her good too. It might wash away her anger and pride. Simon had every right to rule his household, even if he wasn't a deacon in the district. And dinner with Julia and the children would do him good. He'd seldom had the pleasure of time alone with them since she'd arrived.

So Hannah walked through her flock in the wet meadow and along the line of dark woods where leaves and branches sagged with moisture. On she walked near a field of green hay waiting to be cut and then between rows of knee-high corn. At times, she found herself on high ground where she could see the lamp burning in the Lehman window. Eventually she ended up by the river where tree limbs rushed and crashed along in the swift current.

Tired, wet, and hungry, Hannah turned her face to the sky when she couldn't walk another step. "Show me the way, Lord. Have mercy on me and show me the way." When she opened her eyes, she saw a patch of pale blue along the horizon. Growing ever wider as she watched, it promised an end to the deluge in Holmes County.

The slanting rays in that faraway clearing also promised a lifting of Hannah's burdens. Hadn't she been struggling to do it all on her own? Hadn't her independence and willfulness created conflict within her family? Butting heads with her brother-in-law like two barnyard goats wasn't why she had come to Ohio.

When the rain finally dwindled to a few drops, Hannah closed the umbrella—a good idea on Simon's part—and opened her heart. The path, the way, would be made clear to her. She needed only to be still and listen.

~

Water dripped onto the seat and pooled by Seth's feet. He would have to put a fresh bead of sealant at the top of the windshield to stop the leak. But right now he wanted to pick up his daughter, grab a bite to eat in Julia's kitchen, and have a few words with Hannah. He was eager to get to the bottom of this. Why did he hear about the ministerial call from his friend? Hannah was supposed to be his friend too. She should have told him about the warning instead of avoiding the subject. He didn't like secrets, especially not from a woman he had feelings for. She'd already told him about her Scripture reading, so she had no reason to hide the call from the elders.

There was much about Mrs. Brown he didn't know. And now was the time to find those things out before he fell deeply in love.

Seth stomped his boots on the porch mat, drawing the attention of the Millers inside. The sound of scraping chairs and shouts of glee warmed his heart as he opened the back door. A speeding rocket nearly knocked him off his feet.

"*Daed*," Phoebe said, hurtling herself into his arms. He swept her up, and she wrapped her arms tightly around his neck.

"My sweet Phoebe, did I hear you say my name? Did you say *daed?*" he asked softy, cradling her head against his shoulder.

She shook her head no and buried her face in his shirt.

"Well, now, I must be hearing things." He kissed her silky hair and tried to set her down, but the child clung to him like a thistle burr. Phoebe refused to let go of his neck, and her small body was trembling. He stroked her back and uttered the tender endearments that Constance had used, but it was a long time before Phoebe relaxed against his shoulder.

"Seth?" Julia asked. His sister-in-law opened the screen door and joined them on the porch.

"Hello, Julia. I hope you're feeling better today. Is Hannah around? I need to speak with her." He put Phoebe down, but she grabbed his trouser legs with both hands and started to cry. "Phoebe, what is the matter with you? I've been gone only one day. We'll be going home soon. Why are you crying?" The girl only cried harder.

"Hannah's out walking, Seth. In the pasture."

"In the rain?" Seth asked. *Why in the world would she be out in this weather,* he thought, but he placed that last on a long list of more important questions.

"She took an umbrella." Julia attempted a thin smile. "I'm sure she'll be back soon, but there's something I need to discuss with you first." Julia gently extracted Phoebe from Seth's pant leg. "Phoebe, you go into the house. I need to talk to your father alone." Julia used her rare but effective stern voice—the one that seldom failed to get the desired result. Phoebe ran dejectedly inside with a fresh set of sobs.

Seth felt a twinge of unease. "What is it, Julia? What's wrong?"

"It's Phoebe. Something happened when she slept over last night. While Leah was fixing the bed they had shared, she noticed the sheets were wet and called me upstairs."

Seth relaxed against the porch rail and stretched out his legs. For a minute he'd been worried something was seriously wrong. "So she couldn't get herself untangled from the covers and down to the bathroom in time. It happens, Julia. She's only five."

Julia cocked her head to one side as though considering this. "She's almost six, and we're not talking about a little bladder leak or about her not sleeping soundly and simply not waking in time. We're talking about Phoebe wetting the bed just like a toddler without a diaper on. Only she doesn't wear diapers anymore. We had to change the sheets and scrub the pad and mattress. On the next clear day, we'll have to take the mattress to the yard to dry in the hot sun."

Seth blew his breath out in a whistle, feeling ashamed for his little girl without cause and mildly annoyed with Julia. "Isn't a person allowed one mistake every now and then?" he asked. "I'm sorry for the extra work, but it was a one-time accident. Let's not blow this out of proportion." Seth was tired of the bed-wetting discussion and eager to get his daughter home. And something to eat would do him wonders too.

Julia shifted her weight against the doorframe with a grimace of pain, but when she spoke, her words held only sympathy and compassion. "No, this isn't the first time. There have been other incidents. I thought it was a temporary phase, but she's getting worse, not better."

"She's not having this problem at home," Seth said defensively.

"And you would know if she did wet the bed?"

He opened his mouth to argue, to refute her accusation, but closed it like a frog catching a fly. He had been spending so much time away from Phoebe, he easily could have overlooked this. "You're right, Julia," He hung his head with a weary sigh. "I haven't been a good *daed* lately. I'm afraid I've left too much up to you and Hannah. Constance wouldn't be happy with how I've neglected our daughter."

"Oh, pooh. Constance would understand how hard it is to be in several places at once. I'm only bringing this up because I think something is troubling Phoebe. And it goes beyond simply missing her *mamm*. Get to the bottom of this, Seth, and let us know what we can do to help. Hannah's grown mighty fond of Phoebe during the past week and is making good progress with those flash cards. She'll be happy to lend a hand with this too, but Phoebe needs her father right now." Julia leaned over and kissed his cheek.

Seth felt his throat tighten with more emotion than he could handle. *What would I do without my loving family?* "*Danki*, Julia. I'll get Phoebe and take her home, but I'll give everything you said serious thought. She'll have her father back, I promise you. Sorry 'bout the added work she caused."

Julia punched his arm lightly. "Stop it, Seth Miller. No need to worry about that. Lately I've got so many extra hands helping, I'm going to buy myself a box of bonbons and one of those chaise lounges." Just for a moment, she looked like the old Julia, the one before pain had become an everyday occurrence.

208 ~ MARY ELLIS

"I hope you do, so I can see just what a bonbon is," he said, taking hold of her arm. She limped back inside as Seth steadied her.

Hannah still hadn't returned from her walk, but he would tackle that particular mystery another time. Emma packed his meal to go home, and he accepted the basket thankfully, not wishing to eat alone at the table. He wanted to get his little girl home and discover why she was regressing.

"The pain is worse, isn't it?" Seth asked as Julia lowered herself into a chair.

"*Jah*, I saw a specialist in Canton a couple of days ago. He ran tests and determined the arthritis is rheumatoid, worse than the ordinary garden variety. He said quite a bit of damage has been done to my joints, but with the new medicine and physical therapy—plus all the doting-on—I'll be jogging before you know it." The sparkle in her eyes didn't mask the lines of anguish in her face.

"If there's anything I can do to help, Julia, you just let me know. Anything at all." Seth hated that he and his child were adding to her burdens.

"Don't you go waiting on me hand and foot too. I'm not a complete invalid yet." She grinned and looked like the woman who'd married his brother on the hottest day of September he could recall.

Seth leaned down to kiss the top of her head. "And with God's mercy, you never will be." Just as he was about to call Phoebe down from Leah's room, he remembered something. "She spoke. Phoebe said my name—*daed*."

Julia's joy matched his own. "She did? Phoebe is talking again?" Julia clapped her hands together.

"I don't know if it's exactly talking. She said one word last week and one word now before clamming up. But it's a start. We know she didn't lose her voice altogether like I was afraid of."

That was the first time he'd expressed his fear that Phoebe would remain mute forever.

"It's a very good start," Julia agreed. "Wasn't *daed* her first word as a baby?"

Seth grinned. "*Jah,* Constance was a little disappointed. I heard her saying *mamm, mamm, mamm* all day long till Phoebe learned that word too." He hollered up the stairs, "Phoebe, time to go home."

Then he met his sister-in-law's eye. "Take it easy, Julia. Don't do too much. Let others help. They want to, and you deserve it. And *danki* for helping with Phoebe."

"You can thank Hannah. She has spent much more time with her than I have lately."

Phoebe barreled into his outstretched arms, and Seth lifted her to his shoulder.

He left Simon's home with one last perusal of the darkened pasture.

Where is Hannah? Why isn't she back yet? He wanted to wait but also needed to get Phoebe to bed. She had spent too much time at Julia's and not enough in her own home.

He was filled with sorrow with the realization he'd been neglecting his little girl. This was his fault. Phoebe had only one parent, and he was falling down on the job. He always had his mind on the price of corn, the condition of his fields, or a green-eyed widow who had crept into his every waking thought.

On the ride home, Phoebe fell asleep beside him with her fist curled next to her mouth. The sound of her soft snore was oddly reassuring.

He would become a better father.

And he would be a better man.

～

Hannah fully expected the kitchen to be empty when she returned from her rambling. Her sister, however, was sitting at the oak table with a shawl over her nightgown and a cup of tea half gone.

"Julia, go on up to bed. You must be exhausted," Hannah said, hanging up her soggy *kapp*.

"I'm not tired at all. I've slept so much in the past few days, I feel like a bear crawling out from winter hibernation. The new pills might be starting to work too. Watch this," she instructed. She held out her hand and bent each finger in succession from the knuckle. They were only small movements but a big improvement from her near paralysis.

"*Wunderbaar*," Hannah said. "Before you know it, you'll be playing the piano."

Julia arched a brow. "We don't own a piano, sister, and Simon would never allow such a thing."

"Then you'll be back to embroidering." Hannah peeked in the oven to find her dinner still warm under the foil.

"That ham is probably as tough as shoe heels."

"No matter. I'm hungry enough to eat shoe heels right about now." Hannah carried the plate to the table and poured a tall glass of milk. After bowing her head for a silent prayer, she said, "*Danki* for saving my supper. That walk did me a world of good."

"I thought it might. I go sit by the river whenever I feel out-of-sorts. The sound of water always soothes my spirit."

Hannah glanced up from her food, surprised that her sister ever felt bad-tempered, even living with chronic pain. Julia seemed to have been born serene.

"I had my own reason to wait for you." Julia pulled an envelope from the waistband of her skirt. "This came for you today. That brother of ours addressed his letter to you, or I would have opened it by now. Please read it aloud. I'm eager for any news from Lancaster."

Hannah wiped her mouth and fingers and did as she was asked. "You shouldn't have waited. Thomas wouldn't share any secret with me that he didn't want you to hear." She took a sip of milk, cleared her throat, and began to read:

My dear sister,

*I hope all is well with you and Julia and the entire Miller family.
I am looking forward to the harvest so I can come to Ohio for an
overdue visit. It's high time everyone meets Miss Catherine Hostetler,
who by Christmastime will be Mrs. Thomas Kline.*

Hannah paused to eat a bite of cauliflower while Julia hooted
like an owl.

"A wedding!" Julia exclaimed. "A December wedding. Oh, my, I
hope I'll be well enough to travel to Pennsylvania."

"Of course you will be," Hannah said. "The therapies and medications will have worked wonders by then." She took another drink of
milk and continued reading:

*I owe my good fortune all to you, sister. For without your advice, I
would've been destined to life alone on the wonderful farm you sold
me. I took the apples and everything else in the root cellar to Miss
Hostetler for her to put up. She was quite pleased to see me the day I
stopped by. She took me on a tour of her vegetable garden and milking parlor and wash house and woodshed, even though those of the
Hostetlers look just like everybody else's.*

Hannah and Julia broke into peals of laughter. "Ah, to be young
and in love," Julia said. Hannah chose to continue reading:

*I hitched a ride to the next two Sunday singings and asked her
bruder for a ride home. What a good idea that turned out to be
since Catherine has two bruders, which put me in the backseat with
her. We talked all the way back.*

Hannah glanced up at Julia's happy face and winked.

*We are courting, and unless I do something quite stupid between
now and then, I will speak to her parents after the harvest. She is
the answer to my prayers. And I think you will notice Catherine is a
bit like you, sister.*

Hannah gazed up at the ceiling. "Heaven help the poor girl. I hope Thomas is referring to eye color or her taste in cream pies, and not to her temperament."

Julia plucked the letter from Hannah's fingers to finish reading aloud:

I thank God for bringing me Catherine. And I thank Him for not one, but two wise sisters who've saved me from lonely bachelorhood.

> *Your brother,*
> *Thomas*

"A wedding before Christmas!" the two women said together. And Hannah felt her heart fill with hope for the second time in an hour.

"I shall sleep well tonight," said Julia, struggling to her feet. Hannah jumped up to help her. "And please do not dwell on Simon's harsh words. He is overtired from caring for me. This will all blow over and soon will be forgotten. You'll see."

Julia looked so earnest that Hannah merely smiled and nodded. She had no energy to argue even if someone had said the moon was made of milk chocolate. Her Scriptures, her prayers, and then deep, dreamless sleep were the only things she wanted.

Julia started up the steps while Hannah finished the last bites of the shoe-leather ham. "Oh, sister? I almost forgot…Seth was looking for you when he picked up Phoebe. He seemed eager to speak to you. Perhaps he'll stop by tomorrow."

Hannah smiled. Maybe her sleep wouldn't be quite so dreamless after all.

SIXTEEN

Whoever said "a woman's work is never done" had never met a widowed father. Even before the rooster crowed, Seth had brewed his coffee, washed the dishes, and swept the kitchen floor. By the time the petulant bird marched from the henhouse, Seth had fed the horses, milked the cows, and gathered some eggs for breakfast. When Phoebe finally roused and came downstairs rubbing her eyes sleepily, he had ham and eggs spattering in the pan. A stack of toast, slathered with fresh peach preserves, waited on the table.

Phoebe glanced curiously around the tidy room and then up at him.

"Go get washed and dressed before breakfast," Seth said. "And put on one of the pretty *kapp*s Hannah made for you. It's time you start wearing them like Leah. You're a big girl now." As soon as the bathroom door closed behind her, Seth sprinted up the steps to her room. Throwing back the quilt, he felt the bottom sheet from one end of the bed to the other. Bone dry. She'd had no accidents, and no spiteful acts of rebellion either. He relaxed his tense shoulder muscles on the way downstairs. The situation at his brother's probably stemmed from leaving her with Mrs. Lehman or with Julia too often. At home in her own bed, Phoebe had spent a peaceful night.

Seth poured milk for his daughter and refilled his coffee cup.

When Phoebe emerged from the bathroom in a pale green dress, her feet were bare but her head was covered with starched white muslin.

"*Guder mariye*," he said. "Did you have sweet dreams?"

She nodded as she slipped into the opposite chair and reached for toast.

Seth pushed the stack closer and then slid some scrambled eggs and ham onto her plate and a greater portion onto his. "Eat hearty. You'll need lots of strength today."

Her two large brown eyes peered up through thick black lashes.

"*Jah*, you'll be helping me today with chores. I'm not cutting hay yet; it still needs another day to dry. But we will weed the garden, clean the barn stalls, and gather more eggs to take to Aunt Julia's and Aunt Hannah's."

Her bright and cheery face drooped at his mention of the names and then pinched up as though she were sucking on a lemon. Seth put down his fork and steeled his resolve. This wouldn't get any easier the longer he waited. "Don't you still like Aunt Julia and Aunt Hannah, Phoebe?"

Her dark head nodded yes.

"Did something happen at their house—maybe something with your cousins—that upset you?"

A slow lateral nod was her reply.

"Are you just tired of being apart from me...of being away from your *daed*?" Seth held his breath waiting for her answer. He didn't have to wait for long.

Phoebe put down the slice of toast and ran to his side of the table. Crawling into his lap as she had when she was a toddler, she wrapped her arms tightly around his neck. "*Daed*," she said.

One word. The same one she'd spoken yesterday, but it was worth a chest of gold to Seth. "My sweet Phoebe," he whispered next to her ear. "I don't like leaving you all the time, but I can't take you to the fields with me. You could get hurt. Plus, there are too many bugs out there, biting arms and necks. You wouldn't like a nasty deerfly bite, would you?" He pinched her forearm to illustrate his point.

She giggled and reciprocated with her own arm pinching.

"But I promise to start spending more time with you. I know I've been working too hard, and my favorite job is being your pa." He hugged her close while a lump rose in his throat that no amount of coffee could wash down. "Let's finish our ham and eggs so we'll have plenty of energy. Then we'll gather our eggs and take them to Aunt Julia. She's making dumplings today and needs extra eggs, but I'm not leaving you there. You'll be gone from me soon enough when you start school in the fall. Do you think we can find enough to fill the whole basket?"

Phoebe offered an affirmative nod, looking pacified, at least for the moment.

The two finished their breakfasts sitting in the same chair. It might not have been the tidiest way to eat scrambled eggs, but Seth knew this precious time with his daughter was worth crumbs on the kitchen floor.

Seth was glad he'd heard Julia mention making chicken and dumplings for today's supper. He needed an excuse to return to Simon's farm so quickly. His little girl wasn't the only thing weighing heavily on his heart this morning. Thinking about Hannah Brown and what he'd learned from Noah had kept him tossing and turning half the night. *Why didn't she tell me about the threat of shunning?*

If a man and woman had feelings for one another, they shouldn't keep secrets. And he didn't want to dwell on the conclusion that could be drawn from that.

∼

When Hannah saw Seth's mare trotting up the drive, her heart leaped within her chest. Hearing that he'd been looking for her last night eased some of the day's troubles. *Life wasn't meant to be paradise,* she thought. *Our trials, our sorrows, prepare us for what is to come.*

"Hello, Seth; Hi, Phoebe," she called as she set down the basket she'd been using to pick cherries. "A beautiful day, no? Not a rain cloud in sight. The fields should start to dry out and you'll be able to cut hay."

"*Jah,* two good days of sun oughta do it," Seth said, tying his horse to the post. He reached for a covered basket from the backseat. "Phoebe, take these eggs to Aunt Julia and stay in the house for a while. I need to talk to Hannah, and then we'll be going home to our chores." He handed Phoebe the basket. "And don't run with those eggs." The order came at the precise moment the child broke into a gallop across the grass. She immediately slowed her pace to a walk.

Hannah gazed up into his cool eyes, which seemed oddly distant today. "Is something wrong, Seth? Julia said you were looking for me while I was out walking."

"Can't figure why a person needs to walk in the rain, especially when it's getting dark, but that's not really what I came by to ask about."

Hannah felt the blood chill in her veins.

"I was wondering why you didn't see fit to tell me 'bout the ministerial brethren stopping by to talk to you." He looked at her without betraying an ounce of emotion.

"I had planned to. I was just picking the right time." She knew how weak that sounded but couldn't change the truth.

"You had two perfectly fine opportunities but didn't say a word."

"I chose not to discuss the matter at the fundraiser. Laura and Joshua had just announced their engagement and were so filled with joy that I didn't want anything to dampen their high spirits." Then she added in a softer voice, "Besides, I'd just met Laura, and I didn't know Joshua at all. I guess I was reluctant to tell them."

"If you hadn't done anything shameful, you had no reason to feel that way."

Hannah wished they could sit down so he didn't loom so large over her. "But I apparently did do something wrong in the elders' eyes. I had been quoting Scripture from unapproved books. Plus, Joshua is from a different district, and don't forget, I'm still learning the *Ordnung* here."

Seth slapped the leather reins against the hitching rail. "We rode home together from the supper, all alone. There was nobody from other districts then. And I saw you here at dinner the following evening."

"I know," she said. "You're right. I was afraid to tell you."

Seth looked genuinely confused. "Afraid of what, Hannah? You had already told me about your Bible study on the way back from Kidron. I didn't jump off the fishing dock or give you a hard time about it."

Hannah hung her head. He was right. She'd had chances to tell him that she didn't take. She'd been afraid—of what he would say and of what it would do to their fledging relationship. But then again, did they have a relationship? One little kiss didn't make them a courting couple. Seth was acting like he had a right to know her business.

"You've got no cause to get your feathers ruffled just because I was told to stop quoting Scripture." Her tone betrayed the pique building in her veins. "When I was ten I had a willow switch taken to my backside for telling a fib—did you expect to hear about that too?"

Seth breathed in and out through his nostrils, reminding Hannah of an obstinate bull her family once took on loan from another farm. "They threatened you with shunning. Don't you understand how serious that is? You and I...well, we wouldn't be able to sit at table together or ride to Kidron...or anything else." He crossed his arms over his starched white shirt, looking utterly handsome despite the fact the mood had turned sour.

Hannah crossed her arms too and stared at the cows beyond his shoulder. They were contentedly chewing their cud in the tall grass. *How much nicer to be bovine, without the rules, expectations, and responsibilities of life.*

"I understand the significance of their warning. If shunned, I would be an outcast, banned from the district I had hoped to become part of."

Hannah thought about the last occasion she'd been threatened with shunning. Now was the time to tell him she'd once stood up at a congregational meeting and voiced her opinion—something Amish women never did.

Seth's gaze traveled to the kitchen window, and the corners of his mouth turned down. "Woman, I don't know what you're thinking here, but I can't jaw about this any longer right now. I've got my hands full of problems with Phoebe. I need to take her home before she thinks I've gone back on my word."

Her attention snapped back from the cows. "What kind of problems with Phoebe? Let me help. I've grown fond of that little girl. I'll bet if I—"

"No, Hannah." Seth cut her off abruptly. "This is something I must do. She's been spending too much time with you while I have neglected my duties as her father. She's here at Simon's farm more often than she's home."

"I was just trying to help, Seth Miller. It's about time your girl starts talking again." Maybe it was due to the heat and valley humidity, but Hannah found her temper on a short leash.

"I'm not so worried about what will happen this fall in school. I've created a whole new batch of trouble because I keep dropping her off for other people to raise."

Hannah felt as though she'd been kicked in the gut by a plow horse. "You're blaming me for your daughter's problems?" The words came out sounding like a squawk.

"No," he said, his face contorted with sadness. "It's just not something you can help me with. I think Phoebe's worried that you're taking me away from her—that she'll get even less of my attention than she gets right now."

Hannah's spine arched like a cornered tomcat's. "Well, you

can explain to her that that's never going to happen. And if you'll excuse me, I've got better things to do than stand around jawing with you." She stomped off toward the barn where piles and piles of raw wool were waiting to be spun from the shearing she'd had done last week.

She didn't need Seth's approval or his understanding. She had only tried to help with Phoebe—to draw the child from her sad, quiet world and heal her wounded spirit. She'd begun the English instruction so she could be ready to start school in the fall. Amish *kinner* take a big step when they leave the *Deutsch*-speaking home to join an English-speaking world. Phoebe needed to become part of a larger community than the Miller brother farms. But Seth saw her as a bad influence on his daughter since the warning by the district elders. Suddenly Hannah had become unsuitable company for a youngster.

Climbing to her loft where her wool waited to be sorted and spun, Hannah fought back tears for the second time. She felt sick over being cut off from the precious little girl. She'd made a mistake in growing so attached to Phoebe. She'd made an even bigger mistake in growing so attached to Seth. He thought she would never make a good wife. At the moment she didn't know which hurt more.

∼

"Phoebe?" Seth called. "Come outside. We're going home."

Julia heard Seth hollering through the screen door. The child, who'd been playing in the front room with Leah, ran into the kitchen, dragging her doll by the hair.

Julia limped into the back hallway. "Did you find my sister? Did you have a chance to talk to Hannah?"

Seth placed one palm flat against the doorjamb and tapped his toe with impatience, looking cross.

"*Jah*, I found her," he said irritably. "Didn't do me much good."

"Is this about the warning?" Julia asked. Her brother-in-law wouldn't appreciate her nosiness, but too much was at stake here. Julia knew her sister too well.

Seth lifted one dark eyebrow. "It is. I would've thought Hannah could come to me about that instead of letting me hear it from the grapevine." He didn't try to hide his anger or disappointment.

"Did she talk to you now about it? Did she explain what happened and why it's hard for her to talk about it?" Julia whispered the questions. She knew she was crawling out on a thin branch.

"No," he said, drawing out the word. "I suppose she thought it was none of my business."

"Seth, why don't you come in and have some breakfast. Then—"

"No, Julia. I don't have time to argue with a stubborn woman who's made it plain many times where I stand with her." He opened the screen door and took Phoebe by the hand. "And we've already had our breakfast this morning, *danki* just the same."

The two marched off toward their buggy as though late for an appointment.

Julia felt her own breakfast churn in her stomach. She shook her head, trying to think of something to say or do to stop this unfortunate chain of events. But there wasn't a thing she could do. Only Hannah could fix the mess she'd made with Seth.

Even though Emma had done all the chores, Julia managed to putter around the kitchen for hours, wiping down this and cleaning out that, anxiously waiting for her sister. Finally a lint-speckled Hannah walked inside and headed to the sink to wash.

"Shall I make sandwiches for lunch?" she asked. "I'll slice the tomatoes I picked this morning and open a jar of spiced apples."

"No, Hannah. Emma already made egg sandwiches, and the tomatoes are already on a plate. She brought up the last of the canned peaches, not spiced apples." Julia tried to calm her nerves with a few deep breaths.

Drying her hands on the towel, Hannah asked cheerily, "Then what can I do?"

"You can start by telling me why you have no trouble showing love to me and affection for Phoebe, but with everybody else you just run off and hide."

"What are you talking about? I don't run away from anybody." Hannah scraped her palms down the sides of her skirt. "Is this about Seth? I told him I read my Bible—all the chapters—and that I find great solace there."

"Then you should have mentioned the visit from the elders, and it wouldn't have turned into the tangle that you have now."

Hannah lifted her chin higher while her lower lip began to tremble. "I couldn't, Julia. If I started talking about one, I'd have to talk about the other incident. That was a long time ago. It doesn't affect the person I am now."

"But it does, or you wouldn't be sweeping it under the rug. You're still afraid someone will find out and think less of you."

The trembling spread to both of her hands. "And wouldn't they? No man wants a troublesome wife. If I told Seth everything, he would run in the opposite direction. He certainly wouldn't want me near his little girl."

"You're sure of that, Hannah Brown?" Julia mustered every ounce of courage she possessed.

"I'm sure of it, sister."

Julia knew she was going too far but couldn't stop herself. She had watched Hannah repeat the same pattern that had kept her lonely too long. The time had come to speak her mind. "This isn't the only subject you've been avoiding. Why didn't you tell Seth about your work with Phoebe—that you were trying to prepare her to start school. You could have gained his approval and his assistance. Why keep it hidden as though you were afraid to let him know?"

"Because he might not have liked the idea of Phoebe learning English," Hannah said as her hands clenched.

"Then you could have stopped until she went to school, but I think

222 ~ Mary Ellis

you were afraid he'd find out how fond you are of his daughter, how attached you've become."

"He might not want me getting too attached."

"Well, by now you would know for sure how Seth feels instead of guessing. And Seth isn't the only one you run from."

Hannah looked perplexed while a bead of sweat rose above her lip. "What do you mean? Who else do I run from?"

"Simon, my husband." Julia shifted her back against the chair as every joint began to ache at once.

Both of Hannah's hands curled into fists, but she quickly relaxed them and clasped them together. "I don't run from Simon. I spoke with him last night. You witnessed the end of *that* conversation for yourself."

"*Jah*, you talked to him because he approached you. How often do you seek out his counsel on an upsetting matter—not just because he's your brother-in-law but because he's a deacon in your new district?"

Hannah's eyes glazed momentarily as she pondered the question. "Offhand, I can't remember a time, but I'm sure I have at some point."

"I don't think so," Julia said, shaking her head. "You seldom initiate a conversation, and if you have a problem you keep it from him."

Hannah inhaled a strangled breath. "Simon has never thought highly of me. He always assumes the worst if the situation involves me."

"You don't allow him an opportunity to do otherwise. Why didn't you tell him that Seth was giving you a herding dog instead of letting Turnip arrive unannounced? Simon doesn't like surprises."

"I wasn't completely sure Seth would find the right dog."

Julia shook her head dismissively. "And you should've told Simon before you left that I wanted Emma to accompany you to Sugar Creek. Instead, when he came into the house and found me alone with the girls off playing, he thought I was being neglected."

"I had no idea where Simon was on the farm and no time for wild goose chases." Hannah was growing annoyed with the interrogation, but Julia remained steadfast. This conversation was long overdue.

"And speaking of your trip to Sugar Creek—why didn't you explain your reason for going into business with Mrs. Dunn? If Simon knew you planned to use the profits to buy my arthritis medicine, he wouldn't resent your time spent in the barn loft."

"It wouldn't make any difference!" Hannah said. A blush rose up her neck into her cheeks, and she turned the color of a ripe tomato.

"You can't be sure of that. You're so convinced that Simon will misjudge you, you misjudge him first."

Hannah shifted her weight to the other foot and perched one hand on her hip.

But Julia held up a hand to stem any protests. "I'm not saying Simon doesn't jump to conclusions too. He should have come to you about quoting Scripture instead of going straight to the elders. He forms opinions too quickly, but I'm afraid you two share that particular habit. You're both very much alike—that's why you so easily get under each other's skin."

Hannah seemed to deflate like a balloon. "I'll think on what you've said, Julia. I have no wish to argue about your husband."

"And think about telling the truth to Seth. The whole truth, including what happened in Lancaster. If that should come out at some point in the future, you'll again turn a molehill into a mountain." Julia finally released her breath with a *whoosh* as a weight lifted from her shoulders.

Hannah's face furrowed with grief. "No, Julia. You might be my big sister, and this might be your home, but you can't tell me what to do regarding Seth. I have my reasons for not discussing Pennsylvania with him or with anyone else for that matter. That is water long under the bridge. Right now, whatever comes out in the future won't make any difference to him. Seth has already made up his mind about me, and nothing I can say will change it."

As Hannah wiped the tears from under her eyes, Julia suddenly felt mean-spirited. Did she hurt her sister's feelings for no reason whatsoever? Had things fallen apart between Hannah and Seth? Or worse, did she invent this romance between two casual friends out of her own desire to see them married and their families forever joined together?

"I will consider your advice regarding Simon, but about...the other matter, I trust you won't bring up the subject again." Hannah looked as though she would bolt like a startled deer—her usual reaction. Maybe she would flee to the loft or to her favorite spot by the river. But instead she closed her eyes for a full minute and then said, "I'll set the table and get out the sandwiches. If you could ring the farm bell, I believe it's time for lunch." She walked to the refrigerator with a shaky step but with her head held high.

At that moment, Julia had never respected or loved her sister more. She hoped, however, the woman-to-woman chat hadn't done more harm than good.

~

The sandwich lunch with canned peaches and iced tea dragged on for several hours—or so it seemed to Hannah. The boys told fishing stories from their successful morning on the pond in a rowboat. Emma shared ideas about gathering berries, roots, and wildflowers to make various types of natural dyes for the wool. Leah mostly moped, missing the companionship of her cousin Phoebe. Simon, Julia, and Hannah remained quiet, each either content to listen to the three *kinner* or lost in their own thoughts.

Afterward, Julia retired to her room to rest, Emma and Leah cleaned the kitchen, and Hannah went to her room to write a long overdue letter to Thomas. She had plenty of weeding to do in the garden; several ewes needed to have matting cut from their fleeces; and baskets of wool still waited to be spun from the shearing. She had considered spending the afternoon with Emma, searching for natural dye ingredients, but her heart wasn't in it.

The less time she spent with the impressionable young woman, the better. Then it wouldn't be quite so unbearable when they had to go their separate ways. As she had promised, Hannah contemplated Julia's allegations. The conclusion? Her sister was correct on all counts. She could have avoided many problems with Simon if she'd been forthright. She did have the habit of hiding from the man whenever the opportunity allowed. No wonder his opinion of her was so low.

As for Seth Miller...who could blame him for not wanting Phoebe influenced by a woman not known for honesty? Was omitting details of her past the same as telling lies? His withdrawing the child from her life hurt almost as much as the realization she had no future with the dark-haired man who loved sheep, and nature, and being Amish. Almost, but not quite. Seth had burrowed into a heart she'd thought immune to flights of fancy. She loved him, plain and simple.

Disappointed by her behavior, he would never ask to court her now. Not with the elders' reprimand hanging over her head, and not with her own cowardice like a thunderhead on the horizon.

Julia had been right—she was afraid. If she wasn't able to admit the past, she was doomed to repeat the same mistakes.

She would pray for forgiveness. She would ask God for guidance. But she was too weak a woman to face Seth Miller.

In the drowsy stillness of her bedroom, she took out pen and paper. She would write to her brother and tell him she was coming home. Thomas, filled with expectation and joy with his coming marriage, would take her in. Like a maiden aunt or an elderly widow, she would remain in the background in the bride's new home. Hannah would offer advice only when solicited and never overstep her boundaries in Catherine and Thomas' life. The farm belonged to her brother now.

No longer owning the farm didn't bother her. Hannah didn't care about deeds, or mortgages, or bills of sale. What did trouble her about returning to Lancaster County was leaving her sister, her dear nieces and nephews, quiet little Phoebe, and most of all...Seth.

Seth would be the hardest burden to bear, but bear it she must. He did not care for her.

He did not love her.

And she could no longer stay here and be his friend.

SEVENTEEN

Seth's determination to spend more time with his daughter had been easily implemented a day earlier. Together they had weeded the garden, cut lettuce for a salad, and pulled carrots, radishes, and onions. While Seth had cleaned the barn stalls, Phoebe had played with her doll on the hay bales. While Seth had oiled leather harnesses, Phoebe had helped by washing plastic egg cartons so they could be reused. And since it was far too hot and sunny to work the entire day, they swam in the pond and searched for crayfish along the riverbank. For supper they dined on hamburgers and muskmelon and opened the last jar of last year's pickled beets. It had been a very good day.

Today would not be so simple. Yesterday's blistering sun had dried out the hayfield. More of the same weather was predicted for tomorrow. If he cut the field today, the crop could finish drying on the Sabbath while he and Phoebe were at the preaching service. He could rake and start baling on Monday, and by next weekend plant seeds for his second crop.

But what should he do with an-almost-six-year-old who was more curious than any cat he'd ever met? Mrs. Lehman had sent a note with her son indicating she was well enough to resume her babysitting duties. But one day at home wasn't enough time to cure anybody of anything.

"Phoebe," he said, drawing her attention from the cornflakes, "your *daed* needs to cut hay this morning, and it's too dangerous for you to ride on the harvesting implement with me. Do you think you could stay by yourself for a couple hours until lunchtime? You must remain in the house or on the porch. Do not go into any of the barns. You cannot try to cook anything on the stove or light any lamps. You can look at your picture books, play with the dollhouse I built for you, or rock on the porch swing. Nothing else. If you don't think you can do this, I'll take you to Mrs. Lehman's for the day."

Phoebe shook her head vigorously at the mention of the neighbor's name.

"If you're on the porch and someone comes up the driveway that you don't know, go inside and lock the door. Do you understand?"

She nodded her head.

"We'll eat lunch together under the willow tree, okay?"

Another affirmative nod.

"If something happens...if you get sick, or if you need me to come home, you pull the rope on the farm bell real hard like you've done before. Can you do that, Phoebe?"

The shake of her head did nothing to quell the anxiety of leaving his child alone for a couple of hours. "I need you to say it, Phoebe. You must tell me that you understand the rules."

Her dark eyes seemed to grow larger and rounder as she said in a scratchy but clear voice, "Yes, *daed*."

Seth nodded and headed to the barn to hitch up his team of draft horses before he changed his mind. Phoebe was a good girl, but on a farm so many things presented a danger. He prayed hard for the safety and protection of his only child.

When Seth returned to the house at midday, he found his daughter safe and sound. But she wasn't playing on the porch swing or with her dollhouse. Phoebe was sitting on the front room carpet with a pile of white picture cards scattered around her. Seth watched unseen from the doorway as she picked up a card and said the name in two languages. "Barn," she enunciated and then "*scheune*," followed by "dog" and "*hund*." One large card showed the full spectrum of the rainbow with each color identified in *Deutsch* and English. Another pictured numerals, along with corresponding dual names. Seth observed for several minutes, transfixed by the scene before him. He'd heard Phoebe say only three words in the past two years. Now she was speaking not only their Amish dialect of German, but also the language of the English world.

His heart swelled for his little girl and for the green-eyed woman who had spent so much time teaching her. Hannah. As if she didn't have enough to do between tending her flock, building her wool business, and helping Julia run the household, she'd taken it upon herself to bring Phoebe's voice back and prepare her for school while he had stuck his head in the sand like an ostrich.

Seth shook his head and kneeled down on the rug. He picked up a card to show her and asked, "What's this, Phoebe?"

"Rabbit," she enunciated, and then said, "*Kaninchen*." A grin bloomed across her face.

The two of them remained in that position until they'd gone through the whole stack. Only six had stumped her. As they ate their sandwiches under the tree, Phoebe pointed out the sky, barn, tree, and grass and said their names clearly in both languages. She didn't tell any longwinded stories like Henry, didn't sing any church songs as Emma often did, and certainly didn't screech at the sudden appearance of a spider like Leah, but hearing Phoebe say these words took many of Seth's worries away.

"Did Aunt Hannah teach you these?" He tapped the cards into a neat pile.

She nodded and added softy, "*Jah*." She spread the cards out again in the grass.

"That was nice of her to help you. Do you like Hannah?"

She nodded enthusiastically and then crawled into his lap. "*Jah*, I like Hannah."

"Me too," he whispered. He might have elaborated more on the subject, but at the moment speech was impossible. He had his girl back, healed from her silent sorrow, and he had found a woman to love again. Seth Miller was a fortunate man.

He just had an odd way of showing it.

After he put Phoebe down for a nap and instructed her to stay in her room, Seth returned to the hayfield. He cut until suppertime and then reheated leftovers Julia had sent before putting Phoebe to bed. When it was almost too dark to find his way, he walked back to the barn to check on his animals. His crop lay glistening in the moonlight. In tomorrow's sunshine, the green sheaves would dry to become sweet feed for his livestock this winter.

Seth bathed in the cool river and prayed under the stars. He had so much to be thankful for. Every bone in his body hurt from fatigue and strain; his back muscles ached from jostling along the rutted rows; but Seth Miller loved being a farmer.

Tomorrow was the Sabbath—a much-needed day of prayer and rest. Since the preaching service would be at Simon's, he would get to see Hannah Brown. He planned to thank her for providing Phoebe the incentive and encouragement to talk. And maybe he would have the guts to try one more time to win her heart.

～

Sunshine on the Lord's Day was always a special blessing.

Julia rose before dawn to wash, dress, and take her pills. But most of the work to prepare for the service was done. Church would be held in one of the newer outbuildings with a concrete floor. The district had grown to twenty-five families, making the living room too small to handle the crowd. However, the front room was spotless, thanks to Hannah, for mothers nursing infants or anyone else who wished a quiet spot. The church wagon with benches and songbooks had arrived yesterday from the farm that had held the last service.

Men had stopped over after chores to set up the benches and tables that would hold the food. And what food there would be.

Hannah stayed up late roasting brisket for barbeque beef; Emma baked eight pies, both peach and apple; and Julia had made green bean and sweet potato casseroles with Leah's help.

Seth, in his black Sunday hat, and Phoebe, in her white organdy *kapp*, arrived an hour before everyone else. The man looked far too worn out for someone his age.

"Seth Miller, did you cut all those acres of hay in one day?" Julia asked when he stepped inside the kitchen.

"*Jah*, it needed to be done. Who knows how long the weather will hold? Today the hay can dry, and Monday I'll start baling."

"You must be exhausted. Sit across the aisle from me so I can nudge you if you start to nod off." Julia grinned as broadly as the pain allowed.

Seth poured a cup of coffee and sent Phoebe to find Leah. "With my *bruder* preaching the second sermon this morning, I won't need any pinches to stay awake. He always inspires me with his message and the volume of his voice."

"No one naps when Simon preaches." Julia had always loved her husband's sermons.

"I'd best see to the last of the preparations," said Seth. "I brought my twenty-gallon water jug with the spigot and two packages of cups. It's gonna be another hot one today." He peered out the window at the thermometer. "Already eighty, and the sun's still climbing in the sky." His focus kept shifting from the backyard to the steps to the bedrooms to the front room doorway.

"You looking for someone?" Julia asked, moving to the counter for more coffee.

He raked a hand through his freshly washed hair with comb tracks still visible from his morning routine. "If you must know, my favorite, nosy sister-in-law, I'm waiting for Hannah to come downstairs. I'd like a word with her before the service starts."

Julia sipped the strong coffee. Sometimes it seemed to relieve more discomfort than the expensive medications. "She's not up there. She did her chores very early, fixed us breakfast, and then walked over to talk to Mrs. Lee."

"Mrs. Lee?" Seth raked his hair a second time while the back curled over his collar. "Your English neighbor?" he asked.

Julia noticed Seth needed a haircut, but there was no time for that now. "*Jah,* that's right. Hannah said she would be back in plenty of time for the preaching." She was encouraged that Seth still sounded interested in her sister. Their courtship path had been rockier than the riverbed lately.

"Why did she go talk to an English neighbor on a preaching Sunday?" he asked, bending his hat brim back and forth.

"I'm sure I don't know. Despite your fond but accurate description of me, I didn't ask her."

"Of all the times for you to turn over a new leaf, Julia." He shook his head and finished his coffee in a single gulp. Glancing out the window toward the barn, he poured himself another cup. "Confound it. I don't like asking you this, but I've run into a brick wall with that sister of yours. She was talking about willow switches and telling lies, but I really didn't know what she meant. I had promised Phoebe we would spend the day at our house, so that's where I had to go. I think you were right about Phoebe. She was missing me—that's why she had the so-called accidents. The last couple of nights her bed has been bone dry."

Julia smiled with satisfaction. "Glad to hear it. There's always something to worry about raising *kinner.* I had my hands full before Emma started school, but that sure was a long time ago."

"I seemed to have gotten two crises sorted out—Phoebe and my hay crop—but now another situation presents itself that I've been neglecting."

Julia chuckled—only a farmer could lump a little girl and harvesting a field into the same category.

"What is so amusing to you?" Seth asked. The man looked as though his Sunday shoes were pinching his toes. "I'm asking for your help with Hannah. I don't come close to saying the right thing when I'm around her. I get all nervous and tongue-tied and end up just about biting her pretty head off." He glanced once more toward the doorway. "Any advice you could give me to smooth things out over this shunning business would be appreciated. Not that I think it would ever come to that. She never meant any harm quoting the Good Book. Your sister has the purest heart of any woman I've ever known…" Seth drew a breath and added quietly, "…excepting yours, sister." He tried to smile, his first of the morning.

"A pure heart and a pretty face?" Julia asked. "A man couldn't do much better than that."

"That's pretty much the conclusion I came to."

Julia sighed with regret, knowing that this time she couldn't help. Both Hannah and the man before her with hat in hand might run around like blind squirrels romantically, but Hannah's privacy must be respected. If her sister wasn't ready to open her past to Seth, there wasn't anything Julia could do.

"I'm sorry, Seth. Your description of me is often correct, but this time I must mind my own business. You'll have to find your way through this. Anything Hannah told me was told in confidence. I cannot help you."

The expression on his face nearly broke her heart. He gulped his coffee and set the cup in the sink. "I understand. I'll try to speak with Hannah before the service starts. *Danki* for the coffee." He strode outdoors toward the outbuilding looking even more haggard than when he had arrived, despite a double dose of caffeine.

Julia bowed her head and prayed that two blind squirrels might eventually find each other during their mad scramble.

∼

As Hannah walked the road from Mrs. Lee's, several Amish buggies passed her on the way to Simon's farm. The women wore their heavy bonnets, while the men had donned black felt because it was only a few weeks to the biannual communion service. Everyone smiled and waved as they drove by. There wasn't a pointed finger or shaking head or clucking tongue to be seen. Hannah absently wondered whether they had heard of her blunder as she kicked a stone along the gravel berm.

The sun rose over the distant hills, burning off the last dew from the meadows and fields. It would be a warm morning in Simon's outbuilding. Yet even three hours in a stuffy barn didn't daunt her. Hannah liked preaching Sundays—the hymns, the sermons, the prayers. She was lifted up closer to God, and nothing could be better than that.

She hadn't seen Simon this morning before leaving for the neighbor's, but she imagined he would preach one of the sermons. With her mind made up and her path clearly marked, Hannah could enjoy one last church service in Holmes County with her chin up.

God knew her heart, and nothing else mattered. Romans 12:12 came to mind: "Rejoice in our confident hope. Be patient in trouble, and keep on praying."

As two more buggies rolled by, Hannah picked up her pace. Both had stopped to offer her a lift, but she had declined, preferring to walk. This would be the coolest time of the day, and Hannah enjoyed the sounds of birds and insects around her. When she reached the Millers' gravel lane, small groups of men and women were already filing into the barn.

Thank goodness she wasn't late! Hannah took a seat toward the back on the women's side of the congregation. Only smiles and nods greeted her as everyone rose for the opening hymn. During the first hour she concentrated on the High German hymnbook because she didn't know all the words, and then she listened to the bishop's

Scripture readings. During the sermon, she recognized the back of Seth Miller's head with a quiver of alarm.

Would she cross paths with him today? It was too soon. Her emotions too raw to make polite conversation about the weather or prospects for rain. She spotted Julia's stooped shoulders where she sat with her daughters and niece. She hoped the money she would leave behind with Emma would pay for her treatments and pills for a long time to come.

Hannah had no better use for the money. She would not be buying any farm or house in the future. Her home would be with her brother or with her aged parents. Only her flock remained a perplexing dilemma. Hours spent crowded in a livestock trailer at the height of summer could wreak havoc on sheep. Her ewes could miscarry, and many lambs might be lost. Even strong, healthy animals suffered during a hot-weather relocation.

Shaking off her worries about the sheep, Hannah turned her attention to the second sermon. It was Simon's turn, and it took all her determination not to imagine he was directing his admonitions toward her.

Before the building grew too warm, the service concluded and the people wandered out to enjoy the Sabbath. Some looked for their friends to catch up on news; others sought the cool shade of a tree. Children scampered off to play while teens stole surreptitious glances from beneath bonnets and hat brims. Tonight there would be a singing for young people, and Hannah remembered the carefree days of her own youth.

But she possessed no yearning to go back, not with the knowledge of the pain and disappointment yet to come—the days of waiting and praying for a baby. Yet her arms remained empty, and even the affection of one quiet child had been taken away.

Hannah shook off painful memories and hurried into Julia's kitchen. She joined the other women carrying platters of meat, casseroles, trays of veggies, and baskets of baked goods. Soon the tables set up beneath the large oak were laden with a bounty of food.

Hannah retreated inside to clean the kitchen while the menfolk ate. Their voices might be subdued, but their faces revealed pleasure in partaking of a good meal.

"There you are," Julia said from the cellar steps. "I brought up extra pickles to go with the cold ham."

"I'll take them out in a minute," Hannah said over her shoulder. She was up to her elbows in soapsuds, trying to scrape off burned sweet potato.

"I'd saved you a seat on the bench next to me for the service," Julia said, slipping her arm around Hannah's waist.

"Oh, I found a spot in back near a window. I got back from Mrs. Lee's in the nick of time." Hannah scrubbed hard at one particularly burned pan.

"Is everything all right, sister? I hope you have forgiven me for being so blunt yesterday." Julia tightened her embrace.

Hannah left the pan to soak and shut off the water. Turning around, she met her sister's gaze. "There isn't anything to forgive. You said nothing that wasn't true. And it's high time I faced reality." She brushed a kiss across Julia's cheek and reached for the towel. "Do you think the men are finished eating? I'm getting a little hungry."

"Let's go see," Julia said, leaning on Hannah's arm. "I'm hungry enough to finish off everything they left behind."

They walked outdoors arm in arm, joining the other women in the buffet line. Hannah meant what she had said to her sister. She felt only gratitude and love for the person who'd told her the truth.

Hannah's only exaggeration had been her appetite. She tried to eat but ended up just pushing the ham, greens, and potato casserole around her plate. She forced herself to eat a little and then carried her plate to the wash house where women were already busy cleaning up.

"Hannah, may I speak with you a moment?" The familiar voice of Seth Miller stopped her dead in her tracks.

She gazed into his suntanned face. "Hullo, Seth. How goes the hay cutting?"

He swept his hat from his head. "Hannah Brown, I've been searching for you and trying to catch your attention all morning. Now that I finally have it, I don't want to talk about hay." He shifted his weight from foot to foot while he talked.

"Your attention should have been on the morning message, not on me," she said softly.

"True enough, but I've got some things that need to be said. I first want to thank you for helping my girl. She's talking again, and that wouldn't have happened without you. I had ignored the problem, hoping it would go away and pretending nothing was wrong. But plenty was wrong with Phoebe, and you got us back on track."

He looked so sincere, yet so forlorn. Even while thanking her, he had managed to break her heart. "I'm glad that she's talking again," she said, her voice little more than a whisper.

"When I returned from the fields yesterday, I found her practicing those cards you gave her. She was pronouncing each word in *Deutsch* and English. She went from being mute to being bilingual because of you."

"Laura Stoddard gave me those cards. She's used them before with her students."

"Miss Stoddard didn't sit around with my daughter for hours. I'm sure you had better things to do."

Remembering the afternoons spent with Phoebe and the flash cards only made Hannah hurt worse. This surely wouldn't make the move back home any easier.

"You're welcome, Seth. I was happy to do it. You have Emma and Leah to thank too. Now if you'll excuse me, I must help clean up. I can't afford for my reputation in the district to sink any lower."

Hannah wasn't that concerned about her reputation, not anymore. But if she stayed with Seth any longer, she would start to cry. Her emotions were too fresh, too raw to stand around chatting as if he was any other neighbor.

Seth frowned and glanced across the yard. People milling in the shade or congregating in small groups had focused their attention on him and Hannah. Two unmarried people talking to one another tended to cause that in the Amish world. "All right, Hannah. Since the rest of what I've got to say has waited this long, I suppose it can wait till the dishes are done. I'm going to walk the pasture to see if the eye infections have cleared up."

He slapped his hat back on and strode away with determination.

You go mingle with the sheep, Seth Miller. That's one place I don't intend to go.

Hannah made sure that women surrounded her for the remainder of the day while she socialized in the Miller kitchen. Few men wandered inside the house on a fine Sunday afternoon.

The one time she'd spotted Seth walking toward the house, she'd locked herself in the bathroom and hadn't emerged until someone knocked on the door.

Julia would have called her behavior hiding. Hannah thought of it as self-preservation.

At long last the members of the community packed up their casserole dishes and headed to their buggies—home to chores, evening prayers, and a good night's sleep before the start of another busy summer week. Seth too collected Phoebe from a group of *kinner* and left, looking far less enthusiastic than he had outside the wash house.

Hannah watched him leave from her bedroom window. Now she could venture outside to check on her animals' food and water supply. She could walk the pasture without fear of unnecessary conversations or uncomfortable silences. Soon the green, rolling hills of Holmes County would be only a distant memory—a sweet reminiscence like her trip to Cedar Point or her ride on a riverboat before joining the church.

After seeing to her flock, Hannah slipped on her nightgown and unwound her hair from her bun. Gazing at her reflection in the mirror, she brushed out her hair and wondered why she couldn't be just like everyone else. It was to her continued detriment that she went through life hitting her head against stone walls.

After her prayers, and too tired for Bible study, Hannah decided to list ten ways she could become more ordinary in preparation to rejoin the Amish of Lancaster County.

Unfortunately she came up with only three before deep, blissful sleep stole her away to the land of dreams—where all things still were possible.

～

Like the mother of a newborn baby, Hannah awoke to the sound of bawling sheep. But this wasn't a lamb bleating because it had become separated from the ewe. She heard a loud ruckus coming from the pasture that must involve most of the flock. Her first thought was a predator—a coyote or feral dog—as she kicked off the sheet and ran to the window. From her back window overlooking the pasture, she saw a dark massive shape shifting erratically in the moonlight, as though the sheep en masse didn't know which way to flee.

Hannah hurried to the side window. It wasn't a predator that had spooked her sheep but something far more ominous. An eerie yellow-orange light glowed in the open hay window of the barn, while a plume of white smoke curled against the dark sky.

Fire! The shock of seeing a farmer's worst fear gripped her gut and paralyzed her. Then every muscle, bone, and sinew reacted at once. Throwing on her robe, she ran from her room and pounded on Julia and Simon's door and those of the children in succession. "Fire!" she shouted. "Get up! The barn's ablaze!"

Once Emma, Leah, Henry, and Matthew joined their parents in the hallway, Hannah fled down the steps into the kitchen. Shouts, cries, and questions rang from all directions as the family followed her downstairs. Hannah had no answers.

With the six Millers close behind, Hannah ran onto the porch and began frantically ringing the farm bell. She spotted Henry on the steps staring at the barn as flames leaped from the loft window toward the roof. "Here, Henry," she shouted. "Keep pulling the rope. Those who hear the bell will come to help. I'm going to help your pa." Hannah yanked on Adam's old muck boots over her bare feet and hurried toward the largest of Simon's barns.

Smoke began to billow from the doorway as Hannah reached the others. Simon dipped a towel into the water trough and wrapped it around Matthew's mouth and neck and then did the same for himself. "Stay behind me, Matthew, at all times," he ordered as he called over his shoulder. "Do not follow me, Julia!"

"Let me help," Emma called.

"Fill the buckets and drag over the garden hose, Emma," Simon shouted. "Julia, get the gas-powered pump from the under the porch." Then he disappeared into a smoke-filled barn with Matthew right behind him.

Hannah saw no flames on the first level but the smoke made her cough even twenty feet away. While Julia and Emma hurried to fulfill their tasks, Hannah entered the barn and tried to stay as low as possible. She made it as far as the hog pen in the blinding smoke and managed to get the sow and piglets out and headed in the right direction. As soon as the pigs crossed the threshold into the barnyard, four draft horses thundered past her and scattered into the dark night. Hannah had only enough time to jump out of the way. Then Matthew appeared through the smoke, pulling two spring colts by their halters. He let go of the ropes and slapped the horses' rumps once through the doorway. Simon followed close behind, leading his skittish gelding and Julia's frantic mare. Hannah ran forward to help calm Julia's horse.

"Go outside, Hannah," Simon shouted. "Help Julia hook the pump up to the hose. Wet down the roofs of the other buildings so the fire doesn't spread." The two horses held by their leads didn't like pausing inside a burning building. One snorted then lunged against the rope while the other reared up on his hind legs. Simon dodged the horse's hooves by inches. "Please, Hannah, go! These are the last of the animals."

"What about the cows?" she cried, already moving toward the door.

"They're still in the pasture. Everything's out." He pulled hard on the gelding's halter as soon as its hind hooves hit the barn floor, and man and beast followed Hannah out into freedom and fresh air.

Simon released his grip once they were out, but slapped the horses' backsides to keep them from running back into the burning barn. Then he doubled over in a fit of coughing. Hannah also gasped for air as Mr. Lehman hurried toward them.

"Simon, are all the animals out? Are you all right, Mrs. Brown?" asked Mr. Lehman. He grabbed Hannah's elbow as tears streamed from her stinging eyes.

Simon nodded his head, unable to speak.

"*Jah,* I'm fine," Hannah said hoarsely.

Simon supported her other arm, and the three moved back from the unbearable heat. People were arriving by foot, horseback, buggy, and car. At least twenty Amish and English neighbors came to fight the fire in whatever clothes they could pull on in the middle of the night. Black smoke poured from the doorway and hay window. Flames leaped skyward as sections of roof fell in, opening the barn to the heavens. The influx of fresh air fanned the blaze into an inferno. Everyone had to stagger back from the intense heat. The yellow glow against the black sky could be seen for miles.

Simon and Hannah lost little time watching the spectacle, however. "*Danki* for your help with the animals, Hannah," he said, regaining his raspy voice. "I'm going to help Julia bring over the pump to get water from the pond."

"I'll stretch out the hose and drop one end into the pond," Hannah said as she sucked air into her parched lungs.

"I'll get a bucket brigade going to wet down the henhouse and milking parlor, and then I'll aim the hose on the barn's foundation to try to save it," Mr. Lehman called. The three ran off in different directions.

Seth soon arrived with his own gasoline pump and garden hose, and within minutes aimed a steady stream of water on the house and porch roof. The wind carrying sparks and embers could easily spread the blaze to the Miller home.

Mrs. Lee had spotted the orange glow from her bedroom window and called the Winesburg Fire Department. Two trucks arrived within twenty minutes, but by then the barn could not be saved. With one fire department hose trained on the barn to contain the fire and two others on the outbuildings, Mr. Lehman moved his garden hose around to wet down the fencing, vegetable plot, and woodpile. Other folks had their hands full in the pasture stomping out brush fires from burning debris carried on the breeze.

Hannah and Julia joined this group, working side by side with Matthew and Emma. Julia didn't let her *kinner* out of sight. Leah and Henry were ordered to fill jugs of drinking water from the kitchen sink for the firefighters and not leave the porch area. With fire equipment, men, horses, buggies, and cars moving around in the smoke, it wasn't safe for small children to be afoot.

For several hours family, friends, neighbors, and dedicated firefighters fought the blaze and kept it from destroying the house, milking parlor, henhouse, and other outbuildings. The pasture and most of the fencing were also saved, as were the rolling fields of ripe hay and corn.

Weary beyond belief, the Millers stood in their ash-covered barnyard and uttered silent prayers of thanksgiving. As sorrowful as it was to lose a hundred-and-fifty-year-old barn, it could have been so much worse.

EIGHTEEN

The awful, acrid smell hung heavy in the air the next morning. Simon rose to milk the cows and make sure all animals had adequate food and water before returning to bed for a couple more hours of sleep. He had been up until almost dawn putting out the last of the sparks and embers. The horses were in a fenced pasture as far away from the smoldering shell of a barn as they could get. The sow and piglets now resided in a shed off the milk house. The chickens weren't happy about the amount of ash that had fallen into their scratching area but seemed no worse for the ordeal. The cows had remained out in the pasture on the balmy night and didn't seem to notice their winter home had been reduced to a pile of blackened timbers. They chewed the grass with their usual enthusiasm.

The fire department stayed for several hours to make sure nothing ignited from sparks blown by the wind. Before leaving, they soaked a portion of pasture and field downwind of the fire. The exhausted neighbors returned home, mentioning before they left how lucky Simon was not to lose a single animal.

How merciful was the Lord. Simon knew he had been spared, thanks to God…and Hannah's sheep! If their mournful bleating hadn't raised the alarm and awoken Hannah, the fire could easily have spread out of control. He surely would have lost his horses and pigs, and probably a lot more too. He would never call sheep smelly bags of wool again.

Simon looked over the farm that had been handed down to him through four generations of Millers and uttered a prayer of gratitude. Soot and ash would wash away with the next heavy rain. Scorched, trampled grass and flowerbeds would regrow. A barn could be rebuilt. But he might have lost those precious things in life that could never be replaced.

Tears ran down Simon's face as he considered not what was gone, but what still remained. And his tears had nothing to do with the smoke still thick in the humid morning air.

When he walked back indoors, he was startled to find his wife at the sink, starting a pot of coffee. "What are you doing up, Julia? I'm sure you didn't get but three hours of sleep. Go back upstairs."

She raised one brow. "I can't sleep any better than you, husband. Women aren't born with the ability to sleep through calamities any more than men."

He nodded. "I suppose that's true, but rest your mind. The fire is pretty much out in the rubble."

Julia poured cups of coffee and set bread and jam on the table. "I believe we'll have the bread untoasted today."

Despite his strain and fatigue, Simon laughed, furrowing his forehead. "It'll be a long time before I can toast marshmallows with Leah or attend someone's pig roast."

Julia sipped her coffee. "Did the firemen have any ideas how the fire started?" she asked in a quiet voice.

"No. They smelled no accelerant around the barnyard, so they don't think it was arson. It was fairly clear last night—not much chance of a lightning strike. And it certainly wasn't electrical," he added wryly. "So that leaves only spontaneous combustion of a damp hay bale or a careless smoker discarding his cigarette butt."

Julia pondered the possibilities and nodded in agreement.

"I told the fire chief my hay is still in the field," Simon added. "Since

I haven't stored any in the loft yet, that leaves us with the latter likelihood. After yesterday's preaching service, men and boys were milling in and around the barn throughout the day and early evening."

Silence spun out for a few moments.

"We'll probably never know," Julia said.

"A fire investigator will be out this afternoon, but you're right... we'll probably never know for sure. And that might not be so bad. It would be hard to look a young man in the eye knowing he burned down your barn."

Julia looked surprised by his admission.

"Hard," he added, patting her hand, "but not impossible." He took one slice of bread. More food than that he had no appetite for. "Where is Hannah? Is she still asleep? She worked very hard last night. I have much to say to her. I owe her sheep a debt of gratitude."

Julia's expression turned incredulous. "Simon, are you suffering from smoke inhalation?"

"No, *fraa,* I have all my faculties this morning. That's why I need to make amends before I slip back into my old habits."

"I heard her stirring about early, before I came downstairs. Apparently none of the adults could sleep in today. I believe she's gone to check her flock to make sure no sheep got lost during the commotion."

Simon pulled on his long beard, which seemed a tad whiter since last night. "I can find her there then," he said, rising to leave.

"Wait, Simon. Hannah told me she's made up her mind about something." Julia paused and met his eye. "She's moving back to Pennsylvania to live with Thomas until his marriage, and then maybe she'll move home with our folks." Julia's voice held no censure, only a simple statement of facts.

"*Danki* for letting me know. I'll talk to her about that and plenty of other things."

Julia sighed as she leaned back in her chair. "Long overdue, on both of your parts."

"Long overdue," he repeated after the screen door slammed behind him.

Ash and soot covered the pasture as Simon hiked uphill toward the high point where Hannah's flock grazed. Hannah was sitting on a rock outcropping with an open book on her lap. Sheep milled and frolicked all around her, while several lambs lay in the grass by her feet.

She closed the book when he approached and offered a shy smile. Dimples deepened in her cheeks. "Hullo, Simon," she said.

"*Guder mariye*," he answered, taking off his hat. "Mind if I pull up a rock?" He lowered himself onto a nearby boulder.

She looked as surprised as Julia had, either by his arrival or at his attempt at humor. "Of course not," she said.

He reached down and tried to pet a lamb, but it quickly scampered off. The hovering ewe showed her displeasure with a loud *baaa*. "These sheep of yours saved the other farm animals. Their ruckus woke you and me up in enough time to get the livestock out. The fire could've gotten out of hand if not for their bleating. Thank you. I am in your debt—and the sheep's."

Hannah focused on the animals wandering away from the intrusion of a stranger and then back at him. "On behalf of my sheep, you're welcome. They were glad to help."

"I also came out to apologize. I've not given you much chance to explain things since you've been here. I've jumped to a lot of conclusions. Julia told me you've been buying her arthritis medicine. I don't want you spending your sale proceeds on us. Not that I don't appreciate it, but you might want to buy another farm someday, and they don't come cheap."

Hannah was studying him intently. "Simon, I don't plan to buy another house, so I have no better use for my money. I decided to move back to Pennsylvania. Not immediately, of course. I want to help with the barn rebuilding, but as soon thereafter as I can arrange. I just haven't figured out what to do with my flock."

"They're welcome to stay here for as long as you like. Henry won't mind feeding and watering them, plus you know Emma is plumb in love with the lambs. But I'm asking you to reconsider the move and stay with us." He drew a deep breath before continuing. "I've been rigid and judgmental. I should have talked to you before going to the elders. I regret that, Hannah, and ask you to forgive me."

"I haven't exactly behaved without bias myself, Simon. So I accept your apology and offer my own in return." She reached out and grasped his dry, calloused hand.

The gesture deepened his personal sense of guilt.

"But I wish to return home for my own…personal…reasons," she continued. "My wool business is gone—my loom and wheel, my supplies, my stock of wool from the last shearing."

"The loom can be replaced. Since your animals are unhurt, their fleeces will keep growing. That we can be sure of." Simon flattened his palms against his knees while his back rebelled against the low seat with a painful spasm. "The fire inspector will be out this afternoon. I expect him to complete his report and sign a release. Then I can walk to the neighbor's and start calling English waste haulers. We can load up the wreckage and clean the barnyard. I've already sent a letter to Jacob Klobentz, the master barn builder, to stop out when he gets a chance. He'll decide what can be done with the foundation, take measurements, draw up a construction plan, and write up an order to take to the lumberyard. The sooner we don't have to look at this heap of rubble, the better." He stared down at the still-smoking ruin from their high vantage point.

Hannah shook her head. "I'm happy to hear it, but that doesn't change my decision."

"Hear me out, Hannah. We'll build you another workroom in the loft, this one even bigger and better sealed off from the dust down below. We'll put in big sliding windows to let in light and fresh air." He stood up shakily, the boulder finally getting the better of him. "I'll buy you a new loom since you've been spending more than your share of money around here."

Hannah rose to her feet too and held up both palms. "I appreciate the offer. *Danki* kindly, but my mind's made up. I have my reasons for leaving. It isn't because you and I are so much alike we butt heads—according to Julia, anyway. And she knows both of us better than anybody." Hannah smiled at him.

"*Jah*...that she does. I don't know what I'd do without that woman."

"Nor I." Hannah peered at the sun's position to gauge the time. "Shall we start back? I don't want her to worry about us."

Simon took her arm, and they walked slowly through the grass. "Came in thick and green up here on the ridge just like you said it would," he said.

"Long, sunny days can work wonders."

"In more ways than one," he said softly.

They enjoyed the stroll through a July meadow—hawks soaring high on air currents, butterflies flitting from one cornflower to the next, and grasshoppers springing before their footfalls were reminders that life would go on. The black scar on Simon's once pristine farm would heal with time.

"About when do you think the barn raising will be?" she asked. "I'll stay to help Julia organize meals for the workers."

"I'll know more when Jacob stops out to take measurements. I wouldn't even know where to start figuring what materials we would need. He's the barn expert in three counties, but I imagine we'll have a new barn within the month."

"Everyone has his own unique gifts," she murmured.

"When the lumber arrives, he'll come with a crew and do the preliminary layout. I can clean and repair the foundation while that's going on, and get rid of the last of the debris. Julia will write notes to everyone in the area asking for their help once we set a date."

"Will it be on a Saturday?" she asked.

"*Jah,* most likely." Simon cleared his throat before changing the subject. "Hannah, your mind might be made up right now, but don't think you can't change it. We are your family, and you will always be welcome here."

Hannah glanced his way and then back down at her boots as they crossed the dry creek bed on stepping-stones.

Simon had seen tears in her eyes, so he said nothing more. The woes of women had never been his expertise—no more so than what materials to buy to rebuild a three-story barn.

~

As if the horror of a fire hadn't been bad enough, smoke filtered throughout the house though they had kept all windows facing the barn closed. Each garment Hannah took from her closet or drawer had the same acrid smell. Everything needed to be laundered—the curtains, throw rugs, towels, and all the clothing for seven people. Laundry day stretched into three days as two women and two girls washed, hauled, and hung clothes on lines strung far from the house.

Then came the cleaning. Windows, walls, and floors needed to be washed from ash that drifted in on the breeze and settled on every flat surface. Julia tried her best, but her gnarly hands could do only so much. On Friday, after the laundry and most of the cleaning were done, Hannah hitched up the buggy and went to Berlin to shop and refill Julia's prescriptions. Her nieces went along and proved to be a big help as they carefully packed the buggy with groceries.

Hannah hadn't seen Seth since the fire, and that night they hadn't spoken. While she'd been beating out brushfires in the pasture, he'd been spraying down the roof of the house. When she was hauling buckets to soak the garden, he was keeping a steady stream on the barn foundation. Finally, when she could no longer stand up from fatigue, she'd staggered inside, washed her hands and face, and collapsed on the bed. A long, soaking bath would have to wait. Hannah had immediately fallen to sleep and slept five dreamless hours. When she awoke, Seth was gone, and she hadn't seen him since. But that was about to change.

"Uncle Seth is here," Emma said as they arrived home. "That's his buggy."

The girl seemed ecstatic. Hannah felt dizzy and weak-kneed. If not for the fire, she would have been on her way to Pennsylvania. Now she would have to stay at least a couple more weeks. And avoiding the man who raised her heart rate into the danger zone would be impossible.

Seth, along with Simon and the boys, was painting the side of the house that faced the barn. "You missed a spot, Uncle Seth," Emma teased, running to join them.

Seth gave his niece a loose, one-armed hug. "Careful, now, or you'll get paint on your dress."

"*Daed,* can I help? I haven't painted since I was little."

"No, Emma. Your *mamm* and aunt need you in the house," Simon answered without glancing up.

Emma looked cross, an unusual expression for the sweet-tempered girl. But Hannah wasn't surprised Simon didn't let her paint. Amish roles for males and females became specific as one left childhood behind.

Hannah lifted her bags onto the porch and hurried back to the buggy.

"Good afternoon, Hannah. Need a hand with those groceries?" Seth asked. He balanced the paintbrush on the rim of the can.

"No, we can manage just fine. Please don't stop what you're doing." She hadn't meant to sound irritable, but the temperature was ninety-four degrees, her shoes pinched her feet, and she couldn't handle another painful conversation with him.

"As you wish." Seth picked up the brush and dipped it into the can. He applied a long swath of paint with precision and without another glance in her direction.

Hannah marched inside with her bags, sending the girls back for the rest. This would be a long two weeks if he were here underfoot all the time!

But fortunately that proved not to be the case.

Julia announced that they and the children would eat dinner together, but the men planned to work until dark. Seth and Simon ate alone after the rest of the family went upstairs.

During the ensuing days, the yard turned into a hubbub of activity, and Hannah hardly caught even a glimpse of Seth. An English hauler arrived to load the wreckage and cart it away. The master barn builder spent time with Simon compiling lists and returned a week later to supervise the unloading and sorting of the lumber order. After this, his crew came during late afternoons, after their other jobs, for the preliminary construction work. Julia said they were donating their labor for the replacement barn because the fire had been an act of God.

Other people came and went as their schedules allowed. They repaired the fences knocked down by fire equipment, whitewashed the sooty outbuildings, and replanted trampled bushes and shrubs that were away from the barn site.

Hannah stayed busy too. She barely had time to write to Thomas explaining her delay. She also wrote Julia's letters to friends and neighbors announcing the barn raising. Try as she might, Julia couldn't hold a pen even with the physical therapy.

With the big day still a week away, Hannah's curiosity finally got the better of her. When her sister came inside to start another pot of coffee, Hannah mustered some courage. "I've not seen hide nor hair of Seth in more than a week. Isn't he able to help his *bruder*? I hope he hasn't caught that nasty bug going around," Hannah said, concentrating on the potato she was peeling.

Julia dropped the coffee can with a clatter. "*Jah*, he's been over to help. He's cut and raked all Simon's hay and will start baling tomorrow now that he's done with his acres." She stared at Hannah over her shoulder. "He thought if he tended our fields, Simon could spend time with Mr. Klobentz and his crew. There's plenty to decide. If we want any changes made from the original barn layout, now's the time. And Simon needs to direct the men who are patching and painting the foundation and repairing other damage from the fire."

Setting the fresh pot on the stove, Julia crossed her arms over her apron. "Seth harvested our entire crop after finishing his own, without sons to help him, I might add."

Hannah lined up six more potatoes on the table. "A son would've been nice, but I'm sure he wouldn't trade sweet Phoebe for a dozen boys." She selected the next potato to peel.

Julia dropped the coffee mug she was rinsing. It shattered on the cast iron sink bottom.

"Is your arthritis very bad today, sister? If your hands are troubling you, I'll wash those cups after I put these spuds on to boil."

"No, I'll do the cups myself. My hands are no worse than usual. The therapy seems to be helping a bit." Julia cast Hannah a wilting look. "I'm a little curious. You noticed my brother-in-law's absence around the house since the fire. And you are interested enough to inquire about his health. Yet when the man *is* around, you're snappish or act like you've got a thorn in your foot or a mosquito bite where you can't scratch."

Hannah concentrated on her task and attacked another hapless potato zealously. "If you're referring to my shopping trip last week with the girls, I must admit I was overly hot and tired that day. Please pass along my apology to Seth for my rudeness. But in general, I believe I treat Simon's brother with Christian charity and patience."

"Patience and charity might be sufficient for most people, but I'd gotten the idea enough had transpired that he might expect a little affection too," Julia said, tossing the pieces of broken mug into the wastebasket.

"Then I'm afraid you would be mistaken." Hannah carried the bowl of potatoes to the sink to wash.

Julia dried her hands on the towel with more fervor than necessary.

"Then I'm afraid you'll have to apologize to him yourself. I'm done being the referee between two stubborn mules." She threw the towel down on the counter and limped from the room.

Hannah was speechless. *Talk about being snappish.* The shock of the fire and stress of preparing for the barn raising must have frayed Julia's nerves.

As much as possible on a busy farm, Hannah tried to steer clear of her sister's path. She tended her flock and did her share of household chores while keeping a low profile. With the barn gone, hauled away to salvage and landfill, Hannah no longer had a workroom. Spinning wool or working at her loom had always boosted her spirits. Now her only retreat was her bedroom, which was much too hot and stuffy during late July.

With the enormous project fast approaching, Hannah found little time for private contemplation anyway. By the time she reached her room, she usually had enough energy only for prayers before her head hit the pillow. She didn't inquire about Seth Miller after that tense day in the kitchen and also tried not to think about the man. She wasn't quite so successful with the latter.

At long last, the day of the barn raising arrived with blue skies, a gentle breeze, and not a single cloud in sight. By dawn, a few cars and a steady stream of buggies had pulled up their lane. Matthew directed newcomers as to where to park and where to tie up horses. Several round hay stanchions had been set up where horses could eat their fill all day. Henry also carried buckets of water for the equine guests.

No one knew how many people would show up, but by seven o'clock at least two hundred were already milling around the Miller farm. More would come as soon as chores or necessary errands were finished. The bishop asked for silent prayers once the master builder indicated he was ready to start. Simon probably prayed for an injury-free day, with nothing more than splinters or a few smashed thumbs to contend with. Mr. Klobentz probably asked for the mortise and tenon joints to fit together without much shaving and pounding with the sledgehammer. Hannah asked that she could serve her family at the work frolic without too many thoughts about Seth. Soon she wouldn't need to worry about running into him around every corner or twist in the path.

The family that hosted the last preaching service brought over the church wagon. Hannah helped the women set the benches under a large tent where lunch would be served. It wasn't going to rain, so not everyone would have to crowd underneath.

Julia and Simon had rented the chow wagon usually used for weddings that was filled with dishes, trays, and disposable utensils. Food arrived with almost every buggy and car, donated by the workers and other local folk. Hannah and Emma organized young girls to carry cold food to the ice chests in the cellar and nonperishables to the milk house until lunchtime.

Once the steady stream of newcomers slowed, Hannah was able to relax awhile and watch the first walls being raised into place. While some men pushed, others guided with long poles or pulled on ropes from the opposite side. It took at least eighty men to lift the load-bearing center wall, as Mr. Klobentz barked orders in both *Deutsch* and English. Once it was standing, men with sledgehammers drove in oak pegs to anchor the wall, while other carpenters erected braces for support.

Ants in an anthill toiled with no greater harmony and efficiency. Hannah marveled at how quietly the men, other than Mr. Klobentz, worked. Women at a quilting bee had far more things to say. The men were organized into teams, each led by a member of the professional barn crew. With the skeletal frames preassembled by the crew, the teams hoisted wall after wall into place. Hannah watched with fascination as the first and second floors went up and floor joists were laid. Just as Julia called the ladies to set out lunch, Hannah caught sight of Seth clambering like a tree squirrel to set the first roof rafter on the center beam.

A table was set up with basins of water where the men could wash. Then the women loaded the rest of the tables with chicken, meatloaf, roast beef, vegetables, and date-nut pudding for dessert. Straw hats, tool belts, and an occasional English ball cap were left around the barn foundation as the men broke for lunch in shifts. The work on the barn never stopped. As Hannah scooped mashed potatoes onto tray after tray, she wondered how the men would find the right straw hat when they got back.

It took more than two hours to feed the workers, after which the women enjoyed their own meal as the barn materialized before their eyes. Once back to work in the blazing sun, the men passed around a water jug rather than climb down from the rafters for a drink.

Late afternoon was a drowsy time of day for everyone but the builders. Heat shimmered above the metal rooftops, the breeze all but disappeared, and even the birds and insects were too warm to make noise. Women sipped lemonade or dozed in lawn chairs under the sun canopy. Mothers with babies stretched out on quilts under the trees to nap. A few children continued to play in the sunshine, their arms and bare feet already brown as walnut shells.

With the cold foods packed away and the last of the lunch mess cleaned up, Julia went to the front room couch for a much-needed rest. Hannah headed for the shade of a weeping willow with an old patchwork quilt. Her *mamm*'s handiwork had been repaired so many times it was now a bizarre hodgepodge of shapes and colors.

Hannah was glad that this particular tree, away from the main activity yet still in sight of the barn, had gone unclaimed. But she didn't remain alone for long.

Phoebe Miller, barefoot in a soft blue dress and organdy *kapp*, marched across the grass, carrying a plastic sack. The sight of the approaching child filled Hannah with both joy and sorrow. It had been three weeks since she'd seen Phoebe, and the sting of loss still felt fresh. Hannah forced a bright smile. "Hi, Phoebe."

"Hullo, Aunt Hannah," she said, plopping down on the quilt.

Hannah swallowed the lump that had formed in her throat from hearing the affectionate moniker and the sound of the child's voice. "Did you eat a good lunch?"

She shook her head then said, "*Jah,* I ate a hot dog and potato salad." She spoke in *Deutsch,* the language of an Amish home.

"I made that potato salad," Hannah said, hooking a thumb toward her chest. "I hope you found it satisfactory."

Phoebe nodded enthusiastically as she scooted closer on the quilt. "It was yummy." She crossed her legs Indian-style and tucked her dress discretely underneath. Hannah could smell the raspberry scent of her shampoo.

Without warning, Phoebe dumped out the contents of her bag. White flashcards scattered everywhere as the girl put forth a great effort to mix them up. "Will you practice words with me, Aunt Hannah?"

Again, the enviable title. Hannah's throat tightened as air squeezed from her lungs. "I don't really have time to—"

"Please? I want to show you how many words I learned last week." She gazed up with her incredibly expressive dark eyes.

What could she say? That she was no longer interested in her? That she didn't care about her readiness to start school? But revisiting those wonderful afternoons when Hannah still had hopes for a life with Seth would be painful.

Phoebe turned all the cards face up, waiting for a reply.

"All right, but just for a while," Hannah said. "Then I'll need to check on the women in the house." Hannah leaned back on her elbows while the world's most precious child selected a card to hold up.

Phoebe spoke clearly and confidently, card after card, asking about the few she didn't know.

Despite the fact she would soon leave the Ohio Valley behind, and despite the fact Phoebe might be approaching *Rumschpringe* by the time she saw her again, Hannah enjoyed their final language lesson.

When Phoebe finished the pile, she curled into a ball like a cat and fell asleep on Hannah's skirt. In the lazy summer afternoon, Hannah allowed herself a few last dreams of motherhood. She stroked the child's back, humming a lullaby she had learned a long time ago.

Yes, she would miss Phoebe. Almost as much as she would miss her father...the father who from his position high in the roof rafters had just spotted his daughter with Hannah.

Hannah might have been surprised to know that when Seth saw the heartwarming sight, he lost his balance. If not for another worker grabbing his arm, Seth would have surely fallen from his footholds.

But one broken leg might have prevented two broken hearts.

NINETEEN

The view that greeted Hannah from her window that morning filled her heart with joy—a brand new barn.

By four o'clock on Saturday, ninety percent of the barn had been finished. Many people stayed until dark, picking up litter and construction debris. Mr. Klobentz's crew came back on Monday to install barn doors and build the corncribs and animal stalls. Then Simon hired a team of professional Amish housepainters. They finished the job quickly without Simon depending on friends to drop by or taking more time from chores or from his duties as deacon. And their price had been fair. Now that Seth had planted the second crop of hay, Simon could harvest the sweet corn. And it was time to start picking and canning the vegetable garden.

But for a few minutes, Hannah did nothing but enjoy the view of the rolling countryside of Holmes County. She would miss these hills when she returned to the flatter plains of eastern Pennsylvania. Sheep grazing on steep terrain always reminded her of the pastoral scenes in her picture Bible as a child.

Never grow too fond of things of this world. God's greatest creation is the hereafter.

Her grandmother's favorite expression reminded Hannah that she had grown far too fond of a dark-haired man with a gentle kiss and calloused hands, and of his doe-eyed child whose voice sounded like music to Hannah's ears.

At least back in Lancaster County she would have the memories of what had been—auction day in Kidron, ice cream cones in Seth's buggy, talking by the river under the ancient sycamore, seeing his eyes sparkle across the supper table. But she hoped she would never eat another haystack dinner and be reminded of the evening spent with a couple just beginning their life together.

Although she'd been reluctant to move to Ohio and slow to adjust to Simon's ways, Hannah had come to love living in a large family. Her years alone had made her reclusive and sullen—Julia had been right about that. She loved the energy of the children and the camaraderie of a sister. Even Simon's crustiness had grown more dear since his apology last week.

Not that the blame had solely been his. Hannah prayed she could mend her ways once back with Thomas and his bride-to-be. And she prayed God would allow her to find peace at last. But first she had to get through today, and that wouldn't be easy.

She had packed last night before bed except for what she planned to leave behind for Emma and Leah. These were items from her own hope chest that she no longer needed. She hoped the girls could make use of them and remember their aunt fondly. Her trunk of books had been hauled from under the porch and waited next to the driveway under a tarp. Fortunately Simon and his sons had never moved it to the loft as planned, not after the backbreaking escapade with the old plow. Otherwise it too would have burned in the fire.

She'd arranged a ride to the train station with Mr. and Mrs. Lee, who were going to Akron to see a ballgame. Hannah would split the cost of gas despite their protests even if she had to hide the money in the glove box.

Mrs. Lee had tried to talk her into staying, as had Simon, Emma, Leah, Matthew, and even shy Henry. Only Julia hadn't broached the subject with her. Was she glad to see her thorny sibling leave?

Hannah didn't think so, but she didn't have to wait long to discover Julia's true feelings.

Her sister was sitting at the table when Hannah lugged her over-stuffed totebag and purse downstairs. "All set to go?" Julia asked over the rim of her coffee cup.

"*Jah,* if Mathew can bring down my suitcase, I would be much obliged. It's too heavy for Simon's back. Oh, and I left some things wrapped in tissue for Leah and Emma on my bed. Their names are on the packages. If you could make sure they find them after I'm gone."

Julia looked shocked. "You're not planning to tell them good-bye?"

"Of course I am," said Hannah, "but I would prefer to avoid an emotional scene, on my part, when they open the gifts. They're linens from my hope chest that I want your girls to have." Hannah released a sigh.

"Then tell them yourself when you say goodbye. I told you before I wasn't a go-between with you and Seth. And I won't make things easy for you with your nieces either."

Hannah was taken aback. She set her totebag down with a thud. "Do you really think this is easy for me?" she asked. Blood began to pound in her temples. *Why was Julia acting like this—so mean-spirited?*

"*Jah,* I think it must be easy or you wouldn't be running back to Lancaster without trying very hard."

"I have tried, Julia. I've attempted to fit in and make a life for myself, but I have failed."

"You call this failure?" Julia struggled to her feet, using the table for support.

"Wouldn't you? I've practically been shunned by the elders and gossiped about among the women. What would you call it?"

"I call it everyday life. The elders stated their dissatisfaction over a matter, and as I hear it, it's all forgotten. As for the women of our district, women talk when given the opportunity—here, in Lancaster, probably even in Alaska—especially when you give them no chance to like you or even know you. You've been almost a hermit and yet wonder why people are curious." Julia stopped the anticipated protest with an upraised palm. "Yes, you had good reasons to stay close to home or up in your loft—the main reason being me—but that doesn't change human nature."

Hannah nodded her head in agreement, not wanting to disagree. Would their memories of this parting be of another argument?

"And remember, the ladies were very friendly during the barn raising. Those who didn't have a chance to speak to you personally asked about you, not maliciously but with kindness. Some wanted to help you rebuild your workroom. Many left donations with me toward purchasing another loom, and several who own sheep said they'll donate wool from their next shearing so you can fill your order with Mrs. Dunn." Julia's shoulders shook with frustration.

Hannah's mouth dropped open. "I didn't know this. Why didn't you tell me?"

"Because it wouldn't have done any good. When Hannah Brown makes up her mind, there is no changing it." Julia Miller exhibited a rare loss of temper.

Hannah exhaled through her nose like a peeved hen. "That's right, because we both know there's more to my decision than not being the most popular woman in Winesburg. Seth has done everything he can not to cross my path for the past two weeks."

"And you've been a basket of cuddly kittens with him?" Julia braced herself with both hands flat on the table. "You practically spray him with bug repellent if he comes too close."

Hannah looked into Julia's brown eyes, hoping for a bit of consolation—maybe a hint of compassion. When she didn't find the mercy she sought, Hannah dropped her gaze to the floor. "I can't be near him. Feeling as I do about what I ruined between us, I can't go back to being just another shirttail relative."

Julia's expression softened somewhat. "You assume that I don't understand, but I do…perfectly. You're a coward, so go on home. I'll see you at Thomas and Catherine's wedding in December. You are afraid, Hannah—afraid of the past, the present, and the future. Life doesn't treat cowards kindly, and that's why you struggle so much." Julia's words finally ran out and an uncomfortable silence filled the room for a full minute before she asked, "Whatever happened to 'Be still and know that I am Lord?'"

Hannah's eyes filled with tears that flowed down her cheeks unchecked. Her stomach ached, and her throat constricted painfully. "I'm sorry, Julia. Please forgive me. I wish things could have been different." She wrapped her arms around her sister's shoulders and squeezed tightly, for once not mindful of the arthritis. This hug would have to last a long time. "I'm sorry I couldn't be different."

Julia hugged back more fiercely than her disability should have allowed. Tears streaked her face also. "Someday you'll stop running. I just wish it would have been here and now. You will realize you can't hide from yourself. Wherever you go, you take yourself along. I thank God for the wonderful person you are. I only wish you would."

Hannah broke from the embrace. The kitchen felt too hot and airless. She thought she might be sick. Thoughts and emotions tumbled through her mind. *Why can't I be allowed to make one decision for myself?* Picking up her totebag and purse, Hannah headed for the door.

"The girls are in the vegetable patch, picking snap peas and beans. The boys should be painting the paddock fence, and Simon is probably still raking nails from the dirt near the barn," Julia said wearily.

Hannah didn't look back as she walked out the door. She couldn't. This was difficult enough without guilt making it impossible.

Both of her nieces stopped picking and straightened their spines when Hannah approached the garden. With their stiff postures and mournful faces, they resembled soldiers condemned to the gallows.

"So you're really leaving us?" Emma asked, resentment etching her words.

"I must, Emma, though it does burden my heart," Hannah said, glancing between the two. Leah had started to cry. Hannah wouldn't be able to look in that direction again. She much preferred to deal with anger.

"Now that I'm done with school, I thought I could become your apprentice in the wool business, and one day, I would become your partner." Emma stared with blue eyes as cool as the creek in spring.

"I would've liked that if certain things had worked out differently."

"Do you mean with Uncle Seth?" Emma asked.

Hannah was mortified. *Was everything so obvious to all but her?*

"*Jah,* he's a big part of my decision."

Responding to Hannah's surprised expression, Emma replied, "I'm not a baby anymore, aunt. I have eyes that can see what's going on."

"What is going on?" Leah asked, rubbing her face and smearing garden dirt across her cheeks.

"You'll understand when you're older," Emma said, pulling Leah to her side.

Hannah swallowed hard and tried to feign cheeriness. "Since you have such good eyes, I hope you can find the presents I left on my bed for both of you. They are for when you're older and about to have your own homes. In your case, Emma, that's not too far down the road." Hannah's forced smile was starting to grow painful.

"I want to live here with *mamm* and *daed* forever," Leah wailed, starting to cry again.

"Well, that's okay too. You can use them right here at home," Hannah said.

Leah nodded, wiping her nose. Her face was taking on a comic appearance from the streaks of dirt.

Emma tried to wipe Leah's cheeks with her apron. "*Danki,* Aunt Hannah. We're going to miss you 'round here. It won't be the same."

The brave young woman's voice cracked, and she too began to sniffle.

"And I will miss both of you. More than you know," whispered Hannah. It was unanimous—no dry eyes in the bean patch.

Hannah couldn't take another minute of sadness. She pulled her nieces against her chest in an affectionate hug and then picked up her bags and marched to the paddock. There she found Matthew and Henry whitewashing the soot-stained fence.

"Boys, I'm leaving now. Thanks for all your help. I'll see you before you know it at your Uncle Thomas' wedding." It sounded like a practiced speech from a door-to-door saleswoman, but it was all Hannah could manage. She kissed each one on his forehead, which triggered a flood of color up their necks. "Mind your *mamm* and *daed*," she said as she headed toward the barn.

Her brother-in-law was leaning on his long-handled rake. A large pile of rubbish sat beside his wheelbarrow. Simon smiled as she approached. "Ready to go then?" he asked. "Do you want me to take you over to the Lees'?"

"No, they're picking me up any minute now." Hannah noticed how gaunt and aged his face had become. The past few weeks had taken their toll.

He set the rake atop the wheelbarrow and dusted off his hands. "I'll help you load that trunk of yours into their van. It's getting lighter every time I lift it." One corner of his mouth turned up.

Hannah shook her head. "Please don't leave your work. Mr. Lee and I can handle the trunk and—" She forced herself to meet his eye. "I'm having a hard time saying goodbye. Let's just get this over with."

Simon stretched out his thin, weathered hand. "You can always change your mind, Hannah, and come back. You remember that. You belong with us."

Hannah grasped his dry fingers but on impulse threw her arms around his neck and delivered a hug. "Goodbye, Simon. I'll see you in December."

"Oh, my. Had I known you could squeeze my back like that I could've saved a lot of money with the chiropractor." When she released him, his face was beet red as he tugged down his black vest.

"Perhaps spine adjustments should be my new business venture."

"No, you're much too good with sheep." Simon smiled, and Hannah hurried from the barnyard. *Of all the people I never thought I'd miss.*

Mr. and Mrs. Lee were pulling into the drive when Hannah reached the shade where her trunk and suitcase had been set. Mr. Lee backed his van right up to the trunk. The four *kinner* were nowhere to be seen. They had probably gone inside the house, no fonder of long farewells than she.

"All set, Mrs. Brown?" asked Mr. Lee, opening the back of the van.

"Yes, let's be off." Hannah grabbed one handle of the trunk; he took the other; and with a minimum of grunts, they stowed the trunk inside.

Mrs. Lee studied her curiously. "Are you all right, Hannah? You look white as paper."

"I'm okay," she said. "Saying goodbye to six relatives is never quick or easy." Hannah's false bravado fooled no one.

"Are you sure this is what you want to do? Travel back to Pennsylvania before you've decided what to do with your flock? Maybe after the last harvest you'll have time to think things through."

Hannah clenched down on her back molars and stared out the side window. *Not only my Amish community but now the English world is telling me what to do?* However, she said nothing. Her throat had swelled shut as though she'd swallowed a bee. She tried focusing on the scenery as Mr. Lee pulled onto the highway.

Instead of enjoying the trees, ripe fields, and distant hills, Hannah's gaze landed on the sheep that were moving along the ridge. Maybe it was her imagination, but half the flock turned to glare at the passing vehicle.

Hannah dabbed at her nose, drew a deep breath, and gathered her courage. "We have plenty of time before my train departs, and seeing that your ballgame isn't until the evening, might we make one quick stop before we leave Winesburg?"

Mrs. Lee looked at her in the car's rearview mirror. "I believe we can manage that. In fact, I was about to suggest it. Where would you like to go?"

"To Seth Miller's farm, around the corner on Route 158."

A grin deepened the lines by Mrs. Lee's mouth as she began digging around in her purse. The van drove down Seth's road and within minutes turned into his yard. Seth's property adjoined Simon's along the back property line.

"Looks like he's getting ready to go somewhere too," Mr. Lee said.

Seth was leading his mare from the paddock toward his buggy. Hannah noticed he had good clothes on instead of his work duds. Phoebe, with her doll clutched in both hands, stood near the buggy. She waved as the van pulled up the drive.

Seth approached the driver's window. "Good morning," he said, tipping his hat to Mrs. Lee, and then peering into the backseat. "You're leaving already? Phoebe and I were just coming to talk to you, Hannah." He was practically shouting. "Julia said your train wasn't leaving until this afternoon. We almost missed you."

Phoebe stretched up on tiptoes to see inside the van.

Hannah felt trapped in the backseat. "That's why I asked Mr. Lee to stop—so I could say goodbye properly...and ask you a question."

You're a coward, Hannah Brown...You keep running away and hiding...When will you learn you can't hide from yourself?

Julia's words tumbled around her head like a jump rope jingle. Yet Hannah knew every word was true.

Mrs. Lee plopped her overly large handbag on the back of the seat. "I found it," she said, pulling out her cell phone. "Hannah, we've got to run back to the house. I forgot my checkbook, and I'm not exactly sure where it is. Why don't you just call us when you're ready to head to the station? Just push the green button twice, and it'll ring at our house." She shoved the phone into Hannah's hand without pausing for a reply.

Seth opened the van's back door and stood waiting like a valet. There was nothing she could do but get out with her face turning redder by the minute.

He slammed the door shut, and the Lees left as though in a great big hurry.

"There's something I've got to say to you, Hannah Brown," Seth said in a quiet, controlled voice.

"Me too, Aunt Hannah." Even Phoebe's words sounded well starched.

Hannah glanced from one to the other. "All right, but I came here before you found me, so I'm going first."

Seth crossed his arms. His daughter mimicked the gesture.

Hannah wasn't deterred. "I'd like a business partnership with you, Seth Miller. It's too hot to move the flock back to Pennsylvania in a crowded truck. I don't want any sheep to die because of my indecision regarding where I want to live. Besides, they seem to have adjusted nicely to the sparse Ohio grass." She took a quick breath. "Seeing that you're fond of sheep too, and seeing you would like your own flock…we could move mine to your place, along with Turnip, and then you can buy more animals. Once your financial investment matches mine, we'll split all profits down the middle." She exhaled with a whoosh. "Well, what do you think?" she asked, glancing into his sea blue eyes for the first time.

"No," he replied succinctly.

~

Seth stared at the confusing, obtuse, green-eyed woman and had to tamp down his temper. With how he felt, a long-distance business partnership was out of the question for two reasons. First, he would be here in Ohio with the work of feeding, watering, shearing, and doctoring sick animals, besides keeping up with his regular farm chores. She would be back in Lancaster on her *bruder*'s farm, perhaps sitting by a creek reading a book and sipping lemonade. And second, he didn't want a business partner. He wanted a wife. He was in love with her.

"Just no? That's it?" she asked. It was her turn to cross her arms.

"No, that's not it," he said. "Like I told you, I've got plenty to say, but I'll start with I love you."

Her confusing, obtuse green eyes grew round as an owl's.

"I'm not interested in a partnership. I want a wife. And not just any wife—I want you." He started to grin as his words tumbled down like someone shaking an apple tree. Now that he had finally started, there would be no stopping him. "If there's something you don't want to talk about, something from your past, that's okay with me. We're beginning fresh here, the three of us. And we don't need to rehash what's done and gone." He slipped an arm around his daughter's shoulders and waited for Hannah's response. Either way, at least he'd spoken his mind.

"And you waited until *now* to tell me this, Seth Miller? When I'm on my way to the train station?" Her brows knitted together, but she couldn't hide her smile.

"You hadn't gotten on the train yet, Hannah. I still had time. Anyway, I held off because most of the time, those seemed like the last three words you wanted to hear."

Hannah shook her head in agreement. "I did act like that, didn't I?"

"Can I say something now?" Phoebe asked with near urgency.

"I suppose you'd better," Hannah said.

Phoebe looked up at her father first and then said in her sweet voice. "My *daed* says I should thank you for helping me talk again and teaching me English. So *danki*, Aunt Hannah." The child grew suddenly bashful and leaned into Seth's side. "And I wanted to say that I love you too—as much as I love Aunt Julia." She glanced from one adult to the other. "And that's a lot!"

Seth and Hannah laughed, and Seth felt the tension finally drain from his spine. "You go up and sit on the porch swing for a couple of minutes," he said. "Aunt Hannah might have something to say to me and might like a little privacy."

His child bolted for the house. Seth watched her run, as did Hannah, and then he focused solely on the beautiful woman standing before him. "During breakfast this morning, all Phoebe talked about was 'Aunt Hannah said this' and 'Aunt Hannah did that.' Now that you got her started, I can't stop her from talking...about you."

Hannah's lower lip start to quiver, but Seth continued, "When Julia told us you were leaving, Phoebe started crying and said we needed to stop you. I told her we would try. She loves you and I love you. I should've told you awhile ago and taken my chances."

He inhaled a breath. "I can't stop you from moving, but I am here with what I hope is a better offer." He cleared his throat and gazed into eyes that seemed to become greener by the minute. "Hannah Brown, will you marry me?"

She placed her forefinger on her cheek as though to ponder the question. Luckily her decision didn't take long. "*Jah,* I think I will," she said, her face glowing. "In fact, I think I'd love to."

Seth drew her into his arms and hugged her hard enough to bruise ribs.

Hannah didn't seem to mind. "I love you, Seth Miller," she said while buried against his shirt.

She turned up her face, and he kissed her with every ounce of passion he had. Even though he'd once loved a woman as much, he had never loved a woman more. He grew giddy with joy and began kissing the top of her head, her nose, and her lips. When he managed to knock her *kapp* askew, Phoebe came running from the porch at full speed.

"Is she staying, *daed*?" she yelled on the approach.

"She is," he said, and swept his daughter off the ground.

"I am," Hannah agreed, and wrapped her arms around them both.

"Then could we make more cards, Aunt Hannah? I already know all the ones I have," Phoebe declared.

So like a child to reduce things to simple basics, but Seth's heart swelled thinking they would finally become a family. He would have Hannah for his wife, and Phoebe would gain a new mother.

His years of loneliness were over as they stood in his yard wrapped in a three-way hug. Constance would be happy for them. And he was pretty sure Adam would be too. And God might one day bless their union with more *kinner*.

As Hannah tightened her hold on his neck, he kissed her soft pink lips tenderly.

"Hey, that's enough kissing," Phoebe said with a giggle.

Seth stroked the back of his daughter's head. "No, my dear girl, the kissing is just getting started."

Digging around in her apron pocket, Hannah pulled out Mrs. Lee's cell phone. "Do you remember what she said to do?" She studied the phone curiously. "I'd better tell her I plan to miss that train and they can get going to the ballgame."

Seth pressed the green button twice. "When she answers just say you're staying—that you're never leaving. Oh, and when they get a chance could they bring back that heavy trunk and leave it here?"

"Oh, dear, my trunk." She looked momentarily chagrined. "I've caused a big fuss, haven't I? For Simon and Julia, the Lees, and you and Phoebe."

Seth pulled her to his chest and cradled her head. "Not half the fuss if we'd had to go to Lancaster and drag you back."

Phoebe clung not to his pant leg but to Hannah's skirt. "Yeah, if we had to go that far, you'd really be in trouble…because we love you."

The words of a child…simple, to the point, and so true.

TWENTY

Simon had been given one simple task to do by his sister-in-law, and he was failing badly. He had been asked to stand by the loading ramp of the livestock trailer and shoo the sheep inside. The English truck driver remained inside the trailer, chewing a wad of gum and looking in need of a good night's sleep. Hannah, Seth, and Emma worked roundup in the pasture, herding the flock toward the gate. Turnip was having more luck than the humans heading the sheep in the right direction. Seth had erected temporary fencing to form a chute to funnel the critters from the pasture gate to the truck. Matthew and Henry had positioned themselves outside the fence to prod them along.

In Simon's opinion, the plan wasn't working. Only three unhappy ewes stood inside the truck looking down on him. If he wasn't vigilant, they would devise a way to escape, and he'd be left with none. Simon swept off his hat, ran a hand through his hair, and mopped his brow. Today was awfully warm and humid, even for August.

He gazed skyward for a moment and considered praying for help with the sheep. Instead he whispered words of praise and thanks to finally have made peace with Hannah. "Always be humble and gentle. Be patient with each other, making allowance for each other's faults because of your love." The words of Ephesians 4:2 soothed his soul.

His heart had ached when Hannah had left with the Lees. He felt guilty because he had failed her, his wife, and most of all, his God. Pride and stubbornness had soured him, and he was humbled by how easily he had veered off the path.

One fat ewe with her two lambs trailing behind trotted toward him and then marched up the ramp with a gentle prod. He reached down to pat the lamb's head and was rewarded with a pleasant *baaa*. And Simon smelled nothing other than sweet, clean country air. These sheep had finally grown on him. He would miss not seeing them in the field when he lifted the bedroom shade at first light. Their early warning racket had earned them a permanent place in his heart.

Simon shaded his eyes to watch an amusing sight as Hannah and Seth sparred with a particularly determined ram. Hannah with her crook and Seth with a long-handled broom goaded the animal to the gate, but no amount of persuasion could get him into the chute. Despite their predicament, Hannah looked cheerful as she dodged left and right with her *kapp* strings flying.

She certainly had surprised them with her decision to stay. By the time he'd consoled his sobbing, brokenhearted wife and disappointed daughters, Seth's buggy had ambled up his drive, bringing Hannah and her suitcases back home...and without the trunk. He didn't ask where that had ended up. He was happy just to have her back.

A business partnership between his *bruder* and Julia's sister...the more he thought about it, the better the idea sounded. They were two of a kind, as Julia had tried to tell him. Both were ambitious, single-minded, and resourceful, but they were also kind and gentle, and loved the Lord.

It was a good foundation to build a business on, although Simon had secretly hoped the flock would remain at his place instead of relocating to Seth's. He had four children to help with chores—two of which loved sheep. Hannah would have to take the buggy or walk the swampy, insect-infested path to Seth's to tend them. But Simon had said nothing and asked no questions. For once he let Hannah work something out for herself.

"Pa, get ready!" Matthew called. "Here comes a whole bunch."

Simon stopped daydreaming and saw fifteen or twenty sheep charging down the chute toward him. The stubborn ram led the stampede, many of his ewes following behind with their offspring. Simon readied his broom to keep them headed up the ramp. "Wake up, Mr. Taylor. We've got customers," he called to the driver. The animals charged up the ramp where Mr. Taylor herded them into pens.

Soon Hannah, Seth, and Turnip rounded the last of the reluctant into the chute. Seth, with Hannah behind him, scouted on horseback to make sure no stragglers had wandered off. Turnip led the way.

Simon had a couple of minutes to pat some woolly heads and rub a few wet noses.

"Wha'cha doing, *daed?*" Henry asked. They boy looked more worried than curious.

"Just saying goodbye, that's all." He petted one ewe with grass stains around her mouth.

"I didn't think you liked sheep," Henry said, digging his fists deep into his pockets.

"Always remember, son, it's not just a woman's prerogative to change her mind. A man can too."

Henry nodded and climbed onto the top fence rail. "I saw Uncle Seth kissing Aunt Hannah when they thought nobody was lookin'."

"Is that right?" Simon murmured, and finally the mystery of why Hannah was still moving her sheep to Seth's was solved. "Well, I imagine that's their business and not ours. Why don't you check to see if your *mamm* can use your help?"

The boy jumped down and sprinted toward the house as Simon spotted Seth and Hannah coming his way. They were holding hands while Seth's horse trotted alongside them.

"Could we have a word with you, Simon?" Seth asked. They dropped hands but both continued to smile.

"*Jah,* I suppose you've got something to tell me." He gave his white beard a pull.

"I've asked the widow to marry me...well, at least to court me to see if she can tolerate my quirks for the rest of her life." Seth settled his hat on the back of his head to block the sun's glare.

Simon glanced from one to the other. "And what did my sister-in-law have to say about that proposal?" He couldn't stop himself from grinning.

"She said she'd give courting a try, and if we're still speaking to each other in December, maybe we can throw a double wedding with Thomas."

Hannah was finger-combing tangles from the mare's mane and appeared not to be paying much attention.

Seth added, "I'm hoping to talk her into an October wedding, right after the wheat harvest and before we grind the field corn."

Hannah stopped grooming the horse. "Do we have your blessing, Simon?" she asked, not looking him in the eye.

"You don't need my blessing, Hannah, but you certainly have it," he said. "I hope God blesses you both for the rest of your lives."

Seth snaked an arm around Hannah's waist. "He has blessed me already."

The clanging of the farm bell broke the tender moment. "Ma says to come eat lunch or she'll give it to the pigs," Henry called.

The three laughed and started toward the house. Hannah said to Simon, "I'll bet Julia didn't really say it like that."

Simon picked up their pace. "I wouldn't be so sure. She's been in a right fearsome mood this week, and now I know why."

~

The cacophony from cicada, crickets, and tree frogs made conversation almost impossible on their walk after dinner a few days later. Seth was holding Hannah's hand as though he expected her to bolt at any minute.

"I'm not going to run off, Seth. You can lessen your grip a tad," Hannah said.

Seth loosened his grip only slightly. "I'm not taking any chances. Not till I get you wed." His blue eyes looked dark as the midnight sky in the fading light.

"It's almost dark. Where are we heading?" she asked conversationally. As long as they were together and alone, she didn't care if they stood around in the spidery pump house.

Since the announcement of their courtship, the children constantly peppered them with questions, especially Emma. That girl wanted to know everything from whose farm would host the wedding to what Hannah planned to wear and what happened when she became a "double" aunt. At least since their engagement, Julia no longer shook her head and clucked her tongue whenever Hannah was in earshot.

In fact Julia actually smiled at her several times. Her only verbal response on the subject had been: "I told you good things happen when a person shows a little trust. Sometimes you have to step back and allow God to work His miracles."

For Hannah, having Seth and Phoebe become her family was a miracle indeed. Every time Hannah thought about it, her stomach turned fluttery and she got the urge to sing.

"We are heading to your favorite spot by the creek, and I've got my flashlight for the walk back," he said. "Since you're so distracted, Mrs. Brown, you probably couldn't find the way on your own." He released her hand and draped his arm loosely around her shoulders.

"*Jah,* that's true. I've got a lot on my mind, Mr. Miller."

"Hope you're not getting cold feet." His words were soft and gentle.

"I'm not, and I hope you don't either after you hear me out."

Hannah had made up her mind that keeping secrets between two people in love was no way to begin a relationship. He had said it didn't matter and she needn't talk about painful things from the past. But it mattered to her. Her fears had hampered her at every turn. And she had no further desire to be afraid.

They reached the creek that eventually wound its way into the Tuscarawas River. Moss and matted leaves from many past autumns covered the banks. The trunk of an uprooted dead tree made a fine settee for meditation or conversation. Seth sat on the log and pulled Hannah into his arms.

She kissed him and then pulled from his embrace. "Last month wasn't the first time I had been warned by the elders that I might be shunned," she said without preamble. Hannah didn't believe in inching your way into cold water; she preferred to jump into the deep end and get it over with. "Once in Lancaster, I stood up during a congregational meeting and voiced my opinion. Back home, same as in this district, women never do such things. They let their men voice all the opinions as stated in 1 Corinthians 14:34: 'Women should be silent during the church meetings. It is not proper for them to speak.'" Hannah walked two paces away and wiped her palms down her skirt.

"What was the problem that had you so riled up?" Seth asked quietly.

"They were discussing the *Ordnung* for upgrading milking operations in such a way that might allow Grade-A certification for the dairy farmers' milk. Some of the men didn't wish to even consider the new equipment, even though it ran on propane and not electricity. Batteries would be required only for timers and such, and those could be recharged with a solar panel." Hannah glanced back at Seth, who was swatting a mosquito but otherwise seemed unfazed. "A couple of my friends," she continued, "wouldn't be able to stay in dairy farming if they couldn't get a better price than what was being paid by cheese producers."

Seth waited for more of the story, and when none was forthcoming, he said, "That's it? You stood up and voiced your opinion in public?"

Hannah nodded solemnly.

Seth appeared to be fighting back a grin.

"You find my shame amusing, Seth Miller?"

"Not at all. I just imagined you were hiding something far worse." Now he did smile. "I briefly pictured some *Englischer* had seen you wearing shorts, a baseball cap, makeup, and red nail polish at a Phillies ball game. You had been cheering loudly, and they reported *that* back to the ministerial brethren."

Hannah shook her head. "Oh, Seth."

"Or you had cut your hair really short on a whim after sipping some of your pa's apple jack."

She faced him with arms akimbo. "You are truly impossible. How you managed to have a child as angelic as Phoebe is a testimony to Constance's fine qualities."

Seth rose from the log and encircled her in his arms. He brushed a string of kisses across her forehead and down the bridge of her nose. "We'd best get married right away. If we wait until December, you're bound to find out Phoebe is no angel." His lips finally found hers with a sweet kiss.

Hannah allowed herself to be enfolded by his embrace. It felt so good to be cared for, to be part of a couple again.

"I've got my own confession," he said close to her ear.

She stepped away and walked to the log. After seating herself primly she patted the spot next to her. "Come and tell me what you've done." She tried to act serious.

He ran a hand through his hair. "I had a talk with my daughter. She had one of those bed-wetting episodes last week. I thought we were all done with that. I've been spending a lot more time with her." He took a seat on the log. "I sat her down and asked what's going on. I told her she didn't have to worry 'bout your taking all my attention. I've got plenty enough for both of you."

Hannah held her breath as he paused in his story. "What did she say?" she asked.

"She started crying and said she was afraid you would leave her… just like her *mamm* did." Seth stared off into the forest.

No cricket chirped nor owl hooted. The woods, almost dark now, were strangely silent as Hannah mulled this over. A shiver ran up her spine, and her breath caught in her throat. *The child really does love me. And so does her father.*

"Oh, Seth, tell her I'm not leaving. Tell her I'm going to stay and be the best wife and mother in Holmes County." Then Hannah remembered Scripture on pride and added in a soft voice, "At least I'm going to give it a try."

Seth pulled her to her feet and into a hug. "Well, that's good enough for us."

She stood wrapped in his arms in the complete darkness. Night sounds encroached from all sides—rustling leaves, a snapping twig, the mournful cry of a nightjar. But Hannah felt safe and secure, and never more loved in all her life.

～

It probably was a good idea Hannah had agreed to an October wedding instead of marrying back in Lancaster with Thomas in December. For one thing, she didn't want to steal an ounce of attention away from Catherine, a first-time bride. Those two would have plenty of guests to plan and provide for. Catherine came from a very large family, and both had many friends. For another reason, Hannah was amazed how many friends and acquaintances she had in Holmes County—all fairly surprising for a hermit.

As soon as the bishop announced their engagement, she'd received lots of cards and notes from well-wishers. She had met many of these women at the barn raising. And almost all of those who had sheep had followed through with donations of wool so she could fulfill her promise to Mrs. Dunn.

These days she and Emma spun on their new wheel in an empty end of the barn loft. A replacement loom would have to wait. With Emma still so eager to embark on an enterprise with her, Hannah didn't know where the new workroom should be. Probably one at each farm would be the best solution.

Hannah had little time to plan for the upcoming wedding. She and Julia, along with help from Emma, Leah, and Phoebe, had their hands full canning the bounty from the garden. Each of the girls had been assigned her own tasks. Seth, Simon, and the boys were cutting, raking, and baling the second hay crop at both farms. As busy as they were, her eldest niece didn't allow an hour to pass without bringing up the event.

"What do you think of this shade of blue for a wedding dress?" Emma held up a plump blueberry about to go into the blanching kettle. Canned blueberries would offer a nice change from apple and peach pies during the winter.

Hannah turned from the stove where she was sterilizing jars. The fruit was a shade of bright purple. "Emma, that's a tad bright for even a first-time bride—totally inappropriate for a widow getting remarried."

Emma popped the rejected berry into her mouth.

"Why don't you two take the buggy to Sugar Creek tomorrow morning?" Julia asked. "I'll be just fine with my other helpers." She patted Leah's and Phoebe's shoulders as they chopped up tomatoes. "Buy some fabric for your dress so we can work on it in the evenings. Otherwise Emma won't give us one quiet moment."

"You're sure you can manage?" asked Hannah.

"I'm sure." Julia looked more relaxed than she had in a long time. The fearsome mood Simon had described hadn't lasted for long. "You girls go out to the garden and pick the rest of the green beans. We might as well finish them before we turn the kitchen into a sty canning sweet corn."

Emma started to complain, but Julia raised her stern eyebrow. "Go, Emma. I wish a private moment with your aunt."

Reluctantly the three left the steamy kitchen with their baskets.

"Goodness, you would think she'd appreciate a breath of cooler air," Julia said.

"She's worried she will miss something. She's growing up fast." Hannah finished trimming the last of the beets to be pickled, thinking about Seth the entire time.

"Too fast," Julia said, drying her hands. She slipped into the chair across from Hannah. "Another month and we will both be Mrs. Miller..."

"They won't be able to tell which of us baked the *good* pie at the potlucks. That should work to my advantage," Hannah teased.

Julia leaned against the chair back. "I'm proud of you, sister. It took guts to go to Seth's instead of the train station, especially with the Lees right there."

Hannah grinned. "At least I would've been able to get away quickly if he'd ordered me off his property."

"True enough, but I knew he wouldn't do that." Julia stretched her hand across the table. "Are you happy, sister? Do you think you can finally find contentment?"

Hannah set down the paring knife and covered Julia's hand with hers. "*Jah,* I am. And I've already found contentment. Seth and Phoebe make me happier than I deserve to be."

Julia shook her head. "You do deserve it. God doesn't expect us to be perfect. Only to not stop trying."

"I will try each day to make Seth proud."

"Keep turning to the Lord in prayer; all help can be found there." She reached for a tablet and pen. "Now, without Emma interrupting every thought and notion we have, let's write down what you want for your wedding luncheon. The whole district will be here, and Simon will probably invite everyone from the barn raising if we don't stop him."

"I know Simon's viewpoint on fires, but I thought we'd roast a pig a couple of days before the wedding."

Julia furrowed her forehead.

"Not *our* sow...I couldn't live with myself, but Seth can buy one from the packinghouse in Kidron."

"Roast pork, it is," Julia said, jotting it down. "How about baked apples? Fried zucchini? Baked beans?"

"*Jah,* and cucumber salad and corn on the cob."

Julia wrote out the menu and then started listing ingredients in the side margin. "Why don't you order the wedding cake in Sugar Creek with Emma? She would love to help pick that out."

"All right, but I'll try not to be gone too long."

Julia nodded as the girls trooped in, their baskets brimming with green beans.

Warmth spread through Hannah's belly. How nice it was to be part of a family.

~

The most spirited member of the family was in true form the next day. All the way to Sugar Creek, Emma chatted about everything under the sun, asked endless questions about the wedding, and dispensed plentiful advice for someone who'd just turned fifteen. But Hannah was glad for the company and for the extra pair of hands. She had far more wool to deliver to A-Stitch-in-Time than anticipated. It had taken thirty minutes and careful packing to fit it into the open wagon.

"What color will you have the women who'll serve the food wear?" Emma asked.

"They can wear any color they please," Hannah answered, enjoying the first streaks of fall color in the maple leaves.

Emma looked disappointed. "What about the wedding dinner in the evening?" she asked. "You're not planning to serve more of the same roast pork and apples, are you?" She sounded scandalized.

Hannah clucked to the team to pick up the pace. "Our big meal will be at noon, after the wedding service. I have told you what we're having—people will still be too full from that to eat more than maybe some dessert. Remember, my dear niece, this is a second marriage for your uncle and me. Things are to be more subdued."

Emma inhaled deeply, as though ready to admonish Leah for a shortcoming. "I understand, Aunt Hannah, but you have several close friends, such as Miss Stoddard and her fiancé, plus those coming from Lancaster County. Uncle Seth also has many friends that he'll probably want to entertain in a special manner. And what about your English friends, Mr. and Mrs. Lee and Mr. and Mrs. Dunn? Surely you intend to invite Mrs. Dunn, don't you?" She looked at Hannah with her blue eyes shining.

Hannah wondered if the girl had thought of anything else *besides* the wedding lately. "I hadn't considered it, Emma, but that is a good idea. I need to finish the invitations tonight and put them into the mail."

She nodded enthusiastically. "Let's not wait another day! People have to know how to plan. October is a rather busy month compared to December." She folded her hands in her lap and sat quietly... for about one minute. "Since we're inviting your business associate, Mrs. Dunn, what about the Davis family from Charm?" Emma glanced at a passing pickup truck that blasted country music from its radio.

"Who?" Hannah asked, happy to see the "Welcome to Sugar Creek" sign at last. The drive always took longer than she thought it would.

"The English family that raises sheep like we do. We met the son at Mrs. Dunn's store. He invited us to his farm to see their operation, but we never went. Of course, we've had our share of things going on since the fire." Emma busily wiped her hands and face with a towel she'd brought along.

"Emma, you can't be serious. We've never met Mr. and Mrs. Davis. And we were introduced to their son only briefly. You don't invite complete strangers to a wedding."

Emma smoothed down her *kapp* and apron. "It was just an idea, seeing that you and I are in the same line of business as they are. Oh, my, look at that. There's barely room to tie up. Everyone decided to come to Sugar Creek today."

Hannah had reached the central parking area for Amish buggies and wagons, and it was indeed crowded. "There's a bit of shade if I can squeeze in between those two buggies in the back," she said, and clucked to the horse.

Emma jumped down before Hannah could set the hand brake. "I'll fetch water for the horse and meet you inside the fabric shop. I can't wait to see their selection." Emma skipped off, swinging the bucket like a character from a children's book.

Seeing that you and I are in the same line of business? Hannah shook her head. Emma was changing from a child to a young woman before her eyes.

But one had to admire her boundless energy. By the time they left town, they had purchased fabric and notions for her wedding dress in a warm, dark navy, ordered a date-nut cake with walnut buttercream frosting, and arranged to rent a cooking trailer and cooling trailer for the big day. Hannah had argued against both as unnecessary, but in the end she relented. If Simon invited many of the people who had helped on the barn, they would need the rolling kitchen with cookstoves, sinks, and a large supply of dishes, cups, and flatware. The cooling trailer, equipped with propane refrigerators, would keep cold foods safe until serving time. They had also dropped off the spun wool yarn and raw wool at Mrs. Dunn's shop. Mrs. Dunn had read about the fire in the local paper and was willing to wait longer for the natural fabric dyes they'd been working on. Emma verbally invited her to the wedding with far more enthusiasm than necessary. Finally they bought netting for Jordan almonds and paper products at the dollar store. And still Hannah had to practically drag her niece to the buggy.

So much for a quiet wedding...if Emma had her way, the entire Amish population would be invited.

TWENTY-ONE

The sun shone with the slanted, soft rays of early autumn, lending a divine quality to the light. A cool breeze blew from the west, chasing away the last of the summer humidity. Large flocks of migrating birds added happy music from the treetops as Hannah opened her window and inhaled the crisp air on her wedding day. She had slept deep and dreamless, without a worry or troublesome thought. Her sister and niece had already fretted over each small detail, so she could savor this last, special day in their loving home. Hannah was happy beyond what any God-fearing Amish woman had a right to be. She was gaining Seth for a husband and sweet Phoebe for her daughter, while keeping her flock of sheep. And Julia's family would still be just around the corner. Hannah chanted prayers of thanksgiving as she made her bed, lest God think she'd forgotten that everything was by His hand.

After a final deep gulp of brisk air, she closed the window, washed carefully from her pitcher and bowl, and dressed for the occasion. The deep blue dress fit perfectly, a testament to the skill of three women putting their heads together on short notice. She glanced in her small hand mirror and felt happy to see her burnished cheeks and some of her freckles had begun to fade. "A wider brim," she mumbled, brushing her freshly washed hair. "A wider bonnet brim if I'm gonna spend so much time in the fields."

"Who are you talking to, Aunt Hannah?" Emma stuck her head through the doorway and then stepped in and peered around curiously. The young woman was already wearing her bridesmaid dress, which was a lovely soft rose color, suitable for someone who hadn't joined the church yet. She settled herself next to Hannah on the bed, trying not to wrinkle her skirt.

"Just the one silly woman who's in here," Hannah replied, tugging her hairbrush through a nasty tangle.

Emma took the brush away from Hannah and applied it with long, smooth strokes, using her fingers to ease out snarls. "You're not silly, not at all. You're the smartest woman I know. You, and *mamm*, and Miss Stoddard." She reached for the pin box and carefully wound Hannah's hair into a tight, neat bun, pinning it securely. After settling Hannah's new *kapp* in place, Emma tucked stray locks under the heavily starched cloth and leaned back to admire her handiwork. "There you are. Perfect."

"*Danki*, dear one," Hannah said, steadying her nerves with deep breaths. "I have no patience with snarls. I might have yanked a bald spot if you hadn't come to my rescue."

"Even a bald spot wouldn't change a thing," Emma said softly. "You look so beautiful today, Aunt Hannah." Her voice brimmed with emotion. "You shall be the most beautiful bride."

When Hannah looked, she saw tears in Emma's sea blue eyes. "You are sweet, dear child. Every woman looks her best on her wedding day. It is the promise of a new life, a new beginning—all part of God's plan for man and woman."

Emma laid her hand tentatively on her aunt's arm. "Do you think some man will one day choose me?" She sounded like the little girl she so recently was, not the grown woman she was trying so hard to become.

Hannah didn't mean to laugh at so sincere a question but

couldn't help herself. "I do indeed think some lucky young man will choose you, but I know your *daed* is hoping that day will be long in coming."

"What day is that?" Julia asked, joining them in the small bedroom.

"The day you see your eldest daughter wed," Hannah said softly, meeting Julia's eye. Her sister looked well rested today, almost serene. Pain no longer contorted her fine features.

"*Ach,* Simon and I have already decided we'll run any suitors off with that ornery ram of yours. They'll be afraid to venture from their buggies with the sharp horns on that one." Julia laughed from deep in her belly, the way she used to.

Emma rolled her eyes. "See what I'm up against, Aunt Hannah? Now they're putting a watch ram on patrol."

"Tell any future suitors to keep a bag of apples handy at all times," Hannah whispered in Emma's ear as she slipped the brush and pins into the drawer.

"Time for breakfast," Julia announced. "Both of you need to eat something. It'll be a while before the wedding feast. You don't want your stomach growling and drowning out the preacher. Our mamm and Miss Stoddad are already at the table. Do you want those two to finish all the hotcakes I fixed?"

"Where's *daed*?" Hannah asked, hoping she'd get a chance to spend time with her parents today.

"Outside with the men. He has already eaten. Let's hurry."

Hannah and Emma rose to their feet simultaneously. They both eyed one another and then ran for the doorway like schoolgirls on recess. Once in the kitchen, they indeed found mamm and Laura Stoddard with tall stacks of pancakes on their plates. But plenty more waited on Julia's large stoneware platter. Either the men had eaten like sparrows or Julia had fried up several dozen on her stovetop griddle.

Her mother rose to embrace each of them in turn before they settled down to the business of eating.

"A lovely day," Laura said as she took another dainty bite. "Not a rain cloud in sight."

Hannah grinned so broadly it felt as though her face might break. Laura, who'd been instrumental in getting Seth and Hannah back together at the haystack dinner, would stand up for her along with Emma. Because she'd already been baptized, Laura's dress was a deep wine color, but it was still as lovely as Emma's.

Hannah ate two hotcakes and drank a glass of milk. Anything more than that she couldn't handle with her current level of excitement.

Just when butterflies started to take flight in her stomach, Simon opened the back door and announced, "It's time. The bishop is ready to start the preaching service." Wearing his best Sunday clothes with an unusual twinkle in his eye, Simon looked younger than his age by a decade. "Anybody who's coming I s'pose is already here and seated inside. Time to get you hitched, Hannah."

Everyone in the room laughed, but no one more merrily than the bride. "Don't sound so eager, brother-in-law. I'm only moving around the corner," Hannah teased while Julia stacked the breakfast dishes in the sink. Hannah rose from the table and walked with calm assurance out the back door, brushing a light kiss on Simon's cheek on her way by. Emma, looking as though she might float into the wispy clouds overhead, and Laura, glowing with joyous anticipation, followed her down the flagstone path to the barn.

After the three-hour preaching service, the bishop performed the marriage ceremony. While Laura and Emma stood up for Hannah, Joshua and Thomas Kline stood up for Seth. Simon had deemed Matthew too young for the honor.

If the bridegroom was nervous, he didn't show it as Seth Miller pledged to love, honor, and cherish Hannah Brown forever in front of friends, family, and half of Holmes County. Hannah promised to love, honor, and obey the man who had captured her heart. While Simon beamed, Julia cried, Emma sniffled, Leah giggled, Matthew rubbed at a scratchy collar, and Henry appeared fascinated by a bee trapped on the wrong side of the windowpane.

And Hannah? Hannah glowed both inwardly and outwardly, hoping her joy wouldn't seem prideful.

After the service, they moved to the other end of the barn, which had been decorated and set for the noon meal. Hannah looked over the bountiful buffet and the beautifully appointed tables, including a bridal table filled with special cakes and goodies. There were the bowls of Jordan almonds Emma had insisted upon, Julia's blackberry tarts, which had been Hannah's childhood favorite, and the date-nut wedding cake.

As the guests milled about the festive barn, selecting a seat or lining up for the lunch buffet, Seth led his bride to the willow tree for a quiet word. "Well, you've gone and done it, Mrs. Miller. There's no running away now." He brushed kisses across the back of her hand.

"I hope you haven't married me because of my sheep," she said playfully.

He laughed with good humor. "Are you kidding? I only learned to love those smelly bags of wool because I fell in love with you. I pretty much agreed with Simon in the beginning."

Hannah stared into his dark eyes. "You're teasing me, right?"

Seth wrapped his arms around her waist and kissed her tenderly. "Let's just say I *do* like them now, but sheep—same as pickled beets— take some time to grow on a person. But once they do, you never want to be too far away again." He kissed the tip of her nose and added with a wink, "Let's go cut into the chow line. I'm hungry."

Hannah wanted to pinch his ribs or give his beard a good tug, but with Thomas and Catherine heading their way from one direction, and Laura and Joshua from the other, she didn't want the future brides learning any bad habits.

Seth would get away with his mischief this time because Hannah loved him so much. After all, it was their wedding day.

And if God saw fit to grant them a long life together, she would get plenty of chances to get in some pinching and beard pulling.

Singing and visiting lasted all afternoon, and games were played by the younger set. Many a couple strolled hand in hand through the red and golden woodlot and down by the stream. Although wedding gifts were discouraged as it was a second marriage for both, Hannah thanked each woman who brought a bag of sheared wool or dried flowers for making natural dyes. Seth received some new tools from those men who couldn't resist bringing something to the event.

English neighbors and friends began to arrive for the evening meal, parking their cars and trucks in neat rows down by the road. The tables had been reset with dozens of scented votive candles and plenty of lanterns hung from the rafters on gold cords. The rustic barn felt elegant in the soft, warm glow of candlelight.

Dr. and Mrs. Longo stopped in with a certificate for one free farm visit and a large sack of pecans from their recent vacation. Mrs. Dunn and her husband came by, bringing an extra spinning wheel she'd picked up at auction. Mr. and Mrs. Lee arrived with jars of homemade applesauce and grins that didn't cease all evening. Mrs. Lee winked at Hannah each time their gazes met, happy that she helped stop the move back to Pennsylvania. After dark many families wished the couple a safe wedding trip and drifted to their buggies or cars. But a handful of young people stayed until almost midnight, singing, sipping cider, and nibbling desserts.

When no one was looking, Hannah and Seth stole away toward the house, tired but content—not wishing the special day to end but eager for the sweetness yet to come. As they climbed the steps to Hannah's old room, both uttered silent prayers that the love they felt tonight would last a lifetime.

And grow only stronger under God's tender grace.

EPILOGUE

"Welcome home!" A chorus of voices greeted Seth and Hannah as their buggy rolled up Simon's driveway. Henry and Matthew ran from the horse paddock as Julia and Emma stepped out the back door onto the porch.

"Leah!" Phoebe cried from her spot wedged between the new bride and groom. Leah had emerged from the henhouse carrying a full basket of eggs. As soon as Seth set the brake, Hannah let her jump down. "Go see your cousin," Hannah said. Phoebe and Leah ran toward each other at full speed while Leah's basket swung wildly.

"I believe Julia will find those eggs already scrambled," Seth said, helping his wife step down. "Now remember, we're staying only for dinner and to get caught up with the news. No sneaking up to your old room at the end of the evening and falling asleep. You're coming home with me, *fraa*." He brushed a kiss across her forehead and strode off toward his *bruder*.

Simon walked from the barn practically covered with sawdust. "Welcome home," he called, slapping Seth on the back.

Hannah took a minute to glance around the yard. The last of the construction debris was gone from around the barn, and the oaks had turned a deep crimson red. They had been gone for less than two weeks, yet the farm looked somehow different. They had spent their wedding night in Hannah's old bedroom in the Amish tradition and then helped clean up after the wedding festivities. After arranging for Emma and Matthew to manage their chores, Hannah and Seth had left on a honeymoon trip back to Pennsylvania.

Life marches on with a relentless progression of small changes that one overlooks from day to day. Hannah wanted to capture this autumn of happiness in a locket so she might open it in old age for a tender reminiscence.

"Come on," Julia hollered. "Have you forgotten your way to the house? We're eager for some news."

Julia...some things never changed.

Hannah hurried to her sister's open arms and accepted the warm embrace. "How's the arthritis?" Hannah asked.

"Better. I may be able to postpone surgery for a while. Those pills and therapies are working." Truly, her face looked younger, without the weight of chronic pain.

"I'm so happy to hear it," Hannah said, kissing Julia's cheek as they entered the kitchen arm in arm. Emma followed behind them, hanging back with uncharacteristic shyness.

In the kitchen the propane stove had been retired for the season in favor of the cozy woodburner. The room smelled of apples and cinnamon as Hannah spotted two pies cooling on the counter and a plate of oatmeal raisin cookies on the table. She sat down in her old chair and reached for a cookie.

Julia slapped her hand. "Not before dinner. We're having your favorite—chicken and dumplings with corn on the cob. It's the last of it—all the rest has been canned. So enjoy."

"Another day of having others cook for me? I've really enjoyed my honeymoon trip, but poor Seth—he'll suffer while I relearn how to fix a meal."

"Don't worry. It'll all come back to you, just like riding a bicycle. You'll be burning biscuits and overcooking noodles in no time at all." Julia threw her head back and laughed.

Hannah felt her face blush, but she didn't mind her sister's teasing. It was one of the things she had missed. "Who did you pick on while I was staying in Lancaster?" she asked, turning toward Emma. "I hope she didn't turn her mischief on you, dear niece." Hannah reached out to grasp Emma's hand.

Emma had been sitting as quietly as the proverbial church mouse. "No, aunt, don't worry. I hid from her up in my new workroom, just like you used to do."

The three women broke into peals of laughter.

"You've ruined her," Julia said to Hannah. "You took a perfectly fine child and turned her into an adult. Or at least that's what she thinks she is!" Julia slanted Emma a frosty glare that Hannah couldn't help but notice.

"*Mamm* stills thinks I'm a *boppli*," Emma said, rolling her eyes, "but wait till you see what *daed* brought me—I mean us...a loom!" Her voice conveyed plenty of passion. "Wait till you see what a beauty it is. Shall we go now?" Emma started to rise from the table.

"No, dear," Julia said. "It's time for supper. Please go call the men and boys and then find Phoebe and Leah. The loom can wait."

As the young woman left the room, Julia shook her head.

"Has she gotten taller in only two weeks?" asked Hannah. "Something about her is different."

"Maybe. She's growing up all at once now that she's done with school." Briefly an expression of concern crossed Julia's face, but she shook it off. "I want to hear all about home. How are *mamm* and *daed*? Have Thomas and Catherine set their wedding date?

Hannah opened her mouth to answer, but Simon beat her to it. "Take it easy, wife. You're like a runaway freight train headed downhill. Hannah and Seth have just gotten home."

Julia blushed as she rose from the table. "Welcome, Seth. Sit by your bride, and I'll put supper out. I can't help being excited. It's been too long since Simon and I took a trip anywhere!" She patted her husband's shoulder as he lowered himself gingerly into the chair.

Hannah thought his back much worse than it had been.

"What do you mean?" he asked. "Didn't I just take you to Mount Hope last week?" His eyes sparkled with good humor.

Julia rolled her eyes for the second time in fifteen minutes as she set bowls and platters on the table. "I can hardly wait for the wedding. We'll have to stay a full two weeks so I can visit all my relatives and old friends." She passed the platter of chicken to Simon.

He helped himself to a hearty portion. "Then you'll have to come back on the train. I can't expect my neighbors to feed my animals and milk cows for that long."

Phoebe and Leah ran into the kitchen from the back hallway.

"It's about time," Julia scolded. "Now get washed."

As soon as the little girls took their seats, everyone bowed their heads for prayers and then began to eat without restraint.

The touch of Seth's hand on one side and Phoebe's on the other warmed Hannah's heart—almost as much as Julia's delicious chicken and dumplings. "Eat hearty, husband," Hannah instructed Seth. "Starting tomorrow, you'll be stuck with my cooking."

Seth patted his midsection with a grin. "Good. I need to lose a few pounds anyway after that trip to Lancaster County. All your kin ever wanted to do was eat."

Hannah pinched his leg under the table as she addressed her sister. "Our parents are fine. *Mamm*'s eyesight is a little worse, so I bought her a chain to string her glasses around her neck. *Daed* is glad he's finally retiring once everything is harvested. Thomas will run his farm along with his own. Two of Catherine's cousins want to farm and don't have their own land, so they will work for Thomas."

"Thomas said he misses Hannah's sheep and is thinking of adding his own next spring," Seth said, scooping more dumplings onto his plate.

"That's what I keep hearing from my eldest daughter," said Simon, "but I can't see her stomping through a muddy pasture like Hannah does."

Emma frowned. For a moment, the adults had almost forgotten the children were there—they had been so quiet. "Just a few lambs," Emma said. "Maybe Aunt Hannah will part with some of hers come the spring."

"I would love to if your *daed* says it's all right. It'll be payment for tending my flock while we were on our honeymoon trip," Hannah said, "*Danki* very much for that. You did a good job. We stopped at the pasture before coming here, and they all looked healthy."

Emma blushed as she smiled. With her sea blue eyes and wheat-colored hair, the girl was becoming quite pretty, Hannah thought.

Seth slapped Matthew on the back. "I had in mind cash for you, nephew, for your hard work tending my cows and horses," he said. "Is that all right with you?"

The boy nodded as Simon said, "Not too much, Seth. Family doesn't need to pay other family members."

Leah began squirming in her chair. Seth pretended not to notice. "Let's see…that ought to do it. I wonder what Julia has for dessert." He grinned at Hannah while Leah cleared her throat, twice.

"Aren't you forgetting who fed our chickens while we were gone?" Hannah asked. She thought the girl might fall off her chair.

Seth's gaze finally landed on his youngest niece. "Oh, my, that's right." He reached into his pocket and pulled out a ten-dollar bill. "Did you feed those chickens every day?" he asked.

"I did, Uncle Seth," Leah answered with a grin.

"Did you gather the eggs and take them back to your *mamm?*"

"*Jah,* I didn't break a single one."

Seth nodded sagely. "Well, that calls for a bonus." He pulled a bag of blue gummy worms from his pocket. Leah looked positively ecstatic.

Julia cut the pies on the counter and began passing around the slices.

"None for me," Hannah said. "I'm afraid I filled up on your delicious chicken and dumplings, plus I ate two ears of corn."

"Sort of one last meal?" Seth teased.

Hannah pinched his leg again under the table.

"I don't have room for dessert either, Aunt Hannah. Can we go to barn loft now?" Emma asked.

Hannah glanced at Simon and Julia. They both rolled their eyes but said nothing. "Okay, but just for a little while since it'll be dark soon. Then we'll come back and clean up the kitchen. Why don't you come too, Julia, so you're not tempted to start the dishes."

All three women and two little girls left the kitchen for the brisk autumn evening. Emma talked about the dried flowers, tree bark, roots, and berries she'd been experimenting with for natural dyes. Hannah tried to listen, but mainly she enjoyed the companionship of her family again. The inside of the barn had recently been painted yet still retained the smell of freshly cut lumber.

Hannah stopped short when she spotted the new loom in the center of Emma's workroom. It was indeed a beauty. Emma clapped her hands when she saw her aunt's reaction. "I knew you would love it!" she exclaimed. "And it collapses down easily, so it's more movable than your last one."

"Which is a good thing, since it's about to be moved," Julia said.

Emma's sunny expression slipped a notch.

"Why so?" Hannah asked. "It looks right at home here."

"Simon bought this replacement loom for *you*, sister, with his money and the money donated by the ladies during the barn raising. It will be moved to your new home tomorrow." Julia lifted her chin, furrowed her brow, and all but dared Emma to argue with her.

The young woman did not; she only crossed her arms over her apron.

"When Emma earns enough money from her dyes and her wool profits, she can buy her own loom. That is how business works in the world." Julia crossed her arms too, and the mother and daughter seemed to be squaring off like two bulls in a spring pasture.

Hannah suppressed a grin. "Why tomorrow? There's no hurry. I just returned from Lancaster today. I've got enough laundry to keep me busy for a few days."

Julia's head snapped around. "I almost forgot the best part of my news. Laura Stoddard has organized the ladies into a work frolic. About ten women will meet here at nine o'clock."

Hannah lifted her brows questioningly.

"A frolic to help you get the rest of your stuff moved to Seth's—your house now—and caught up with your laundry, cleaning, and baking once we get over there." Julia looked as pleased as a cat in the cream. "Seth and Simon will be available to help, we'll have at least five wagons here, so it'll be a good time to move the loom. By day's end you'll be all set up and caught up in your new life."

"*Danki*, Julia," Hannah croaked in a hushed tone. The friendly gesture from the women had left her almost speechless.

Her better half did not suffer from the same affliction, however. "Looks like I've gotten a governor's reprieve with the other ladies comin' over…one is bound to fix us supper," Seth said, stepping into the loft.

Hannah perched her fists on her hips and opened her mouth to howl, but Seth swooped in for a kiss instead. He kissed her until Hannah forgot what she was irritated about.

"I think it's time for you two lovebirds to go home," Julia said.

"My sentiments exactly." Seth swept Hannah into his arms and carried her down the stairs.

"Good night," Hannah called over his shoulder. "See you tomorrow at nine. And *danki* for everything."

Her last words were lost in the crisp night air as Seth had already hauled her out the door.

Julia and Emma stood watching them go, both with tears in their eyes.

~

One week later Hannah and Phoebe drove the buggy home from

Julia's. They had been helping her with fall cleaning. It had been such a blessing when the work frolic moved her to Seth's that she had to return the favor. She, Emma, and Julia cleaned the house from top to bottom, while Simon and the boys washed the outside windows. The house sparkled, Julia was pleased, and Hannah felt tired but satisfied. All she wanted to do was reheat yesterday's stew in the oven and soak in a hot tub while Phoebe took her nap.

"Look, *mamm,*" Phoebe said.

Hannah was so taken aback with joy every time the child called her *mamm* she didn't notice anything else. Then Hannah spotted a shiny new, dark green pickup parked in the driveway. *With any luck, they are lost tourists and only need directions,* she thought, too tired for any visitors.

"A truck," Phoebe said in *Deutsch* and English.

School had begun, and Miss Stoddard was very pleased with Phoebe's progress.

"It certainly is," Hannah murmured, parking the buggy in front of the barn. "Stay with me. We don't know who it is." Hannah jumped down and tied the reins to a post. When she turned around, a young man got out of the truck in clean blue jeans, a flannel shirt, and a ball cap. She didn't recognize him until he took off the cap.

"Mrs. Brown? You might not remember me. I'm James Davis. We met in Sugar Creek at Mrs. Dunn's store."

Hannah relaxed and smiled. "Yes, I remember you, a fellow sheep farmer," she added with a smile. "I am Mrs. Miller now, and this is my daughter, Phoebe." Hannah tried to extricate the child from her skirt, but she clung like sticky tape.

The boy grinned with a dazzlingly bright smile and cleared his throat. "Is Emma here, ma'am? May I speak with her?"

Hannah looked confused.

"I had told Emma that I usually drive to Mount Eaton on Tuesday afternoons. I cut my grandparents' grass and see if they need anything done around the house. My grandpa can't climb ladders anymore."

James Davis stood there looking earnest as he waited for this to make sense to Hannah.

But it did not. Hannah shrugged her shoulders and smiled pleasantly. She didn't wish to appear rude but couldn't fathom what his visit to Mount Eaton had to do with her family.

James blushed slightly and shuffled his feet. "Your niece told me to stop here—at her aunt and uncle's farm—to see your sheep and check out your operation—any Tuesday on my way home from Grandma's. Emma said she'd be happy to show me your flock."

"Perhaps another time, James. Emma is not here. She's home with her parents." Hannah nodded her head politely and walked onto the porch. When she glanced over her shoulder, young Mr. Davis was headed back to his pickup truck.

You want to see our sheep indeed, she thought. Hannah watched him drive away as an unsettled feeling grew in the pit of her stomach.

But before long the fragrant pot of stew was simmering on the stove. Phoebe was setting the table, and soon Seth would be back from town, where he'd delivered the last of his own sweet corn. He would greet her with a hug and a kiss and praise her culinary attempts enthusiastically, even though she was only heating up leftovers.

Hannah felt a surge of joy and contentment sweep over her, chasing away any and all worries. She had found her home, her place, and her purpose in the world.

She was happy at last.

And God would watch over her dear niece Emma too.

All things in this world are by His Hand. She needn't worry about a thing again.

About the Author

~

Mary Ellis grew up close to the eastern Ohio Amish Community, Geauga County, where her parents often took her to farmers' markets and woodworking fairs. She and her husband now live in Medina County, close to the largest population of Amish families, and enjoy the simple way of life.